tHe

biG

MaNgo

Norman Kelley

Akashic Books
New York, NY

This is a work of fiction. All names, characters, places, and incidents are the product of the author's imagination. Any resemblance to real events or persons, living or dead, is entirely coincidental.

Published by Akashic Books
©2000 Norman Kelley

Art assistance by Greg Wilson
Author photo by Reynold C. Kerr

ISBN: 1-888451-10-6
Library of Congress Catalog Card Number: 00-101835

Akashic Books
PO Box 1456
New York, NY 10009
email: Akashic7@aol.com
website: www.akashicbooks.com

To my great-grandmother Selena Woodfolk Stevens and grandmother Equilla Green; to my sister Patricia Anne Kelley and nieces Ava Marie Kelley and Justine Danielle Kelley.

And to my other sisters...
Grace Brill, Adriane Fugh-Berman, Sheree Thomas, Claudia Lemaire, Karen Tyndale, Carla Becker, Sherri Carter, Britt Arbelius, Julie Patton, Karen Rizvi, Cynthia Washington, Shelly Brody, Carol Amoruso, Jennifer Williamson Catania, Georgene Shelton, Selena White Persico, Isa Bakker, Celina Davis, Michelle Linton, Opal Linton, Stella Leung, Annie Thurow, Debbie Dyson, Danielle Frater, Pagan Kennedy, Barbara Lowe, Barbara Mogulescu, Christine Caulder, Mrs. Bowls, Edith Rich, Sally Howley, Tyra Ferrell, Nancy Neal, Utrice Leid, Mieke Vadersall, Janis Russell, Rosa Sandoval, Sara Bernstein, Leigh Henderson, Kate Pfordresher, Karen Lengel, Uta Piper, Donna Baines, Michelle Puryear, Portia Bowers-Yakub, Johanna Ingalls, Jennifer Washburn, Kara Gilmour, Kyra Sinkowsky, Alexis Scott, Vanessa Shannon, Tracy Locke, Marcia Savin, Betsy Feist, Shadi Sheybani, Toni Short, Jacquelyn Woodworth, Nancy Reynolds, Kathy Gallagher, Ann Filloramo, Lesley Yulkowski, Maquita Moody, Isabell Dominati & Olivia Miller, Claire, Shereen & Leona Miller, Rena Nowacoski, Arlene Lopez, Naomi Zauderer, Nina Leichter, Rosemary Halligan, and Nina Simone
...Conscious and unacknowledged members of the Bad Girls International.

Also, I wish to thank David Shirley for his editorial stewardship. Like a farmer in a mango grove, he knew what to cut and harvest. Truly, a gentleman and a scholar.

Power concedes nothing without demand. It never did and it never will. Find out just what any people will quietly submit to and you have found out the exact measure of injustice and wrong which will be imposed upon them.

— Frederick Douglass

He had all the right enemies: the army, the business elite, the church, and, of course, the grandest and most formidable enemy of them all, the United States government. From the beginning of his presidency, Father Pierre-Pierre Bernard's constituency had consisted entirely of the poor: the black, tan, and mulatto masses of the island-nation of Misericordia. Known affectionately by his people as Pepe, Father Bernard preached the tenets of liberation theology, calling for the emancipation and empowerment of les miserables, as the wretched citizens of Misericordia were called.

A slight, bespectacled and bearded man, Father Bernard tried to reach the elite of his country with the same message of mercy and compassion once proclaimed by Nestor Morgan, the semi-illiterate slave general who had liberated his people from foreign rule during the 18th century. Rallying the island's slaves to rise up against more than two centuries of colonial oppression by the Spanish, English, and French, Morgan established the new republic as "the land of mercy," a refuge for former slaves throughout the New World.

Tragically, the "infernal nigger nation," as it was named by its slave-holding neighbors to the north and south, had difficulty surviv-

ing from the start. Within its borders, a new group of ruling elites quickly arose: the fou blancs, *or crazy whites, who controlled most of the land and imitated the speech and religion of the former European colonists. The illiterate masses had only one language: Kreole, a colorful hybrid of Yoruba, French, Spanish, English, and Caribe. The poor also practiced the indigenous religion of voudoux, which blended Catholicism and the various Yoruba deities. When Morgan struggled to protect the meager property holdings of the rural masses from the insurgent middle class, he was ambushed and killed by a small army of* fou blanc *guerillas. As he returned one evening without escort from one of his frequent clandestine visits to one of his many mistresses, Morgan's horse stopped at a clearing several miles outside the capital, when it sensed something out of the ordinary on a trail it had traversed many times before. The creature snorted and reared itself. A fusillade dislodged Morgan from his saddle, but not from the stirrup, and the frightened animal galloped all the way to the streets of the city with his master dragging behind.*

From that day onward, Misericordia's history would be based on one faction usurping another—black against tan, tan against mulatto, and tan and mulatto against black—with new leaders appearing and falling at a dizzying pace. "Stability" did not return to the island until 1920, with the bombastic arrival of the United States Marines and the violent installation of a series of puppet regimes that lasted until the mid-1950s. The marines trained the New Model Army of Misericordia and an interregnum of nickel and dime despots assumed the office of El Presidente. Propped up by the U.S. government, the army and the ruling business elite quickly turned "the land of mercy" into an unforgiving nightmare for the poor, illiterate masses.

American rule in Misericordia was finally interrupted by the political ascension of Dr. Henri Triomphe in 1954. An oafish, overweight country physician who dabbled in Negritude and developed an esoteric philosophy called "Afrotism," Triomphe was an unlikely political savior. Afrotism—or Triomphism, as it was later called—was based on the theory that the black peazants, the descendants of the African slaves, were the true repository of everything that was pure and virtuous in Misericordia. In direct defiance of the Eurocentrism of the fou blancs, *Triomphe wrote and spoke exclusively in Kreole and extolled the practice of voudoux by the Maerican masses.*

Scorned by the fou blancs, *Triomphe slowly built a network of followers and supporters in the middle and peazant classes, eventually winning popular election in 1954. Determined to overcome the influence of the island's mulatto elite, Triomphe immediately mobilized a volunteer civic group known as the Presidential Aides, men and women who "assisted" the president in the various and multifaceted tasks of* le regeneration *of the black nation. The "Papas," as they came to be known and feared, scoured the island, searching for—and forcibly removing—anything or anyone that was not considered* authentique *by the strict standards of Triomphism.*

Soon, virtually every aspect of Maerican life had been transformed by Triomphism—from the mandatory education of the formerly illiterate masses in the grammar and philosophy of Kreole to the virtual enslavement of all cultural and political dissenters. After Castro's assumption of power in Cuba, Triomphe clamped down even harder on the mulatto elite. Former business and political leaders were savagely tortured in the basement of the Presidential Palace in the capital city of Port Henri, while the mutilated bodies of progressive democrats were strewn by the Papas through the streets of the capitol. As the deposed fou blancs *and middle-class landowners fled the island in droves, the U.S. government secretly applauded the heavy-handed rule of the "butcher of blacks" to the south. As long as Triomphe remained in power, there was little danger of a progressive, Cuban-style insurrection in the land of mercy.*

After tyrannizing his people for more than twenty years, Triomphe became the island's first dictator to die in bed—of natural causes. Following Triomphe's death, his son Henri II assumed the Maerican "throne" and sought to rule the country as a dictator with a human face—and an entrepreneurial imagination. The younger Triomphe's plan was to open the island to its wealthy neighbors as a voudoux Disneyland, a center of gambling and other indigenous pleasures for tourists and a source of cheap, docile labor for foreign corporations and investors.

In spite of Henri's grand ambitions, the situation in Misericordia began to deteriorate during the economic crisis of the 1980s. Earlier in the decade, the new ruling elite had seized the small arable plots of land that had been farmed by the peazants since the days of the revolution. When a massive swine flu epidemic swept across the Caribbean, the

3

Kreole pig, the mainstay of much of the population, was killed off in large numbers. In response to the crisis, the U.S. government began supplying its own herds of swine, konchon blanc, *to the island. But the rural peazants, who typically earned less than $250 a year, could hardly afford the expensive wheat germ diet required to feed the animals, and so began a slow, steady exodus of the impoverished masses from the heights of the mountainous hillsides to the dark slums of the cities.*

Arriving in the island's urban centers, the former peazants were introduced to the compelling Kreole sermons of Father Pierre-Pierre Bernard and the incendiary songs of Bob Marley, telling them to "get up, stand up" for their rights. The political movement inspired by Bernard was called the Lava-lava, named for the molten rock that once flowed down from a now-dormant volcano, consuming the island and destroying everything in its path. According to Bernard and the island's other liberationists, the pressure of the suffering masses had reached its boiling point, and the island was once again about to erupt.

As Henri II began to lose power in the late 1980s, Bernard and his liberationist followers provided the moral and intellectual background for a radical course of action among the masses. Barricades went up. Students marched. Leaflets appeared everywhere, denouncing the regime. The Papas, the traditional dogs of repression, conducted a brutal reign of terror throughout the island: killing, raping, plundering, and bombing virtually everything in sight. But the poor, led by Father Bernard, refused to retreat. They formed a "black flood of misery," as Bernard himself described it, filling the streets of Port Henri and other major cities with their protests and fighting back whenever they were attacked. Essentially unarmed, they defended themselves with rocks, stones, bricks, and the new weapon of choice among the urban masses: the necklace, an ignited tire filled with gasoline.

When violence eventually erupted and blood began to soak the streets, the island's deposed but powerful fou blanc *elite and their allies in the U.S. government quickly decided that Henri's time was up. Early one morning, the gates to Mt. Henri, the palatial fortress that overlooked the city, slowly opened and Henri Triomphe, seated behind the wheel of his Mercedes-Benz, led a motorcade that consisted of his wife, the fashion-conscious Margot, along with the couple's children and personal entourage. The procession descended slowly and arduously toward the airport, where a U.S. military transport airplane awaited. Thou-*

4

sands of Maericans lined the streets and stared at the cars in silence. Along the way, Henri's entourage was pelted by an endless torrent of garbage, spit, and feces, the limousine's windshield wipers struggling futilely to clear the way. Henri retaliated to this indignity with his own parting gesture, zipping down the fly of his Armani suit and urinating on his motherland before ascending the ramp of the avian behemoth.

Though won through the sacrifice of the people, round one of the revolution was claimed by that great fount of democratic insurrection around the world, the United States. True to Misericordian history, the island's generals, propped up by the U.S. government, began ruling the roost under the guise of a government of National Unity, derisively referred to as "Triomphalism without Triomphe" by Father Bernard and his followers. "Watch those monkeys," Bernard told his parishioners as the generals re-instituted the violence and repression that had characterized the former regime. "Notice that the tails they are cutting off are not their own." Instead of public executions or simply killing people on the streets, the Papas preferred to take their victims into custody, where they tortured and killed them in private. It was simple policy: no body, no crime. Just the memories of those who had disappeared.

Abandoned by the church for his radical position, Father Bernard became the people's choice. The flood of the Lava-lava could not be stopped. With a platform that espoused "a walk from despair to the simplicity of poverty with respect, love, and dignity," Bernard won more than seventy-five percent of the vote in a general election against the suave World Bank official, Franz Petain. But Bernard, for all his ideological zeal, had few talents as a political leader. He stopped the violence against the island's people, but he seemed ill-equipped to make the tough decisions that were necessary to restore order and economic stability to Misericordia. Within a year, the island seemed ready to erupt once again.

CHAPTER ONE

"Nina Halligan?" asked the voice on the other end of the phone. It was a man's voice, a Caribbean voice, distinct and refined, slowly encasing its vowels in American English.

"Speaking," I said, as I applied polish to the shoe that I was holding, the receiver cradled between my shoulder and my neck. I had noticed a scuff a few moments before as I bent over to retrieve a paper clip that I had dropped, and I was never one to leave a job undone.

"Allo, I am Father Bernard."

My attention was still on the stubborn blemish on my shoe, and I failed at first to catch the name. After applying one last stroke of the brush, I slipped on the heel and stood up to admire my shine. "I beg your pardon? Who?" I asked.

"Father Bernard."

I sat back down. "What can I do for you, Father?"

"Well," he started hesitantly, "I would like to speak to you about an important matter."

"Shoot," I replied casually.

"Huh?" He sounded confused.

"I'm listening. What can I do for you?"

"Well, I would like for you to come to Washington, Miss Halligan."

I suddenly realized that I wasn't just talking to a priest in some tiny Brooklyn parish. "Excuse me. What did you say your name was?" I pricked up my ear to make sure I didn't miss it this time.

"I'm Father Pierre-Pierre Bernard, the President of Misericordia," he answered immediately, in a very sweet and unpretentious manner.

"What can I do for you, Mr. President?" Needless to say, I was surprised to hear from the man.

"Well. I read your article about my country. A copy was sent to me recently. You are a very wise woman."

"Thank you, sir. It's kind of you to say so, but I'm not a policy expert, Mr. President. I only went down to your country and reported what I saw. I don't have any expertise—"

"My dear sister, that's why I would want to speak to you. You're right in what you say. But perhaps I need a new perspective. Would you honor my people and myself by coming to Washington?" His voice became very low and intense. "I need help, Miss Halligan."

"Are you in trouble, sir?" I inquired. A warning light blinked somewhere in the back of my mind.

"Well, yes. I've lost something."

"What's that, Mr. President?" I reached for a pen and a pad, ready to jot down a list of particulars.

"My country," he sighed heavily, "and I'm wondering if you could help me get it back."

I listened carefully to Bernard's story, though I knew most of what he had to say already, having traveled to Misericordia in the past on both business and pleasure, and recently written an article on the events of his country. Bernard had been a powerful preacher and grassroots liberation theologian, who had inspired his people to rebel against the last remnants of the brutal Triomphe regime that had tyrannized the island for decades. But for all his religious and political passion, the man cowered in the face of the harsh realities of Maerican political and economic life. Instead of making tough, decisive decisions, he hesitated in the face of each new challenge, carefully weighing the merits and the consequences, while events in his country continued without him. Within a year, he had lost favor with many of his followers and had easily been deposed by yet another coup.

During the days of the Bernard regime, I had actually traveled to Misericordia, at the request of my sister-in-law Miriam Butler, a medical coordinator for the Committee to Aid the People of Misericordia, to observe the plight of the island's people. As an unannounced human rights observer, I recorded the violations I had witnessed and filed copies of my report at the appropriate non-governmental and governmental agencies back in the United States. Based on my experience on the island, I had recently written an article for a new uptown journal, the *New York Drum*, in which I had argued that President Bernard's greatest mistake to date was his decision to come to Washington. If he really wanted to lead his people, I insisted in my article, he would have to break free, once and for all, from the big brother to the north.

And yet, here the man was, sitting in a plush Georgetown apartment, considering a deal with the U.S. government—the same government that he suspected of inciting the coup that deposed him—to return him to power. I winced now, as I listened to him weigh the advantages and disadvantages of a strategic partnership with the inside-the-beltway crowd. Once again, Bernard was having difficulty making an important decision. Only this time, he seemed to be looking to me to provide him with the answer.

I hadn't thought much about my article on Bernard and Misericordia since it came out. I had problems enough of my own, after all. My own personal demons. I had recently ended a relationship with my former lover, Dexter Pierson, now a reporter with the *Drum*. And apart from my work as a private investigator, there was my teaching and my recent responsibilities supervising the publication of a series of books by my late husband, Lee.

Sure, Bernard needed help, I thought. But since when do

you ask a charter member of the Bad Girls International to engage in international statecraft? That would be like expecting U.S. president Jeff Benton to respond enthusiastically to a kiss from his wife.

After the call, I leaned back in my chair and began to swivel. It was a bit overwhelming that a president, even a deposed one, would call and ask for my help. I ain't the marines, after all, much less the United Nations. Someone must have been *seriously* dropping my name in order to get Bernard's attention. And that someone had to have been Miriam.

In addition to my article in the *Drum*, Bernard may also have seen another article of mine in *Misericordia Progres*, a newspaper published in New York for the Maerican émigrè community. But in spite of his flattering comments, that certainly wouldn't have been enough to get him to call me. Before we had ended the phone conversation, I had told him that my only connection with the government—with the White House, to be precise—was through my friendship with presidential aide Michael Debord, the husband of one of my best friends, Gale Simmons. That wasn't exactly true, I had realized after I hung up. The current First Lady had been an instructor of mine at law school years earlier. But the two of us hadn't really kept in touch in recent years. And apart from the personal connections, I had absolutely no foreign policy experience; nor did I have any connection with influential backers at corporate-sponsored think tanks. So, why me? Bernard must have had some good reason for seeking me out. I just couldn't figure out what it was.

"Nina?" Zimbawe Kincaid, my assistant, knocked softly on the door to my office, which was slightly ajar. An exquisitely dark woman, Zee was letting me know that she had arrived at work and was now in the outer office. "Officer of the day reporting."

Months earlier, someone had tried to radically remove me from the premises with a shotgun. Since then, it had become a house rule to announce your presence upon entering—or risk suffering a precautionary gunshot. "Thanks, Zee. How are you?"

"Oh... I'm fine," Zee said. She sounded unusually subdued,

but I wasn't in the mood to pry. "I'm going to take care of some of the bills and correspondence."

"Okay. Thanks." She was about to return to the outer office when a question occurred to me. "Zee?"

"Yes."

"You know any students from Misericordia?" I pointed to the chair next to my desk.

"Some," she said, taking a seat.

"What's the word on Pepe Bernard?"

"Oh, I don't know," she shrugged. "Depends on whom you ask."

"Right, dear. I'm asking you."

Zee rested her elbow on the chair's arm, cradling her chin in her palm. "Well, he's considered progressive. The people—the majority of the population—love him."

"What about the other students at the Graduate Center. I gather that most of them are middle class or upper class."

"Oh, some of them think he's done the country some good; some believe that he's a clerical demagogue," said Zee. "Others think he's weak, that he blew a real chance to protect democracy for his people."

That got my attention. "How exactly did he do that?"

She leaned back into the chair and casually crossed her arms. "Some feel he should have armed the masses. The Maerican army is basically a criminal enterprise; they're used to doing as they please, shaking down the people at will. They would have been psychologically unprepared if Bernard had persuaded people to fight back."

"But, Zee," I interjected, "the army has the guns."

"Yes, exactly, but Bernard had the people. They would have been willing to fight to the death for him and the idea that Misericordia was theirs to defend. They scared Triomphe, Jr. out of the country when they took to the streets before, and a lot of people think they were ready to defend themselves again against the coup. Bernard really missed the boat in not recognizing this—not acting on it. Guns aren't everything, Nina. Look, the U.S. had a superior military force in Vietnam, but the Vietnamese won because it was their country and they were willing to die to defend it."

And now the Vietnamese government is selling the country to Nike, I thought with a shrug.

"At least that's what they say at school," said Zee, sensing my distraction. "What's up? Why are you interested in Bernard?"

"He called me."

Zee stared at me incredulously. "Pepe Bernard?"

"Just before you walked in, girlfriend."

"What—"

"What did he say? He told me that he had lost his country."

"He's certainly right about that. Now he's exiled in a Georgetown townhouse and getting slammed by Rory Buchanan." Zee rolled her eyes as she mentioned the distinguished senator from South Carolina, the chairman of the Senate Foreign Relations Committee and head of what some called the Fascist International.

We sat in silence for a moment. "Nina, why did he call you?"

I smiled inwardly as she zeroed in on the same question that had been bothering me. "That, my good woman, is what I've been asking myself ever since I hung up from talking with him. Maybe he thinks I'm running a missing country bureau, Zee."

"Any real thoughts about it?"

"Only speculative. Miriam," I answered.

"Your in-law?" she replied.

"Well," I said, picking up the phone and punching out the numbers, "there's only one way to find out." Zee rose, bowed her head, and made the faux arabesque hand movements that generally signaled her withdrawal.

Miriam was in transition. For years, she had worked at Harlem Hospital as a primary care pediatrician. But the hospital fell into private hands, yet another cost-cutting casualty of the current reign of Mayor Kevin Carlucci, affectionately known by the more sophisticated denizens of New York as "Il Duce." As the wife of a successful investment banker—my brother Earl, to be precise—Miriam didn't have to look for work immediately. Instead, she took to the streets and began organizing community-based clinics, first in Harlem and then throughout the city. Miriam's clinics were staffed by volunteers from the French-based organization, Doctors Without Borders.

It was difficult, tiresome, and frustrating work. Some people criticized Miriam for providing direct aid to poor communities without pushing for new laws and public policies to improve the situation. But Miriam had given up on begging the government for the assistance that she needed to do her work. Instead, she taught her patients how to initiate their own health programs and maintain a healthier style of living by giving up cigarettes, eating more fruits and vegetables, cutting back on alcohol, exercising, and staying away from fatty, fried, and processed foods. Simple stuff, but the basis of a healthy life.

I was thinking about the changes she had been through when I heard her voice on the other end of the telephone. "Miriam," I responded immediately, "President Bernard called. He wants me to come to some swinging soirée that you're arranging for him."

"Oh, did he?" she said, not surprised. "That's marvelous. I'm assuming you won't turn down a command request?"

"What's the deal, girl?"

"I told him to invite you to the reception, Nina."

"I figured as much, Miriam. But why did he call me?" I insisted. "He doesn't know me, but he has the impression—at least I gathered he does—that I may be able to facilitate his return to office. You wouldn't by any chance know why he thinks that?"

Miriam paused for a second. "I...uh...uh...may have intimated that you could get things done."

"Get things done?" I echoed.

"Yes. Gary told me about how you got Reverend Tower—"

"Hold it!" I interrupted her at once, unsure about the security of her telephone line. "We need to talk, Miriam. What's your schedule like today?"

It turned out that Miriam was planning to come to the city that afternoon on business. She wouldn't be free until the evening, so we agreed to meet at *Byron's* in Tribeca at 8 p.m. We said our good-byes and I hung up the telephone. I sighed, rose from my chair, and stepped into the outer office in my stockinged feet. Zee was at the keyboard tapping away. As usual, she was switching back and forth on the screen between the firm's business and schoolwork of her own—in this case, an esoteric study on Islamic identity and post-modernity.

"Do we have any aspirin?" I asked.

"Yes." She opened the top drawer of the desk and pulled out a small black plastic bottle. I dumped a couple of tablets into my palm and retrieved a cup of water from the kitchenette.

"What's with Miriam?" Zee's eyes were shifting back and forth between the two documents.

"I'll find out in greater detail later tonight—but she's the one, all right."

"She had the president call you?" asked Zee.

"Seems so. And she almost mentioned the Tower affair over the phone—"

Zee's dark eyes narrowed as she turned her face toward me. "Over the phone?"

I raised a hopefully reassuring palm. "I cut her off at the pass."

Zee wiped an imaginary streak of sweat from her brow. There were certain aspects regarding my dislodging of Paul Tower from the Black Christian Network that we did not want to become common knowledge. If the truth got out, our names would have been right up there next to Anita Hill's in the Hall of Treasonous Black Bitches. I didn't know how much Miriam knew, but she obviously knew something. Probably from Gary, I thought, who was around for the reverend's denouement. The Tower affair was something I did not want to experience again, either as a private citizen or a private investigator. Hell, I'd gladly work overtime and lower my fee to help a welfare mom get back her check. But when it comes to matters of state with real political consequences? Not interested.

"I'm seeing Miriam tonight at *Byron's* to scope out the 411."

"Are you going to D.C.—to the reception?"

"I don't think so," I shook my head. "Miriam is really wrapped up in the doings in the Carib. She's family, so I'm checking it all out for myself. It's the least I can do for her—and her father."

* * *

Byron's was patronized by a black professional crowd that wore its income on its sleeves. Lots of suited-up brothers with Denzel Washington or Tupac Shakur profiles, looking like *GQ* fashion plates. Positively no *real* hip-hoppers allowed. No baggy jeans. No oversized shirts. No Timberland boots.

Upon entering the place, I squeezed my buttocks through the tightly packed tables on the floor—dodging the lustful stares of the well-groomed brothers and the disapproving glares from the sisters at their sides—as I made my way toward the upstairs lounge. The place was equipped with all the standard accoutrements of a fat capitalist hangout: plush carpets, banker lamps, burgundy-colored overstuffed chairs. Apparently Byron, the restaurant's namesake and my former brother-in-law, was still wrestling with the room's decor. Original paintings by Romare Bearden and William Johnson shared the wall space with tacky, stylized photo portraits of Colin Powell, Kweisi Mfume, and other Afro alpha males. No one seemed to notice, however. The denizens of this secluded upper chamber were always busy conducting or concluding deals in the corners of the dimly lit rooms. A perfect place, I thought, for Miriam and me to talk things over. I found myself an unoccupied corner and sank into an overstuffed chair. As a waitron took my order, I felt the vibration from the music down below. I slipped off my heels and dug my feet into the carpet. My feet and my body were beginning to relax, all right, but my mind still had serious misgivings about what was to follow.

The game was over, I thought to myself, and the people down below didn't seem to have a clue. The era that spawned the new black middle class—that had made this whole gathering possible—was already past. It had been stomped out decisively by Boothe Wainwright's "Agenda for a New America." Across the country, Republicans were shutting down program after program designed to help blacks, and things were about to get pretty bleak pretty fast. But the denizens of *Byron's* were completely oblivious to the new order that was coming. Sleek and sweet, preoccupied with getting over, the reality of the first bite had yet to sear their flesh. These, after all, were the spiritual descendants of the Rev. Reggie Baxter and Mel Farmington, a generation of cats and kittens who were functionally incapable of thinking beyond the dead-end muddle of black politics. Better to party up and hope for the best than to duck down and run for cover. Seated upstairs, I felt the decadent pulse of the *func de siècle* surging up through my toes.

I twirled the rocks in my glass of Jack Daniel's Black, sipped greedily on the stirrer, and waited for Miriam. As I mused over my post-civil rights apocalyptic philosophy, I suddenly saw Miriam approaching out of the corner of my eye. She was toting a large green canvas shoulder bag and looked as if she were returning from the trenches. Upon reaching me, Miriam dropped the bag, which thudded softly onto the carpet, and plopped down into a chair across from me.

"Sorry I'm late," she apologized, looking tired but curiously satisfied. A full body, who walked with great purpose and enthusiasm, Miriam had the kind of glow that comes with the conviction that one is fighting the good fight. It was also the same look that I had seen on the faces of many of the nuns who tortured me in Catholic school. "Been here long?" she asked.

I looked at my watch. "Not really. How goes it?"

"Never a dull moment," she shrugged. "Folks uptown want me to form a commission."

"For what?" I tried to flag Marilyn, the waitron, in the semi-darkness. I caught her eye just as she was turning away from a table of three men.

"The shoot-out and the fire at *Johnnae's*," explained Miriam.

Weeks earlier, a woman had walked into *Johnnae's*—a popular beauty shop on 125th Street in Harlem—shot and killed the owner, and torched the place in one fell swoop, before being shot to death herself by the police. Johnnae was a black subtenant of Goode's, a discount store with whom he shared the building. Recently, the landlord, a local black church, had dramatically raised the rent to fatten its coffers and expand its presence in the neighborhood, and Goode's had responded by raising the rent on *Johnnae's*. What was largely a business matter between landlords and tenants quickly mushroomed into an all-out racial quagmire when black residents got wind of a rumor

that the actual owner of Goode's was Jewish—which was un-
true. It didn't help that Dr. Walid Afreeka—described and de-
nounced by many (including me) as a professional race racket-
eer—was right smack dab in the middle of it all. Afreeka had
waddled his roly-poly presence, along with his big mouth, right
out onto the picket line; he was even accused by some people
(though not by me) of instigating the event by spreading the
false rumor about Goode's. The woman responsible for the
killing and the blaze had been a member of the picket line that
had marched in front of *Johnnae's* with Afreeka. All in all, twelve
people died at the "Massacre at *Johnnae's*," as it was named by
Harlem's pugnacious *New York Drum*.

"What do they want with you?" I asked.

"My credibility, I suppose."

I slowly shook my head. "Watch it, girl. Il Duce and the
commissioner are having a field day with this. Can you blame
them? Walid set himself up for this, with that big, fat mouth of
his." Afreeka, I thought to myself, didn't have a clue what he
was fighting for anymore; the man was running on empty, a
frightening example of just how far so-called black leadership
had deteriorated in this country during the past twenty years.

"I know," she said, running a hand through her mass of
graying hair. "They want to make it solely a case of black anti-
Semitism and take the moral high ground—completely ignoring
the underlying cause of it all, the way that Harlem is being swallowed up—"

"And the exact role of Goode's Discount Store?" I asked.
Miriam winced. Most of the people who had died in that fire
had been women, Latin-American women. And it had been the
black church—and Goode's—who had started the whole thing
by raising their rents.

The waitron handed Miriam the bourbon she had ordered,
and we both sipped our drinks quietly and pondered the tragic
mess that had occurred uptown. That and the other tragic mess
that we were preparing ourselves to discuss.

"Okay," I said, tapping the table to open the subject to discussion. "What's the deal?"

Miriam locked her fingers together and wedged herself more

comfortably into the chair. "President Bernard needs help."

"I thought he was getting that from Uncle Sam."

"Nina, you know as well as I do that the government—our government—is trying to pressure President Bernard into disavowing the Lava-lava movement. They see the whole thing as a low-rent communist plot. It's like what Noam Chomsky has been saying all along," she said.

"What's that?" I was startled to hear Miriam, a moderate Democrat, citing Chomsky.

"The U.S. doesn't condone any sort of development outside of the free-market sphere," Miriam reported.

"Miriam, you aren't suddenly finding fault with our glorious free enterprise system?" I asked, feigning shock at her newfound revolutionary analysis. "You have to remember my dear, that I'm a petit bourgeois capitalist and you're married to *un grande* capitalist!"

"Nina, this is serious!" she said reproachfully.

"Honey, a little levity never hurt anyone." But I couldn't help thinking seriously about our country's track record for thwarting "rogue regimes": Guatemala, Nicaragua, the Dominican Republic, Chile, Grenada. The only one that got away was Cuba—and it was still paying a heavy price for its nationalism and antiquated communism. The queer thing was that if Cuba was guilty of being a totalitarian regime—and it was—then what about China, the ancestral homeland of my dearest friend, Anna? The difference was that China was a vast market of commercial possibility, and human rights could take a flying leap out the window when it came up against our paramount commercial interests.

"Okay, Chomsky is right. What does that have to do with me? Why does Pepe Bernard want to see me?"

Miriam casually looked around the room before she spoke. "The president—he's needs to speak to someone who isn't into policy."

"Okay. I'm not," said I. "What does that mean, though? What is it that he's looking for?"

"Practical knowledge," she replied. "You know?"

I stared at my sister-in-law. "No, I don't. What does that

have to do with me?"

"Nina, please." She gave me a "you know exactly what I'm talking about" look.

"No, Miriam. What are you alluding to?"

"Look, Gary didn't tell me everything, but—"

"Tell you about *what*?" I was wearing my Polly Poker face, perfected during my years of on-the-job training as a Brooklyn prosecutor.

"Tower."

"And?"

"Gary said that you had come across confidential material." Her voice began taking on the low, quasi-conspiratorial tone that people use when they feel they're dealing with something *deep*. "Gary also read about a break-in at Tower's hospital in Queens. The paper reported that it looked to investigators as if a commando operation had gone on. One or two people were dead. He never said anything exactly, but he came to the conclusion that you were dealing with some big-time shit—and surviving."

I almost laughed, particularly at the word "surviving." If she only knew what an emotional and mental wreck I was because of it all, ready to snap off someone's head. And I almost had. I had actually frightened away my former assistant—struck her and drove her away. Yes, as Robert Nesta Marley once said, I'm a survivor. A black survivor.

"That you could get things done, Nina," I heard her say, snapping me out of my inner monologue.

"I don't know what you're talking about, Miriam," I lied. She knew something, all right, but I was convinced she didn't know enough to do anything with it.

"Look, Nina, you're the pro. I'm new at this," she laughingly confessed, sensing that I wasn't going to take the bait. "I can't bullshit you. I know it and you know it."

"Miriam, dear, you're already doing enough with the committee."

"It's not enough, Nina. Look at the butchery that's taking place!"

The junta had unleashed a ferocious terror campaign

against the popular forces in Misericordia. Anyone suspected of being a Lava-lavaista—or even a sympathizer—was harassed, tortured, executed, exiled, or raped. Rape had become the choice weapon of terror and humiliation, aimed, of course, at the weakest link in the social chain, women. Prior to the revolution that won the island's slave population their freedom, whites often raped black women with impunity. It was perfectly acceptable for slave owners to get in their "strokes" with a "sugar cane bitch" (as slave women were called) and then return home to the more relaxed and refined company of their wives. Now the military and the Papas used rape to dehumanize the women they attacked—and the men who were powerless to help them. It was nicknamed the "Bosnian Technique."

The crisis in Misericordia was considered an internal matter; the leaders of the junta played the sovereignty card to shield the terror from international scrutiny and to block intervention. The United Nations was understandably reluctant to get involved, having recently been burned in Somalia, Rwanda, and Bosnia. Afraid that their own internal problems might be exposed by their involvement in the crisis, the Caribbean island-nations weren't eager to intervene either. The same was true of that colossus to the north, the Organization of American States, whose members had plenty of sins of their own to conceal.

For Miriam, Misericordia wasn't just another grotesque dose of nightly news about a nation gone mad, the incomprehensibility of a voudoux-plagued nation. This was personal. It concerned her family, her father and mother's legacy. It was personal for me, too. It was exactly the sort of bloody mess that I was determined to stay away from.

"It's not enough," she reiterated under the influence of her second drink of the evening, her fist pounding the chair's leather arm.

"Miriam," I sighed, "I can understand your feelings about the situation, but this is out of my league and, unfortunately, out of your hands."

"My hands?"

"Yes. Look, this is the kind of situation where the Maericans will have to get themselves out of—"

"You mean idly stand by?"

"I mean that they rose up against the French, the Spanish, and the English and fought them for years and won," I reminded her.

"Nina, this time is different!" she retorted, stoked by the liquor. "They didn't have the CIA scheming against them in the past! The junta is doing the U.S. a big favor by getting rid of the movement that got Father Bernard into office! They don't like him because he's against privatization and structural adjustment, and all those modern-day Jesse Jameses like the World Bank and the International Monetary Fund!"

"You forgot the World Trade Organization," I added.

"Them, too!" Miriam was upset, and understandably so. Nasty people were doing undemocratically nasty things. "Okay, okay," I began. "What do you want me to do? Or, what is it that you think I can do?"

"Some of us—"

"Us?"

"Yes. The committee. We decided that a third force—"

"A *third force*?" My dear sister-in-law was eerily beginning to sound like Pyle from Graham Greene's *The Quiet American*, who ushered in a reign of terror by arming a so-called "third force."

"Yes. We decided that a third force was needed to even things—"

"To do *what*?" I wanted Miriam to cut to the chase.

"To equip the popular forces with the requisite tools of liberation," she finished.

"Weapons?"

"I'm speaking about the requisite tools of liberation," she insisted. This woman had already picked up the lingo of plausible denial: stick obstinately to something that sounds benign.

"Miriam, first, I'm not an arms merchant or a mercenary. Second, the government has a slew of laws: the Neutrality Act, the Logan Act, arms export laws, and the Omnibus Counter-Terrorism Act. You are talking about serious butt-spanking if caught and convicted—and I ain't talking about no English butt-spanking, either! We're talking about serious welts on the tush!"

"Now, Nina, someone like you knows people who, uh, can wiggle—"

"Yeah, and I prosecuted their Celtic asses during my D.A. days. Their Irish posteriors are wiggling upstate. Case closed."

"Nina, these are *our* people."

"Look, *sister*, don't start waving the red, black, and green in my face. You're talking about sticking your hand into a bloody cauldron where foreign policy and national security are cooked up, and you and the committee don't know what the hell you're doing!"

"Then help us!" she pleaded. Miriam's eyes widened with anguish. "Help us. Help them. They are your people, too."

"Miriam, don't start." I closed my eyes, moving my head from side to side. She was going to do a black attack.

"But it's true."

"Miriam, I'm not Maerican. I'm an American. What you're talking about, with all due respect, is a Carib thang."

"Nina, all black people are Caribbean."

"Oh, really now? I felt my eyebrows arching upward to my hairline. "Since when?" Some of the "Afro-Caribbeans" I knew wanted to hot-foot it away from any association with us blacks who were born here in the States. We were perceived as bringing down the race. Carving out the perceived differences between us had become something of a cottage industry as of late.

"At some point, sooner or later, all black folks, either as slaves or post-colonials, passed through the West Indies."

I was getting tired of this line of reasoning. "Stop it. Stop it! This sort of sophistry is beneath you."

"Sophistry?! Are we or are we not an African people?" Miriam challenged. She wasn't just playing the black card; she was playing the full deck.

"We are an African-American people," I countered, "but the American strain in *me* understands certain domestic laws that the African in *you* seems all too willing to ignore!"

Miriam sank back into her chair, deflated. Suddenly, a gleam of enticement entered into her eyes. "We have funds," she assured me throatily.

"Good," I replied. "You're going to need them to bail your

collection of asses out of jail if you go ahead with this, Miriam!"

"Stop speaking to me as if I'm Monique or Yolanda," she snapped, invoking the names of her two daughters. "Obviously, you don't think I know what I'm doing."

"Well, you are approaching me, aren't you? Miriam, I'm trying to look out for your best interest. You have a husband and three children."

"A career, a nice home," she mocked.

"And a city of Lisa Bartholomés who depend on you," I said, reminding her of the six-year-old Latina child who was allegedly beaten to death by her mother, yet another example of the financial stewardship of Il Duce and the city's Child Welfare Office. "You already have enough on your plate right here. Let the Maericans sort this out. If President Bernard is a real political leader, he'll rally his people to rise up and fight. Nestor Morgan did, after all."

"They have guns, Nina," Miriam reminded me.

"Look, tinplate, pocketbook desperadoes like the security force in Misericordia have a habit of running scared the minute the folks they've been bullying become righteously riled. They can't take the real heat of the people's wrath. I've seen neighborhoods in Brooklyn rise up and put the fear of God into the thugs who had been terrorizing them. But it's people themselves who have to make the decision about what they want to do and what they're willing to risk."

"They need help, Nina," she said softly.

"Yes, they do," I sadly agreed. "But they don't need more Americans meddling into their affairs. Stay out, Miriam. Do what you can here!"

Miriam eyed me coldly. "Tell that to George Plunkett."

"Plunkett? What about him?"

"He's been speaking to the president about an invasion."

"To Bernard?"

"No, to Benton."

George Plunkett, a Chicago Democrat, was the chairman of the newly renamed but politically eviscerated African-American Congressional Caucus. After Boothe and his new Republican rough riders took over the House, they immediately eliminated funding for the black caucus. And the only thing the black congressional leadership could do in response was to change its name—from "Black" to "African-American." Plunkett seemed to be shopping for a big-ticket item to prove the Caucus's mettle. I seriously doubted that President Jeffrey Benton would be likely to make any sudden moves on behalf of a black country. But I have been wrong about other things.

"Bernard isn't listening to him, is he?"

"He's considering his options."

"He would countenance an American invasion of Misericordia?"

"Desperate circumstances call for desperate measures," said Miriam, as she showed me the bottom of her glass.

Indeed, I thought. These are the times that try a woman's soul.

CHAPTER TWO

I left Miriam with a non-committal: I didn't say yes, but I didn't rule it out entirely. As I drove uptown, I thought about the P factor: Plunkett. Rep. Plunkett had resolved to make the AACC "a fighting organization." The battlefield he had chosen was foreign policy, perhaps the last area of so-called white male expertise. Forget the fact that Boothe and his boys were currently dismantling the entire domestic agenda legacy of Roosevelt and Johnson. Plunkett was following a monkey-see, monkey-do strategy, staking his own claim to the foreign policy muscle already wielded by the commander-in-chief. The choice of Misericordia was a stroke of genius, I thought. He'll take black minds off the incompetence of black leadership at home by focusing on black misery across the sea. The one unseemly glitch was Plunkett's current role as an apologist for the military dictatorship in Nigeria, a brutal regime that had been called "the open sore of a continent" by that nation's exiled Nobel laureate, Wole Soyinka.

Shuddering at the brewing madness and the utter moral bankruptcy of so-called leadership on the Hill, I parked my car, attached my "club" to the steering wheel, and got out. The evening air felt pleasantly cool, temporarily diluting the stale aroma of male urine that usually lingered in the city's corners and alleyways from early spring to late fall. I stopped at a convenience store to pick up a carton of milk and then headed back to my apartment building.

As I inserted my keys into the lock of my apartment door, I heard an angry voice cursing and shouting in Chinese. I swung open the door and saw Anna, her back turned away from me, shouting into the telephone. She wheeled around as I entered the room and closed the door behind me. Her face was contorted with rage, her cheeks flushed with anger and covered with tears. She spewed forth a torrent of verbal abuse—the only Chinese I could recognize was the phrase, "incestuous turtles"—and slammed down the phone. Anna had gone to Chicago to check out an art exhibit showcasing young, multicultural artists and wasn't expected back for a day or so. Although we share keys to each other's apartments, her presence in my apartment was still a total surprise.

"Anna?" I asked cautiously. "What's going on? What happened? What are you doing here?"

Anna, her eyes tightly closed, raised a hand to interrupt. "Nin, you're asking too many questions too quickly." She began sobbing uncontrollably. "I caught that bitch fucking someone else!"

"Who? Shinyun?"

"Yes!" Anna hissed between tears. "Medic!"

She wanted a drink. I tossed my briefcase on the couch. "Sit down," I told her as I walked across the room. In the kitchen, I placed the milk in the refrigerator and knelt to retrieve a bottle of whiskey that was stored below the counter. As I reached for the glasses in the cupboard, Anna came into the kitchen and weakly leaned against the doorjamb. The woman had taken some major blows recently, following her announcement to her mother, the surviving head of her family, that she was gay. The fire from that major revelation had scorched much of the Chinese community from Manhattan and Queens to Hong Kong, Taiwan, and mainland China.

No longer respected as one of the leading members of the up-and-coming generation of Chinese Americans, Anna suffered a dramatic drop in the number of Chinese and Asian clients that she represented, and found herself suddenly isolated from all the mainstream civic organizations in the Asian community. Adding insult to injury, she was even asked to return her Miss Chinatown beauty queen award. And now the news about her lover, Shinyun.

Always resilient, Anna decided to use her savings to abandon her failing practice and to pursue an even riskier career as an artist rep and gallery owner. Anna and Shinyun, her Taiwanese lover, had moved into Shinyun's East Village apartment together, converting Anna's Upper West Side apartment into a small gallery. Anna threw herself into her new work, going to galleries and shows almost every night, meeting and greeting people in her office and over lunch, networking and jawboning on the phone endlessly. Shy and with a limited command of English, Shinyun was left handling the basic maintenance of the gallery. It was tedious, unrewarding work, and she soon began to feel neglected by Anna, who was fast becoming a hot item in the artistic and gay and lesbian communities.

Anna, I had thought and said at the time, was spending too much time politicking and too little time taking care of her relationship with Shinyun. She mistakenly thought that just living together was enough to keep the home fires burning and was too preoccupied with her work to see what was happening with Shinyun. I could see it coming from the start. Anna still felt she had to prove herself, to create a new identity to make up for what she felt she had lost when she was cut off from her family and friends. She still hadn't given up on a city council seat and maybe even a crack at the mayor's office. Il Duce wouldn't—couldn't—be there forever. Term limits would eventually see to that.

I guided Anna back into the living room, sat her down in the armchair, and plopped myself down on the couch. I poured her a drink, which she gulped down quickly, sighing deeply. Her eyes were puffy and swollen from crying. As she ran her fingers through her black hair, I noticed a streak of gray that hadn't been there before.

"You're getting old, Anna," I kidded, trying to lighten the mood. Both of us were only thirty-five, after all.

"That's the least of my worries," she said sourly.

"You want to talk about it?"

"What's to say? Can I have another?"

"Sure." I poured us both a drink. "Was that Shinyun you were reading the riot act to?"

"The bitch, you mean," Anna spat. She swallowed hard and placed the glass smack down on the middle of a *Vanity Fair*, the perfect coaster. "Well," she began, "Chicago was a bust; nothing really interesting at the exhibit. As usual, identity politics begets identity art, which is to say, bad art. I came home early and went straight to the apartment from the airport, thinking that Shinyun would be there. I walked in and heard someone moaning in our bedroom where—"

"—Where you have brought other women yourself," I reminded her. Anna had been experimenting recklessly with her newfound gay artiste lifestyle for some time now. "So, now you caught *her* with another woman."

"Less than that," she replied. "A man."

"What?"

"She was with a dick! Rolando's to be precise!"

"Oh, my God," I heard myself say. I poured myself another drink. This was a shock. Anna had been looking for a new Basquiat, a young painter whom she could promote as a hot, sexy, artistic stud. She had recently found him in a young brother who went by the single name, Rolando. The two of us had actually "discovered" him selling his neo-primitive paintings around Astor Place. With his dark skin and long dreds, Rolando was a ruggedly handsome manchild. He had perfected a seductively monosyllabic drone that consisted more of grunts than words; a root of licorice dangled constantly from his full lips. The brother was hot, all right, and Anna had left him in the care of Shinyun, while she promoted him to the media machine as a "primitive genius." Apparently, primitive genius also implied primitive urges, both for Rolando and for Shinyun, who had clearly become more flexible in her sexual orientation

"God, Nina, if only I'd had your gun," Anna moaned.

"Well, I can understand you wanting to shoot him—"

"Fuck that! I'm talking about that cunt! I've got to keep Rolando!"

For a moment I wasn't sure I'd heard her correctly. "Anna, Rolando was sticking your woman."

"I know, I know, but I have to remain calm and play my cards carefully, Nina. He's my meal ticket, after all. If I put him on the map as a painter, my career as an artist rep will be established," she rationalized. "I have to use that bitch fucker!"

"What about Shinyun? Don't you think you two should have a cooling-off period and try to work this out?"

"Why are you so concerned about her?!" Anna snarled like a wounded animal. "That bitch is getting more dick than you!"

I flinched inwardly. "Anna, I know you are under a great deal of stress with everything that's happened, but don't you ever speak to me that way. You're in *my* house, drinking *my* liquor, and, figuratively speaking at least, crying on *my* shoulder. The bar is closed!" I reached over and snatched the glass from her hand. I gathered up the whiskey and my glass and strode furiously into the kitchen. The girl-talk session had ended. I wasn't in the mood for that type of abuse, not even from a wounded friend.

I placed the bottle down hard on the counter, rinsed the glasses with warm water, and placed them in the dish rack. Anna's words had cut me so deeply because they were true. Shinyun *was* getting more than me. And my occasional digital forays into my lower erogenous zones had started to leave me wanting. I sighed heavily as Anna stepped into the kitchen.

"Nina, I'm sorry," she sputtered. "You're right. I'm being an ungrateful bitch. I'm sorry."

"Apology accepted." I turned and offered her a wet hand. "Let's get your things and bring them into Donna's room."

Anna brought in her overnight bag as I made up Donna's old bed. It was hard. Months ago I had buried Donna in my family plot after she died in a shootout in Pennsylvania with the New Nation movement. Hakim. Eve Shandlin. All dead and now added to a growing list of race martyrs. I snapped open the sheet. Anna grabbed her end and fitted it over the corners of the mattress.

"What's been going on with you?" she asked, as I handed her a pillowcase.

"Nothing much. Miriam wants to get me involved in that madness in Misericordia. Check this out. She wants me to organize a third force." I tossed Anna a light cotton, powder-blue blanket, which she opened and spread over the mattress. With that finished, she sat down on the bed and began removing her shoes, as I leaned against the wall near the door.

"I don't get it. What's this third force?" Anna stopped and thought. "A guerrilla army?! Is she trying to lasso you into that? Is she crazy or what?! She's never heard of the Counter-terrorism Act?"

"Thank you, Anna." I bowed. "I tried to tell her the exact same thing, and she started waving the red, black, and green in front of my face. Anyway, President Bernard wants to meet with yours truly."

"Why?" Anna asked, unbuttoning her blouse.

"His excellency the president believes I have deep insight into the black scheme of things—along with direct access to the requisite tools of liberation."

"Weapons?" asked Anna, as she stepped out of her skirt.

"Uh huh."

She zipped open her bag, removed a toilet kit, and then made her way toward the bathroom. "Honey, just remember this," she said, stopping at the door. "Your family can get you killed."

"Does that include your friends?"

"*Certainement*," she replied in her best French accent. "As the Mexicans say: all your friends are false; all your enemies are real. Ciao."

With that, Anna stepped into the bathroom, and I retreated to my own room to catch some Z's.

When I reached my office the next morning, I found several messages on my answering machine—all from Miriam. I was flipping open my newspaper when the phone rang.

"Nina!" she shouted into the receiver.

Good god, girl, I thought, it's too early in the morning to be popping my ears like this.

"Did you hear what happened?" she asked breathlessly. "There was a another coup in Misericordia!"

"No, I haven't seen anything. I was just flipping through the *Times*."

"Fuck that—"

"Miriam, your language," I tsked.

"Nina, turn on your television! Luc's daddy is now running the country!"

I almost dropped the phone again. Now she was really pushing my button. I reached for my remote and switched on the TV, moving from one channel to another until I found the White House spokeswoman Valerie Compote on the screen. A law school classmate of Anna's and mine, Valerie was giving the standard party line that the White House was closely monitoring the situation in Misericordia and the Benton Administration was committed to the lawful return of President Bernard. Then the network switched from Washington to Port Henri.

A press conference was being held by General Estaban Malmundo, the father of a man I had once dated, loved, and incessantly fucked. (I'm sorry but that's the way it was.) Standing at a podium before a huge picture of Nestor Morgan on his horse, Gen. Malmundo was taking questions from the press. He didn't look at all like a general, however, dressed as he was in a white double-breasted suit with a red carnation in his lapel. Smart move, I thought, both politically and sartorially.

"Uh oh, Miriam. I think this is Triomphalism without Triomphe."

"Exactly," she replied.

I watched the performance intently. The general, a bronzed, athletic-looking man of about sixty, smiled beatifically at the cameras and spoke about "establishing an atmosphere conducive to democratic rejuvenation." When reporters questioned him about the possible return of President Bernard, the general replied that such a politically charged move would have to be carefully negotiated.

"You see, Nina! He's just about power," my sister-in-law said over the phone.

"Well, you don't think he did it because he felt a deep love for the masses and wanted to stop the bloodshed, do you?"

"He just represents the same old mulatto elite."

"No doubt about that, but at least they made up their minds; they have a plan," I countered.

"What do you mean?"

"Simply put, Miriam, while Bernard is playing Hamlet, the elite has decided to replace the blood-soaked junta with a guy who's not likely to deposit dead political opponents on the streets of Misericordia." The whole dead body thing, I reminded her, was bad for both tourism and the gambling industry.

"President Bernard is trying very hard to weigh his options," she defended.

"What options? He's been preempted! Can't you see it? Benton would much rather deal with Malmundo. Your boy simply doesn't have a plan, Miriam."

"Well, he would if he could get help from—"

"Wait a minute," I interrupted. The camera was pulling back to film the introduction of a group of men who were standing alongside the general. "I think the general is introducing his cabinet—"

"He can't do that! He doesn't have the constitutional authority to do that!" Miriam exploded.

"He has something better—the country! He doesn't need constitutional authority, Miriam. Oh, wait—there's Luc!"

After the introduction of the ministers of law, economics, and security—the latter, an enormous man named Hobson—Luc finally appeared. He was still the same deep golden nigga I became entranced with in college. His sharp features were inherited from his French and Spanish ancestors; his color and hair, from the Africans. He looked like a bronze god, standing proudly there before the cameras.

Luc was widely known as a human rights advocate. In fact, he had once helped me in my own investigation. It was certainly a gamble for his father to appoint him to a high-level cabinet position. It was also a big risk for Luc. After all, he was attaching his good name to an, at worst, illegal regime and, at best, an interim, caretaker's government. I was sure he had some kind of plan, some good reason for sticking his neck out like this. But I couldn't for the life of me figure out what it was.

"Damn," said Miriam. "Luc has sold out."

"I don't think so, Miriam," I countered. "Luc Malmundo has too much integrity for that."

"Nina, my eyes aren't deceiving me the way your heart is — he's on his old man's staff! He's a fucking *comprador* sell-out!"

That touched a nerve. "Look, Miriam, I have enough critical wherewithal to make a rational assessment. Luc is a cock hound, a Latin lover, a ladies man — no doubt about it — but the man has principles!"

"Don't make me laugh; my lips are chapped," Miriam sneered condescendingly.

"Look, dear," I said through clenched teeth, "Lucious Garcia Francisco Malmundo cares about his country and his people as much as Pepe Bernard — certainly as much as you do! At least he's willing to crawl into the belly of the beast to do something about it. Are you saying to me that Luc isn't progressive? Huh? Are you going to deny that it was Luc who prevented the president from being murdered — the traditional Maerican farewell treatment for their fallen chief executives?! You just don't get it, Dr. Butler. You honestly can't see the difference between Luc and Pepe?"

"What's that?"

"El Presidente is waiting for a plan of action and Luc, I feel confident, already has one. It may not work and it may cost him his life, but at least he's not acting the chump to that tower of moral principles, Jeff Benton!"

"No, he's being used as a cloak for his father's sinister policies," Miriam spat back.

"Luc would never lend his support to a corrupt agenda," I snapped, trying to convince myself. "He has been vocal in the past about stopping the bloodshed!"

"Perhaps his father has promised him the presidency, a Malmundo dynasty," Miriam countered. "After all, I'm from there —"

"Get the fuck out of here, you pompous *bogusita*!" I said,

pacing angrily around my desk with the phone. "You were born in Nuevo York—raised in Queens. So don't get ethnic or extra-national on me! Miriam, you're rapidly developing the type of closed, ideological mindset that rejects potential allies outright just because they're not pure on every bloody issue. And besides, if Luc was interested in building a dynasty, he would have picked the military or the security apparatus—not education!"

"Okay, Nina, you've made your point—"

"I'm not finished, sister dear. I'm going to come and meet El Presidente—"

"Terrific!"

"—and show you what a dick-beaten chump he is!"

With that, I slammed down the phone and tried to calm myself with the memory of Luc's strong arms and moist lips.

CHAPTER THREE

A few days later I landed at Reagan International Airport outside of Washington, D.C., where I was greeted by Gale Simmons, one of my dearest friends from way back when. A professor of history and political science at Howard University, Gale was a leading member of the intellectual, post-modern jet set. The girl could rap the P-mod talk till she was blue in the face: semiotics, deconstruction, post-structuralism, you name it. Gale's leading competitor as a po-mo feminist celebrity was nellie marcos, for years the reigning black feminist and a charter member of what my late husband Lee used to call the Niggerati, a posse of celebrity intellectuals who made their fame and fortune explaining black issues to white audiences.

When it came to explaining what currently passed for an intellectual class in America, I usually just shrugged my shoulders in disbelief. But my friend Gale was into it thick and slick, jet-setting regularly from Paris to Lagos to Tokyo to Los Angeles with the informal calling card, "Have Theory, Will Travel." Regarded by many of her peers as an "intellectual newscaster," she preferred sexy female power suits and relaxed hairstyles to the common Afro ensembles and braids of the black multitude. With her smooth caramel complexion, keen negroid features, and thick wavy black hair, she exuded professionalism. Her cat-like gray eyes and high cheek bones added an element of sex appeal. A regular on television panel discussions and newscasts, in op-ed pieces, and at socialist, feminist, neo-socialist, and post-feminist conferences, Gale also cranked out a steady stream of indecipherable tomes that no one outside the academic priest-hood could possibly comprehend. "Terminally irrelevant but career enhancing," had been Lee's one disinterested review.

Gee, as I had called her for years, was trying to get me to take my new academic position seriously. I had only been teaching at Manhattan Borough Community College for a year and a half; as an adjunct, I was still fairly low in the academic scheme of things. But I just wasn't interested in Gale's line of bullshit, the so-called life of the mind.

Besides, my late husband had left behind a literary bonanza of manuscripts, the first of which to be published was already netting me a small fortune. Lee had first gained notoriety—as well as infamy in some people's minds—with *Prophetic Accommodation*, in which he argued that Christianity had had a negative, as well as a positive, effect on blacks. With the help of Lee's best friend, Toshiro Fleming, I was currently editing *The Niggerati*, about so-called black public intellectuals; *Pet Negroes*, about black conservatives; and *Betrayal of the People*, an analytical study of how the civil rights movement won the battle but lost the war. The real kicker would be *Blacked into a Corner: The Decline of Black Nationalism*. I planned to use the money from Lee's books to fund the Lee Halligan Foundation, to promote his concept of "progressive nationalism" nationwide, and to give out scholarships in my children's names.

"Nina, I can help you get a treatise published," Gale bragged good-naturedly, zooming through Washington in her black Mercedes sedan, the embossed license plate garishly proclaiming: THEORY ONE.

"On what, pray tell?" I gazed out the window and suddenly remembered the last time I was here. Dexter and I were looking for some documents and ended up having to kill an NYPD captain, who was stalking us in a warehouse in the northeast quadrant of the city.

"I don't know, Nina. You can do a post-fem analysis of your years as a brother-buster. The legal Terry McMillian who busts head-moe hoodlums! Pow! That's for Anita, Clarence! Pow!"

"Gee, please. I'm supposed to be pumping my progressive black woman credentials. I already make some men nervous as it is." Besides, I didn't need an extra income from writing, and I certainly wasn't interested in being a celebrity intellectual. Fuck theory. The point is to change the world, not analyze it to death.

"What do you mean? You always used to make the niggas drool, you and your fine Anita Baker-looking self," said Gale. "You're just a darker version of that fine-looking sister, Nina."

"I'm damaged goods, Gee," I confided.

"You mean the thing about Lee and the kids?"

"Yep," I gulped. I felt a surge of grief coming forward, but I held it back and softly swallowed it.

Gee kept her eyes on the Connecticut Avenue traffic as we headed uptown. She slowly nodded her head. "Still rough, huh?"

"Yeah," I sighed. "I also think about Donna a great deal."

"Seeing anybody?"

I bounced my head on my shoulders. "Yes and no; maybe so."

"What's his name, rank, and condom size?" she winked, weaving the car past the slugs on the avenue. "C'mon, girl, details. Details!"

For all her supposed worldly sophistication, Gale could be quite vulgar. I told her about Dexter, how we had worked on the "Black Heat" aspect of the Martin case and how the Tower angle had developed. Gale pulled suddenly over to the curb, brakes screeching. The whole thing happened so fast that I thought she was having car trouble.

"Wait a minute! Wait a minute!" she said, swerving in her seat to look at me.

"What's wrong?!" I asked, anxiously looking about the car.

"You mean to tell me that, in addition to schtupping this guy, Dexter, you two also took down De Lawd?!"

"That's confidential, Gale!" This was the kind of thing that I was going out of my way to keep from Miriam, and, of course, here I was blabbing it to Gale the first chance I got.

"Confidential?! What the fuck for? You know how many niggas have been trying to expose that faker? Yipeeee!" she shrieked.

Needless to say, Gale was beside herself, absolutely ecstatic about Tower and the circumstances of his demise. Everyone knew that he had abruptly resigned from the Black Christian Network, turning it over to Veronica Martin and her daughter, Malika, who also happened to be the wife and daughter of the man from whose organization Tower had stolen money. Very few people knew why it all had happened, however. I had the "smoking gun"—a film of Paul Tower conspiring with NYPD captain Harold Kirby to kill Malik Martin. Kirby was the same man who had tried to kill Dexter and me. The same man who we had ended up killing ourselves.

"Girl, you're the baddest black woman in America. The baddest woman, period," Gale beamed as she switched the key in the ignition. "Nina, the nigga killer. Do it, girl. Word!"

"Gale!"

"Oh, we have to be PC when we speaketh of the noble tribe of African-Americans, lost here in Babylon. Particularly the Black Man. Puh-leese!"

"Look, it's not something I'm proud of. Or ashamed of, for that matter. It just had serious repercussions for my life; that's all. Now Dexter doesn't want to see me—or at least has difficulties seeing me."

"What's wrong? I'd figure you two would be into some serious power stroking after taking down the most prominent black MAN in America. Boom! You're dead, sucker! Took down the Tower of power. Word up!"

"Gee, it's complicated. His wife was killed up in Harlem, a robbery victim."

"And?" She made it seem as if losing a loved one was an ordinary and everyday occurrence.

"He feels that I'm a little too close to that kind of violence."

"Oh, a sensitive brother," she replied, with a slight veil of contempt.

Yes, I thought. Maybe that's why I found him attractive in the first place. We were silent for a brief moment, and it was a brief moment that I was enjoying.

"You pack a gun, Nina?" Gale looked at me with a gleam of perverse curiosity.

"Sometimes," I shrugged. "I don't like them, but they do come in handy sometimes." The image of me as a poster girl for the National Rifle Association suddenly popped into my head: *Hi, you don't know me, but my name is Nina Halligan. They call me the Screaming Madonna. Since my family was brutally murdered, I now use handguns myself. If only my husband had one at the time he was attacked, he could have used it to protect his life and the lives of our children.*

I pulled a black-pronged Chinese star out of my purse. "I use these. They are illegal but very effective."

"What's that?" She quickly looked at it and then returned her eyes to the road ahead.

"Martial arts throwing star." Gale took the star from me, bringing it quickly round to her face as she drove. "Damn, girl, you turned into a black macho mama."

"Femo," I corrected, using the word Anna employed to describe a tough woman. "Femo."

"I like bitch better," she countered.

"You and every knucklehead standing on the corner with his crotch down to his ankle," I retorted. "Smokin' blunts and drinkin' forties."

"No, hear me out."

"Hear you out? Are you going to rationalize, theorize thirteen-year-olds referring to women and young girls as bitches and 'hos?" I asked. "Get real, girl."

Gale drove the Benz into the driveway of her home, situated in a very posh, leafy, upper-middle-class section of northwest Washington. She turned off the motor and looked me square in the eyes. "You see, I'm working on a thing called the B-theory."

"Different from black theory?" I asked. I knew what the B meant, and she knew that I knew that she knew that I knew.

But I wasn't going to bite.

"You see, Nina, the black woman, today's successful black woman, is afraid of sex and being associated with sex. Where's our black Madonna? We no longer enjoy sex. These days, white girls are getting all the black dick."

"If I have to listen to this," I said, shaking my head as I left the car. I closed the door and held onto my black nylon carry-on bag, "I need to be under the influence."

Half an hour later, my shoes off and my feet propped up on a comfortable couch, I listened to a sick, demented, twisted, whacked-out woman—one of my best friends, mind you, and my daughter Ayesha's godmother—lay out the "theory of the bitch."

"Pussy, Nina, it's all about pussy."

I reached for the bottle of red wine. I'll listen to anything if I'm suitably buzzed. Well, almost anything.

"Somewhere—I don't know how—but the black woman and the white woman have exchanged places. These days, white women not only get to proclaim themselves as an oppressed minority, but they even get to represent hot pussy. White women, for God's sake, who were once the epitome of chastity and idealized feminine beauty."

"Do you want us to represent hot pussy?"

"I think we have to stop being afraid of sex," she defended. "The black woman is the epitome of fecundity."

"Who's afraid of sex? Too much sex is the problem with some of our younger sisters, especially the poorer ones. Too many of those girls are having babies they shouldn't be having," I argued. "Baby mothers."

"Exactly! The lower classes aren't afraid of their bodies— they enjoy fucking! Do any of the Hundred Noble Black Sisters enjoy sex?" Gale puckered her mouth and blew, as if she were ripping the air with a sudden posterior burst. "Nooo. They want to make policy." Gale began arranging items on the coffee table in a condescendingly prissy and formal way. "Policy," she mimicked. "All those women want executive leadership roles at the NAACP and those other institutions…"

I shrugged. "So what's wrong with that? Most of the people

who make up the association are women. Sixty percent is the figure, I think."

"But, you see," said Gale, pulling her feet up from the floor and tucking them underneath herself, "the NAACP is dead! It isn't going anywhere. It's successfully fulfilled its historic mission: to create a *comprador* class of Negroes who are more interested in being white than being black, and in snuggling up as close as possible to whites who wield power. You think Reggie Baxter is interested in power? Mel Farmington?"

"Paul Tower was."

"Yes! But you took him down, and he was a throwback to the old 'head nigger in charge' syndrome. Now, Anita Hill—"

"What about her?"

"I think she was scared of the power she had."

"What the hell are you talking about? I remember the woman getting slapped around on Capitol Hill."

Gale looked at me steadily. "The power she possessed as a black woman—a very dark black woman. You know, the darker the berry—"

"Uh huh..."

"She should have thrown that bull of a brother down on the floor and made him worship her. Ripped off his pants, pulled his bad boy out and worked him, worked him good!" Gale threw her head back and laughed. "Now, that's the real power that today's black woman possesses but is afraid to use. Power to the pussy!"

Mentally I had disconnected from her presentation. The whole thing was the result of too much Deep Theory, I thought. Next season she'll do a 180-degree turn and be theorizing about the positive aspects of female genital mutilation.

"Now," continued Gale, "he's married to a white woman and every time he thinks about the black race, he sees that gray sister and becomes confused. White women are willing to work the power they have. Today's black woman? No wonder the brothers call us bitches. They can still smell it, but we can't!"

"What the hell have you been drinking?"

"Well, that's going to be my presentation at the International Feminist Forum. nellie marcos is planning to present a paper on 'Feminism, Women of Color, and Sexual Representation,' but yours truly is going to bust a real move with pussy." She raised her eyebrows with mirth. "This is what I call X-rated theory."

"Stolen from Funkadelic album covers, I bet."

The front door opened and closed, and Michael Debord, Gale's husband, walked into the living room. He looked tired and discouraged, carrying his Nike gym bag in one hand and his attaché case in the other. Ever since I'd first met him, Michael had always been the "golden" black man: a Harvard undergrad, Yale Law School, handsome, and athletic. Now he was a highly praised presidential assistant in an administration that was going down the tubes. He had hitched his star to Jeff Benton, the only Democrat to find his way to the White House in twelve years. A master of the election campaign, Benton was a klutz when it actually came to governing the country, leaving it to trusted assistants like Michael to keep him on track.

"Hey, Nina." He came over to me and kissed me on the cheek. I could smell the faint scent of cologne beneath his five o'clock shadow. Michael kissed Gale's puckered lips and then plopped down in a comfortable armchair. "You look good, sister."

"You don't," I replied, perhaps more honestly than he had expected. I shook my head before continuing. "That dude ain't worth it, Michael. Nina says so."

Michael smiled. "I can read the same tired story in the *Times* and the *Post* every day, Nina. He opened his collar and began pulling off his tie. "So what's the 411 about you talking to Bernard?" Gale had put out some crackers, cheese, and paté, and Michael was strategically eyeing a morsel across the table.

"Beats me, Michael. He read some article I wrote and thinks I'm this year's Franz Fanon."

"And you really don't have any clue?" he asked, momentarily eyeing me instead of the food, before ripping off a fistful of bread and smearing it with paté.

"The man said he lost his country."

"Bernard and his metaphors!" said an exasperated Michael.

"I don't think that is a metaphor, Michael," I replied. The

man is in exile. He was kicked out of his country, and the jerk you work for is dicking him around."

"Is that what you're going to tell him?" A twinkle appeared in his eyes.

Realizing that I'd been baited, I shifted quickly into my lawyer's mode. "That's confidential, Mr. Debord."

"Bernard is intransigent, stubborn," countered Michael, ever the point man for his high-placed patron.

"You'll never hear people say that about Jeff Benton," laughed Gale. "Our fearless leader. Mr. Backbone!"

Michael ignored her and continued with me. "He seems to be expanding his contacts and options."

"Oh?"

"Yeah. Rep. George Plunkett, the chairman of the newly renamed," he rolled his eyes, "African-American Congressional Caucus, is attending the swinging soirée, along with Maurice North."

"Maurice North," said Gale. Her jaw dropped.

North was the reigning dean of the Niggerati. Ensconced at Yale's Frederick Douglass Center, which houses the university's black studies department, he supposedly represented the cutting edge of postmodern "black thought," with a distinctly multiracial twist—also called "deep black bullshit" by his less receptive, and more perceptive, readers. As a Christian and former divinity student, North was into healing—and not the kind that Marvin Gaye used to sing about. His key words were dialogue, consensus, and rapprochement, all thinly veiled euphemisms for not saying anything that would offend whites. These were the people, after all, who read his books and watched him on *Charlie Rose*. I had to admit: the man could put on a dazzling performance with his black prophetic histrionics, his postmodern lexicon and social democratic theorizing, sprinkled with vocabulary that neither blacks nor whites without graduate degrees could begin to fathom. To me, though, he was a bad version of Richard Pryor doing a gutbucket preacher.

As an improvisational socialist and radical democrat at Yale, North supplemented his million-dollar lecture income by sharing an occasional podium with David Goldstein, editor of the post-talmudic review, *The New Jew*, and dubbed by some of the more cynical members of the press corps as Claire Foster Benton's "court Jew." The whole thing was just too nauseating for words. The real showstopper was the pathetic display in which the two would publicly slobber over blacks' and Jews' once-grand civil rights alliance, completely ignoring the critical changes in both groups in the intervening years. There was something particularly unseemly about the North-Goldstein road show, recalling the Duke and the Dauphin, Mark Twain's colorful con artists in *Huckleberry Finn*. But the Duke and the Dauphin were crooks to the core, all too aware of the cons they perpetrated. North and Goldstein actually seemed to believe the post-civil rights, New Age babble they were spouting.

But who was I to argue with success? Several of North's books were currently on the *New York Times* best-seller list. Was this what passed for serious thought in contemporary America? I shook my head incredulously, thinking of North's recent success and the rise in popularity and importance of the type of anemic drivel that he produced.

Meanwhile, Gale was certainly in no mood to miss a North sighting at the Bernard soirée. It infuriated her that I, an academic nobody, had somehow been invited instead of her. I could read the "Why you?" look on her face. She simply couldn't understand that this was a matter of practical, not theoretical, knowledge.

"How do you know about this? The guest list?" I knew that Miriam was putting this together and that she wasn't sharing it with the White House.

"Well, you know, we know things," Michael said, with a not-too-concealed insider's smirk.

"You fatherfuckers are spying on him," I said. Gale and I looked first at each other and then at Michael. "Check your man out, Gee. He gets his reports from the CIA."

"Come on, the guy's a liberation theologian."

"Oooh, the new terrorism," said Gale. "Wow, cross-wielding priests exciting the masses. Scary stuff, Michael. They might even get the masses to take the Bible seriously! Booo."

"Hey, they are doing it, and they call it fundamentalism," I cracked. "But it's not as scary as Islamic fundamentalism, the new communism. From commissars to mullahs. See it live on Five!"

"Look, Misericordia could be another Cuba," he defended.

"And what's wrong with that?" she asked.

"Gale, don't play radical *hausfrau* while you're sitting up here in the lap of luxury..."

"I *use* my privileged position," she said defensively.

"For the masses? Right," Michael scoffed, turning to me. "Did she tell you her B-theory?"

I nodded my head and sipped my wine.

"That's how she spends her non-academic time: helping the niggas," Michael crowed. He stood up, removed his coat, and started to leave the room. "I got real problems," he said as he prepared to mount the stairwell to the second floor. "This guy is a possible wacko—"

"That's CIA propaganda, Mike, and you know it," I said loudly. The agency had leaked a scurrilous and bogus report—supplied by Bernard's enemies in Misericordia—and Rory Buchanan, chairman of the Senate Foreign Relations Committee, had no compunction about quoting from it before television cameras."

"You're damn right, I know it. But do you think all those corn-fed white folks out in Des Moines know it? Sure the shit is printed for the elites in the *Times*, but by the time it finds its way into the *Post*, *Newsweek*, and the like, and gets blasted across the television networks, there's just one message that gets lodged into most people's brains—the image of a crazy nigga from a country called Misery!"

"So, tell me this. Why are you guys beating up on him when General Malmundo is the real culprit? It was Malmundo who seized power from the general who had kicked out Bernard, a man who had been democratically elected."

"You want to know why, Nina?" said Gale, picking up our glasses and the remainder of the food from the coffee table. "Misericordia is a nation of niggas—nothing more, nothing less. And niggas don't count with this administration—except during elections. And then all they're supposed to do is vote and shut the fuck up!"

"Typical left-wing conspiracy propaganda!" said Michael, charging angrily back into the room and almost tripping over a hassock. The situation between the two of them was really beginning to heat up.

"Oh, come on, Mike!" argued Gale. "You know that any time a big story breaks involving crime, drugs, welfare abuse, or teenage pregnancy, Jeff Benton winds up at the pulpit of some black church, symbolically linking all of America's social problems with the so-called black pathology. When was the last time you heard him at a country club or in a corporate board room speaking about the pathologies of the white corporate elite?! Their greed?! Or about the abuses of the white overclass?! Hell, no. He's too busy with his hand in his donors' pockets. He sold out black folks even before he got into office, from the moment he made the decision to send Maerican refugees back to their burning house!"

"Benton called them economic refugees, not political refugees," I added. "Denying the political reality they faced."

The president's man was about to protest once again, but Gale suddenly intervened, placing a wine-soaked finger to his lips and then kissing him. "Michael, enough for the moment, baby. We have a guest. Get ready for dinner."

Exhausted, he peeled himself reluctantly away from her and headed slowly upstairs. We listened to his heavy, uneven footsteps as he trudged across the second floor.

"Gale, Michael is beginning to look old and sounds like a stranger." I gathered up a bottle and some plates and followed her into the kitchen.

"I know," sighed Gale. "The deeper Benton goes, the stranger Michael sounds sometimes. This is the price we pay for integration. We now have the luxury of telling lies for white folks to our own people." Gale scraped the remains of the food off the plates and into the sink, and the garbage disposal went to work on the afternoon's refuse.

As I helped set the dinner table, Michael came bouncing down the stairs, dressed in a fresh suit and tie. He didn't look off-duty. "Oh, I didn't know this was semi-formal," I said, surprised.

"It's not. I'm going back to the White House—I was beeped. I'm sorry, Nina. Tomorrow night I'll take you and Gale out to dinner."

"Thanks, Mike, but I already have a previous engagement. Remember? I dine and wine with El Presidente tomorrow night."

"Yeah, that's right." Michael looked at me for a second, the kind of look that meant that he needed to confide in me about something. "Nina, after you speak to Bernard—"

"Yes...?"

Gale stepped in from the kitchen. "Michael?"

She saw him dressed for the office, and an angry scowl spread across her face.

"Not again!" she shouted, as she placed a dish of Caribbean ox-tail stew on a heat pad at the center of the dining room table.

Michael looked at me and smiled weakly. "Excuse us." He led his enraged wife back into the kitchen, behind closed doors.

"You tell that son of bitch that you have a wife who would like to have a family!" I could hear Gale's voice clearly through the wall. "Jesus, Michael, what are trying to do to us, baby? We never see each other."

I knew what Gale and Michael were going through all too well. Lee and I had been through this in my early days as an assistant district attorney, attending midnight arraignments and late-night work sessions with my colleagues. Disturbed by the memories stirred up by their conversation, I decided to retreat into the living room.

As I was flipping through *Lingua Franca*, an utterly useless, niche-market magazine for the academically inclined, Michael, briefcase in hand, stormed past me and out of the house. He then re-entered the house almost immediately, charging upstairs in a huff. A few minutes later, he flew out the door again without uttering a word to either of us. I felt sorry for the man—and his wife. Jeff Benton wasn't worth it.

After Michael's second departure, Gale entered the room and plopped down in the beige-striped armchair to the right of the coffee table. Still furious about the sudden change of events, she said nothing for minutes. She reached over to a beautifully carved, amber-wood box and pulled out one of her death sticks. Smoke streamed out of her nostrils as she laid her head back against the chair.

"Want to take a guess about what our sex life is like?" she finally broke the silence.

"No," said I, "but I'm sure the present reality—whatever it is—can't possibly live up to your vivid imagination."

"Nina, I'm beyond imagining. A woman's gotta have—"

"Please, Gale, don't start quoting that fifteen-cent auteur," I replied, quickly forestalling any further references to a certain black filmmaker whose work I didn't admire.

She shook her head. "I'm quoting Bobby Womack," she said authoritatively.

"How long has this been going on?" A little embarrassed by my mistaken assumption, I did my best to one-up her.

"How long has Benton been fucking up?" she answered my question with a question. "'The president needs me,' Michael tells me. Well, so do I. I'm his wife, goddammit. We've had to schedule fuck sessions at downtown hotels just so he can be near the president!" Gale crossed her legs dramatically, her foot bobbing up and down in front of me. "Luckily, I've been able to get some of my needs met."

"An affair?"

"Plural, not singular. Yes," she replied nonchalantly. "They have a way of presenting themselves at academic conferences."

"Ah, yes, those academic fuck fairs."

"For those of us who engage in the life of the mind, physical respite is a welcomed relief," she sniffed. "After all, intellectuals are different. We require different sort of stimuli."

"So what are these postmodern studs like?"

"Pathetic, Nina. Give me a rough and tumble nigga any day, someone who never even heard of Foucault. Theoretical depth has its price, you know. The old compensation factor."

"Compensation factor?" I had no idea where she was going with this.

"Yeah, you know. Big theory, little dick. Or else they don't know squat about pleasing a woman. Don't believe any of the hype about the connection between intelligence and esoteric sex, although I did say otherwise once upon a time. It's all bullshit. Want some controlled substance?"

"Pot? Sure." I welcomed the opportunity to turn our conversation in a sillier, more relaxed direction.

Gale stubbed out the cigarette and pulled a joint from the bottom of her finely carved box.

"Don't you think that's kind of risky, Gee? Suppose some suspicious Republicans started snooping around your private life?"

"Live dangerously, Nina. But you already do that, don't you?" She handed me the blunt and lit me up. I inhaled deeply, holding the smoke as long as I could. As we say in the street, the shit was good. We passed the joint back and forth for a while, and then my girlfriend decided to drop her bomb.

"Anyway, Nina, since yours truly hasn't been getting properly stroked by her truly beloved, and since none of the available intellectuals are up for the down stroke, I've had to improvise." Gale tossed me a wicked grin.

"Improvise what?"

"I'll show you," she said. Gale took a lung-full of pot and rose from the chair.

"Can't you just tell me?" The last time a girlfriend showed me something, Anna and I wound up in bed together. Maybe men know something we don't, I thought, being such lousy communicators. Unlike us, they don't feel the need to share every goddamn thing. They know when to shut up.

Gale enthusiastically skipped up the stairs, shouting back as she reached the second floor, "Open another bottle of wine."

I went into the kitchen, retrieved a bottle of Merlot and a couple of glasses, and returned to my seat on the couch. I was uncorking the bottle when Gale returned—popping *my* top before I had a chance to finish with the wine.

Standing front and center of the stairway, Gale was decked out in a black leather halter and matching hot pants. The low-cut halter swooped down to reveal her nipples; a silver stud decorated her navel. Beneath the hot pants, she wore black sheer stockings and fucking six-inch heels. Around her neck, she wore a dog collar with spikes, and black leather gloves covered her arms up to her elbows. Bowing to Afrocentrism, I supposed, she wore a black leather kufi, beaded with cowrie shells, rakishly angled atop her head. She looked viciously stunning as she slapped a riding crop across her gloved hand. She was nasty, all right. Too nasty.

"Well?" she asked expectantly. "I'm a sex diva."

I gulped deeply from my second glass of wine. "You are whacked!"

"No, that's what I do to them, Nina. *They* get whacked!" She brought the crop down into the palm of her hand, and the sharp sound cracked the air.

As stunning as she was, the woman had gone somewhere over the rainbow—and, from what I could tell, it definitely wasn't Kansas. "What the hell are you doing, Gee? You don't go out like that, do you?"

"I do, too. I put on a black leather coat. You know, Nazi black and down to my ankles during winter. A black cotton duster during the spring. Then I walk the streets and pull 'em up to the bumper."

"Pull who?"

"Johns, silly. I don't know who the fuck they are!"

My head sank into my hand. "Gale, you've gone overboard! Do you mean to tell me that you're tricking?"

"Uh, not for money. But I do get paid," she said, as she sat a foot or so away from me. "I give the money to the United Negro College Fund. Lord knows they need it." She took a sip of the wine. "It's a role, Nina. Like you being a private eye."

"I'm not playing a role, Gale. That's what I do for a living. And how could you possibly compare my work with your S/M frolics!"

"I gather you don't approve?"

"Well," I sighed, "I don't think a university professor and the wife of a high-level White House official—"

"Fuck Jeff Benton!" she shouted. "I'm a married woman who's entitled to a decent sex life!"

Gale was starting to scare me. I understood her sexual and emotional frustration; in my own way, I was going through the same thing. But the S/M trip? It was unbelievable to sit there and come face to face with the kinky lives of the emerging black professional class—in the persons of Michael and Gale. Suddenly I realized just how dramatically my normal world had been disrupted when my husband Lee and my two children had been murdered three years before. Slowly, unbeknownst to me, I had slipped deeper and deeper into the darkness. I now found myself in a strange world where people exposed themselves to me in ways that I simply couldn't comprehend or measure. In some ways, I'd even become a stranger to myself. None of the things on which I had staked my life—work, friendship, family, and achievement—had survived one bloody night of carnage in Brooklyn.

"Gale, do you really want to be doing this?" I asked in as unthreatening a tone as possible, trying to connect with her.

She hung her head low for a second and looked up at me. "Honestly, I don't know. I like the attention, you know. I like making men drool over me. Everyone wants to feel powerful, Nina. Sometimes I'm a little confused by it all. I really don't know how I feel."

"So, why don't you get out of those clothes and we'll have dinner and—uh—talk about it? Okay? I mean, I don't know if you want to do that, but that's all I have to offer."

"Okay," Gale answered solemnly. She rose and went upstairs.

I went into the kitchen and put the rest of the dinner on the table. Gale returned, dressed in a denim shirt and slacks. We sat down and prepared to eat.

"Nina, I know this is going to sound weird, but can we say a blessing?"

"Sure. But I think you probably should remove the bitch collar from around your neck before you invoke the Lord's name."

CHAPTER FOUR

The next morning, Gale regaled me with tales of the skin trade as we sat on the back porch and ate breakfast. In each of the stories she shared, she discretely concealed the actual names of the upper-class and ruling-elite white males — congressmen, lobbyists, business executives, lawyers, judges, military officers — whose flesh she had seared. But for even an occasional Newshour viewer like myself, most of the men's true identities were painfully obvious.

Gale was happy and animated as she told me the sordid details. The fact that Michael had not come home the night before didn't seem to faze her at all, since he often slept downtown when he was doing an all-nighter for Benton.

"They all want to be told what naughty white boys they are," laughed Gale as she sipped her coffee. "And they want a big black mama to punish them."

"None were black?" I asked.

"Hell no, girl! You think a brother is going to allow a sister to tie his ass up and whip him? No way, Kunta Kinte! Niggas do the beating 'round here."

"Or the cops," I added, thinking of the beatings and shootings of black suspects by the police, especially back in New York. The situation was so bad that Amnesty International had recently issued an official report, which the *New York Times*, an impassioned advocate of human rights in other people's countries, had practically buried in the metropolitan section.

"Well, that's the assigned social/sexual role," Gale clicked effortlessly into her po-mo feminist rhetoric. "The privilege of regulating and punishing the black male body is assigned to the white working class. The elites come up with the policies, and the constabulary forces take care of the intimidation, incarceration, and annihilation of the black male." Decked out in a yellow DKNY suit, looking very much like a high-toned business executive, Gale was always quite comfortable intellectualizing about sex, violence, and the politics thereof.

"And what about you, Nina?" she asked.

"What about me?" This was the feminist show-and-tell part that I really didn't like at all. Gale was looking for a kink exchange; she wanted to know about some deep, dark secret of mine. The truth of the matter was that my girlfriend was an intellectual voyeur who loved to peek into the hidden recesses of other people's emotional and sexual lives. Evidently, she often did a lot more that peek.

"You know what I mean, Nina. You've seen me in my compromised glory." She yawned and stretched her arms upwardly. "Surely an experienced woman like yourself...."

Gale wanted details, something that would titillate. I thought about my brief tryst with Anna but decided that wouldn't be enough to inflame her imagination. The whole thing was too innocent and sweet to register on her kinkometer. I knew I didn't have to say anything. But Gale seemed hellbent on being entertained, and I decided to give her something she could really sink her teeth into.

"I killed somebody," I said.

"What?!" Gale was excited. I had confessed to transgressing a major taboo, the taking of a human life. "Who? What?"

"You must realize I can't go into details about it. After all, my profession requires a certain amount of discretion."

"Yes, of course. I understand." She paused reflectively before continuing, "You really did?"

The girl simply couldn't believe it. For all her foul-mouthed bravado, her own stories were about playing roles and acting out fantasies. At the end of the day—or night—she and her clients went back to their normal lives and their normal identities. Nothing had changed, really. But now she suddenly found herself in the presence of someone who had gone beyond role playing, beyond fantasy construction. In a small way, I had played God by taking away another person's right to exist, and Gale was beside herself with amazement and curiosity.

I simply nodded, waiting for the ubiquitous question of every grief-hunting reporter or talk-show host. I didn't have to wait for long.

"How did you feel about it?"

The killing was in self-defense, I assured myself before responding to her. The need to rescue a client had meant going up against a man who was armed and dangerous, a man who had killed before and would no doubt kill again if I didn't stop him. But I knew there was a lot more to it than that. I was out for blood, desperate to avenge the murder of my husband and my two children. And in killing a man, I had become a killer myself. And here I was opening up to Gale—and planning to do it again.

"Not good, Gee. I've been through it as a victim. It's nothing to be proud of," I began. "I'm not a marine. I haven't gone through the sort of psychological conditioning that turns a civilian into a soldier. I once thought I was special because I was on the move as a dynamic and politically aspiring prosecutor. You know, the new black generation. But when my children died, I was suddenly faced with how utterly mortal and insignificant I was. Now I think a great deal of finding the man who ordered the murder of my family."

Gale looked at me with a pained expression on her face. It was obvious that she wasn't prepared to hear what I was saying. Without the protection of a pretentious, overblown discourse on power, deconstruction, and the meaning of human life, the simple reality of my suffering and confusion was just too much for her to bear. This was the raw stuff of human history, after all, something about which academics, for all their clever phrases and theoretical swagger, have precious little to say. In a sense, what I was sharing with her had destroyed me, and Gale clearly didn't want to hear about it.

"Nina, have you told anyone else?" she said, trying to find a way out of the conversation.

"A few people know what happened. And now you."

She gripped my hand. "I'm sorry, Nina. I...I won't say a word." Gale had wanted a bomb, and that's exactly what she got. "I have to go." She looked at her watch and rose. "Nina?"

I was removing the morning's dishes. "Hmm?"

"Thank you. For being my friend." Gale sounded as if she were about to offer me a humanity award or something. "Your sense of grief and humility has taught me a very important les—"

The doorbell suddenly chimed.

I moved toward the door.

"No, no. I'll get it. As a matter of fact, you shouldn't even be cleaning the table."

"It's no big deal, Gee. You have to get to work and I'm lounging around until the afternoon." The doorbell chimed again.

"Excuse me," said Gale as she left the porch. "I do want to finish what I was saying before."

"I'll be in the kitchen or out here." It was nice sitting outside. Gale and Michael had a rather large backyard that was frequently used to host lawn parties and barbecues. Lee, the children, and I had stayed there many times in the past, and I clearly remembered the children running up to me from the small clump of trees at the far end of the yard. Sitting there helped me realize just how claustrophobic one can become living in New York, enclosed in one four-walled world after another. My thoughts were interrupted, however, by the sound of Gale's voice, loudly calling my name. I was so lost in my own reveries that I thought for a moment I was hearing Lee calling out to me from the distnace or the gentle voices of my children playing in the yard.

Gale was standing with two other people when I entered

the living room, a black man and a white woman. Gale stood in front of the large bookcase that dominated the room. As she turned to face me, I could see that she was visibly shaken, wringing her hands. From the somber faces of the other two, I immediately knew what had happened. The Big D. Death. Someone close to her had died.

"Michael's been..." Gale's voice broke, "murdered." I went over to her and held her hand. "I just can't believe it. My Michael is gone." Her eyes began flooding with tears. She let out a long sigh and did her best to compose herself. "Nina, this is Detective Lance, District of Columbia Police Department."

I nodded and Detective Lance did the same. He possessed a long face and a washed-out, brown-skinned complexion. Except for that long face of his, he was suitably nondescript. Perfect for surveillance.

"And this is Carol Bridges, Michael's assistant at the White House," continued Gale. The young woman was a petite blonde with boyishly cropped hair, her pretty face hidden behind wire-framed glasses that would surely put off any cruising male gaze. She wore a smart, charcoal gray suit and her heels gave her height and presence.

I mustered up a slight social smile and announced my name to both of them. The police had found Michael in Meridian Hill Park—dubbed Malcolm X Park by many black folks in the area—and had called the White House immediately. Ms. Bridges had been sent with the police to provide a humane and friendly face to the proceedings.

"Well," Gale looked at the police officer, "I guess I need to come downtown and identify the body. Right?"

"Yes, Mrs. Debord," he answered. "We need to ask you some questions."

Gale nodded her head. "Let me gather up my things and call the office."

"Certainly," said the police officer. "I'll be in my car." A professional to the core, he turned on his heels and left the home quietly.

Carol Bridges made a few tentative steps towards Gale. "Gale, is there anything I can do?"

"No, Carol. Thank you. I'll call you. Thanks for coming." Gale turned to me and I read the confusion in her eyes.

"If you like, I'll come down with you," I offered.

"Please," she sighed. "I don't know where to begin."

"We'll get through this together, Gale. I'm sorry," I offered. She was holding up well for the moment, but it would only be a matter of time before the devastation set in.

Carol Bridges took her leave as gracefully as possible and returned to her office at 1600 Pennsylvania Avenue. While Detective Lance waited in his car, Gale went into her study to phone the university and cry. I took the time to head upstairs and change into a white blouse, dark slacks, and an even darker jacket. It was all too much, I thought, as I slipped into my clothes. Last night, Gale was dressed in black leather; in a day or so she'd be wearing funeral black. God could be so random and unmerciful. Was Gale paying the price for stepping out on Michael? I had no answers—and certainly wasn't going to judge.

Gale held up well until we arrived at the medical examiner's office. Her knees buckled and her feet slipped from beneath her as the short, bespeckled man rolled out Michael's body. Half of Michael's head had been blown away by the gunfire. I did my best to hold her up, but it was all I could do to stay on my feet.

"Steady. Steady, girl," I softly said.

"Who would do this to him?" she asked. "Why? Michael never hurt anyone, Nina."

"I know. I know," were the only words of comfort I could offer as we walked down the hallway that led from the medical examiner's office to the center of the precinct. The hall was eerily silent for a people-oriented establishment like a police precinct, and our slow, high-heeled footsteps seemed even more pronounced. Finally, Detective Lance led us through the office door of a Captain Amos Durk.

Durk ushered us respectfully toward the straight-backed chairs that lined the front of his desk. He was of average height and dark, with broadly flared nostrils. A seasoned veteran, he immediately got down to the matter at hand, the death of Michael William Debord.

"What time did your husband leave? How did he seem before he left the house? What did you discuss? Did he say where he was going? Were you and Mrs. Halligan the only people he spoke to before he left the house? Did he have any known enemies? Who were his friends? Did he frequent clubs? Did he use drugs?"

The questions came so rapidly and mindlessly that Gale barely had time to think about her answers, until—

"Did you know your husband was a homosexual?"

"I beg your pardon?" Gale suddenly lowered her handkerchief from her face and looked straight at the captain. I half expected her to rise from the chair and slap Durk across the face. "My husband was not gay," she said emphatically. "What are you alluding to?"

"I'm sorry, Mrs. Debord, but there was—"

"There was *what*?" snapped Gale.

Durk was seated at his desk with his fingers entwined, staring straight ahead, unblinking in the face of yet one more ugly reality. "Semen was found in his rectum."

"My husband was not—"

"And in his mouth."

Gale was silent. I rose from my chair and stood behind her, placing my hand tentatively on her shoulder. She immediately gripped it. Her whole world was being radically altered, perceptions challenged and changed.

"Mrs. Debord—" said Capt. Durk as he rose.

"Simmons," corrected Gale. "We were a professional couple. I use my own name."

"Ma'am," he continued, sitting on the edge of his desk like a folksy attorney, "I don't take pleasure in this. But people in my department have discovered things, physical residues that imply certain things."

"Such as?" challenged Gale.

Durk looked first at me and then at Gale. "That your husband was having sex with a man and had been using drugs. Heroin was found in his bloodstream."

"Not my Michael!" cried Gale. "He was clean! He was clean! He wasn't some cheap hood! He was somebody important."

"Mrs. Debord," he paused to correct himself. "Excuse me, Ms. Simmons, you would be shocked to learn about what goes on among many powerful men in this city. But it's something I see every day, you see. The kink factor—"

"That's enough, captain," I broke in, more incredulous than angry at his choice of words. But it was too late. Gale was weeping, instantly transformed into the newly minted widow that she had become. Of course, she knew about the kink factor. She herself was a kinkette, but not her Michael.

"I'm sorry," he apologized. Durk turned, leaned over his desk, and picked up a calling card from a tray, handing it to me as I helped Gale to her feet. Placing the card inside my inner breast pocket, my fingers brushed across something unfamiliar, a computer disk that I hadn't put there. Someone else had.

As soon as the police drove us back to Gale's house, I convinced Gale to take a nap, and went right to work. In the privacy of the guest room, I pulled out my Powerbook, slipped in the disk, translated it, and discovered that I had Michael's journal. I then remembered that he had wanted to speak to me after seeing President Bernard, and that prior to his leaving he had reentered the house and gone back upstairs. Had he slipped the disk into my coat then? If so, did he expect that something would happen that night, that he might not be returning? I opened the file and read several entries, spanning from January to October, right up to the day before his death.

The first entry, January 25th, casually mentioned Richard Stone, the controversial political consultant who had helped Jeff Benton out of a previous political jam while he was governor of a southwestern state. Stone had recently signed on as a special consultant to the president. According to Michael, the staff was less than pleased with Stone's presence, which they interpreted as representing a move on the president's part toward a more politically calculated approach to policy decisions.

February 19th. Michael's beat at the White House was Misericordia. On this particular day, he described his meeting with President Bernard. Publicly, the POTUS—White House speak for "President of the United States"—was committed to returning President Bernard to his office in Misericordia. Off the record, everything had changed with the appearance of Stone, who was now sitting in on policy discussions regarding Misericordia and other affairs of state. Michael viewed Stone's presence with increasing suspicion.

Subsequent entries described Stone's growing role in developing policy toward Misericordia. To Michael, Stone was little more than a hired gun, the living embodiment of Machiavelli's belief that anything and everything was justified in a great leader's pursuit of power.

In one entry, Michael described Stone physically, whom—with his long, strawberry blond hair, designer sunglasses, expensive Italian suits, turtlenecks, and trademark three-day growth of beard—Michael deplored as the epitome of faux New York sophistication. According to Michael, the president admired Stone's complete lack of core convictions, characterizing it as "flexibility." As the weeks passed, flexibility came more and more to define the Benton administration.

When Stone was actually asked to sit in on a formal policy meeting, Michael voiced his concern to the White House chief of staff, Pamela Hurston. Hurston sympathized with his concerns but stressed the president's growing desire for "fresh input" in policy decisions. As Michael would soon learn, Hurston was in no position to challenge Stone's influence with the president. Within a few weeks, she, along with Valerie Compote, the White House spokeswoman, became the first overt victims of Stone's increasing control over the inner circle of the oval office.

Michael realized that he had been squeezed out of that inner circle when Stone persuaded Benton to recognize the coup by General Malmundo as the de facto government of Misericordia. In the timeless Beltway tradition of back-channel politics, Michael actually learned of the change in policy via a call from a news reporter who was fishing for leads on the "tilt." Michael assured the reporter incorrectly that no such policy change was currently being considered. As the official White House adviser on the "Misery" situation, Michael expected his position to carry weight with the president. "But what if the president has changed his mind about me?" Michael worried in his journal after returning home that evening. This wasn't out of the realm of possibility, since Mr. Backbone was widely understood to be a person likely to change his positions whenever it was politically expedient. He was known to reward his enemies, but punish his friends.

The next day, the new chief of staff, Coke McClure, an old boy from the cash-and-carry New Democrats Institute, tried to assure Michael that no fundamental policy change had occurred. When Michael attempted to coordinate meetings between the deposed president and Benton, however, McClure abruptly informed him that the State Department would now be handling the situation at the sub-cabinet level. This meant that someone other than the secretary of state, the national security advisor, or the POTUS himself would be taking the lead on the issue. Michael now had little doubt that it was Stone who was directing U.S. policy in Misericorida. What he simply couldn't comprehend, however, was Benton's rationale for abandoning his previous position and diverting so much of his authority to a shady, opportunistic character like Stone.

Scrolling down a few more entries, I read a report of alleged drug dealing by the Malmundo regime. The illegal activities highlighted in the report were glossed over by Benton's new foreign policy elite as an "aberrant exercise committed by wayward officers." Subsequent entries mentioned Michael's meetings with staff of the Senate and House intelligence committees to discuss the reports of drug dealing in Misericordia, as well as a private meeting between Michael and Sam Archer, a former DEA agent. Yet none of the reports of drug-running by the Malmundo regime were sufficient to tilt the Benton administration back towards Bernard. From the harsh, cynical tone of Michael's self-reporting, it was clear that he was getting closer and closer to the breaking point, as far as his commitment to the Benton administration was concerned.

The last entry in Michael's journal, made the day before he was killed, mentioned a scheduled meeting with someone named MF that evening. That could only be Miriam, I reasoned, remembering that her middle name was Francesca. Michael was probably using only her first two initials as a cover in case someone broke into his computer. Michael mentioned that he was going back to the White House before the meeting. Had he gone there and then met Miriam? Or was that a smoke-screen as well?

"Nina?"

I turned, startled from my reading and reflection, to see Gale standing in the doorway in her slip. Her eyes were still puffy and swollen from crying.

"I couldn't sleep," she said haltingly. "So I turned on the television and..."

"What, Gale?" I asked, noticing how shaken she was.

"That cracker is having a press conference and bad-mouthing Michael even before he's buried."

I got up from the chair and followed her into the bedroom. A White House press conference was being broadcast on television, starring, front and center, the chief magistrate of the republic himself, the ultimate postmodern prince, Jeffrey T. Benton. Always at his smarmy, cynical best when conveying sympathy, he stood calmly at the presidential podium and fielded questions about the late Michael Debord, a young man whom he characterized as "troubled."

"Let me reiterate," he said in his smooth and soothing southwestern drawl, "this is a tragedy, the death of Michael Debord. He was once a fine worker and valued member of this administration. Our hearts go out to his widow, Gale. But—just as a reminder—the circumstances of his death cannot and will not be condoned by this administration. The fact is that our random drug security testing had recently revealed that Michael was taking drugs—"

"That motherfucking liar!" screamed Gale, and a high-heeled shoe smacked Jeffrey Benton's televised head.

"At the time of his death, he was already being removed from his assignments and was about to be asked to leave the White House," continued the president.

Gale was seething. "Look, Nina! Look what they're trying to do to Michael. They're already promoting the same bullshit that Durk was trying to tell me. Something else happened, Nina."

"What do you think happened, Gale?" I asked, keeping an eye on Benton's masterful but cynical performance on the screen.

"I don't know, but I know that the whole thing is some type of cover-up."

"Cover-up?" That certainly got my attention. The magic word in American political culture.

"A goddamn, motherfucking, nigga-baiting cover-up," she replied, pressing the remote and ending the news conference, at least in her bedroom. She tossed the remote down on the bed and picked up a gold-colored terrycloth robe. Gale tightened the belt with such determined vehemence that I could easily imagine her black hands around Benton's white throat.

"Covering up what?"

"I don't know, Nina," Gale said. "I was hoping you would find out."

"You want an investigation?"

"You better believe it, girl! Something is going down and my man isn't going to take the weight for this bullshit. What are your rates?"

"You don't have to pay me a thing."

"I'm not a welfare case, Nina," she said testily. "I'm a woman with money."

"Okay," I said slowly, and then assured her that she would get the full Halligan treatment. "But let's get this straight. If I start investigating the Benton administration on your behalf—and you're probably right about the whole cover-up thing—they may start coming after you."

"HA!" she said bitterly. "What the fuck can they do to me now? Michael is dead. Let them! They don't have anything on me."

"Well, let's make sure they don't," I replied.

We went downstairs, gathered up her marijuana, and flushed it down the toilet. We then made an early fall fire in the living room fireplace and ended her career as an S&M diva once and for all. She tossed in her black leather wardrobe and accessories, and I used the poker to make sure that the flames got every article.

"Guess I'll now be performing my new role as a widow with more sincerity and conviction than I performed my role as a married woman," said Gale without the slightest trace of irony.

I rose from my knees and watched the fire eat the last of the stockings and brassieres. Satisfied that no traces of Gale's past indiscretions remained in the fireplace, I placed the poker back in its cast-iron stand and turned to face Gale. "Now you're a black widow, too, and the two of us together are deadlier than any first wives' club. Much more deadly."

CHAPTER FIVE

The next day was busy. I informed Gale about the disk that Michael had slipped into my coat and about his situation at the White House. Now she was even more convinced that something else had been going on. While she made funeral arrangements, I fended off reporters who wanted to know about Michael's "secret life," as it was being described in the media. Refusing to take Gale's repeated "Fuck off!" as an answer, the press had set up a line of television cameras on the sidewalk in front of the house. I enlisted the services of my faithful cousin Bass (pronounced "base") Pilgrim, a massive hulk of a man, who guarded the property line, and stationed several of his most trusted, and intimidating, cronies along the backdoors and windows.

Next, I located Sam Archer, the former DEA agent, and gave him a call. I told him that Michael had mentioned him in his journal and that I needed to talk to him. We agreed to meet at Union Station at 3 p.m. Later, I planned to stop by Bernard's swinging soirée to see if I could find out what my dear sister-in-law knew.

A few years earlier, Union Station had been renovated as a showcase piece for the "new" Washington, D.C., after years of deterioration from drugs, mismanagement, and limited home rule. No longer the sleepy station for an increasingly obsolete mass-transit system, Union Station now hosted cafés, bars, boutiques, leisure-wear outlets, movie theaters, coffee bars, and the like. An emerging Mecca for urban sophisticates on the move. Arriving a few minutes early, I sat at a small corner table in a stylish bar and nursed a glass of red wine, waiting for Mr. Archer.

It was the first moment I'd had to myself since Michael's death. I'd been preoccupied with helping Gale get through her trauma, an experience that I well understood. But I still wasn't as confident as Gale that there had actually been a cover-up. Maybe Michael did use drugs. Many professionals do, after all, and Gale was having a sex problem of her own. If Michael did have a drug problem, that might have played a role in Gale's decision to step out of her marriage to get her needs met. Could Gale's insistence that the whole thing was a cover-up be some type of cover-up of her own—to conceal the tragic outcome of a troubled marriage, both from me and from herself?

As I reached for my glass, I felt the presence of a shadow over me. I looked up to see an unimposing man of average height and medium build. He wore a tan gabardine suit that would have blended perfectly with the changing leaves of Washington during the fall. He accented the suit with a dark brown fedora.

The man spoke first. "Nina Halligan?" He held out his left hand, catching me off-guard. "Yes. Mr. Archer?" I answered, shaking his hand.

As he nodded his response, I noticed that the right sleeve of his coat was pinned snugly to his side. Then it struck me. This wasn't just any Sam Archer. This was *the* Sam Archer, also known as "Armless Archer." A legend in the drug end of federal law enforcement, Archer's career had been brutally terminated when his right arm was shoved down a garbage disposal in a Mexico City suburb by drug dealers who had kidnapped and tortured him following a failed investigation. Other agents claimed that Archer had simply become too cocky, repeatedly taking risks that compromised both his investigation and his safety. But Archer told a different story, insisting that he had been sold out by his own people—the U.S. government—because he was about to expose the fact that the CIA was colluding with drug traffickers in the region. Predictably, Archer's charges eventually resulted in his forced retirement from the DEA, and he soon took to writing books on the failed drug policies of Republican and Democratic administrations, and the social consequences of unfair drug-sentencing laws. His claim of CIA involvement put him outside the pale of standard Beltway discourse on drug policy. The conventional wisdom around the capital was that Archer's bleeding arm had drained just a little too much of the blood from his brain.

"Sit down, Mr. Archer," I gestured toward the other chair. "May I buy you a drink?"

"Yes, you may, Ms. Halligan." He removed his hat to reveal graying black hair, deep, inset eyes, and a prominent brow. He definitely reminded me of someone—some famous figure from American history?—but I couldn't tap my memory banks for the image. He ordered a Cutty Sark and raised his glass.

"To Michael Debord," he said quietly.

"To Michael," I echoed. For the first time, it really struck me that my friend was gone. No more friendly debates with Michael on the future of the race. No two-couple vacations—well, that ended a few years back. No more girl talk about husband-swapping or whose man was the better cook in the kitchen—or in bed. Like Lee, like Andy and Ayesha, Michael was now gone. I quietly sipped my wine and tried to get on with the business at hand. "As I mentioned over the phone, Mr. Archer—"

"Please," he interjected. "Call me Sam. Even my enemies do."

A slight smile appeared on my face as I continued, "Michael had mentioned speaking to you in his diary. I'm conducting a preliminary investigation on behalf of Mrs. Simmons, Michael's widow."

"She doesn't buy it either, huh?"

"Buy what, Mr. Archer—Sam?"

"The bullshit that the press is trying to snow the public with about Mike's death." Archer moved the chair in which he was seated a few inches back from the table, making room for himself. He unbuttoned his coat. An innocent move on his part, but it made me think that, being a southpaw, he would almost certainly be carrying his heater on his left side. Just a fleeting thought.

"You think otherwise?" I inquired.

"Mike wasn't a faggot," he said emphatically. "He was a dedicated public servant. A patriot!"

At least he and Gale agreed about Michael's sexuality at the time of death, I thought, before pressing on with my inquiry. "What about the police report."

"That semen bullshit?" he contemptuously snorted.

I looked at him. The police had alluded to a gay angle in the press, that Michael had been found in Meridian Hill Park with his trousers down. The park was known as a cruising ground for black gays, but nothing had been said about semen. "How did you find out about that?"

"Simple. Contacts." Armless cracked a knowing smile.

Yeah, I thought, someone like you would have contacts. Perhaps the sort of contacts that Michael found useful. "Michael told you about his concerns? About Misericordia?"

Archer nodded. "Yep. He did. I told him it sounded like standard operational policy."

"Standard operational policy?" I echoed incredulously.

"Yep," he sighed. "Mike was astounded that even after it had been reported by the press—and the CIA and State Department knew full well that the Malmundo regime was engaging in drug-trafficking—the Bentonistas still wanted to deal with the scum suckers. I tried to assure him that it was just their natural way of doing things. The American people always get sold out, one way or another. It's the timeless wonder of Washington."

I wasn't completely convinced by Archer's cynicism. As he picked up his drink, I detected a sinister smirk that may have signaled his own disgust and revulsion for the sordid affairs of "our" nation's government, and maybe even his own naïveté about thinking otherwise once upon a time.

"Let me get this straight," I said, bringing my chair confidentially closer to the table. "The White House knows that Malmundo is dirty and they preferred him to Bernard?"

"Yep."

"Why?"

"Bernard is honest but ineffectual," Archer explained.

"Ineffectual for what? The drug dealing?"

"Maybe," he said cryptically.

"Maybe what else?"

"Other things also..." Archer shrugged his shoulders and I suddenly realized just who it was that he resembled: Joe McCarthy, the notorious junior senator from Wisconsin and infamous red-baiter.

"Like what, Sam?" I pushed.

"Stone."

"What about him? He's just pushing the Malmundo regime," I argued. "The question is why?"

"Well, that's what Mike was trying to find out," he replied. "That's why he's in his present condition."

True, I thought, but a bit cold just the same.

"It's a nasty business, young lady," said Archer, noticing my disapproval of his last remark. "Truth-hunting is a cold path in hell. It's where, as the Mexicans say, 'All your friends are false and all your enemies are real.'"

That saying was certainly gaining currency in my book. I kept waiting to hear, *Are you now or have you ever been a member of the Communist Party?*

"Is that what he discussed with you, Mr. Archer?" I pulled myself together and continued my questioning.

"Now, how did we get from Sam to Mr. Archer?" He was being flirtatious.

"Easy. I don't feel that you're being too forthcoming in your information and that forecloses any first name basis on my part, bub." Archie was really beginning to annoy me. He was doing the "girlie push" on me, the sort of bullying that men often do when they encounter a woman on what they had presumed to be their turf. "You have something to sell, mister? Put it on the table and name your price!"

His eyes suddenly flashed with anger. "Look, I'm not a cheap shamus looking for cash! I earned this," he jerked his amputated limb, "in the service of my country!"

I swirled around my purse, flipped open my wallet, and slapped down a photo of my family. "To paraphrase Willy the Shake, murdered in one motherfucking fell swoop," I replied through clenched teeth. "Do we need to get into case histories and describe the intimate atrocities of our lives?"

Archer turned the photo around and looked at it. "Nice family," he sighed.

"Yeah, I thought so, too." I was getting ready to bolt. This guy was a one-armed jerk.

"I heard about you," he continued. "Mike told me that you might be getting involved and that I should help you. I just needed to know if you were half the woman he described."

"When did he tell you that I'd be getting involved?"

"He left a message on my answering machine, earlier in the evening before you last saw him," responded Archer, taking out a pipe and tucking in some tobacco. He took his time lighting his pipe and then tossed the match carelessly into the ashtray.

"Then he may have known that something was about to go down. But what?"

"You ever heard of the Butt Fuck Boys?" he asked nonchalantly. He jutted his chin upward and blew smoke circles.

I directed a blank stare at Archer and cursed myself for getting involved in this goddamn business. One of the routine tortures of the profession was learning to master the idiotic names that criminals often used. "The butt fucking what?"

"The Butt Fuck Boys," he said a second time, a bit embarrassed. The phrase "butt fuck" didn't roll easily off the tongue of a macho man like Archer, especially with "boys" bringing up the rear.

"Waiter!" I shouted. "No, Sam. Enlighten me, but only after the waitron has taken our order."

"This one is on me, Halligan." Archer kept the pipe in his mouth and fished around in his coat pocket, finally withdrawing a twenty-dollar bill. After the waiter took our order, Archer filled me in on the subject of the Butt Fuck Boys. "Like any smart leader, Malmundo doesn't do his own dirty work. He allows a gang called—"

"—The Butt Fuck Boys," I heard myself say.

"Right. They do all the dirty work and pass the profits through a sham business that Malmundo controls," continued Archer. "Basically, they are an offshoot of the Papas. Oscar Peltrano is *El Capitano*, but no one sees him. He has a reputation as a doodoo priest."

"Voudoux," I corrected.

"Same difference," he countered with a shrug, sipping and smoking with his one good arm.

"Okay. What's the connection?" I insisted.

"Hold your horses, young lady. I'm getting there. Ever heard of PBH?" he asked.

I shook my head, no.

"That's surprising."

"I'm black and brilliant, but I can't keep up on everything, Mr. Sam," I said wryly.

"Okay, what was Nolan Grayston's firm before he became Benton's Commerce errand boy?" he queried me. "You *are* up on your current black history, I take it?"

Archer's problem, I surmised, was that he for some reason assumed that I wouldn't slap him. "Pewter, Bale and Hewitt," I answered. "Wait a minute." It was beginning to make sense.

Nolan Grayston, soon-to-have-been-indicted Secretary of Commerce, had recently died in a jet crash while on a corporate shopping mission over the Middle East. Grayston had been a key political strategist during Benton's presidential campaign and was rumored to have been tipping around some potentially shady deals. He was the sort of black face in which the black bourgeoisie exalted. He had really "made it," after all. A major partner at the law firm of Pewter, Bale and Hewitt, Grayston had also done some work for the unsavory Triomphe regime during its most blood-curdling days.

"PBH is a subsidiary of the firm, right?" I tried to make the connection.

Arched winked. "You *are* black and brilliant—beautiful, too." He sipped, puffed, and continued. "Okay. The suits got embarrassed about the stuff over Triomphe and decided to create PBH as a public relations firm that would handle cases of that sort. Now, guess who also works for PBH as a consultant?"

"Stone?" I guessed.

"Right. Now, Stone has his own agency that specializes in sensitive operations—black bag operations, dirty tricks, industrial espionage, and the like. PBH funnels the sensitive stuff to him. He was also a CIA asset. Guess who PBH has as a client?"

"Malmundo?"

"But deeper," said Archer. "EarthChem."

EarthChem was a major pharmaceutical biotechnology company that was also a *muy*, *muy* major player in the political realm, especially in campaign financing. They were the corporate example of socialism for the rich and free enterprise for the poor. They gave to everyone and owned everything. I chewed on this for a few seconds until a question surfaced. "Okay, Sam, where do the Boys come in?"

"Mike couldn't figure out why Stone was really pushing Malmundo. He knew the client angle and all that, but there wasn't that much coke going out of there. Stone still does some work for PBH, and EarthChem is a major account at PBH. There must be something that EarthChem wants and, whatever it is, a policy change in regard to Misericordia is necessary."

"Any idea what that change is, special agent?"

"That," sighed Archer, "may have died with Mike. He was trying to find that out. Peltrano iced him because he was getting too close to finding out that Malmundo has some sort of deal in the making with EarthChem. Peltrano sent his dogs."

"But why the—" I couldn't find the right words to describe what they had done to Michael.

"The technique of discrediting? Simple, if you think about it. The idea in the trade is that nobody will take the word of a dead faggot."

"That's sick," I said.

"But effective. Look, Mike was trying to connect the various threads in the conspiracy, but is the press interested in that?

Fuck no. All they're interested in are the details of his secret life?!" Archer sneered. You could tell he'd tasted this same bile many times before. Cases thwarted and colleagues ambushed, shot in the back.

"Has anyone tried to alert the press?" I asked. "Is there a story here?"

"Of course! Those lazy cocksuckers!" he scoffed. "They want you to do all their leg-work for them, provide them with documented handouts before they get interested. Fucking bastards!" Armless threw back the rest of his Sark. "Want another?"

"Uh, no thanks." I pegged him as a bitter drinking man and didn't want to go his route. My bad attitude doesn't require any potent stimulants.

"You may find this interesting. As macabre as the Boys are, they follow a pattern. Remember what Nate Ford used to do? Didn't Ford used to cut off the tongue of an informer or the relative of an enemy and—"

"Please!!" I slammed the table with a palm. I knew where he was going and I had already been there. I didn't want to hear it. My husband had been mutilated that way. His tongue carved out, rolled like sushi, and stuffed into his rectum. And the bastards did the same and worse to my babies. Nate Ford. I collected myself. "So, what are you telling me, Mr. Archer?"

Archer looked at me. He knew exactly what he was doing and what had been done to me. He dished out his tip and returned his fedora to his head. He pulled the brim down and looked me squarely in the eye.

"Nate Ford is Oscar Peltrano. Good day, Ms. Halligan. If I can be of any further assistance, don't hesitate to call."

With that he rose and left the room, the aroma of his tobacco floating in the air. Still shuddering with my rage and my painful memories, I remained in my seat for several minutes, trying to compose myself, to keep from being consumed with hatred. This was the new Nina, after all, a few years older and more in control. I no longer went off blindly at the drop of a hat, screaming and hollering at a blood-drenched moon. This wasn't a time to rant and rave; it was a time to think. Archer had given me some important bits of information about what was going on with Michael, but he had also given me even greater incentive to take care of a big issue in my life.

I picked up my package, an outfit I had purchased for the funeral, and left the bar. I made my way into the cavernous waiting room of the station. Commuters, train passengers, expectant loved ones and friends, shoppers and workers on after-hour engagements—all crisscrossed and collided into each other as I made my way through the crowd. As I walked to the entrance, the afternoon sun shone through the large grated and ornate windows, toning the place in an amber light. I stepped up to the taxi lane and climbed into a car that I knew was waiting solely for me.

Archer dropped some bombs on me all right, the biggest and most explosive one concerning the shared identities of Oscar Peltrano and Nate Ford. That was definitely news I could use. Now I wished that I'd only accepted a dollar from Gale. I might not be capable of keeping my personal concerns separated from the case. After all, if Ford was actually Peltrano—and if he had ordered Michael's assassination—then my own personal vendetta and solving the circumstances of his death really did converge. What threw me for a loop, though, was the 411 about EarthChem.

What was the deal? What did EarthChem desire that would lead to a collusion of interest with Malmundo and Ford—and be worth killing Michael over? EarthChem was a leading pharmaceutical company and was on the cutting edge of biotechnology. The firm's motto, according to critics, was "clone it and own it." Its controversial policy—according to critics of the World Trade Organization—was to patent, clone, and then claim the exclusive rights of various types of plant, animal, and human DNA. And in the process, they specialized in ripping off the indigenous folk medicines of so-called underdeveloped nations, withholding access to their "perfected" products and information from the very people from whom they had stolen the idea in the first place. Misericordia perfectly conformed to the profile of an exploited nation—zero GNP, political instability, a greedy elite population, desperate but crafty masses skilled at improvising to survive. But what did it have organically that EarthChem was interested in? That's what I needed to know.

"—Right here, miss?" the taxi driver interrupted my train of thought.

I realized that we were already back at Gale's neighborhood on Van Ness, but we were sitting in front of the wrong house. "This isn't it, driver. It's up a bit more." There was a large crowd assembled where the driver had parked, completely blocking the view of the house.

"This is the address you gave, ma'am, 3814 Van Ness Street," insisted the driver, who spoke in an Eastern European accent.

I examined the crowd more closely. There were picket signs, televisions vans and camera men, television news reporters, police officers at barricades. I heard heated voices and began to read the words on the signs. "Don't Put Mike Debord Back in the Closet!" "Benton's Sinner Besmirches the Country!" "Abomination in the Eyes of Our Lord!" "Black Gay and Lesbian Alliance for Mike Debord, RIP!" "Benton's Drug Policy Died in Debord's Veins—and Ass!"

My God, I thought, this is Gale's place after all. I simply hadn't recognized it for the crowd.

"Driver, pull over to the other side of the street," I ordered. The cabbie drove on and parked beneath a large elm, fully adorned with autumnal leaves. "Just a moment," I told him. I sat back and looked over my shoulder and out the back window. A bloody circus. Archer was right. If the Peltrano technique was to discredit Michael, it was working like a charm. Damn.

I opened my purse, pulled out my cellular, and dialed Gale's number. "Hello? Gale?"

"Nina," she said. "Where are you, girl?"

"Watching the show from across the street in the cab," I answered.

"Oh, I see you. I'm upstairs in the front bedroom."

I looked up at the windows. We waved in each other's direction, but I wasn't sure if she could see me. "Are you all right?"

"Oh, these motherfuckers," she nearly shrieked. "It's not enough that Michael's dead. Everyone has to use him for their own purpose. We can't even mourn in peace!"

"Yeah," I sighed. "I'm coming in."

"Tell the driver to make a left and come into the alley," she said.

"Okay. Just tell Bass that I'm coming through the back. See you in a few minutes. Bye."

I relayed Gale's instructions to the driver. We drove into the alley, to the back fence behind the house. I paid the man, hopped out of the car, and went through the gate of the brick wall that ended the Debord's expanse of property. I walked up the stone path and then passed through the clump of trees at the end of the yard. Kicking a large pile of leaves that had recently accumulated up in the air before me, I heard the sound of someone else walking through the leaves and turned to see a large, dark-skinned man.

The man must have been one of Bass's associates. In addition to his formidable size, he looked as if he'd recently been beaten about the face with a bag of nickels. He was wearing a black trench coat, and I noticed that he was plugged into a portable tape player-radio.

"I'm Nina," I said.

"Yeah, the boss told you were his cuz—and cute." He broke into a salacious smile and quickly undressed me with his eyes in a way that only brothers could do. "I'm Oval."

Snatching a page from Zee, I quickly decided to establish my authority, letting him know in no uncertain terms that my bod was off-limits. "Is this your post, Oval?"

"Yep. A couple dudes from the media been circulatin' about, but I showed somethin'." He pulled back the coat to reveal a police baton.

"Good." I was about to turn.

"Yo, sister. Can I have a word with you?"

"Well, uh," I began. I looked back at the house. I saw someone peering through the window who did not look like Gale. "I have to get back to the house. Gale, Ms. Simmons, needs me, uh, Oval."

"Won't take but a minute, sister," he said with a smooth authority. He quickly walked over to me and crossed into my zone, that space that I never allow strangers to enter. "Is it true what they sayin' 'bout this dude?"

"Who? Michael?" I was slightly caught off guard, thinking he was going to make a pass.

"Yeah." He looked around. "I mean, the dude didn't have any bitch in him, did he?"

"No, Oval, but would it matter if he did?" I said.

"Well, yeah, sister. I ain't down with this faggot shit—"

"Oval," I snapped. "I'm not paying you for your opinions! That sister had her man taken away from her and she needs some serious backup. If you have doubts about my late friend's masculinity, then I'll have Bass relieve you. Is that clear?"

"Look, sister, I didn't mean to offend you. I...uh...I just wanted to know the deal," he said, stepping back to his original position beneath the trees. "I'm cool. I was merely inquiring about his original black man status, you know."

"So, I'm not going to have to worry about you, am I? Bass said you were reliable. Don't make him out to be a liar or poor judge of character."

"No problem, sister. I got your back. You don't have to worry about me. Oval Dupree is on the scene." He reached into his coat and switched on his tape player.

Suddenly curious, I asked what he was listening to.

"*Hardcore* by Li'l Kim," he said, giving me a mouthful of gold-encased teeth. "I gots Rah Digga and Foxy Brown, too."

Well, I thought to myself, as my daddy once told me: It takes a bitch to make a male dog a good watchdog.

"Carry on." I turned on my heels and tried to execute an authoritative strut towards the stairs and into the house. If Oval had learned the name of the gang that killed Michael, he would have had a dick fit. Luckily, the gals were keeping him physically stimulated, if not intellectually occupied. For some reason, I found myself cursing Sam Archer's name as I entered the back door. I was simply disgusted by all the propaganda around this case.

When I entered the kitchen, I was greeted at the door by Naomi, Gale's younger sister, who had somehow become a grown woman since the last time I had seen her.

"Oh, Nina," she sighed, "this is horrible."

We gave each other a hug.

"Hey, let's not get too discombobulated," I said. "We have to stay strong for Gale."

"I know," she agreed. "But first Lee and now Michael. God, what is happening to us? Why us?"

I sighed. "Come on." We walked into the living room through the hall that led to the front of the house. Hearing the sound of the protesters through the walls, I decided that I would have to find a way to get rid of them all at once, for the sake of my own sanity as well as Gale's. Gale was probably holed up in her bedroom or study, trying to block out the scene. We went upstairs. "I like your hair-style, Nao."

"I don't have any, Nina."

"That's what I like about it." Naomi's head was closely cropped and it showed the contour of her skull. Unlike some of the brothers and sisters who were completely bald, Naomi had a run of fuzz over her head. With her dangling looped earrings, she really looked very *Africano*.

"Gale said you were investigating Michael's death," she said as we reached the top of the stairs.

"Yes. I can't talk about it right now, Nao. I haven't sorted it out yet."

We walked a few paces, and she suddenly stopped.

"Nina, you don't believe the sick stuff they're saying about Michael, do you?"

I looked at her. "Nao? Not you, too?"

"Nina, it's all over the media," she replied.

"What is?" asked another voice.

We both looked in the direction of the voice and saw Gale standing before us. She was wearing a black T-shirt and black denim jeans. I peered at Naomi and gave her a special look. "About this mess outside," I said to Gale. "How long has this been going on?"

"Too long! Since you left," Gale answered. She looked tired and drained, the snap gone out of her. It was completely under-standable. Here she was cooped up in her own home, dealing with death, funeral arrangements, and a knot of unwanted knuckleheads congregated together in her front yard. "What did you find out, Nina?"

I turned to Naomi. "Your sister and I have to speak. Why don't you fix us some tea and we'll be down in a few minutes."

"Yes," added Gale. "We'll have it up here."

"Why not in the living room?" I asked.

"Nina, I can't sit in my motherfucking living room!" Gale replied. "I called the police and they just put up the barricades and blabbered on about *their* constitutional rights to express *their* views! The media's goddamn right to block my mother-fucking driveway!"

"We will have tea in the living room—without the yahoos. Mark my words, the big mamou has spoken," I said. "Go, child," I said to Naomi. I approached Gale and gently took her by the arm and into her room, closing the door behind us.

In her bedroom I tossed my package onto the bed, in-structing her to sit down at her vanity desk while I sat on the edge of the bed and told her all that I knew, everything I'd learned from Archer: Stone. Malmundo. Peltrano. PBH. Earth-Chem.

"What does EarthChem have to do with this?"

"I don't know," I shrugged. "But Archer seems to think that, whatever it is, it's the key to Michael's death. Stone was pushing the change in recognizing the junta because the Mal-mundo regime is having some sort of relationship with Earth-Chem or is willing to give EarthChem what it wants."

"What's that?"

I shrugged my shoulders. "I haven't a clue. But it must be big, so big that Benton is willing to bend over to a heavy political con-tributor like EarthChem and risk being called soft on drugs."

"What's the next move?" she asked.

"I'm going to see what's shaking at Bernard's capital-in-exile. Miriam was mentioned in Michael's diary and she may have a piece of the puzzle. After all, whatever they want has to do with Misericordia. We just have to find out what it is."

Naomi knocked on the door and entered, as I was about to stretch out onto the bed. "Tea will be ready in a few minutes." She closed the door and went back downstairs.

"Okay," said Gale. "What are you going to do about that?" She jerked her head towards the chanting that had drifted up to the room and could be heard from outside her window.

I picked up the phone and asked for Carol Bridges at the White House. I waited and then spoke to her. "Hello. Carol Bridges? Nina Halligan... I'm fine... Gale? She would be in a lot better shape if she didn't have to deal with inconsiderate protesters... I know. But the police don't seem to be interested in a widow's peace of mind while she prepares the burial of her loved one... I understand, Carol. I know the president doesn't control the D.C. police. But no widow preparing for the funeral of her husband should have to go through this. First, the slander... I understand you have no power, but the president does. And Mr. Richard Stone seems to exert a certain degree of influence over presidential affairs. So you tell Mr. President or Mr. Stone, whomever you run into first, one simple word: EarthChem... Yes, EarthChem. I don't think certain parties are going to want to see Gale or myself stepping onto the front lawn and speaking to the assembled protesters and media about EarthChem and Misericordia in the same breath... Thank you. Good-bye."

"Well?" asked Gale expectantly.

"Just a test, my dear."

Archer was right. Michael was hot on the trail of something. Within five minutes, as Gale, Naomi, and I watched from the living room, a District of Columbia police car pulled up. A high-ranking officer in a white shirt got out and ordered the protesters and camera crews to leave. No ifs. No ands. No buts. Go. First amendment rights or no first amendment rights. Clear out or face arrest. They grumbled. They complained. They invoked constitutional and sovereign citizenship rights. But they did leave.

Michael had been fucked with, murdered, and now, with this sick and slick character assassination, fucked over. Well, as my daddy once said, when people fuck with you, you have to fuck with them right back.

Tea was served.

CHAPTER SIX

It had been forty-eight hours since I last checked in with Zee. I planned to call her in New York before I left for Bernard's "capital" about some research I needed her to do on Richard Stone and EarthChem. She called me first.

"Anna's been arrested," she informed me. "I heard about the killing in Washington and thought you would have your hands full. That's why I didn't call you before."

"Arrested for what?"

"Assault and battery."

"Who? Shinyun?"

"And Rolando," she added. "She's walking around with a shiner and fat lip, skipper."

"God," I sighed. "Where is she?"

"She's back at your place. I spent the night there with her. She's a wreck, Nina. So am I."

"What's happened?" There was clearly something going on with Zee. She'd been spending a great deal of time at the office lately and had been very quiet. Granted, she'd always been a very quiet woman, but she was normally friendly and personable as well.

"I broke up with Ibrahim."

Ibrahim Mossoud was an Egyptian whom she had met at school, a member of the Egyptian ruling circle. From what Zee had told me, her own skin complexion—she was gorgeously black with luminous eyes—would be a problem with an haute bourgeois Cairn family. The pairing had also caused a stir with some members of Zee's family, who were very progressive but ardent black nationalists. But Ibrahim was a Muslim and that was more important to Zee. And besides, Ibrahim was a progressive Muslim, who was willing to deal with her as an equal and not keep her locked up in some modern form of purdah, the Islamic tradition of restricting women to the house or under the watchful eye of men. A very nice young man with an eye toward the diplomatic service, Ibrahim wanted to follow in the footsteps of his uncle, the former secretary general of the United Nations.

"I met his family and they didn't like the line-up," she snapped bitterly. "They used to trade in people like me, Nina. His mother described me as an over-educated Nubian slave girl."

"Zee!" I was shocked for her sake. "To hell with them. You don't need that kind of abuse, sister."

"They think something is wrong with me because I'm an army officer, Nina. They were so cruel and disrespectful," she choked. "It wouldn't be so bad if I didn't love him so much."

"What about Ibrahim?" I inquired. "What did he say?"

"Nina," she began, "I need a man. I can defend myself, but I want a man who's proud of me and not ashamed of my race or what I do. His parents have money. He may love me, but they control the flow of cash."

"Look, I'll be back in New York the day after tomorrow. We'll go out and talk. I promise. Okay?"

"Okay. Yes. I would like that. I need to sort this out with someone else. What about Anna?"

"I'll call her, but please check in on her for me the first chance you get. And before I forget, I also need you to do some research for me." I gave her my targets of inquiry and ended the call. Anna did not answer when I called my apartment, so I left a message for her to call me at Gale's.

It wasn't like Anna to punch someone. She must have finally reached her limit over her breakup with Shinyun. Her cold-blooded calculations to retain Rolando were just a front to protect her from her own feelings, I thought. Anna was a very complex person. She could be as tough as nails one moment and a Wanda Weepy the next. I didn't like the idea of her running around the city like a loose cannon. I had originally hoped that I could rely on Zee to keep an eye on her, but Zee clearly had her own problems. And, as luck would have it, so did I.

The deposed president of Misericordia was holding court in a brownstone building that was modeled after the Ca'd'Oro in Venice, built in a romanesque revival style with arched windows and columns that appeared from a distance to be arabesques. Above the windows was a frieze depicting some long-forgotten epic of conquerors and the vanquished.

The building was located in a fashionable section of Georgetown on Q Street. My first stop upon entering the building was the security desk. I introduced myself, gave the man at the desk a calling card and ID. He made a telephone call, announcing my name into the mouthpiece. The securitron waved me through. I was asked to deposit my clutch purse, watch, and jewelry into a plastic box before proceeding through a security gate to be X-rayed for any potentially dangerous metal.

After my belongings were returned to me, I was led up a sweeping set of stairs by another securitron. At the top of the stairs, I was greeted by my target for the evening.

"Nina, you made it," Miriam gushed, acting as if my arrival was unanticipated.

"Doubted it, huh?" I asked. "Ye of little faith."

Miriam became solemn. "Well, given the circumstances..." she trailed off and then shifted gears. "How's Gale?"

"Surviving. Surviving," I said. "You're certainly more than appropriately decked out for the occasion." Miriam was splendidly attired in a wine-colored knit dress with a gorgeously draped and wrapped bodice. The dress was flared and extended down to her ankles. Her hair was tastefully arranged in a series of complex, lusciously thick braids, forming tentacle-like arches.

"I'm playing hostess for the president, since he doesn't have a wife," she said. "Come. Let me take you to the reception room. The other guests have arrived."

A series of elaborate paintings, wall-sized epics depicting the Misericordian revolution, flanked the carpeted hallway that led to the reception room. I stopped briefly at one of the paintings, a classic military man on a horse with upraised front legs. I turned to Miriam.

"Miri, is that Nestor Morgan?"

"Yes."

Something about the painting didn't seem right. Morgan, who according to historical accounts was a black slave, was painted with fair skin and Caucasian features. I reasoned that this was probably a pre-Triomphe rendition and decided to let it pass.

Guards stood at the entrance as we entered the room. It was an enormous room painted light gray with gold trim; a chandelier hung from above. One end of the room formed an alcove. Across from the entrance, a set of French doors led out to a patio or garden.

I had assumed this would be a policy party, composed of a few choice talking heads and policy wonks. I soon realized, however, that it had turned into something else entirely. To my surprise, the room was scattered with a significant portion of "the gang of one hundred," popularly regarded as the most influential African-Americans. Television cameras were everywhere. Bernard and his advisers, including Miriam, were suddenly into "show and tell," that postmodern malaise of imagery and symbolism over substance, blood, and sweat.

"Miri, what's with the cameras?" I said as we walked to a buffet table feted with dishes of Caribbean food. A gloved waitron offered me a glass of wine. "I thought the president just wanted some discrete advice, to talk about the requisite tools of liberation."

Miriam gave me her tightest smile, inadvertently signaling that she was about to lie or at least try to feed me something she herself didn't really believe. "President Bernard feels that after the recent coup we need to highlight the situation and get more media coverage. So we invited Ebony Television Network to film it."

"Miriam, you aren't going to talk about 'the requisite tools of liberation' on TV, are you?" I asked.

"Oh, God, no, Nina," she replied, taking a sip from her wine and waving at someone across the room. "You'll have a private audience with the president and some of his most trusted advisers."

"The same trusted advisers who came up with the idea to televise this?" I asked with a certain level of pained incredulity.

"Yes," she replied flatly. "It pays to advertise."

My original assessment had been correct. Malmundo and the elite had a plan that enabled them to take over the country. Bernard, on the other hand, was simply using television to create a simulacrum of himself as an engaged president, rallying his people against homegrown despots. This smoke-and-mirrors routine might inspire the professional émigré community, but it sure as hell wouldn't do squat for the multitude back home who were being decimated. I quickly scrubbed any idea of giving Bernard my advice.

"Really tragic about Michael, huh?" I began.

Miriam avoided my eyes for a hot second and then looked at me. "Michael was trying to get the process going—the negotiations with Malmundo," she said. "I don't know what's going to happen now that he's gone."

"From what I understand, the White House is thinking about tilting towards the Malmundo regime," I added. "Unofficially recognizing it. Is that true?"

"That's what we were told—unofficially," answered Miriam. "I spoke to Michael and he felt that there was a subtle policy change or shift going on in the Benton Administration. Things changed after the second coup—and changed quickly."

"How so?"

"No one from the administration was allowed to be in contact with us—I mean the president was cold-shouldered. The crisis was deprioritized."

Miriam's eyes darted around the room, taking in the assembled black glamorati. As she waved and smiled, I realized the extent to which Miriam had become a power groupie. No longer satisfied with being a medical doctor, mother, and wife, she was trying to carve out a new role for herself, one I felt would have disastrous consequences if she didn't wake up and face the facts about the team she was backing.

I was about to zero in when she turned to me and said: "It's a mess, Nina. This whole thing is a mess. Michael's death and...." Her voice trailed off into a whisper.

I finally had my opening. "Michael Debord mentioned you in a diary he'd been keeping and was scheduled to see you the night he was—"

"Nina, I have to go," she stopped me. "The president's assistant, Chantal, wants me."

With that, Miriam glided across the room and began conversing with a light-skinned woman, about thirty years old and perfectly dressed for television. She wore a black lace evening dress with a dangerously low *décolleté*. Her hair was pulled into a bun. The sleeves of her dress were sheer lace and the body, up to the bust line, was fully lined to discourage peering eyes. She was more striking than pretty. I watched the way she gestured dramatically with her hands as she spoke, with the kind of broad, sweeping motions that I would normally associate with French people or Italians.

Miriam turned a quick glance at me. The woman knew I was dead on her ass, and she also knew that she couldn't shake me, even if she tried. The two of them departed through the French doors that led outside the building. I put down my drink and was about to shift into gear when I bumped into the epitome of rotundity itself—Dr. Walid Afreeka, professional mouth-for-hire, in the process of helping his ample self to the spread at the buffet table.

"Nina! What the hell are you doin' here?" said the portly professor, recent celebrity of the massacre at *Johnnae's*. Under the circumstances, I would have expected him to be keeping a low profile, but he must have surfaced the moment he heard the television camera's motor running. He may also have been trying to beef up his "foreign policy" credentials by assisting Misericordia. After all, he did wonders for the brothers and sisters in Harlem.

"Sorry, doc, I have to make my way to the ladies' room," I said as I squeezed my way through the room that was becoming more congested with foreign policy wannabes. "Incited any other conflagrations of late, doc?"

"That's not fair, counselor!" he protested, fingers greased with jerk chicken sauce. "I wasn't talkin' that talk on the days when I was on the picket line."

"No, just about 'alien merchants,'" I reminded him of his aggressive use of what many people considered to be code words for Jews and other non-blacks.

That settled it. The whole evening was a bad idea if Dr. Afreeka had been invited. Afreeka had certain credibility with some folks in the black community. But he was too much of a student of Reggie Baxter, and both men were mainly interested in running their mouths. My political cynicism had begun to deepen under Lee's influence. We had both steadily sickened of charismatic black religious leadership, especially after De Lawd.

As I made my way across the room, I took stock of the "prestigious" assembly. Everybody was there. Maurice North, Gresham Hopkins, and nellie marcos predictably represented the intellectual elite, the Niggerati. Constance Mortimer, the executive director of the Black Women's Council and the unofficial inheritor of Paul Tower's ongoing tirade against so-called gangsta rap, was front and center. Rep. George Plunkett, the chairman of the pussy-whipped—if not dick-beaten—African-American Congressional Caucus, was also in attendance. By his side was the new director of the NAACP, Touré Shaka, a former congressman who, seeing the writing on the wall, had opted for the leadership of a flaccid NAACP over an irrelevant rump of a congressional caucus. Smart move, I thought, one that would probably earn him directorships on Fortune 500 corporate boards where he could beg whites for money.

Moving through the crowd, I kept hearing snatches of conversations that reminded me of the background effects on Quincy Jones's version of *What's Going On*. The place had too much bonhomie—too much clinking of glasses—to be taken seriously as a gathering of great black minds. All the people there were just too fat and too impressed with themselves and their proximity to the princes of power. The smug air of the room—the stench of self-satisfaction—wafted toward me, propelling me outside and toward Miriam.

I crossed the room, passed through the same French doors that Miriam and the other woman had exited a few moments earlier, and found myself in the middle of a formal garden. Earlier in the year, the garden would surely have been in full bloom. Now, in the midst of October's Indian summer, the garden's greenery was slowly edging into a harsh shade of brown. Still, it was a nice place to have a party. The sun was setting and the garden was lit by the warm glow of security lights. Scanning the area, I walked around the corner of a large hedge of bushes to a somewhat secluded part of the garden. I heard the sound of water gushing and voices. Deciding to be discrete, I peeked around the hedge and saw my sister-in-law standing before a water fountain with a party of three: President Bernard, Chantal, and another woman whom I didn't recognize. Chantal and the other woman were exchanging verbal fireworks. El Presidente said nothing, listening intently as the two women zigzagged back and forth among what sounded like a mix of French, Kreole, and English.

The other woman looked as if she was in her mid-twenties. She wore a white blouse and dark trousers over her curvaceous figure. She was, as the menfolk in my daddy's day would have said, "healthy," a perfect example of what songster Kid Creole would call "pulchritudinous." She was as dark as me, but her features were different, more European. Eyeing her more closely, I decided that she was probably of Carib descent. She wore wire-framed glasses and short, black hair.

Bernard was short, shorter than all three women. His small frame was encased in a dark blue, double-breasted suit. He had bulbous eyes and a large head covered with crinkly black hair. He seemed like a trapped man listening to loved ones fighting; he appeared to lack either the authority or the courage to intercede.

It was actually Miriam who kept trying to intercede and

broker the debate, and it was from her that I learned the other woman's name.

"Look," said Miriam, "this isn't the time or place to be having this discussion. Fanon, I think you ought to wait until the end of—"

"This *is* the time!" countered the woman named Fanon. "We have wasted precious time trying to deal with the Americans, and it seems that they have made up their minds and want to deal with Malmundo and not Pepe. This is a farce! You expect these counterfeit blacks here to intercede on our behalf?"

Hit it girl, I thought. She'd already scoped out the fakirs.

"Fanon, my dear," said Chantal. "We have to be realistic. The best chance for the president to return to our country as the rightful democratic leader is by pushing for negotiations. I share your disappointment and disgust in having to deal with General Malmundo, but we have to play the cards that we've been dealt."

"We should have played our hand a year ago," said Fanon, "and prepared the people for a fight. Now, the man that our people elected—at a great sacrifice—gets to play Hamlet and be made a fool of by the Benton administration in the process!"

"This is not the time for your cheap Marxism," snarled Chantal.

"You're the one he's been listening too," replied Fanon, her finger in Chantal's face. "Pepe isn't going to tell you about his doubts because you've succeeded in poisoning him with your bloody love darts. Our country is lost because of you and your stupid bourgeois ideas about trying to work with the Americans!"

"The people that Dr. Maurice North and I have assembled here are the leading minds in the African-American communities," defended Chantal.

"In America. Period," added Miriam.

"Dr. North is from the Frederick Douglass Center," continued Chantal, "and has connections to the White House. We have to negotiate—"

"It's too late for that!" countered the revolutionary. "Look what happened to Michael Debord—and he was an American."

"What happened to Mr. Debord was an isolated event," said Chantal.

"HA!" responded Fanon. She had fire, this woman. "It was an assassination!"

"According to the newspaper, Michael Debord was the victim of a homosexual tryst gone bad," offered the president.

"It was a set-up," hissed Fanon. "I don't believe for a second that happened. It's so convenient that the only American who was willing to stand by us is now dead. That means we have to take what they offer, and that probably means nothing at all!"

I wondered why she thought his death was a set-up, an assassination.

"Not if we sit down and discuss this with them as business people," countered Chantal.

"Business? Business?! This is our country we're speaking about. Not some bloody piece of real estate. My God, Chantal, you really do think like them, like an American. You fucking bloody reductionist!"

"Fanon," began Chantal, addressing the other woman as if she were a wayward child, "one has to be pragmatic. It is now time for us to be realistic and try to salvage—"

"The hell with that! It's time for *Dechoukaj*! *Dechoukaj*! *DE-CHOUKAJ*!" she loudly proclaimed.

"God, you're impossible, Fanon!" said Chantal.

"Good. That means I stand the greater chance of getting something done," she countered. "I admit to being creatively maladjusted, and I won't participate in a farce with a group of bogus blacks who can't—or won't—protect their own people! I'm leaving, Pepe. You lost our country, but at least you got something out of this—a wife!"

I heard her soft footsteps on the lawn and decided to duck around another hedge. She passed by without noticing me.

"Marisol!" cried the president. "Miriam, stop her. I can't have my family break up like this. We have to stay together during this crisis. I need all of you."

"Pepe, let her go," said Chantal, dropping the presidential title. "Fanon and Raoul are impossible to work with. Besides, she has nowhere to go and will be back."

"Miriam," said the president. "Bring her back. We have to settle this as a people. As a nation."

"Yes, your excellency," said Miriam, sounding as if she'd switched her allegiance to a foreign potentate.

I waited for her to round the hedge and stepped up quickly behind her, placing my hand over her mouth. She was startled, but I held onto her firmly, edging her back to where I'd been standing.

"Nina! What the hell are you doing?" she exclaimed after I released her.

"What's going on?" I asked

"Between Chantal and Fanon?"

"Yes."

"Oh, just a dispute about policy."

"Oh, really now? Sounds a bit more intimate to me," I said. "Particularly the marriage aspect."

Miriam's eyes widened enough under the subdued light for me to see that she was shocked. "Nina, you were spying on us."

"I'm merely letting you know about my wonderful surveillance skills," I said sweetly.

"I brought you here to help us, not spy on us!"

"I want to know about you and Michael Debord on the night of his death," I said. She tried to wrangle free, but I tightened my grip on her wrist. The woman wasn't going anywhere.

"Look, the president asked me to get his daughter."

"What? Who? Fanon? That sneaky clerical," I muttered and smiled.

"Adopted, Nina," explained Miriam. "Adopted. He raised her and a boy, Raoul, when they were young *urcheros*. Father Bernard worked at an orphanage with young children from the street and adopted two of them, Fanon and Raoul. Now, I have to go."

"Not until you tell me about—"

"Look, I don't know what you're talking about!" she protested.

"Michael wrote in his diary that he was going to see you the night of his death."

"Me?"

"Yes. He said he was going to meet MF—as in Miriam Francesca."

Miriam looked puzzled for a moment, but then offered a slight smile. "Not me, Nina. Fanon. Marisol Fanon. She prefers to be called Fanon in honor of Franz Fanon, as well as another famous revolutionary who lived in Misericordia years ago, another Marisol."

"The president's kid?"

"Well, it wasn't me, Nina. Now, I have to go and find her, and if you want speak to her, maybe you'll assist me."

"Lead the way," I said. We walked across the garden, entered the reception room, and found that it was even more packed than before. Bernard and Chantal had returned to the room and were greeting the guests in the alcove. A television crew was filming them. As I craned my neck to look for Fanon, I pondered Bernard's predicament.

Bernard was an interesting case. While most other political leaders were supremely confident in their abilities to lead, Bernard was a creature of the crowd, the masses. As a former parish priest, he was an embodiment of the people's moods, feelings, and sentiments. Raised in the shanties of Port Henri, he never forgot his people; he drew sustenance from them and they from him. But the strong connection between the two was also a shared weakness; one could not function without the other. Separated, they both floundered. Exiled, Bernard simply could not decide on a course of action. He had let himself be trapped by the grand illusion of Washington-as-savior, surrounded by a circle of middle-class progressives who actually believed that his power to rule his people could only be restored by Jeff Benton.

Miriam and I circled the room repeatedly, but Fanon was nowhere to be found.

"Maybe she left already," said Miriam. "Maybe she has the brains to get out of this."

"What do you mean?"

Miriam looked around her. There were knots of people milling about. "I need to get a drink. Like one?"

I caught her meaning right away. "Sure, Miri."

We squeezed ourselves through the crowd and over to the table where we were each handed a second glass of wine. Dr. Afreeka was still feasting at the trough; his badly fitted suit was speckled with crumbs and stains. The two of us moved farther down to a corner at the end of the table.

"So?" I prompted.

"There's a power struggle going on," she said.

"Let me guess. Hmmm. Chantal and Fanon? The two most important women in the president's life. How exciting."

"Don't be mean, Nina. Pepe feels bad about what's going on. He just can't make up his mind about what to do about it," admitted Miriam. "He's trying to make the right decision for Misericordia."

"Now, why doesn't that surprise me? I suppose Chantal is helping him do that?"

"Yes." Miriam sipped her wine and looked at the other end of the room. "Fanon is of the faction back home that's always argued that the people should have been armed and prepared for a battle to defend what they had just won."

"Well, that was never done and now it's too late," I replied. "If the Benton administration is going to recognize Malmundo—unofficially, of course—then it will only be a matter of time before it unfreezes Maerican assets. Malmundo then gets the gold, so to speak."

"That's why Chantal is advocating negotiations."

"Who the hell is she?" I said in a tone that let Miriam know that I didn't like her. She was slick. In fact, she reminded me of myself when I was a slickette.

"I told you. His assistant."

"And future wife. Uh huh, he's going to quit the priesthood?"

"He already has."

"Check that out." I glanced up at her. "Tell me more about this star child—Chantal...?"

"Laurent," Miriam filled in. "She's of the Laurent family in Misericordia. Haute bourgeoisie. The family has money in textiles. Export-import."

"Drugs. Money laundering." I remembered the name now.

Her family—maybe not her, but maybe—had their hands in everything that was dirty, as well as clean.

Miriam frowned. "I don't know anything about that, Nina."

"I do. I've heard things. Read DEA reports. Nothing conclusive about her, just enough to give a whiff of corruption," I said.

Miriam looked back over at the couple, who were still greeting their guests. "She's studied under Dr. North at Harvard and has given lectures at the Douglass Center. She got him here and he's brought in the rest of his intellectual colleagues. They have access to the media and can interpret black culture to whites."

"You mean *market* black culture to whites," I said, responding to her take on the Niggerati.

"What?" she asked, my sarcasm sailing right over her head.

"Skip it. What do you know about Oscar Peltrano?" I asked.

She shrugged her shoulders. "Nothing. Who is he?"

"Supposedly a big, big-time drug dealer in league with Malmundo," I said. "What about EarthChem?"

"Huh? EarthChem? The pharmaceutical company?"

"Yes. You know, the firm that claims to be doing harmonious things with the earth and chemicals."

"What do they have to do with Michael?" she wanted to know.

"It seems that Michael was closing in on a scandal involving the firm and Jeffy-boy's change in policy. Exactly what, I don't know."

Miriam shook her head in confusion. "I don't know anything about that."

"Did Bernard or Chantal or Fanon ever mention Earth-Chem? Its influence or its presence in Misericordia?"

"No. They are always arguing about what tactics to choose."

"Figures. Yet Fanon doesn't believe the story about Michael's death. What about you, Miriam? What do you think?"

"I don't know, Nina. I think the whole thing slipped out of our hands. Something funny is going on, but I don't know what. I just have a bad feeling that everything that I ever cared about has been wiped off the map and that no one is concerned about anything except for cutting the best deal."

"What about Fanon?" I asked. "What's her story?"

"Nothing much. Father Bernard found her searching for food in a garbage dump and took her in. The boy, Raoul, was about to be executed by Triomphe's police for stealing. Bernard intervened and saved his life. He's been devoted to both of them, a true father. He even got them to start attending school, and tutored them in French and English. Taught them everything he knows."

"Luckily, Fanon hasn't picked up her adopted father's trait of indecisiveness," I said.

We heard voices from the other end of the room. Our attention drifted in the direction of the president's voice.

"My friends, I am honored that you have chosen to heed the call of my country," began the president in his Caribbean lilt. "As some of you may know, things have taken a sudden turn of events in Misericordia. It is time to stop the violence. In the spirit of doing so, I have instructed officials who represent me to contact General Malmundo to see if we can begin a dialogue. We must end Misericordia's legacy of civil war."

It was over. Whatever they had thought previously—arming the masses or not—had been tossed aside. Chantal had won. The American Way was ruling the day. Bernard was going to sue for peace, negotiate; I suspected that Malmundo would laugh, if not spit in his face. No, Malmundo was a gentleman. He would merely laugh.

"Miriam, is Bernard p-whipped?" I decided to ask before I left. "I mean, the man has only recently begun getting some serious attention. And you know how guys are when they get some."

"What?!" responded Miriam. She looked at me as if I had transgressed a boundary—and I had.

"Pussywhipped," I reiterated. You know, can't get his head out from between the legs. Dick deep into *le fuck*?"

Nonplussed, Miriam looked at me. "Nina, what are you saying? I can't believe you said that!"

"Yeah, well, it's obvious, Miriam. He's gotten used to the

taste and can't make up his mind about what to do. And his new heartthrob—excuse me, dick-throb—is calling the shots."

"My God, that's an incredibly sexist statement!" Miriam replied. "Girl, you usually hold your liquor better than that."

"Crude but accurate," I retorted. "Personally, if it were fortifying him to be bold and bad—making active decisions on the behalf of his people—I'd be all for getting his mojo working. But this Chantal put a spell on him."

"If that's the kind of advice you were going to give him—" she tried to interrupt.

"As a matter of fact, his whole advisory team is made of up women, isn't it? Chantal. Fanon. You."

"Are you implying that a team of women shouldn't be a man's key advisers?"

"I'm not saying anything of that nature, Miriam. I'm just identifying the true dynamic of the president's decision-making process," I explained. "Two-thirds of his team don't know what the hell they're doing, and the one who understands the real conditions on the ground, back in Misericordia, understands that North is merely collecting another fat lecture fee."

Miriam's mouth hung open. I placed my fingers beneath her chin, gently pushing it upward and closing her mouth. I said good night and slipped out of the room. As I went through the door, I questioned the guards about Fanon and learned that she had a good fifteen-minute head start on me.

CHAPTER SEVEN

I hailed a taxi and headed east along Q Street, past the elegant townhouses and apartment buildings of Georgetown. I immediately dismissed Bernard and his problem from my thoughts, focusing instead on Fanon and her whereabouts. Before I left the reception, Miriam had given me an address for her in Takoma Park, Maryland, and I was determined to find her tonight.

Although I wasn't at all surprised about the political turn of events, I felt bad for Miriam. She had banked a great deal on the revolution that never was. Now she was beginning to see that the whole thing was out of her hands and that even Bernard had become a hostage to Washington. The man was worse than pussywhipped; he was useless.

The taxi made a left onto Connecticut Avenue. The drive from Dupont Circle to Florida Avenue had a decidedly French-boulevard effect, with a dense line of shady trees and a host of shops. We stopped at a traffic light and waited. On the right side of the street was the Washington Hilton Hotel, situated on a small hill. The light changed and the taxi stayed in the left lane to avoid veering off onto Columbia Road, which led through a neighborhood known as Adams Morgan.

As the taxi slowly climbed up the hill, I turned to the right and saw a woman dressed similarly to Marisol Fanon cresting the hill. I told the driver to pull over. I paid him, left the cab, and stood beneath a statue in the night air. I watched the woman as she walked, convinced that it was Fanon. I began to shadow her from across the street as she headed into Adams Morgan. I stayed to her left, on the opposite side of the street, and followed her as she passed a series of apartment buildings, a 7-Eleven, a supermarket, and several restaurants. The woman stopped and looked in my direction at the oncoming traffic. She waited for the cars to pass and then crossed to my side of the street. I continued following her as she crossed another corner, made a right on Lanier Street, and then turned into the entrance of an apartment building. In what seemed like a single motion, she pressed a buzzer and entered the building.

I walked up to the building and looked at the names of the occupants. Carol Bridges, Michael's assistant, resided on the eleventh floor. Oh, happy day, I thought, slipping in a "credit card"—a flat piece of metal—over the door latch and entering the lobby, with its octagonal tile floors and ochre-colored walls.

The elevator ride was slow, giving my creative little mind time to speculate. The elevator floor was painted the same color as the lobby and had an old, musty apartment-hall smell. The eagle landed on the eleventh floor, and I walked down the hallway until I found 11-F. I stood at the door and listened to the faint voices inside. I was about to pull a listening scope from the small purse that was slung across my shoulder, but the sudden appearance of a pair of young zebras, a black-white couple who were leaving their apartment, prompted me to knock on the door instead. Just as the couple passed, an eye popped into the door's peephole.

"Yes?"

"Carol Bridges?" I asked.

"Yes?"

"I'm Nina Halligan. You met me the other day when you came to Michael's house. I would like to speak to you." Pause.

"I'm really tired, Ms. Halligan. I've had a long day. I'm

sorry, but..."

"I'm trying to find out about Michael, Carol. To find out who killed him." Another pause.

"I—I'm sorry, Ms. Halligan, but I'm not in the mood to talk. Maybe later."

"But you're not too tired to speak to Fanon, huh?"

"I'm sorry, but I—"

I banged louder on the door. "*Dechoukaj!*" I shouted. *Dechoukaj*, remembering my extremely limited Kreole, meant loosing or uprooting. It had recently become a keyword for the popular movement in Misericordia. To them it meant revolution.

"What?" said the voice from the other side of the door.

"Fanon, I know that you were supposed to see Michael the night of his death. Sooner or later you're going to have to deal with me—"

Before I could finish, the latches and bolts were cast aside. The door opened narrowly, and I saw Fanon's pretty but stern face—along with her nasty-looking automatic pistol. Must be the right place.

"Ms. Halligan, please join us," she said smoothly. She opened the door and stepped aside to allow me in.

Carol was dressed in a maroon T-shirt and rust-colored jeans, sans shoes. A day or so ago, she looked like a sleek young woman. But without her professional attire, she looked heavier, full-breasted with generous hips. She had a nervous smile on her face as she stood there in the living room next to a desk that housed a computer and reams of untidy paper. Behind her was a bookcase, on top of which rested a photo. Mr. Backbone, the president himself, stood front and center of a White House staff that included Carol and Michael.

"What do you want, Ms. Halligan?" said Carol. I noticed that she wasn't wearing her glasses.

Pointing to Fanon, I said: "Her, and information."

"Just who are you, miss?" asked Fanon. She had an edge to her voice that let me know that she would pull the trigger if given a reason.

"May I?" I held up my purse and opened it. I showed her a

card announcing my profession. She briefly examined it and then handed it to Carol. While both women were looking away, I slipped an electronic device with a sharply pronged point out of my pocket and cradled it snuggly in my palm.

"Gale Simmons, Michael Debord's widow," I said to Fanon, "hired me to investigate her husband's death. Before Michael died, he slipped me a copy of his diary on a computer disk. In it, he mentioned a scheduled meeting with an MF. First, I thought it was Miriam Butler, since the first two initials of her full name are MF, but then she suggested that it might have been you."

The two women shifted away from the desk and towards one another in the center of the room. They spoke too quietly for me to understand what they were saying.

"Please confer," I said casually, as I turned to the bookcase and implanted the bug underneath a shelf, feigning interest in a bulky, pseudo-philosophical tome by the current vice president.

"How do we know we can trust her?" said Fanon, who kept a close eye on me. I turned and smiled.

"This is just getting to be too much!" said Carol. She was distraught, running her fingers nervously through her hair.

"What is?" I asked.

"The whole thing—Michael's death!" Carol walked around in circles and then plopped down on a love seat. She appeared exhausted.

I looked at Fanon, who was still holding the gun. I sensed that she wasn't really into this any more than Carol. "*You* want to tell me about it?"

Fanon looked at Carol, who returned her look pleadingly. "Okay," she sighed in her Misericordian accent. Resigned, Fanon sat down in an armchair. But it was Carol who spoke first.

"Michael was here on the night that he was murdered," began Carol.

"He told us—Gale and me—that he was going back to the White House," I said. "That was at 8 p.m., I thought, and the medical examiner placed his death at somewhere between 11 p.m. and 1 a.m. When did he get to your place?"

"Around half past 8?" Carol said. "But that was a cover. And a lie."

"A cover and a lie?" I echoed. "Pray tell?"

Carol and Fanon exchanged nervous glances.

"Girls, we're all adults here."

"Is this confidential?" asked the blonde.

"Absolutely. But please, what happened?"

Carol sighed. "Michael and I were having an affair."

I burst out laughing. "Everybody is convinced that Michael was smoking someone else's cigar, and the whole time he was having an affair with you!"

"It's not funny," she said unsmilingly. "And I resent your racist insinuation, Ms. Halligan. You can take that attitude of yours elsewhere."

She was right about my insinuation that she was a gray girl. I crossed my arms and looked at her. "Carol, I don't want to besmirch your love for Michael, but you two were engaged in an illicit affair. I mean, after all, the man was married. Now do you want me to tell his widow that he was a natural-born man hours before his death? You have the power to save his reputation from the stain of alleged faggotry. Are you willing to do that?"

Carol squirmed uncomfortably on the love seat. I wanted to be sympathetic, but she had schtupped my friend's late husband after all. And besides, she didn't rise to the challenge I presented to her. I didn't think she would. No one stands up for true love nowadays; everyone just fucks and runs.

"Okay, what *was* going on?" I continued. "You said that it was all a lie and a cover. He was lying about going back to the White House to see you? What about the cover? A cover for what?" I looked at Fanon.

"Michael was going to meet me at Cafedon, up the street, on the corner of Columbia and Ontario," said Fanon, still holding the gun limply in her hand.

"Why? Another tryst?"

"No. I had some information for him about a project in Misericordia," she said.

"EarthChem?" I ventured.

She simply nodded her head.

"What about EarthChem?" I was finally closing in on something tangible—a real "McGuffin." Before Fanon could answer me, the telephone rang on the desk where I was leaning. I stood up as Carol crossed the floor to answer it. I walked over to a bookcase across the room.

"What?" said Carol. "Are you sure it's them?!" She carried the phone to the window and looked down on Lanier Street. "Thanks." She turned and looked at us.

I gave her a quizzical look. "A problem?"

"The Secret Service just entered the building. That was my neighbor who lives across the street. I've been followed a lot lately. They came and asked her about me. I think they are trying to build some case against Michael, and since I was his assistant..."

I looked at her and Fanon. Something else was up, but—

"Please, go. They shouldn't find you here. Take the stairway up to the roof. I'll come and get you when they leave."

Carol ushered us out the door and we walked across the hall, passing in front of the elevators. As we cornered the hallway, I heard the elevator arriving. The gate and door opened, and two dark suits over white bodies disembarked.

Fanon and I hurried upstairs, pushed open the door, and stepped out into the night. From the roof, I could see the crossroads of Adams Morgan, the intersection of Columbia Road and 18th Street.

I opened my purse and pulled out a palm-sized listening device that doubled as a radio. I inserted the tear-drop earphones and switched on the device. Fanon, who had wandered over to the far side of the roof, was clueless about my little intrusion on her friend's privacy. I could only make out bits and pieces of the conversation downstairs.

"Am I under arrest or not, Agent Brennan?"

"Miss, we're told to bring you down for questioning."

There was a pause.

"I'm going to call my attorney and have him meet me at...."

I heard her pressing the buttons on the telephone.

"Don't do that," said the man called Brennan.

"I have a right to have an attorney present," Carol protested.

"Look, bitch," someone else snarled.

"You're not the Secret Service! Just who—?"

I jumped. Her answer was met with two muffled gun shots—silencers. I heard a crash and then her body thudding onto the floor.

"Fanon!"

She walked over quickly, and I grabbed her wrist.

"Carol's been shot."

She looked at me. "What? How do you—"

Fanon saw the listening device in my hand.

"You're a fucking spy!" she screamed, pulling out her gun again. "*Puta!*"

I grabbed her gun hand and smashed it down over my upright knee, breaking her grip. The gun skipped across the roof without firing.

"Listen to me!" I said, shaking her. "I'm not a spy! I don't work for the CIA or the FBI! Michael was my friend. I only planted the bug because I didn't know if you or Carol were going to tell me what I need to know. Now we need to get out of here. If you start acting like a crazy witch, I'll throw your ass off the roof."

She stood there trying to figure out if I was on the level. Keeping my eyes on her, I picked up her gun from the tar roof and looked over the top and down at the street. Though it was dark, I could make out the two suits leaving the building and entering a car. They drove from their parked position on Lanier, stopped at the intersection, and then made a very energetic right onto 18th Street, screeching their tires as they did.

Carol's door was locked when we arrived back downstairs. I pulled out one of my "jeweler's tools" and picked the lock. Carol was face down, blood seeping from her gaping mouth. The force of the gunfire had ripped through the bookcase, and there were books and knick-knacks all over the floor. I put on a pair of thin black leather gloves and turned her body over.

"You think of everything, don't you?" said Fanon.

I searched for a pulse in Carol's neck and wrist. Nothing. I went over to the phone, called the police, and told them that I heard gunshots in apartment 11-F. I gave them the street. I did not leave my name. After that I reached beneath the desk, pulled off the bug, and wiped everything clean of handprints. I pulled Fanon out of the room, leaving Carol lying in a pool of blood with the photo of Benton and the White House staff near her soon-to-be-cold fingers.

We left the building, walked across the street, and stepped into an alley behind a savings and loan building on the corner of 18th Street and Columbia. I pushed Fanon deeper into the alley and around a crook in the wall, to get us out of eyesight of passing strangers. I heard a sound behind me and quickly turned to my left to check my rear. Nothing. I turned to Fanon to finish my questioning about Michael. But she had her own point to make—a vicious four-inch, gleaming blade of steel.

"*Puta*," she hissed at me, "get out of my way."

I stood there in silence, waiting. It was her move. She shifted to the left, but I blocked her path. She paused for a moment and then lunged at me. I jumped back, grabbed her wrist with my left hand, and quickly turned around, swinging my back into her and ramming my elbow into her solar plexus. Momentarily stunned, she released the blade, which flew into a corner, frightening a stray cat from beneath a stack of wooden food crates.

I forced her right had behind her back, yanked it higher toward her shoulder blade, and grabbed a fist full of flaxen hair. Pressed against the brick wall, with a potential madwoman on her back, Fanon suddenly became much more cooperative.

"Okay," I breathed into her ear, "you're going to tell me about the information you were going to give to Michael. *Tú comprendes?*"

"*Sí*," she hissed through clenched teeth.

I twisted her arm slightly, just to make sure I'd made my point.

"The People's Liberation Army of Misericordia overran a campsite in one of our liberated zones. We first thought it was the army making a foray into our territory, but..."

"But what?" I said hurriedly. "I don't have all night."

"Please," her voiced cracked, "you're hurting me. I'll tell you what you want. Just stop hurting me."

I loosened my grip a bit but kept her arm in the same position, her face pressed against the wall. "Go on."

"It was a small unit of the army protecting some American scientists from a U. S. company who had been doing research in Misericordia."

"What kind of research?"

"I don't know. Genetics, I think. We killed the soldiers, capturing the scientists and their documentation. That's what I had for Michael."

"And that's what I want—and now. I want those papers. Now! Tonight!"

"They're at my place," she said.

I let her go and stood back. Fanon slowly turned. I could see that I had driven her to tears. "We're going to go to your place, and I'm getting those documents and out of your life. Just remember this: fuck with me and I'll cripple you. Is that understood?"

"*Sí,*" was her only response.

I stooped to pick up the knife and we then walked out of the alley and back onto the street. As I raised my hand to flag a Capitol Cab, I heard the police sirens and saw a couple of D.C. police vehicles and an ambulance arriving to pick up the latest casualty of the war in Misericordia.

It was only a fifteen- or twenty-minute drive to Takoma, Maryland, just across the District line. Fanon told me while we rode that Michael had not shown up for their planned meeting at 11:30 p.m. at Cafedon on the night of his murder.

We finally arrived at the house where she lived with other Maerican exiles. I told the cabbie to keep his motor running. My plan was to pick up the package, hop back into the car, and head straight to Gale's place. I followed Fanon upstairs to her room, where she pulled an envelope from a desk drawer and handed it to me. I made her sit on her bed with her hands on her knees while I opened the package and studied its contents. It mostly consisted of handwritten notes in scientific jargon— on EarthChem stationery. There was also a preliminary report. I said thanks and left, warning her not to get up from the bed until I left the house.

As I entered the taxi, I chucked her weapons on the lawn of her house. I pulled the documents out of the package, examining them in the moonlight. There were a couple of photographs and a report with a cover letter. I suddenly noticed the chirping of crickets. It was a sweet childhood sound that I'd managed to ignore since my return to D.C.—but then I'd been a very busy woman.

The taxi pulled up at Gale's house and let me out. I noticed two men sitting in a dark, late-model Lincoln Continental parked near the house, but I was too preoccupied with Carol's death and the new information from Fanon to give them more than a passing glance.

Going up the walkway to Gale's porch, I heard someone rushing up behind me on the sidewalk pavement. I turned and saw two white, sandy-haired men running toward me. Both men shouted in unison: "Secret Service!" But I knew at once they were bogus, since they withdrew their guns from the waistbands of their pants. No holsters. Very unprofessional.

I shouted, "BASS!" at the top of my lungs, diving past the sudden spray of bullets and over a low redbrick wall that separated Gale's property from her neighbor's. My cousin Bass was standing on the front porch in a dark corner, wearing a long black duster. Bass refused to go into the house until I was safely home each evening; that was his rule. He calmly walked down the steps and into the line of fire, withdrew two 9mm pistols, each with a fourteen-clip magazine, and returned the men's fire. He took three quick hits in his chest but continued walking towards the men. He shot one of the suits in the neck, sending blood spurting from the wound as he collapsed. The other man caught a slug in the head and spun around, spastically firing his gun into the pavement. A second slug from Bass knocked the man off his feet. Lights switched on up and down the street, and dogs began barking furiously.

Bass walked over to where the men were lying in the street and kicked their guns away. He then slowly ambled over to me, unbuttoning his coat and shirt to reveal a white concealment vest with three embedded slugs.

"It was quiet until *you* came home," he said in his raspy voice, smiling down at me and placing a licorice root in his mouth.

CHAPTER EIGHT

Needless to say, Gale's neighbors weren't happy to have their night's sleep punctured by the sound of rapid gunfire, not to mention the reappearance of the police in the neighborhood and two corpses in the middle of the street. I told the questioning officer that I had arrived at Gale's after making stops at Bernard's residence and Fanon's apartment. As a seasoned officer of the court, I neglected, of course, to mention my brief visit to Carol Bridges' place. As soon as the police finished with me, I called Fanon and told her everything that had happened and that I had informed the police that we spent the evening at her place—not Carol's. Luckily, her roommates came home after I'd been there. Fanon was going to keep a very low profile. Maybe even return to Misericordia—via the underground.

I had informed the police that the men who fired on me had identified themselves as Secret Service agents. Soon it was all over the news that two vaunted Secret Service agents "had been cut down in the second twist to the macabre Debord murder." I managed to shake things up even further by sending the police—anonymously, of course—the tape of Carol Bridges' murder. Suddenly, the police started checking things, questioning people everywhere. Who were they? Why were these two posing as Secret Service agents? It turned out, not surprisingly, that the bullets that hit Bass were discovered to be similar to the ones that killed Carol.

Few people failed to notice that Carol was the second White House assistant to have been killed in a week's time—and the third member of the Benton administration to have died, after Michael and Nolan Grayston. Sniffing around the bodies of three dead Democrats, Representative Owen Greeley, the Republican chairman of the House Oversight Committee on Governmental Affairs, wasted no time in convening a hearing into the matter. His motives? No one could say for sure, but it seemed like a perfect opportunity to embarrass the president.

Reading the newspapers was difficult since I had sprained my left arm and shoulder when I went over the wall. Propped up against pillows on my living room couch, I perused the newspapers' ubiquitous coverage of the Debord-Bridges murders. Fortunately, I wasn't mentioned too often in the news accounts, and was only photographed a single time, wearing a hat, veil, and sunglasses at Michael's funeral. Witnessing the barrage of press coverage at the funeral, I had decided to get out of Dodge—anticipating a possible subpoena from Congress—assuring Gale that I was still on assignment, following some leads out of town. I didn't tell her about Michael and Carol, a moot point, I reasoned, now that both of them were dead. I'd set Gale straight about everything—at least everything she needed to know—once the case was closed.

Reclining on my living room couch, I was surprised to hear the doorknob suddenly turn. I reached instinctively into my arm-sling, which had lately been serving as a holster. Anna entered the apartment with an armful of groceries and immediately read the look on my face. Her gaze slid quickly down to my good hand, which was gripping the butt of my gun.

"You are such a suspicious woman," she clucked, closing the door with her foot and then locking it from the inside. "Honestly."

"That's what keeps me alive," I replied. I released the gun

and continued with my reading. Anna went into the kitchen and began putting away the groceries.

"Anything interesting?" she asked from the kitchen. I heard her opening the refrigerator and the cupboards, stocking the shelves.

"Not really. The press is still trying to figure what's what. The Republicans are giving Benton a hard time, of course," I reported. "That son of a dick deserves it."

"You really don't like him, do you?" she asked from the kitchen.

Anna already knew the answer: I detested Jeff Benton and everything he stood for, which was anything that was politically expedient. Don't get me wrong, I had campaigned for that ambulating piece of shit when he ran against President Digby and had defended him passionately to Lee on a number of occasions. Lee, of course, could see the writing on the wall—that Benton was the stalking horse who would help the Democratic Party make its final transformation away from working- and middle-class people and become a sophisticated collection plate.

Oh, my baby saw it coming, all right. But when I was a new jack Democrat and hoping for a political career, Benton was "my man." His wife, Claire, had even been my (and Anna's) law professor and mentor at NYU. But she, too, had become a power freak, just like her Jeffy-boy. Everyone knew that Benton had schtupped other women, but he was Claire's ticket to the White House and nothing was going to interfere with that. The two had cut a deal to keep the marriage together for political expediency—and dear old Claire had lost her soul in the process. At least in my opinion.

"No, honey," I snapped back at Anna. "I wouldn't even blow him with *your* mouth."

"Oooh." Anna poked her head out of the kitchen, a wicked gleam in her eyes. "Well, what about Claire?"

"Now that I would reserve for your juices and your sluices alone." Within some sapphic quarters, Claire was considered a high-powered fuck. She had also hired some queer people for her staff, causing her a lot of grief from the political right's P.C.

squad. When she refused to cave in to the pressure from the right and dismiss her gay staff members, conservative pundits began spreading prurient tales of dyke covens in the White House and at Camp David. To her credit, Claire stood by her people till the end.

Tiring of the *"New York Slime,"* I stood up, left my sitting position on the couch, and stood in the kitchen doorway, my gun still tucked into my sling. Anna was reaching up to put something in the cupboard.

"What's up?" She placed a container of soy and rice milk into the refrigerator and then returned to stocking the cupboards.

"Nothing much." I stood in the doorway and watched her graceful domestic extensions. Anna's left eye was still purplish; the swelling in her lip had receded somewhat. Sensing that I was inspecting her, she turned and looked at me suspiciously.

"What are you looking at?"

"You know," I began, "you really are too old to be getting into girl scraps."

"Me?! Look the fuck at you!" she said, jerking her head at my slinged arm.

"I got this in the line of duty. You, my dear, got yours because of booty. But I'll put my gun away—I feel so much safer knowing that the Imperial Tigress of China is here to protect me."

"Oh, please," snarled Anna, slamming shut a cupboard and walking brusquely past me into the living room. "You sound as if I don't have a life!"

"You've got a life, all right, honey," I shouted back over my shoulder on my way to my bedroom, "and it's kicking your ass." I knelt down at the side of my bed, pulled the weapon from my sling, and holstered it beneath the bed.

When I returned to the living room, Anna was listening to Björk on the stereo, a sparsely produced but hard-driving tune called "An Army of Me," about an unsympathetic kick-ass bitch. (Was she trying to tell me something?) With her feet propped up on the coffee table, the Tigress was lighting a cigarette— something I'd never seen her do before. We exchanged glances as I lowered the volume on the stereo.

"New life, new habits," she said to me. "Mind if I smoke?"

"Not at all, honey," I said. "Mind if I fart?"

"Don't get cute," she replied, blowing a stream of smoke from her nostrils.

I cracked open a window. A cigarette I could deal with, I suppose, but a cigar would severely test our friendship. I sat back down on the couch. Anna's head rested on the armchair's back and she gazed up at the ceiling. She puffed on her death-stick and the smoke streamed out from her nostrils. Her Chinese features and the smoke coursing from her nose suggested the image of a crippled dragon. As she threw back her head, I noticed something different about her hair.

"Hey, you're letting your hair grow longer."

"Yeah, all them white dykes—my sappho sisters—have short hair as their signature coiffure. I decided I had to break from the pack." Anna sat up and looked at me.

"So, what caused the fireworks between you and Shinyun?" I asked. I'd been back a couple days licking my own wounds, and hadn't inquired about the chain of events that led to her bruising.

Anna said nothing for a second. She reached over, picked up a saucer that she was using as an ashtray, and flicked the cigarette. "Shinyun called me and said she thought that we needed to have a civilized airing of our difficulties. I said okay and went over. Get this, Nin," she began, leaning toward me with her cigarette dangling from her lips, Bogart-style.

Needless to say, I pricked up my ears.

"The bitch was fucking with me! She opened the door, decked out in Vickie's Secret lingerie and with a goddamn smirk on her face. Meaning that I hadn't pleased her the way her new buck stud does. And then I realized that he was there in the bedroom and she had just finished blowing him. I went ballistic. I mean, the bitch had purposely got me down there just to throw shit in my face! I wanted to wipe that fucking smirk off her stupid face." She blew out a last trail of smoke and reclined. "I know I haven't been an angel, but I didn't try to fuck with her—not like that."

I didn't respond.

"I'm going solo. I spent the last three years with Winston Chao and now with Shinyun. Maybe I need time to sort things out for myself, to experiment unencumbered for a while."

"So what am I going to do with you when I'm gone?"

"What do you mean?" she asked, a look of panic spreading across her face. "You going somewhere without me?"

"Yep. To the Big Mango—Misericordia."

"Nina, I thought you were through with Miriam and El Presidente."

"I am. But I'm still working for Gale and—"

"So what's doing?"

"Nate Ford," I slowly replied.

"What does he have to do with Gale?" Anna quickly put out the cigarette in the saucer and looked at me. "And you, no doubt, have murder on your mind."

"No. No," I hesitated for a moment. "I'm going to seek justice—"

"And then kill the son of a bitch."

"Judge, jury, and a bitch of an executioner," I confessed. "Do you really blame me?"

"No, Nina. I know as well as anyone what you've been through," she sighed. "How do you know he's there anyway?"

"I don't really, but a reliable source—"

"How reliable?"

"Lost his arm in the drug war."

"Armless Archer?!"

"The one and only."

"Shit," replied Anna. She knew Archer all too well. "Damn."

"What?"

"Jesus Christ, Nina."

"I'll be back."

"I know that. I'm just worried about losing you the other way."

"Meaning what?"

Anna's dark eyes darted away from my face and returned in a flash. "You go down there and kill this guy, and you'll be picking up just where he left off."

I started to answer, to defend myself, but she interrupted

before I could open my mouth.

"No, Nina! It doesn't work like that. Ford's been fucking with your mind, and if you go down with the sole intention of killing him, how different are you from him? It takes a savage to kill a savage. A beast. I know you're not like him now, but what will you be like if you do succeed in killing him? Think about it."

In my heart of hearts I knew that she was right, but there was a dark corner in me, a dark crevice that didn't want to listen to all her moaning and moralizing about evil and justice. This was revenge, all right, revenge pure and simple. And I knew that it was wrong of me to lust after the bastard's death, but I had to go and see if he was there.

"Well, just how badly do you want to be my guardian angel?" I blurted out, without thinking about what I was saying.

"What?"

"Come with me and save my soul, keep me from ripping out the bastard's heart and making him eat it right in front of me."

Anna folded her arms and looked me straight in the eye, arching an eyebrow as she did. "Girl, you better come up with a better way of asking me for an extended date."

"Anna, this ain't a vacation," I informed her. "Misericordia is a ride and a half."

"Maybe not for you, but it would be an art expedition for me, as well as an adventure. Maybe I'll find myself a Basquiat down there." She laughed as she said it, but I knew that she wasn't joking.

Anna was probably right about my motives for trailing Ford to Misericordia. And I also had to think about Gale. I couldn't allow my own drive for revenge to get in the way of solving the mystery of Michael's death. But one thing was certain, however I chose to cut the cards: I had to go. I could sort the rest out once I got there.

"Anna, I have to warn you. Misericordia is no easy walk. There is a real reign of terror going on. Even if the junta under Luc's daddy is a bit more subtle and refined in its techniques."

"Hmmm," said Anna, thinking it over one last time. "Oh, well. Great art is often born out of adversity and violence.

When do we fly and die?"

I told her that I was planning on leaving in a couple of days. Anna said that would be enough time for her to settle some of her matters and fly down with me. Sensing that this was a momentous occasion, another page in the annals of our friendship, I went to the kitchen and retrieved some whiskey—called "tea that burns" by a bootlegging uncle of Anna's—and poured us each a shot. We raised our glasses in a toast.

"To McFate," said Anna.

"McFate," I echoed.

CHAPTER NINE

My aim in the days before I left for Misericordia should have been clear and true—shuttle down to Misericordia and blow the object of my hatred away, maybe catching a little sun and sand on the side. But things started getting funky, really funky, right before I left, and I suddenly found myself being torn in all directions. The Father, the Son, and the Holy Ghost couldn't hold me together or keep me focused by the time Anna and I boarded the plane at JFK.

The first big blow involved Zee—and her father.

I was waiting for Zee in the sub-basement of her father Mustapha's electronics store on Canal Street where my situation room (nicknamed "the womb") was located. I had given Zee the documents that I had wrangled from Fanon about EarthChem's activities in Misericordia and had hoped that she could help me decipher some type of lead about what Michael was up to at the time of his death. Zee and I had scheduled a session for 2 p.m. to discuss her breakup with Ibrahim. But the woman never showed up, unusual for Zee, who was normally punctual and professional to a fault.

I was phoning upstairs to Mustapha's store to find out what had happened when I heard the door slide open. I turned quickly, expecting the worst, but Mustapha entered, handing me a diskette inside a plastic case.

"This is for you, Nina. It's from Zee. Her report."

I thanked him and took the disk. Mustapha, who is generally a very genial and gracious host, seemed worried and preoccupied. "Mustapha," I offered delicately, aware of his reluctance to discuss family matters, "is something wrong? Has something happened with Zee?"

"IN PARIS!" he blurted out. His fat, powerful hand danced anxiously over his black dome and down to his face as he began pacing the floor in front of me. At first he said nothing. I decided to give him all the time and space he needed to open up.

Mustapha walked around and around, his hands buried in his pockets, tucking things in, straightening computer terminals. With all his fidgeting, I shifted my stance, trying to get more comfortable.

"Don't leave here, sister!" he said desperately, mistaking my intentions. "I need to speak to you. You have to tell me what happened," he said, pointing a finger at me.

"News to me," I said. "I knew she was feeling blue about—"

"That playboy!" snapped the colonel. Zee had told me that her father didn't like the idea that she was in love with a fair-skinned, rich Muslim, the son of a family that holds dark-skinned Americans in disdain. Mustapha was a proud man, in no mood to be nice to people who condescended to him and his family, not even for his daughter's sake. He had always followed Malcolm X's edict: Be peaceful. Be courteous. Obey the law. Respect everyone. But if someone puts his hands on you or your loved ones, send him to the cemetery. He raised his children the same way. No need to be loud and wrong. Instead, be quiet and diligent, and break arms efficiently.

Zee was a dutiful daughter, even to the point of following her father into the military. She was already en route to becoming a well-established young scholar in Islamic and African matters. Her father had every reason to be proud of her. But as a woman, she needed and wanted something that neither the military nor being the apple of her father's eye would give her, a progressive Muslim man whom she could love.

"Mustapha, what happened?"

"Zee has run off to Paris to be with that Egyptian gigolo!"

"When did she leave?" I asked.

"Last night. She sneaked out like some har—"

"I'll smite thee," I warned, fearing he was about to call Zee a whore.

"Ach! Of course, you'd take her side. I should have known."

"Mustapha, let's not become nigorant," I responded. "Is she going to marry him?"

"That's what I fear."

"Mustapha, Mustapha." I rose and went over to him. "Your daughter is in love. Try to put yourself in her shoes. You're both such strong-willed and opinionated people. How do you expect her to please the two most important men in her life, and herself, all at the same time? She knows that you don't approve of him."

"These people hold us in contempt, Nina. The mother condones the genocidal war in the Sudan! I don't even put up with that bullshit!" he thundered. "These people have contempt for us. I already get enough of that kaka from white folks here. I won't take it from foreigners! It's bad enough that two-bit Indian émigré is writing racist crap about us. I'm not going to take it from these Egyptians. I won't. And I won't have my daughter taken from me!"

I waited to make sure that he had finished his harangue before I responded. "Calm down, Brother Mustapha." I gently guided him over to the lounge, sat him down, and placed myself in the chair next to him. "Calm down. It's not the end of the world. You raised your daughter right. She simply wants to be with the man she loves."

"How can you say that after she upped and left us? Not a word to her mother?" he shot back, very much the wounded father. "Acting like a sinful woman."

"Oh, please, Mustapha. Zee isn't some virginal sylph untouched by a man's hands. The girl's been around the block," I said. "Let's face it. If this had been your son, you'd think nothing of it, but because she's a female—" I stopped myself, realizing that I was probably pushing things too far. "She's a grown woman; all twenty-seven years of her. Beautiful, intelligent, strong-willed. And very much like her father. She has to make her own mistakes—if the love she feels now is, in fact, a mistake."

Mustapha settled back, thinking about what had been said, and then responded. "You counsel well, my sister, but I'd sleep better if you'd do something for me."

"Yes?"

"Go to Paris and bring her back."

"I'm not going to embarrass myself and try to bring home a woman who's a Ranger in the United States Army. Be for real, Mustapha!"

"Nina," said Mustapha, pleadingly, "she's my only daughter and I care about her dearly."

"Good. 'Cause if the gods find favor upon you, she'll make you a righteous grandfather," I announced, looking down at him, arms folded across my chest.

"Then you won't grant my request?"

"Sorry. I have my own rendezvous with destiny to attend to. I'm afraid you and Zee will have to fend for yourselves this time."

As I drove back uptown, I tried to sympathize with Mustapha's fear of losing his child. But it was simply the natural state of things, after all: Children grow up, leave home, pick mates of their own, and then get on with the business of living *their* lives. Just as it is; just as it's always been; just as it should be. Mustapha didn't know how privileged he was to see his children come of age and leave him behind. Some of us weren't so lucky.

CHAPTER TEN

I returned to my office on West 14th Street to attend to some last-minute details before leaving for Misericordia. Anna had picked up our tickets in advance and was out tying up some loose ends of her own. I turned off the lights and was about to step out the door when the telephone rang. Normally, I would have just continued out the door, but I'd been trying without success to reach Gale for days. I listened to the answering machine and heard instead the voice of another old friend.

"Hello, Nina? This is Claire. Claire Foster Benton. I'm in New York."

I hesitated for a moment. Why would SHE be calling me? Granted, she was an old friend and mentor. But we had completely lost contact since she became the First Lady. I picked up the phone and switched off the machine.

"Claire, it's Nina. What a surprise."

"Hello, Nina," said the First Lady. "I'm in New York. Is it possible for us to get together? I know it's on short notice, but..."

I thought immediately of the press and the Secret Service.

I didn't want any part of that traveling circus. Not to mention that I was about to leave for Misericordia to track down a lead that might implicate her husband's administration. "To be honest, Claire, I'm kind of booked. I'm heading out of the country."

"Nina, we must talk. I'm not here on official business. No one knows I'm in New York."

"You mean you're traveling naked?"

"Yes. No press. No bloodhounds. I need to speak to you. It's about our friend, Gale."

Uh oh. My client, my responsibility. "Okay," I sighed. "Where are you staying?"

"The usual place, the Blackmoor Arms Hotel."

I agreed to meet her and then hung up. I thought briefly about my impending trip as I walked back into my office, pressed the plate beneath my desk, and retrieved my gun. The voice on the other end of the telephone certainly sounded like Claire Benton, but I wasn't taking any chances.

The Blackmoor was located on East 63rd Street. It was owned by Richard Foster, Claire's father, who had been a very successful hotelier until his death. The Blackmoor was one of a series of pricey, niche hotels around the city that catered to specific clients. The elder Foster had owned several of these hotels, as well as a fair share of the larger, more traditional facilities that catered to the average traveling tourist. Claire had actually lived at the Blackmoor when she taught at NYU law school and was estranged from her philandering governor husband. I had gotten to know the place pretty well at the time, attending parties and discussion sessions as a law student of hers and later just hanging out as a friend. If Claire was staying at the Blackmoor rather than at the presidential suite at the Waldorf-Astoria, she was definitely in New York on less-than-official business.

I announced myself to the doorman, trying to shake off the unexpected coldness that had descended upon the city, and was directed immediately to the top floor of the modestly structured six-story building. I rang the buzzer and my old friend Claire Foster Benton, a woman vilified by her enemies as "Macbitch," the unofficial co-president of the United States, answered the door. She looked trim and sleek in a red sweater and loden-colored trousers. Years ago she had worn eyeglasses and had taken to wearing contact lenses when in the public eye, but at the door she was wearing her spectacles again. Her blond hair, broken at her shoulders, framed her high cheek bones and accented her German ancestry.

"Nina," she said pleasantly as I entered the room. She closed the door, took my hand, and squeezed it. "It's so good to see you." Years ago we would have embraced, but that was no longer acceptable now that she had ascended to the role of consort for our civilian king.

"It's nice to see you, Claire," I responded stiffly.

She led me into a living room that I'd been in many times before. It was a very warm room with parquet floors, oak furniture, and majestic bookcases. The walls had several modern and Italian paintings—all originals. Several Botticellis. A Picasso here. A Van Gogh there. And several African sculptures and masks, as well as classical Greek and Roman vases and other archaeological artifacts scattered throughout. On the coffee table, I noticed several official-looking leather-bound portfolios marked "Claire Foster Benton." Briefing reports, I assumed.

The entire apartment reeked of the old money to which Claire had been accustomed as a child, before she married into the nouveau riche world of her husband and the other entrepreneurs in his family. Now she found herself surrounded by people who could only approach art as an investment, who simply couldn't appreciate the more refined and intangible aesthetic qualities that transformed the mind and soul.

Claire had prepared coffee, and I asked for some skim milk when she offered me the aromatic brew. The room was glowingly warm, the wood crackling steadily and slowly crumbling into red embers in the fireplace. It was nice and cozy, a perfect place to spend a chilly night with an old friend.

"Needless to say, Nina, the president and I were dumbstruck with grief over Michael's death. He was a valued friend and a highly esteemed member of the administration."

I sipped my coffee and kept my responses as monosyllabic as possible.

"Our hearts go out to Gale and we do feel her pain," said the First Lady. "Of course, I can understand her reluctance to face the harsh reality of it all, that she perceives her husband in an entirely different way from what the facts reveal. I can well understand that."

To put it crudely, I thought, Michael was a dead nigga-junky-faggot who had disgraced himself, his wife, his family, his friends, his country, his people, and most importantly, of course, the president who had once trusted him.

"It's a shame that it came to such a tragic end. I wouldn't have wished that on anyone. I mean, how do you get up and go on with your life under such circumstances?" Claire asked.

I honestly couldn't figure out if she was being ironic or truly sympathetic.

Claire's hair was cut shorter than when I knew her before, and strands of gray flecked her locks. I noticed that lines were slowly etching their way into her once-immaculately clear skin.

"You have to go on with your life, Nina. *You* did, after all. Gale has got to face reality and get on with her life. But getting on with her life doesn't give her the right to make spurious attacks on others," she said with the harsh, inhuman finality of a New England school marm.

"By 'others,' I assume you mean none other than the president himself?" I sipped my coffee. I knew where this was coming from. This was no girl-to-girl talk between old friends. Jeff Benton sent *his* girl—Claire—to talk to one of *her* old girls—me—in the hopes that I could talk some sense into to *my* girlfriend, Gale. This was the old girl network in service of the great white dick. An appendage that was Claire's department.

Claire placed her coffee cup down on the table and comfortably sat back into the golden-striped couch. To make herself more comfortable, she lifted one leg from the floor and tucked it beneath her right thigh. She was trying to shift our conversation into a warm and fuzzy mode. Just two old friends—mentor and student—spending the evening together. It shouldn't have been that far-fetched of a proposition. At one time, Claire and I actually were close: I admired her as a very down-home and unpretentious sophisticate, and she viewed me as a very gifted and hard-working student. We used to hang out together, listening to music and checking out clubs, or just sitting around talking about law and politics. In fact, we had once been so close that rumors about us began circulating around school.

I shrugged it off at the time. I was quite certain about the type of plumbing I enjoyed, and it always involved outside fixtures. But Claire had clearly been disturbed by the stories. She was, after all, a woman with a troubled marriage to a relatively young, up-and-coming Southwestern governor, and the mother of a young boy.

We'd confided in one another at the time about our men problems. She had left her husband and his home state when she discovered that the bastard was having an affair, and I was busy going loco over Luc Malmundo. Neither of our men seemed to be able to keep their hands off of other women. But we thought that they were the most exciting men—physically, sexually, and intellectually—that we had ever met. In retrospect, I'd have to say that my late husband, Lee, was the most intellectually stimulating man I've ever known. The sad truth is that, during my frantic days of prosecuting and politicking in Brooklyn, I hadn't paid that much attention to Lee's intellectual output. It wasn't until after his death, when I heard Paul Tower quoting him, that I went back, read his books, and discovered what a brain I'd married.

"Nina, the things that she is saying about the president," she continued. "I mean, years ago no one would have given them any thought or credence, but in this era of paranoid conspiracism—"

"Well, Claire, the fact that you're paranoid doesn't mean that someone isn't out to get you," I quipped.

Claire looked at me. She couldn't figure out if I was just making an innocent crack or if I had really become one of "them"—a member of the mob, the masses, the amorphous public held in contempt by the policy elites, the only ones who truly understood the issues. Well, maybe I had gone over to the other side. Maybe Claire hadn't done a good enough job in recruiting me when she had the chance. It had taken me years to understand that one of the salient effects of integration was to recruit enough "Negroes" to administer and speak on behalf of policies that benefitted the overclass. I ought to know; I had been a true, fast-track Negress myself. Until the fateful evening in Brooklyn when I rudely received my own wake-up call.

"You don't believe these stories about a conspiracy from the White House, do you?" She was on the verge of being angry. "Oh my God, Nina, not you, too?"

"Claire, I have a friend from way back when who has a dead husband and wants some answers—"

"Well, she isn't going to get them by accusing the president of killing her husband when the reality was that Michael had a drug problem. That's a fact!"

I leaned back against the couch arm. "Is it, Claire? Or is it a manufactured fact?"

"Meaning what?" Claire asked skeptically.

"Meaning that for someone who was described as a drug addict, Michael, according to an independent autopsy report, did not exhibit any sustained evidence of habitual drug use. He was shown to have heroin in his system for that night, but there was absolutely no evidence of repeated drug use over an extended period of time. Once he was dead, the White House released a story about him testing positive for drugs. Of course, when Gale tried to get her autopsy report released to the public, not one newspaper or television station picked up on it. He was just another dead black man, as far as they were concerned, and a dead homo to boot. Case closed."

"Nina, you don't believe the president had anything to do with Michael's death, do you?" she asked, her face tightening into a mask of disbelief.

"I'm investigating that, Claire," I told her. "I do know that Michael was very concerned that the administration's policy toward Misericordia radically changed when Richard Stone came aboard."

"There has been no real policy change with regard to Misericordia, Nina. The president supports the return of President Bernard." She rose, walked over to the fireplace, and placed another log in the fire. "We have national security concerns that have to be taken into consideration."

"Yeah, sure," I snorted. "Cheap labor."

"What was that you said?" she asked, as she rose and wiped her hand on her trousers.

"Cheap labor," I repeated. "Misericordia is a reliable source of cheap labor for powerful multinational companies, like Disney."

"Oh, Nina, please." She was in no mood to hear yet another angry diatribe against American imperialism. "Don't give me what's left of the left: standard anti-Americanism."

"And EarthChem," I tossed out nonchalantly, curious to see her reaction.

"What about EarthChem?" said Claire. The First Lady had gone over to the liquor cabinet and opened it.

"You tell me, Claire."

"If I have to tell you, then you really don't know anything," she said sweetly over her shoulder. "Jack Daniel's?"

"No, thanks." I quickly pulled out a bug and fastened it beneath the lip of her wooden coffee table, as she turned away from me. I was being bad, but that's what people pay me for.

"What's wrong, Nina?" Claire poured herself a drink and walked back over to the fire. "Think I'll poison you?" Her back was still turned to me, but I could hear the contempt in her voice loud and clear.

I said nothing. After all, she was the one who'd called me.

"I think you really don't know what you're talking about— about EarthChem."

"What about Richard Stone?" I said. "The man shills for EarthChem. And it just so happens that when he gets to 1600, there's a sudden change in the direction of the wind. Michael is killed and two suits running around D.C. claiming to be Secret Service agents kill Carol Bridges. You figure it out, Claire. It may be easy enough to explain away a dead nigga, but not some white girl!"

"Don't go ghetto on me, Nina! Your black credentials don't impress me." The First Lady closed her eyes condescendingly. "There are certain things that you don't understand, Nina."

I rose from the couch and calmly stepped over to her.

"Look, don't pull that executive privilege *mysterioso* bullshit on me. You're not talking to Sally Smalltown. My God, Claire, what has happened to you? You were the one who always talked about public service being one of the highest callings of a citizen, especially if one is privileged. And here you are fronting for a morally bankrupt politician! You run around promoting your book, *The Politics of Community*, talking about safeguarding the future of children, while your husband the president cuts all the programs designed to protect children! What kind of bullshit do you expect me to swallow?"

"Oh, excuse me, Miss Politically Pristine," snapped Claire. "You're the conniving cunt who suddenly decided that you were for the death penalty when your father-in-law was murdered! It became so convenient to change your position, Nina, when you were positioning yourself for political office. Ray's death was just an opportune time."

"That was then and this is now, Claire," I replied. "Let's deal with the issues as they are now."

Ignoring me, the First Lady continued. "It made such good copy in the *New York Toast*. 'Ex-prosecutor sees the light. Favors Death Penalty. Pull the switch!' You were even strategic enough to question the left's slobbering over Omal Abdul Salim's incarnation as the messiah of death row. Smart move. That transformed you from being a soft quishy liberal to a candidate with law-and-order bona fides. Bravo, Nina. I know Lee enjoyed you fucking over his father at his graveside!" She clapped her hands.

Claire enjoyed dredging up my less-than-stellar foray into political whoredom. After Ray Belmont, Lee's adopted father, had been murdered, I changed my position on the death penalty, citing my father-in-law's death, yet knowing full well that he abhorred the death penalty. But no matter how much of a sleazebucket I had been, damaging my marriage in the process, it didn't change the fact that Claire herself was married to a man who not only found the death penalty politically expedient; he would bend over and take it up the wazoo, elbow-deep, as long as the giver was clutching a fist full of dollars. And I'd let her know that in no uncertain terms.

A white flash slashed through the air and across my cheek,

stinging me. I instinctively grabbed Claire by her sweater with both of my hands and slammed her against the mantle. We were both shocked by her action, and my reaction. Our eyes locked, and for a single, hot moment, a glimmer of delight and desire appeared in her eyes. She tried to struggle free, but I held onto her tightly. I was afraid, shocked that I had lost control. This was the wife of the most powerful man in the world, after all, no matter how little I may personally have thought of the bastard.

"Take your goddamn hands off of me!" she finally hissed imperiously. "This is a security breach!"

"Are you going to be a good girl? Are you going to behave yourself and act like a proper First Lady?" Claire began to twist and turn. Her hands gripped my forearms and her nails tried to rip the fabric of my denim jacket. I pushed her away and stepped back. We had crossed a bridge of some sort and there clearly was no turning back, nothing left between us. I turned away to leave.

"Nina Halligan, don't you dare leave here until I've finished with you!" she said in her best Bette Davis tone of voice.

I turned and starred at her. First Lady or not, the woman's impertinence caught me off-guard. I wondered what she'd been smoking, let alone drinking. "Just who in the hell do you think you're speaking to?"

"I'm going to say this and say it once: We're finished! But you hear me on this. Drop this matter with Gale Simmons and get that stupid bitch to shut up!"

"And if I don't?" Her attitude was beginning to change my complexion.

"You don't know what you're dealing with, Nina!"

"I have a good idea, Mrs. Benton," I spat. "I have a damn good idea."

"This is about national security!"

"Oh, please," I mocked. "And that means you people have a license to kill?"

Claire crossed the room, picked up one of the leather portfolios I had noticed before, and threw it down at my feet. "A group of American scientists—"

"Employees of EarthChem," I interjected.

"Were kidnapped by the so-called People's Liberation Army of Misericordia, a terrorist organization."

"Wait a minute," I began. "The corporation that employs your husband!"

"Don't interrupt me, Nina!" she snapped. "The president is going to invoke the Counter-terrorism Act. That means individuals who have contributed money to terrorist groups will be subjected to arrest and prosecution. The Justice Department will begin looking into the affairs of the Committee to Support the Maerican People, a committee to which Miriam Butler, your sister-in-law, actively belongs. An organization that tried to infiltrate and influence the Maerican embassy, organizing a third force!"

I shook my head in disbelief. This was how they were going to try to get me to drop Gale.

"And I will remind you, my dear friend, that your brother, a prominent investor, has allowed his home to be used as a fundraising depot for this third force. The Security and Exchange Commission may want to look into that as well. Imagine the headlines."

The television news spots floated ominously before my eyes. People's lives would be ruined, all right, even a totally innocent party like my brother's boss, Charles Warren. The deal was simple: dump Gale, and my brother and his wife would be left alone.

"Well, Nina?" There was a trickle of a smile on her face; the satisfaction of cornering an adversary.

"I'll give you an answer tomorrow."

"Tonight, Nina. Tonight! Now!"

I didn't know what to do. I felt my body tensing; the cold iron of my gun pressed annoyingly against the small of my back. I had come here expecting an ambush and I had gotten one, all right, one that couldn't be handled in a hard-dick fashion. But there was one thing I was certain about: I would not submit to extortion, family or no family.

"Well, Nina?" the First Lady of the Republic demanded.

"Claire," I began, sadly wagging my head. "You've become an *empty* bra. Ciao."

I walked. Claire kept calling after me well into the hallway. I kept stepping. I had a lot to do, after all, and several other people to protect. I was so preoccupied with the conversation as I rode down to the lobby that I almost walked into the man who had been waiting there for the elevator.

Richard Stone.

He smiled. "Interesting conversation, hmmm?" Ever the roué, he sported a three-day beard, and his longish blond hair broke at the upturned collar of his expensive leather barn jacket. He stepped around me and entered the elevator, pressing the button not with a gloved finger, but a riding crop. "Too bad you're leaving so early. Say hello to Gary and Miriam. Ciao."

The door closed before I could smash my fist into his *GQ* face and immaculate dental work. He had been listening to our conversation the whole time. But two could play at that game.

Sliding into my car, I pulled out my transmitter unit and began searching for the frequency that would give me their conversation. I pressed the recording mechanism and listened:

"I don't want do this, Richard," moaned the First Lady.

"Claire, you have to follow through with your threat. This is how you discipline your inferiors," said Stone, superciliously. "Are you afraid of her? A nickel-and-dime prosecutor turned private investigator? Some comely doxy off the street?"

"Nina is very resourceful," informed Claire. "In a way, she doesn't have anything to lose."

"Maybe she doesn't, but her brother and his family do."

"I don't know about this, Richard. And why Carol Bridges? Why her?!"

"Loose ends had to be tied up, Claire. Things went awry," he sighed, explaining things in that condescending tone that men use when they think that we don't understand the way the real world works.

"Nina suspects something."

"Then we'll have to see to her, too."

"No," said Claire. There was a slight crack in her voice. "You leave her out of it. Leave Nina alone."

"Do you want four more years in the White House, Claire, or don't you? It's quite simple really. EarthChem wants a quiet countryside. Fair trade. Come here, love."

For a few minutes I heard nothing. Then, just the feverish sound of someone slurping and sucking, a man moaning.

"Hmmm. That's right, you First Bitch. Suck it. Unnnhhhh. Take off your clothes, wench."

My mouth dropped open. I couldn't believe what I was hearing. Claire?! I turned up the volume and the sound filled the car.

Stone became more and more authoritative and abusive with each moment of pleasure. This was the modulated command of class, of male domination. It disturbed me to think that this was probably the only kind of attention that Claire was getting from a man these days, from a control freak like Stone. But you had to hand it to the bastard: If you could face fuck the wife of the president of the United States, you must have something going for you. A gross, disgusting, singularly unappealing something, to be sure. But something, just the same.

"Strip!" said Stone. He had apparently zippered up his pants and was setting the stage for the evening's next activity.

For a few minutes there was nothing but the rustling of clothes being removed and the sound of the fire blazing.

"On the coffee table!" he commanded. "I have to teach you once again how to be hard."

I didn't want to believe what was about to happen. Not to Claire Foster Benton. In spite of our differences, I had always admired her as someone who was clearheaded, forthright, and never afraid to let her will and her intelligence shine. But after years of taking public abuse on behalf of her husband, she now seemed more at home on the rack than on the podium. I could hear it all too clearly: the hiss of Stone's riding crop as it viciously slapped into Claire's behind; the low, pleading moan of her voice, begging for more. There was absolutely no doubt about it: Claire was enjoying every minute of her humiliation. But I also knew that she hated herself as well.

CHAPTER ELEVEN

"Nina?"

"Hmmm?" I was looking out the window of the American Airlines jet, the clouds carpeting the sky as the plane streaked toward Misericordia. Anna and I had boarded the plane at JFK for an 11 o'clock flight the following morning. There weren't many people on the plane after it stopped in Miami and then continued to our destination. The seats in front of and behind us were vacant. Anna was thumbing through one of her gay gals magazines and I was ruminating on Claire Benton and how she "saved" my family. With what I had recorded, I was confident that I would be able to protect Miriam from prosecution under the Counter-terrorism Act and safeguard my brother and his affairs from the wide net of the Justice Department.

Before we left, I had a courier deliver the tape to the First Lady at the Blackmoor, along with the message: "Back off or I'll send this tape to every media outlet I can think of—including *Hustler* and Matt Drudge. And for God's sake, get help." I made additional copies of the tape and placed them in the vault of the Womb, along with instructions to Mustapha that the tapes were to be released to the public in the now-unlikely event that either Miriam or Gary were charged by the government in my absence while in Misericordia—or in the somewhat more plausible scenario of my own sudden death.

"Nina?" asked Anna. She had placed the magazine on her lap and was looking straight at me.

"I don't know, Anna," I began. "This stuff—"

"You mean, Claire and her peccadilloes?"

"Ssshhh." I popped my head up and looked around the cabin. There didn't appear to be any prying ears nearby, but Anna and I were discussing something that could bring down the government. "Not only Claire, but Gale, too," I continued in a low voice. "Excuse my sexual provincialism, but I'm from the fuck and suck school. At least Gale is not on the receiving end, but Claire? I don't understand it, Anna. For me, sex is about pleasure."

"But if something can bring you pleasure, it can also bring you pain," Anna sagely informed me. "Girls just wanna have fun. And pain, at least for some people, can be exquisitely pleasurable."

I looked skeptically at my friend, informing her that she could park herself on the other side of the plane if she was going to dole out any more of that type of sophomoric wisdom.

"How do you know it isn't pleasurable on some level?" she challenged, refusing to give in. "I mean, at least for them. No two people operate on the same sexual level. As for Claire, I think this Stone guy pierced her veil."

"How so?" Anna had crossed certain sexual barriers that a meat-and-potato lover like myself couldn't even begin to comprehend.

"Look," said Anna, picking up her magazine again and beginning to leaf through it, "Claire is a very powerful woman politically. She hitched her star to a guy who's a genius at politicking but a run-of-the-mill president. Claire has more guts than he does."

"Or so we thought. We co-dependents of the Claire Foster Benton Club."

"Yeah, well, okay," conceded Anna. "She doesn't have the guts to stand and run for political office, but the First Bitch is a powerful woman, and I suspect she got bored with all those genuflecting males and females around the White House. And then along came the Stone-man."

"And?"

"Ba-da-boom, ba-da-bing. Stone is a power freak and doesn't have any compunction about it. He's obviously up on his dead-white-male classics: Machiavelli and the Marquis de Sade. Let's face it. He's running the White House and fucking Claire. Maybe Claire realized that—given a choice between the two most powerful men in her life—Stone was the real alpha male. As they say in the S/M community, the guy is a very heavy top. Maybe he saw that Claire, as a bottom, needed a release."

"Release? Release from what?"

"The burden of being a superwoman. Mother. Lawyer. Co-president. The bad little girl getting whipped by daddy. The First Girlfriend maybe finds delight in being a politically incorrect, groveling, submissive, supine female. All the things we are taught to hate, we modern New Women. It's subversive. The way it's subversive for us lesbians—just some of us, mind you—using dildoes, the ultimate transgression to hard-line lesbian-feminist sensibilities. Didn't Gale say her biggest freaks were generals, CEOs, national politicians? These guys want a release from the pressures of being at the top by taking their turn on the bottom."

"I don't know, Anna."

"Look, Nin, I'm just speculating. At the very least, maybe she's just role-playing. But it is a very dangerous sort of role-playing. I mean, people are turning up dead. Mike Debord. Carol Bridges. And now Claire trying to force you off the investigation. Now that's kinky."

I looked out the window and thought about everything that had been dropped on me recently. Then another thought hit me.

"Anna?"

"Hmmm?" She was mildly engrossed in her magazine. "Yes, my pet?"

"You...uh...aren't...uh... I mean, you aren't into this scene, are you?"

Anna smiled and looked at me. "No, girl. I'm not the submissive type. I may have succumbed to the model minority syndrome, but I'm not a submissive Asian female. Neither top nor bottom. I fluctuate." Her eyes suddenly focused on an image in her magazine. "But I'd be willing to consider just about anything with her!"

Her eyes were glued to a photograph of Magdalena VillaRosa, the Maerican chanteuse. Magdalena, known as "La Bomba" among the Maerican locals, was the descendant of a French plantation family that had left Misericordia for France after the revolution and then returned years later. The VillaRosas, it seemed, had spent too many years soaking up the Maerican culture and lifestyle; they just couldn't live happily back in France without their blacks.

Along with many other former plantation families who remained in Misericordia, the VillaRosas intermarried among themselves, occasionally crossing racial lines to avoid the risk of regressive genes. Magdalena was a sublime example of the terrifying impact of miscegenation on certain island men, driving them to kill one another in a sex-crazed frenzy. Looking at the picture, it wasn't that difficult to understand what drove them to a murderous rampage. The woman was gorgeous, with her delectable, café-au-lait skin, her wavy red hair, her hard but sensual body. In spite of her questionable pipes, she could also sing quite fluently in French, Spanish, English, and Kreole, and had become Misericordia's one true international attraction. She was currently starring in a much-heralded house show at the Hôtel Nestoire, formerly called the Triomphe, and Hollywood was plying her with film offers, not one of which had yet to catch her fancy.

Her legend as a Caribbean sex goddess had been permanently sealed when two generals had argued over her company at a party, drawn pistols, and shot one another to death.

"Fools!" Magdalena cried out at the time, "I was woman enough for both of them!"

Disgusted with the violence and possessiveness of men, she soon took to the sensible sex, women, breaking a string of international hearts along the way. As described in the local tabloids, she discarded her lovers on the beaches of the

Caribbean, after ravishing them the way the sea does the sand. Since Magdalena was of the elite class, her sexual transgressions were mostly overlooked, while lower-class Maerican lesbians and gays, called *masisi* by the populace, were publicly ridiculed and locked up as subversives—some even summarily executed when Misericordia was blamed for the AIDS epidemic. Gays were seen as undermining the tourist industry—and besmirching the swaggering image of the Caribbean male.

"Now, I could be a bottom for this woman," crooned Anna. "We are definitely checking her out at the Hôtel Nestoire. Mark that on our social calendar."

I was about to say something when I remembered that I had purchased a *Vanity Fair* at the airport. I retrieved it from the compartment in the back of the seat in front of me and began flipping through the pages. My magazine also had an article about Magdalena VillaRosa, but the setting was different from the one Anna had been reading. In Anna's girl-world magazine, Magdalena was framed on all sides by her all-woman band and back-up singers, and was definitely giving out some serious sapphic signifiers. But the *VF* piece pictured her at various locations, all in the company of attractive men. Anna looked over at my magazine.

"Damn, this woman's got her marketing strategy figured out!" said Anna. "Go ahead, girl. Do it to death."

"Yeah, she's working both sides of the street," I said with amusement, until I turned a page and I saw a photo I didn't like. Anna noticed the abrupt change in my demeanor.

"What's wrong?"

I said nothing and placed the magazine back where I found it. Anna reached over me, pulled it out, and thumbed through the pages until she came across the photograph of Magdalena in a serious saliva exchange with the only man alive who could drive me crazy: Luc Malmundo. Fuck love, I thought. I was here to kill someone.

CHAPTER TWELVE

The airport spread out along the Misericordian coastline, five miles outside the capital city of Port Henri. En route, Anna and I had slipped off our shoes and socks, replacing them with sandals. Descending from the cabin, we were greeted by the island's warm, luxurious climate. Almost immediately, I felt my body's normal constrictions beginning to loosen up, and found myself being seduced by the tropical groove of the Caribbean. The smell of the ocean air filled my nostrils. The island was a sweet and succulent mango, oozing with juice as well as blood.

The place had changed since the last time I was there. Things actually worked. Planes landed and took off on time. New runways were being constructed everywhere, along with a new control tower and several new terminal buildings. Passengers were moving about the complex with an ease and confidence that suggested we were no longer victims of a slow and excruciating form of extortion, bribery, and banditry. It was hard to believe that Misericordia, for many years a cruel example of kleptocracy run amok, could have changed so quickly and dramatically.

For years—beginning with the grand old man of theft, Triomphe—the Miseri elite had siphoned off international development money earmarked for structural improvements to fatten their own coffers. To satisfy the prying eyes of donors, projects were always begun—concrete poured and runways half paved—but rarely completed. The pilfering elite also generated off-the-book revenues by franchising customs and other money-collecting governmental operations to obsequious relatives, cronies, and other incompetents, whose single responsibility was to deliver kickbacks to the ruling class.

I was down here to find a killer and to investigate the murder of a friend's husband, but I felt as if I were on vacation in a place where time seemed to stand still—and responsibilities fell away like autumn leaves along the George Washington Parkway. It was a curious sensation—while it lasted. Strolling through the main terminal, I was greeted by a sign that abruptly reminded me that I was in a nation gripped by political turmoil, whose people were suffering under a police state. In bold, black letters, the sign announced:

OBSERVE!

LISTEN!

REPORT!

—STATE SECTION OF PRESIDENTIAL AIDES—

"Travel tips for newcomers, huh?" said Anna. Each of us had taken our luggage on board—a single shoulder-strapped carry-on. A very nice, efficient, and darkly handsome young man with a rolling accent welcomed me at the customs desk, becoming even more solicitous when he looked at my passport and noticed my name.

"Ah, my dear lady, you are Nina Halligan."

I couldn't deny what was printed on my passport, but I felt suddenly apprehensive about what would happen next. "Correct," I admitted.

"Dr. Malmundo," said the official, "called and left word that he would be here to pick you up."

"Luc?" I said. "Dr. Lucious Malmundo?"

"Yes. Our highly esteemed Minister of Education." He

smiled brightly, showing off a remarkably white set of teeth. Nice bite, I thought. I felt a salacious tickle up my spine as I imagined their imprint on my shoulders and ass.

I shouldn't have been surprised to hear that Luc would be meeting us. I had e-mailed the luscious one earlier in the week, telling him about our travel plans. I had checked my e-mail for messages right before Anna and I left Misericordia, and he hadn't responded at the time. But Luc was like that, completely unpredictable. I still felt a little uneasy to hear that he was meeting us there without making arrangements beforehand.

"Madam," said the young man, breaking my train of suspicion, "please, we have the VIP Lounge waiting for you."

"I'm here with my friend," I said, indicating Anna, who was standing behind me.

Infused with the new can-do spirit of the Maerican Department of Tourism, the young man smiled again, not missing a beat, and responded at once in that rolling Caribbean accent that made me think of ocean waves lapping on the shore. "But of course, madam. A friend of a friend of Dr. Malmundo's is welcomed as you are and will be treated accordingly."

The man picked up a phone at the desk. He spoke a few words into it, and a woman dressed in the vibrant colors of the peazant class immediately appeared at the desk. "Gertrude, please take Dr. Malmundo's guests to the VIP Lounge."

The woman smiled benignly. "Please, follow me."

As I bent down to pick up my luggage, Anna whispered throatily in my ear, "I like this country, Nina." She moved quickly ahead of me, eagerly following the VIP hostess. I caught up to her with a few large, awkward steps.

"Anna," I said in a low whisper, "you better chill your ass. This is a very traditional society when it comes to sexual roles and preferences."

"I can be discrete," she said, her eyes fixed eagerly on the undulating behind of our hostess, the woman's buttocks twitching seductively beneath her green stripped skirt. Damn, I thought, if I walked like that back home, I'd have every male dog within sight lapping after my trail.

"Just be careful about how you show your enthusiasm for

our sex. Same-sex activity is considered subversive here and you can easily be thrown to the Papas."

"The what?" Her eyes were still firmly fixed on the lower regions of the woman in front of us, who was now leading us down a bending hallway. To our left was a long train of glass that curved along the hallway; from the inside we could see palm trees dotting the runways of the Nestor Morgan International Airport.

"Those guys at the door," I pointed out. We had come to an entrance leading in from outside the terminal to another carrier's desk. Near the door stood several darkly clad men with gray fedoras, Ray Bans, and foreign automatic rifles slung ominously across their shoulders. To set themselves off from the regular armed forces, who strictly adhered to formal military decorum, the Papas often dangled licorice sticks or tooth picks from their mouths, tooling them carefully around as if to underscore their deadly insouciance.

"Those fuckers," I whispered under my breath. "They mutilate *masisi*—gay men—and are given license to rape gay women, just to show them what they've missed. Catch my drift?"

"I sure do," said my friend, who slowed down—not under the influence of the wisdom that I was imparting—but because she had become completely entranced by the smile of our hostess as she showed us into the VIP Lounge.

The entire room was outfitted with wicker, *tres cher* furnishings, from what I could tell. A wet bar and a complete entertainment unit occupied one corner, and tropical plants and flowers dotted the floor. A ceiling fan slowly stirred an infectious aroma across the room, an odor that I couldn't readily identify but that was clearly meant to make one feel relaxed. Someone certainly knew his or her olfactory sciences, as well as their therapeutic applications.

If China Cat had been beside herself before, she was reduced to fluttering insanity when our original hostess was joined by two equally lovely examples of Maerican womanhood. The three young goddesses stood before us: one black, one honey brown, one *crème de cacao*.

They welcomed us in Kreole, laid our bags aside, and led us to reclining chairs, where we were offered an array of tropical juices: papaya, guava, coconut. We sipped the refreshments and reclined like bitch goddesses in paradise. Our sandals were removed and our feet were lowered into a warm solution of sea moss; our hands were placed in porcelain bowls of the same solution, and warm, moist terry-cloth towels were spread across our faces. I completely surrendered to the moment. Five stars, I thought.

"This is nice," I heard Anna purr. "So nice."

"Amen," was all I could manage in response. At some point, the natural opiates in my brain were released and I fell fast asleep, or at least part of me did. In the distance, I heard a door opening and a set of footsteps leaving and entering the room. A voice called out to us in that now-familiar, rolling Caribbean lilt.

"Ladies," said the full set of teeth from before, "a new situation has arisen."

"Yes. What's that?" I asked. My head was still resting against the chair, my ears filled with the imaginary sound of the sea against the shore.

"You are now the guest of the People's Liberation Army of Misericordia!" he proclaimed.

I slowly raised my head, unfurling the towel with my left hand and keeping my right hand in the bowl of sea moss. The custom official's smile had disappeared and an automatic pistol was pointing sternly at my face.

Anna's natural opiates must have been working double time; she was still totally snoozed out.

"Wake that bitch up!" the man viciously barked, jerking the gun in her direction.

"Anna! Anna!"

"Huh? What? Is Luc here?" She slowly raised herself, removing the towel from her face, and found herself face to face with the man holding the gun. "What the hell?"

"You are prisoners of the People's Liberation Army of Misericordia!" he informed us bluntly. "I'm the man from PLAM!"

Anna frowned, looked at me, and then at our toothsome friend. "This certainly isn't the vaunted Maerican hospitality

I've heard so much about," she protested.

"You are friends of Luc Malmundo," he began.

"But we are not U.S. government officials. We're just Luc Malmundo's personal friends. Kidnapping us will not influence American policies," I tried to explain, as my fingers slowly crept up to the outer rim of the bowl.

"We are not interested in influencing your government's policies," he replied. "We've heard enough American lies! It's the fascist dictatorship of the Malmundo regime that we seek to overthrow."

Anna and I exchanged looks. "That makes sense," I heard girlfriend say. "But I think you have the wrong bait. General Malmundo isn't going to give a fuck about us."

"Luc Malmundo may feel differently, though. At least you had better hope—"

I flipped my wrist suddenly and the bowl crashed into the middle of the custom official's forehead. I pounced on his gun arm at once, as he fired a wild shot into the ceiling. Anna didn't need any instructions. As I kneed the official in the groin, she lifted a reclining chair above her head and smashed it through the window behind us. I slammed a side-palm blow into the bastard's neck, and he fell to the floor, his weapon dropping to his side. Anna bolted through the window like an Olympic diver. I turned, jumped onto the reclining chair on which I'd been resting before, and flew straight out of the window and directly on top of Anna, who was still groggy from her abrupt flight from the lounge.

Rising unsteadily, I suddenly realized three things. First, we had no shoes, and the ground was blisteringly hot—a big disadvantage when one is being chased. Secondly, various points of gunfire had ignited inside and outside the airport. Lastly—and most disturbingly—all of the gunfire was directed at us.

Mr. Teeth and his rebel buddies were standing angrily at the shattered window, their weapons pointed straight at us. I grabbed Anna by the hand and scurried across the verdant lawn outside the terminal. The only obstacle blocking our escape path was a waist-high fence.

"We gotta go up and over," I shouted as we approached the

fence, building up speed as we went.

"Tell me something I don't know, Nee."

I cleared the fence first, completely oblivious to a large limo that had just pulled up on the other side. My thick skull crashed into the glistening hood of the car, and I rolled over the car and onto the grass beyond.

"Nina!" The rich, male voice that called me certainly didn't come from Anna. It was Luc! He rushed out of the car and ran toward me, pulling me up on my naked feet. Anna immediately appeared on my other side, and we dashed toward the car in a crouched position as the gunfire increased. The two of them shoved me into the front of the car, where Luc discovered that his driver had been shot through his open window, the back of his head blown away a la JFK. Luc dragged the man's body away, squeezed behind the wheel, and stepped on the gas.

I sat back in the seat and covered my throbbing head with my hands. For a few seconds, we drove along the runway, away from the terminal. From out of nowhere, a vehicle appeared behind us, an American-made recreational four-wheel drive. The passengers lowered their windows and began firing at us, as Luc stepped on the brakes and swerved the limo momentarily out of their line of fire.

"Get down!" he shouted, as the rebels raked the right side of the car. "Don't worry; it's bulletproof!" he screamed above the noise, trying to comfort us.

"Yeah, but for how fucking long?" I asked. My question was answered much too quickly for comfort as we felt a sudden jolt behind us and turned to see a black plume of smoke racing toward the car. The rebels had somehow gotten their hands on a bazooka-style rocket launcher, and they clearly weren't firing blanks.

"Son of a dead-dicked dog," swore Anna, as the first blast exploded over our heads. "The fatherfuckers are shooting rockets at us! Puh-lease, tell me this is a fucking SUV commercial gone berserk!" Anna began swearing in Mandarin.

"Obatala!" said Luc, invoking a Yoruba divinity. "Now I really have to do some serious fucking driving! *Merde*! *Coño*! Shit!"

We drove back along the runway in the direction of the terminal with the four-wheeler hot on our trail. Luc, crouched over the steering wheel of the car, reached desperately beneath the seat for something with his right hand.

"Nina!" he shouted. "Look beneath the seat. There's a comparment with..."

I fumbled around for a moment until I found the compartment. Opening it, I pulled out an M-16 rifle.

"You got it?" he asked, swerving to avoid another unsuccessful missile launch that crashed along the side of the road. Although the missile missed us by a wide margin, the explosion savagely pelted the side of the limousine with gravel and up-turned earth.

"Luc," Anna was white with fear, blood draining from her face, "I know you're doing the best you can, but that was getting too goddamn close!"

"Luc?" I said, as I pulled out a magazine and slid it into place. The gun was ready and I was ready, but there was still one thing I needed to know. "Baby, what's with you and Magdalena? I saw you two together in *Vanity Fair*!"

"What?" He swerved to the left as my hand caught hold of his right leg and then his balls.

"Nina! *Chica*, are you fucking crazy!" He looked first at me and then at the rearview mirror, keeping track of the pursuing vehicle.

"Nee-na!" said Anna, who was nervously looking over her shoulder at the rebels, who were still trying to get a bead on us. "This isn't the time for that!"

"This is between Luc and me, Anna!"

"Eat me!" screeched Anna, reaching over the seat and snatching the rifle from my hands. She flicked the safety latch and shouted "Roof!" at the top of her lungs.

Luc pressed the control panel and the sun suddenly beamed into the car, brightening the darkness within, but doing little to lighten the growing tension between Luc and me—or my sudden lapse into madness. Raising herself unsteadily to her feet, Anna began firing rapid rounds at our pursuers. The four-wheel swerved abruptly behind us.

"Hey, she's good," said Luc.

"Taught her everything she knows," I responded.

"And then some," said Anna with a grim wink, as she continued firing.

The rebels regrouped and reloaded, and another missile tore up the road beside our car's front left wheel. Luc pulled to his right and then to his left, jolting Anna from side to side. She continued firing throughout, but the rebels had fallen back—out of our range, but not the bazooka's. Our pursuers, I surmised, realized that they had the advantage and were preparing to use it. The only thing saving us at the moment was their abysmal marksmanship. If they couldn't hit us from short range, I tried to reassure myself, how in the hell were they going to find the target from way back there?

Before I could answer my own question, however, the entire pursuit had ended. We heard a tremendous explosion behind us, and the ground rumbled violently beneath our car. For a moment, we all assumed that we had been hit. But our limousine was still racing along the runway, not through the air. Meanwhile, the four-wheeler behind us was doing side flips along the road, engulfed in a ball of black smoke and orange flames, shards of metal hanging from its sides like flailed human flesh. I heard a loud roar above us; looking up through the sunroof, I saw a Cobra helicopter hovering in the sky directly above us. At that same moment, the telephone in Luc's car rang. He picked up the receiver.

"Yes," he said nonchalantly, "we're okay. A bit frazzled, but we're fine... Yes. I'll head back to the terminal... Fine. *Muchas gracias*. I'll see you at the palace later." The conversation ended, and Luc slowed the car's speed to what seemed like a crawl.

"Who the hell was that?" I asked. "Obatala?"

"On the phone or in the air?" Luc replied, as he removed a handkerchief from the inside pocket of his jacket.

"Both." I took the handkerchief from him and began mopping his brow and face.

"That was the general—my father."

"On the phone?" asked Anna, who sat exhausted in the back seat, the weapon across her lap. Her cotton T-shirt was drenched with sweat and stained by the grease and sulfur from the weapon. Her black hair, also matted with sweat, was slicked back and featured a dangling cowlick that I'd never seen on her before. She looked like a Hong Kong babe in a John Woo film.

"Yes, and in the chopper," replied Luc. "He heard that there was an ambush at the airport and rushed out here with an air cavalry detail. He just wanted to make sure that we were all right."

He paused for a moment and then offered an exhausted smile. "You know, being a dictator's son can definitely have its advantages."

CHAPTER THIRTEEN

As we circled back towards the terminal, I looked behind me and saw the upturned car in flames, smoke rising from its black, mangled carcass. In the distance, I could hear the wailing sirens of a fire truck approaching the wreckage. Up ahead, steady streams of smoke were rising from various points along the airport terminals, all of which appeared to have sustained major damage. One entire wing of the complex had been reduced to a smoking hull, while most of the buildings were pockmarked by gunfire. I suspected, as I watched a team of helicopters receding from the airport, that the bulk of the damage had been caused by the immense firepower of the notorious "air cavalry" of the New Model Army of Misericordia.

Luc sighed and shook his head. "It's started."

"What?" asked Anna.

"The war," he replied. "This attack—"

"It turned into an attack when they failed to kidnap us," I interjected.

Luc turned to me quickly. "They were trying to kidnap you? The rebels?"

"Yes. They knew who I was," I said. "We were escorted to the VIP lounge as your guests and then told that everything had suddenly changed, that we were now being taken as prisoners."

Luc steered the car back onto the road that led to the terminal. We passed piles of dead bodies—soldiers, rebels, and civilians—a traffic jam of ruined vehicles, and a steady line of reinforcements from the army. Accompanying the military progression were several black sedans from the State Section of Presidential Aides, the dreaded Papas.

"Maybe there is still a chance," he said, more to himself. "If they were coming to kidnap you, then it wasn't an attack."

"Right," I agreed, not fully understanding the implications of what he had said. "What was it then?"

"I suspect that this was the brilliant planning of Raoul," confided Luc.

"Who is he?" asked Anna. Relaxed, she cradled the M-16 in her arms.

"One of the founding members of PLAM!, as well as President Bernard's adopted son," he said. "And a total dickhead. This is the sort of maneuver that he would pull. A typically moronic leftist guerrilla tactic. Abduct an innocent third party and hold them hostage. Stupid asshole! Marisol would never have stooped to something as stupid as this."

"Marisol Fanon?" I asked. I'd slammed her against a wall a few nights before, and, if I remembered correctly, she was Pepe Bernard's adopted daughter.

"Yes." Luc turned into a parking area that was flooded with khaki-colored soldiers and dark-suited agents of the state. He killed the engine and turned to me. He was still as handsome as ever, fleshing out in his mid-thirties into a nice hunk of a man. "So how is it that you know Marisol, Nina? She's the most wanted woman on the island."

"We met in Washington, D.C.," I responded.

"Regarding what?" he asked.

"Going to tell me about Magdalena?"

"Look," he began testily, "just what the hell are you two doing down here anyway?" He threw an angry look at me and then another one over his shoulder at Anna.

I informed the newly appointed minister of education that I was, in fact, on assignment in his country—and that I had come here in search of the killer of Michael Debord, whom Luc had also known in college.

"Yeah. I heard about Mike," he sighed. "But what makes you think that his assassin is down here?"

"Luc, you know me. I always do my homework. I got leads. I have names."

"I read that it was a homo tryst gone—"

"That's a goddamn lie, Luc," I said, cutting him off. "He was investigating a sudden change in U.S. policy toward Misericordia."

"So?"

"And it had something to do with EarthChem."

Luc closed his eyes and slowly shook his head.

"And I believe that Oscar Peltrano, an alleged associate of your father, was also somehow involved."

With the mention of Peltrano, Luc lowered his head to the top of the steering wheel. "I'm afraid you came down here at the wrong time, Nina," he sighed. "Things down here are about to explode—as you can well see."

We watched as soldiers and Papas escorted captured rebels into the back of canvas-covered trucks, their hands raised and placed behind their heads. The rebel soldiers were very young, most of them barely out of their teens. They represented the second or third generation, the recently uprooted peazant class, who had migrated to the cities after they lost their land, trying desperately to eke out a living. Some had taken up a life of petty crime just to make ends meet. Stateside, many would already have found their way into the new prison industrial complex that was devouring young black men by truckloads. Yet the militant history of Misericordia had led these boys and men to politicize their anger and frustration—and to take up arms together against the current regime.

"Nina, I have to send you two back. I really don't want you down here," Luc continued. "It's just too dangerous."

"Luc, did you hear what I said? The man who may have killed one of your best friends is engaging in drug town frolics."

"Nina, you don't understand—"

"Then explain," I snapped. "Enlighten me!"

"*Chica*," he started again, in a more measured tone, "my comrades and I are trying to persuade all the different factions here to sit down and negotiate peace. At great risk to my reputation as a human rights advocate and educator, I took a position in my father's administration, hoping that I could somehow counsel my father to a wiser and more humane course of action. Now this. Now you! I don't like it, and I want you out of here as soon as possible. Both of you on the next flight to Miami!"

"Are you trying to make me one of your enemies, Luc? Is that what you're trying to do?" I wasn't planning to budge my ass out of Misericordia any time soon. If I had to, I'd go underground.

"I have enough enemies, *chica*," he laughed good-naturedly, trying to conceal his growing frustration with me. "But as you know only too well, only your friends and your family can really hurt you; you never let your enemies get close enough to you to hit you where it really hurts." He paused for a moment, becoming more serious. "Besides, I'm a marked man, Nina."

"Luc," I reached over and gripped his arm. "Who has marked you?" I'd instinctively slipped into my protective mode.

"Everyone," he said bitterly. "Elements of the army. Hobson."

"The chief of the presidential aides," I relayed back to Anna.

"And now the rebels. I get death threats all the time. I don't dare spend more than two nights at a place. And now you're here, looking good—no doubt about it—but smelling of death and disaster."

That cut me, and Luc knew it. He knew that I knew exactly what he meant. I turned to Anna. "You feel brave enough to go and get our stuff?"

That was the only hint she needed that I wanted to talk with Luc by myself. "Sure," she said without hesitating.

"I'll have somebody go with you," Luc said to her.

"Thanks." Anna looked at me and winked, as she passed me the M-16. "I'm not going to need this—I think."

Anna squeezed my shoulder as she got out of the car. Luc

left the vehicle for a moment and instructed a nearby officer to escort Anna into the terminal. I was about to remove the magazine from the rifle, but immediately thought better of it. I placed the weapon back into the chamber beneath the seat, and Luc got back into the car. The moment he returned, I could see that things were different than before; he was smiling a broad, unguarded smile.

"It's so good to see you," he said.

"Then act like it." I was thrilled to see the change in his attitude, but I still needed some reassuring.

In college, Luc and I simply couldn't keep our hands off of each other, constantly devouring each other sexually everywhere we went—in our dorm rooms, in the park, between the book stacks in the library, in the back seats of cars. And here we were again—more than ten years later—with the same sexual energy welling up between us. And no better at restraining ourselves than before.

I slid over close to him, wrapped my arms around his neck, and lost myself in his mouth and his embrace. The limosine's windows were darkly tinted, shielding our rediscovered passion from the eyes of the soldiers outside. Luc's hands and lips roamed freely across my body, as I fumbled clumsily with his zipper.

Several minutes passed before Luc resumed his argument from before.

"*Chica*, I have to send you back. I know you're down here to find Peltrano and kill him."

His fingers were still caressing my erect nipples. "Believe me, beautiful, I'm not...thinking about killing anybody right now."

"Yes, but later," he said, nuzzling my hair with his nose. His nostrils searched for my scent amongst my braided locks.

"Later," I breathed heavily, "could be reserved for you and me." I pulled away and grasped his face firmly between my hands. "I want to be with you, Luc. If what you said before about being a marked man is true, I couldn't possibly leave you. I'll forget about my business, my mission, for the time being. Just let me be with you. Let me help you."

"You'll forget about Peltrano—about Ford?" he asked me between kisses.

Oh, God, I thought, swallowing hard. He knew that Peltrano was Ford. "Yes."

"You would forget about what he did? Sanctioning Lee's death? Andrew's? Ayesha's?"

I nodded, and he reached over and wiped a tear from my cheek. For a moment I felt both trapped and released, cornered by the past but somehow freed by the demands of the present. Could I possibly abandon my quest to avenge the deaths of Lee and the children? Could I drop it all, just like that, for the possibility of a single night of passion? All I knew was that my hatred for Ford had closed me off to the future—while just seeing Luc again had somehow opened things up again. Could I possibly think now about the future? Even a dangerous and precarious future with Luc?

The man bowed his head and kissed my hand. "You are truly a remarkable woman, but I couldn't ask you to abandon your duty to your family or your client. I won't ask you to sacrifice your integrity, Nina. What would either of us be if we lost that?"

"Look, I'll go back, but I just want a little time here with you before I do," I finally said, biting his lips. "Is that too much to ask?" I ran my finger over his neatly trimmed moustache.

Luc was wrestling with himself. I could see how badly he wanted to be with me but that he also feared exposing me to danger.

"What about Anna?"

"She's resourceful, believe me; she'll be happy to be spending her time looking at Maerican art." However, she would more than likely be finding someone to explore her inner regions.

Luc remained silent for a few more seconds, tenderly caressing my hand.

"Baby," I put my hand up to his face. "Even a condemned man gets a last request. *No es verdad?*"

He agreed to my terms, and I kissed him passionately. But Anna and I were leaving in just forty-eight hours, he reminded me. Two days.

Before we could continue, Anna opened the door to the car and handed me my day bag. She looked horrible, an expression of white terror on her blood-drained face.

"What happened, Anna?"

It took her a few minutes to let it all out. "I saw three flowers of Misericordia lying dead in a pool of blood outside. Oh, God, Nina. All of those beautiful women who waited on us are dead!"

Luc just looked at me. He knew he didn't need to say anything more. Anna had made his point for him. I moved to the back seat with Anna and let her cry on my shoulder. Luc turned the key in the ignition and stepped on the gas, as I tried to wipe away my friend's bitter tears.

We drove along Nestor Morgan Boulevard to the city, escorted all the way by an armored truck and a military jeep with a .50-caliber machine gun. Luc took the time to fill me in on the situation in Misericordia, as well as "the kiss" with Magdalena.

"I was set up," he explained sheepishly.

"Pussy-whacked?" I asked skeptically, caressing the back of his neck as he drove.

"Yeah, something like that." Luc looked at me quickly as we turned onto a steep upgrade in the road. We were slowly climbing the highest point on the northern shore of the island, en route to the presidential palace. I tightened my grip on his neck to signal my non-belief in his story.

"Look," he said, "you have to understand something. Some of my allies were assassinated. All of them were progressive people. But Maggie is the leader of a conservative element of the elite, and someone took a shot at her, too. It looked like things were about to get ugly. All hell was breaking loose, Nina."

"So what's with the kiss?" I asked for the umpteenth time, unable to see any connection between the political unrest in Misericordia and Luc's lip-wrestling episode with Magdalena.

"Maggie called me over and said that we should talk. She knew that I had been trying to put together a coalition of people across the political spectrum. I honestly believed she wanted to talk about that. I arrived at her place and was greeted by a team of reporters and photographers—and, of course, by Maggie, who corralled me into a kiss. The kiss you saw in the article. It was supposed to be a warning to her would-be assassins, to imply that she was now under my father's protection. The whole thing was no big deal, Nina. I grew up with Maggie and—"

"Oh, the first fuck, huh?"

"You know, my dear, it is so unbecoming to hear you speaking like one of those hoodlums you've prosecuted in the past," he said disapprovingly. "*Tu sabes, chica?*"

"*Sí, popi,*" I replied, giving his neck an extra pinch.

"I'm going to smack your ass if you don't behave yourself, *chica.*"

"Oooh, I can hardly wait," I said, doing my best to impersonate a submissively drooling female. I could see myself smiling in the reflection of his mirror-sunglasses.

"Okay, enough of this," said Anna. "What about this first fuck?"

I winked at Anna. She wanted to know the 411, too. Gossip. We want it. We need it. We love it.

Luc sighed. "This isn't about a fuck or a kiss! It was about political expediency. Things have badly deteriorated since Bernard left the country. In the past, the elite and the military had concentrated their energies on grinding down the poor. But now something different was happening. The island's elites actually began turning on themselves. Each group carved out its own turf, its own sphere of influence. Somebody took a shot at Magdalena and that someone wasn't one of the progressives."

"Why not?" asked Anna.

"Because none of them actually have the balls to do that," he responded, looking up at her in the rearview mirror. "They all left and went to Washington."

"And those who were in Washington and came back," I added, "are on a different agenda."

"Exactly," said Luc. "La Bomba—Magdalena—was scared. She knew it wasn't me or any of my allies. As a human rights advocate, I have forsworn violence—"

"I'm sure that has made your father, Smilin' Jack Malmundo, extremely happy," I said. I thought about what Luc had said before about "spheres of influence." A euphemism for drugs, no doubt.

"That's a different story; we're different men, my father and I," he quickly said. "But Maggie feared that it was PLAM! who was after her, and she needed some cover quick."

"Your lips? Negro, please!"

He shrugged his shoulders and followed the armored truck as it passed beneath a grove of palms, the national tree of Misericordia. The languid heat had finally begun to abate; the air was cooler and the sky clearer as we left the thick vegetation of the humid coastal lowlands.

"I was the last man standing who had any credibility at all, but, of course, that ended when I joined my father's administration," Luc reflected. "I stupidly thought I could get him to change, to influence the elite and do something for our people, but all that was thrown out the window when the guerrillas tried to kidnap you two. Now it's just a matter of time. The history of Misericordia is nothing more than a history of civil wars. God against all and every man for himself. Our destiny, it seems."

Atop the cliff overlooking the capital and the harbor that faced the Caribbean Sea, the motorcade arrived at the gate of the presidential palace. The palace, almost a carbon copy of the Parthenon, was sitting on an enormous rock outcropping that descended toward the cliff and was surrounded on all sides by a moat. Beyond the moat was a beautiful formal garden of native tropical flowers.

The car drove up to the front of the palace. We disembarked and were greeted at once by the Keeper of the House. He announced that General Malmundo was expecting us in thirty minutes, giving us plenty of time to freshen ourselves after our "harrowing experience." A staff member led us to our sumptuous rooms. Anna was dropped off first, and I told her that we'd come by to get her in twenty minutes. Luc and I kissed briefly inside the door of my own room. After he left, I rested for a few minutes on the bed before dragging myself into the Louis XIV bathroom to prepare myself to meet a real big daddy.

Luc had instructed us to dress casually. I wore a simple white blouse, blue linen trousers, and loafers; Anna switched into sage-colored slacks and a blush pink, boxy waffle top. Perfect ensembles, I thought, for meeting a dictator.

Luc led us down the most pretentiously massive hall in the annals of Caribbean architecture. One could easily have run a convoy of tanks down the corridors of the place. As we approached the general's office, Luc began to fill us in on him.

"Listen," he fumbled with his words as our steps resounded through the hallway, "you have to understand something about my father. He likes to—"

A piercing cry of "AGGGGGGGGGGHHHHH!" echoed through the hall and circled our skulls.

I jumped closer to Luc. "What the hell?" We stopped, as the cry reverberated throughout the hall.

"My father," Luc sighed. "Shall we continue?"

"Not without some type of explanation," said Anna, holding onto me.

"My father enjoys hurting people," he said calmly and continued guiding us. We turned a corner to witness two soldiers dragging away a small, light-skinned black man. The skin, muscles, and tendons of both of the man's hands looked as if they had been pulled up and ripped apart. Everything was pulled back and exposed to the bone. The sleeves of his torn white coat were soaked in blood up to the elbows.

"That was the former manager of the airport," said Luc sadly. "Prior to this, he was regarded as a fine administrator."

We reached two huge doors that would have looked more appropriate on the entrance to a French castle. Two guards snapped to attention as we prepared to enter the inner sanctum of General Estaban "Smilin' Jack" Malmundo. It took us several more minutes to reach the end of the room, which must have been twice the length of a football field.

The general was being fitted into his military waist jacket by a busty female valet. As we drew closer to the general, I watched the valet place a black cloth over a blood-soaked, stainless steel device that must have been used to torture the general's previous guest. The valet carried the instrument away on a silver tray. The general was handsome like his son, in his sixties, with smooth, glistening brown skin. His closely cropped gray hair was thinning. He still had a powerful athletic build, the product of years of ascetic military discipline. Was this how Luc would look in thirty years? It was certainly an appealing thought.

The man's attire was suitably Pattonesque: spit-shined, black riding boots; khaki jodhpurs, a riding crop tucked neatly into the right one; and a pair of ivory-handled, 9mm Glock pistols holstered on either side of his waist. Beneath his Eisenhower waistcoat, he wore a khaki shirt with an olive-colored silk ascot. He certainly looked impressive, I thought, but could the man actually command a military force? After all, he had only recently encountered his first real military opposition— and that had been PLAM!

He seemed extremely pleased with himself and his recent performance—and why not? Here he stood in his element. Behind him stretched a magnificent view of the island. The portraits of distinguished black leaders covered an entire wall of his cavernous lair: Kwame Nkrumah, Jomo Kenyatta, Gamel Nasser, Martin Luther King, Malcolm X, Adam Clayton Powell, Frederick Douglass, Nelson Mandela, Booker T. Washington, W. E. B. DuBois, Elijah Muhammad, Nehru, Idi Amin, and Louis Farrakhan. Not a single woman among them.

The other wall was crowded with busts and portraits of celebrated warriors of all races and nationalities: Ghenghis Khan; Alexander the Great; Julius Caesar; Hanibal; Frederick the Great; Shaka Zulu; Korea's Admiral Yee; Lords Nelson and Wellington; Napoleon; John Paul Jones; Simón Bolívar, the liberator of South America; Admirals Perry, Farragut, and Nimitz; the Union's Grant, Sherman, and Sheridan; the Confederacy's Lee, Jackson, and Forrest; Crazy Horse, Sitting Bull, Cochise, and Geronimo; Generals Pershing, Eisenhower, Patton, MacArthur, Marshall, and Montgomery; Field Marshall Erwin Rommel; Admiral Yamamoto; Soviet Marshall Georgi Zhukov; and Vietnam's Giap, who had mastered the French at Dien Bien Phu and served as the architect of America's defeat. These were the men with whom he compared himself.

True to his name, Malmundo smiled graciously as we approached. Luc introduced us formally, according to protocol. "General, allow me to introduce you to two friends of mine, Señora Nina Halligan..."

The general clicked his heels, bowed, and kissed my freely extended hand. "General, it's a pleasure to meet you," I lied. It felt as if Dracula himself was grazing my skin with his lips.

"And Señorita Anna Gong." Girlfriend was really getting the treatment from the general. He was giving her *the look*. He'd probably plowed through plenty of black women in his time—but a Chinese babe, that would be something special.

"General," Anna responded, almost without expression. She was still thinking about those gorgeous dead women back at the airport, I suspected.

He leaned against the edge of his desk and gestured for us to sit. Luc remained standing, about an arm's length away from me.

"Those who tried to abduct you," he smiled benevolently, "will be found and punished. I swear it. This is my personal pledge to you. There will be no terrorism on this island. No more banditry!" he said, slapping his palm with the riding crop. "Not under my watch, my command!"

An unusual number of riding crops had been popping up in my life recently.

"I'm trying to bring some order back to this island," the general continued vehemently, "after the woeful mismanagement by that communist priest!"

"Oh, then you're not planning to negotiate a power-sharing arrangement with President Bernard?" I asked.

"Certainly not!" he snapped. "The man is a communist. In no way should he be viewed as responsible or trustworthy. Washington shares my view, though they won't say so openly. I'm convinced that the terrorists who accosted you were nothing more than a provocateur wing of Bernard supporters. A futile attempt to bring back socialism to the island. A bankrupt idea!"

"But the president won more than sixty percent of the vote, General," I argued. "A large number of people must feel he has something to say." I knew that arguing with him would be useless, but I wanted to hear for myself how the man reasoned.

"But it's the remaining thirty percent that matter," he corrected me with a smile.

"Meaning what?" asked Anna.

"Meaning that some people are gold, some are silver, and some are bronze," he answered with the cryptic arrogance of a dictator. He stared at Anna like a treasured lotus blossom on which he soon planned to be nibbling.

Anna had no idea what he was talking about. She looked toward Luc and me, hoping one of us would fill her in.

"Plato's *Republic*," I said. Anna nodded her head, suddenly remembering her classics.

"Correct!" said the general. "I've been reading it. A masterful book of philosophical insight on leadership and power."

"The handbook of all totalitarian regimes—both left and right," I added. It was easy to see that the general, picturing himself as a Caribbean philosopher-king, shared Plato and Socrates' contempt for democracy.

The man shrugged. "But most people are either gold, silver, or bronze. *No es verdad?*"

"And it's usually the bronze ones who get it in the neck," I responded.

"And rightly so," General Malmundo agreed. "Rightly so. Some people are naturally on the bottom."

"Bronze, General, is usually the color that is attributed to people of color like ourselves," I added.

"Is that so?" For a single, rare moment, the general actually seemed to be honestly reflecting on what I had said. "Hmmm. I never knew that."

The general stood, preparing to make a command decision. "Excuse me," he said, then strode around to his side of the desk. He spoke forcefully into the intercom, brandishing his riding crop. "Gather up all copies of the subversive literature, *The Republic*, by the notorious communist Plato, and have them incinerated!"

"You're going to have *The Republic* burned?" asked Luc. As a committed educator on an island where books were already scarce, the very idea of it shocked and sickened him.

"Yes! I will not tolerate insults to our people." he answered. He then turned back to the intercom. "This will commence immediately!"

He snapped off the machine, strutted back over to us, and placed his jodhpured buttocks on the edge of the desk, his arms crossed in satisfaction. The man was, after all, a faithful student of the Henri Triomphe school of reductive racial reasoning.

Smilin' Jack sized us up. "Well, since you're friends of my son, let's direct our discussion to a subject that's of interest to him, education."

When we finally escaped the general's pedantic ramblings on education and propaganda, I announced to Luc that neither Anna nor I had any intention of spending a single night in the home of a torturer and book-burning fanatic.

"Look, you have to stay," pleaded Luc. "You can't insult him by leaving."

"Just watch us," Anna and I informed him. Both of us were on a girl vibe and wanted to get the hell out of there.

Entering Anna's room, I noticed that girlfriend had already packed her bags. Her own work completed, she then stood guard beside the door of my room, as I busied myself with my own bags and continued to set Luc straight on our newly altered plans for the evening.

"Look, beautiful," I said, stuffing the pants I had dirtied during the earlier shootout into the bag, "he's got his eyes on Anna and it's only a matter of time. At some point during the night, he's going to do a midnight creep into her room. In his mind, he's our rescuer, our knight in shining armor, and he's got the scent of a man who expects a hero's reward."

"And I'm sleeping with Nina!" said Miss Lotus Blossom. "I'm not sleeping alone with that guy in this place—his palace. Forget that!"

"And if girlfriend here is sharing the other side of my bed," I said, cocking him a raised eyebrow, "guess what's not going to happen tonight?"

"Don't mind me. I'll watch," Anna announced, her eyes flashing with delight. "I can mark it off as research for the Chinese compendium on the mating habits of inter-American Africans."

Luc immediately called Casa de Esperanza, the inn where our original reservations had been made, and confirmed our arrival. He announced to the clerk that he would deliver us there himself. *Tout de suite*!

CHAPTER FOURTEEN

Luc's plans to influence the direction of the new government had been interrupted by the PLAM! assault and the general's decision to permanently suspend negotiations with President Bernard. The three of us sat in silence as we drove into Port Henri, watching the stark hills dissolve into a vast expanse of green grass, palm trees, and stinking slums.

Luc was a frustrated man who was born to lead. But he was determined not to do it the old-fashioned Maerican way—by violence and coups and bloodshed. A modern man, he preferred to achieve power through money, media, and charisma. Luc was a member of the Miseri elite, after all; he had been educated in the States and regarded himself as one of the chosen few. But Luc understood the hard lessons of modern history that his predecessors had failed to grasp. He knew that "*nada sera como antes*"—nothing will be as it was. Misericordia was due for a change, a change toward democracy and popular rule, and he was determined that the multitude would remember him as their champion, as a man who had pushed history forward, not tried futilely to hold it back.

Luc was sincere in his desire to do something for the people, to get the boot of the state off the necks of the peazants. But like all modern leaders, his desire was tinged with self-interest. He was also disturbed to see the New Misericordia slipping back into its familiar pattern of violence and bloodshed. Even more disturbing was the fact that the one man in the way of Luc's success, in the way of popular rule in Misericordia, was his own father. The implications were positively Shakespearean.

Casa de Esperanza was a large hacienda in the old French section of the city. The area was known for its two- and three-story wooden buildings of pink, aqua blue, and yellow, each with wide double doors and balconies. Casa de Esperanza had a warm, old feeling about it that recalled the sensation of walking in to a relative's home after a long journey. The place featured classical and *nuevo* flamenco music, as well as ample doses of new African vibes. Singers Ishmael Lowe of Sierra Leone and Geoffrey Oryema of Uganda blared forth from the powerful sound system. The decor was distinctly New World Spain, with decoratively carved wooden chairs throughout and an elegant fountain bubbling at the center of the lobby. Subtle African figurines, from the Yoruba and Benin kingdoms, were placed in corners or discrete niches.

The owner, Esperanza Pomona, a café-au-lait-skinned woman in her late thirties or early forties, greeted us at the door. She had raven-colored hair, accented by a glorious white streak. I attributed her hospitality to Luc. The man was right: Being the son of a dictator did have its advantages. At the front desk in the lobby sat a man of subtle Arab descent, who was introduced to us as Salim. He called for an assistant and our bags were taken. Doña Esperanza then led us downstairs and through a hallway to our adjoining rooms.

"*Bienvenidos. Mi casa es su casa,*" she said in a very throaty voice, after she showed us our rooms and the garden that led to an outside sunken tub that was hidden by walls that blocked off the view of the other's business. "Please don't hesitate to call upon me for anything."

"*Muchas gracias,*" I said. Doña Esperanza left, and I turned to Luc, who was looking out of the door into the private garden. I knew he had things on his mind. I left him standing alone and went through the door connecting my room to Anna's. I heard the shower running in the bathroom and knocked on the door.

"Who is it?" Anna bellowed.

"Me," I said as I poked my head in. "I'm going to be taking a siesta—"

"With Luc?" Anna asked.

"Yeah," I said, somewhat embarrassed about my obvious intention. I wasn't even waiting until nightfall. "Do you mind?"

"Enjoy yourself," she said over the sound of the water. "You deserve it."

"Thanks," I gasped, eager to return to Luc.

"Nina?" The water suddenly stopped.

"Yes?"

"I love you."

Uh oh, I thought. This was not the time to be having one of our Nina and Anna moments.

"I just wanted to say that," explained Anna, "because I felt we almost bought the farm today—at the airport. You're really special to me, Nina."

I smiled. "Anna, not now. Not now. There'll be plenty of time for this later. I'm about to get it the old-fashioned way."

Anna paused. She pulled back the curtain and stuck out her soapy, wet head. "I know," she pouted. "I just wanted to tell you; that's all."

I entered the bathroom, stuck my head into the shower and wrapped my arms around her neck. I winked and said nothing. I only smiled. But Anna was right. We had almost died, and it was hard not to take stock of things, to get a little misty-eyed. Not to mention the fact that I was also getting soaked from Anna's wet hair and the spray of the shower.

"Listen," I said, after pecking her on the forehead, "I have to go and make you an aunty." I grabbed a towel and dried off my face and arms.

"Have fun," she smiled, then called out after me, "Hey! What do you mean by make me aunty? Nina?"

* * *

My hands were braced against his chest, rubbing his hair and his nipples. I felt my body tighten as my buttocks rose and fell to meet his thrusts. This was the release I had been searching for, a way to get beyond myself, to push past the violence and death that had plagued me for so long.

I sat up and tweaked the nipples of my breasts. My skin was coated with sweat. A wild tingling coursed through my body and up to my brain as Luc forced himself deeper and deeper inside me. "My God...oh God... Unnnhhh."

My body began convulsing and I lost all sense of time and place and perspective. Somewhere in the back of my consciousness, I sensed that Luc had withdrawn from me, that his dark form had descended beneath me, across me, exploring my body's hidden secrets. I floated downward with him, kissing his forehead, his eyelashes, his nose, before losing his image to my own deepening desire. As Luc's fingers and lips sailed across my skin, I found myself drifting into a lost place within myself, a place where body and soul, thought and desire, past and present, were all indistinguishable. This was the place Jimi Hendrix once described as a sea of forgotten teardrops.

I rested on my stomach, a pillow strategically angled beneath my waist and my rear, as Luc's tongue began snaking its way up from my toes, lapping the soles of my feet and tracking the curve of my calves and thighs. I gasped as he finally found the dark mound between my legs.

"Talk to me, baby," I purred. "Talk to me. Hmmm."

"This is going to be hard, *chica*," he replied, breathing heavily, licking my ear. He was poising himself for a rear entry, and I was completely at his mercy.

"I have confidence in you. Hmmm," I purred, locking my feet around his legs as his hands clasped my hips. "I don't care how you do it, but do it," I growled over my shoulder before burying my face in the pillow.

I jerked my arms fiercely behind my back, and he forced himself inside me, entering me with such overwhelming force that I could manage only a muffled cry.

I floated in and out of consciousness, holding onto Luc as

long as I could. Suddenly I noticed that he was gone. I rolled around in bed, reaching for him futilely. A sense of panic came over me and I opened my eyes. The sun had lowered, darkening the room slightly. It took my eyes a few seconds to adjust to the absence of light. From the other side of the mosquito net, I saw a figure looking down on me. I smiled contentedly. He hadn't left.

"Baby," I cooed. "Come here."

He didn't move, though, but stood still, continuing to look at me from outside the net.

"Luc, is there something wrong?" I sat up in the bed. The linen sheet slid from my breasts as I reached over and parted the net.

All at once, I could see that it wasn't Luc standing on the other side of the net. It was my dead husband, Lee!

"Bitch!" he hissed and slapped me back onto the bed. "You fucking whore. You were supposed to be avenging us! Your family! But you're down here spreading your legs like a trifling 'ho. A skeezer!"

Lee struck me a second time and I fell back onto the bed. I found myself spread-eagled, strapped to the posts by leather thongs. Lee rose above me and ripped off the netting around the bed. He opened his mouth and spat blood all over me. I screamed. His bloody spit burned like acid.

"You slut!" Lee grabbed his male thang, which immediately grew into a long whip. He held it in his hand and snapped it. "Look at her!" he shouted to someone on the other side of the room. I looked to my right and saw Andrew and Ayesha, their eyes flaming with contempt at seeing their mother, naked and degraded.

"What is she?!" he demanded of them.

"A whore!" they cried. The cock-whip cut me across my chest, spewing more blood, burning my skin.

"Noooo!" Writhing in physical and emotional pain, I pleadingly looked at the creatures who were my children. "I'm your mother!"

Another slash stung my face and cut across my throat.

"Is she?!" my enraged husband countered. "Is she really a mother?"

"Noooo! She's a bitch in heat!!" the children screamed. "A slut!!"

Another slash stripped a layer of skin from my torso. I screamed louder and louder with each crack of the whip.

Drenched in sweat, I opened my eyes and saw Anna above me, gently trying to rouse me from my nightmare. She handed me a glass of water, which I drank greedily before gathering the courage to look around the room.

"Bad dream, huh?" She stood over me as I raised myself into a sitting position.

I was still completely confused and disoriented from the afternoon of intense lovemaking and the harrowing dream that followed. "Where's Luc? Is he gone?"

"Yes. He left about forty minutes ago," she replied. "He said he had to attend to some business at the ministry and that he would join us later for dinner."

I nodded my head in silence, allowing the news to register. Luc was a government official, after all; he did have to get back to work.

"I had a really horrible, horrible dream that Lee was here. He was whipping me, Anna."

"Oh God, Nina."

"And the children were here, too. They called me an unfit mother, said all sorts of terrible things. Jesus," I sighed, beginning to lift myself out of the bed. Anna handed me my robe, which was draped across a chair. She then turned her head, allowing me a moment of modesty.

"Thanks." I put on the robe and instinctively reached inside to touch my skin, to see if it had any welts. I couldn't find anything, at least nothing external. I'd had bad dreams about Lee and the children before, dreams of loss and vengeance, even guilt. But nothing like this. This one shook the very foundation of my being.

"A real bad one, huh?" Anna asked sympathetically.

I merely nodded and then trudged off to the bathroom for a cold, bracing shower.

Half an hour later we were sitting at the bar downstairs. Siesta was over and the cocktail session had begun. There were a few other patrons at the bar, seated at the tables, and the overhead ceiling fan was swishing and swirling the air about. It was cooler and generally quiet, only a low murmur of voices here and there. Salim, Doña Esperanza's right-hand man, was doing double duty as bartender, washing glasses, cleaning the counter, and attending to us and another couple at the bar. He was a small buzz of activity. I watched him attentively, trying to avoid the ugly truth that lurked beneath my dream.

"Nina, tell me what's going on." Anna's words jolted me from my revelries.

"The dream or with us being here?" I replied, sipping on a gin and tonic.

"Both. What's the deal? When I left you two, Luc was about to boot us out of the country," she said, then sipped her palm wine. "When I returned, it was obvious that a true pheromonal experience had taken place."

"It was that thick, huh?"

"Uh huh," she nodded seductively. "It was definitely your scent."

"Anna," I blushed. "What are you talking about?"

"I know your scent, buddy girl."

"I told him that I'd forget about my reasons for being here," I confessed reluctantly. "That I wanted to be with him. I told him that I'd forget about Ford being here."

"Then you had that dream."

"Yeah, and spare me the analysis, will you? You don't have to be a discredited Freudian to figure out the symbolism, either." I was trapped between two contradictory impulses: love and vengeance. And it was getting harder and harder to tell where one ended and the other began. Had my desire to find Nate Ford merely been a smokescreen to protect me from the fact that I had been disloyal to Lee? That I was still in love with Luc? Did I come to Misericordia to investigate Michael's death? Or did I really come here to find Luc again? To lose myself in his arms? Sure, I wanted to kill that son of a dick, Ford. But was that all there was to it? Lee and the children were gone, and I wanted something that memories and revenge couldn't provide. Lust? Love? Perhaps another chance at family? Was I missing something? Did I really want to be a mother again? And if I did, would I be betraying Lee and the children?

"Talk to me, Nina," interrupted Anna.

"Huh?" I turned and faced her.

"You zoned out," she said, lifting her drink to her lips. "*Que pasa?*"

"Maybe it's time for me to forget my quest for Ford," I replied quietly. "It's eating me up inside, warping me."

Anna stopped abruptly, her narrow, almond-shaped eyes widening to a size that I'd never seen before. "What did you say?"

"Maybe it's time for me to stop thinking about all this killing shit."

"Nina," said Anna, as she placed her hand on my forearm and began gently stroking it.

"I think what was troubling me about Claire was that I didn't want to deal with my own demons," I confessed. "I just feel—"

"Guilty," she finished, "about Lee and the kids?"

"Yes."

"Nina, I think Lee would like for you to go on with your life, to find someone and be happy."

"He didn't seem that way in my dream, Anna."

"That's because the Lee who appeared in your dream was *you* beating yourself, feeling guilty about Luc and punishing yourself," she reasoned. "I don't think it had anything to do with Lee and the way he would have felt, Nina."

"Maybe I have a thanatos thang," I replied.

"What?"

"Death," I explained. "I'm trying to deal with the memory of one dead man by looking for his killer, while trying to grasp a few fleeting moments with another man who says he's been marked for death. I mean, what the hell is that all about?"

Anna thought about it for a few seconds. "Well, you do have a tendency to emotionally complicate your life."

"Tell me about it," I replied to the obvious. "McFate."

I noticed that Salim was still busy with his work, lining the recently washed glasses in a neat row along the bar. He looked up, saw me looking at him, and smiled. He was a nice looking man. I smiled as he reached across the bar and picked up a newspaper that someone had left earlier. When he lifted the newspaper, I glimpsed a folded section of the newspaper's headline.

"Salim, may I see that for a second?" I pointed to the newspaper.

"Yes, ma'selle," he replied. When he handed the newspaper to me, our hands touched. Zzzzzz! A charge. I looked away, embarrassed, wondering if he had noticed it, too. I shook my head and tried to get on with business.

The headline read: "Murdered: Japanese Executive in Gay Love Tryst Gone Bad." There was a photo of a body, a pool of blood flowing out from the head. It was the kind of thing I was used to seeing as a former assistant district attorney. What caught my eye was the victim's exposed buttocks and the protruding black dildo. I thought immediately about Michael's death and what Archer had told me about the BF Boys. Had they struck again? I also remembered that Zee had written in her report that roughly twenty-five percent of EarthChem's stocks were owned by a Japanese firm. The firm was the dead man's employer. Was there a connection? I also found it intriguing that the story was written by my old friend, François Belancourt. François had left Misericordia two years earlier, when the junta exiled President Bernard. Apparently, he was back. If there was anyone who knew *le* 411, it was my friend François. I finished my drink and turned to Anna.

"Come on, let's get our purses and our passports," I said to her.

"What's up?"

"Shopping."

CHAPTER FIFTEEN

We crossed Liberation Plaza and found ourselves right smack in the middle of the Maerican multitude, a western hemispheric version of a West African village. Luckily, it was the end of the day, and the crowd had thinned out a bit from the midday rush. The remaining people were milling around the fountain of the Liberator. The peazant women were selling their fruits and cuts of goat and pig meat. Nearby stands offered cold guava, papaya juices, and tropical fruit drinks. Others featured various folk-art objects: African-Caribbean masks, charms, chickens for sacrifices, bracelets. In the midst of it all, the kill-and-go squads, Papas on motor scooters and jeeps, zipped ominously about the city.

Along the way to the offices of the newspaper, *Maerican Progres*, we were propositioned repeatedly by the island's male population. "*Mira*. Psst. *Hola, mamasitas! Chulpa mi pinga! Bonjour,* ma'selles."

The newspaper was housed in an old-style, sand-colored colonial building that looked as if it had absorbed numerous gunshots over the years. Two men stood at the door, looking more like bodyguards than agents of the state, and checked our passports as we entered. Things had degenerated to the point that the island had become an armed camp with everyone loading and locking their weapons, with armed thugs posing as government functionaries. Inside we were greeted by François' assistant, Gerard, who led us immediately to François' office.

"Nina, *ma chérie!*" exclaimed the ever-exuberant François, a tall, lanky man with heavily creased, black folds along his jaw line. A veteran in the fight to make his country a democratic, law-abiding republic, François had survived numerous bombings and assassination attempts, and had once had his stomach pumped for poison. He had left Misericordia after the first junta took over the country and exiled himself in Toronto.

"*Bon jour*, François," I responded, kissing him, Maerican-style, on both cheeks. "What the hell are you doing back here?"

He winked. "That's what I should be asking you, *ma chérie.*"

"François, this is my partner, Anna Gong," I introduced. "Anna, François Belancourt." He offered us chairs in his sparse office.

"Charmed," he replied, as he seated himself behind his paper-scattered desk. "So let's dispense with the usual tropical pleasantries, Nina. What the fuck are you doing here?"

I snapped open the newspaper and placed it on his desk. "I read the paper. Now tell me the real story."

"What's there to it?" he shrugged. "It's in black and white."

"Black and yellow," I replied, "with a dildo sticking out of his tush."

"Nina, your language," he teased. "I remember you as being more refined."

"And I remember you as being someone in the know," I shot back.

François looked at me sternly. "Close the door."

Anna leaned backwards in her chair and pushed the door closed, immediately silencing the clacking din of the old-fashioned newsroom typewriters.

"Okay, but first," began the newspaperman, "why do you want to know?"

"I'm investigating the assassination of Michael Debord, a

White House aide."

"And not the FBI?"

"I am the FBI."

"*Quel?*"

"Fierce. Black. Intrepid." I leaned near his desk. "I go where other bitches fear to tread." I snapped my fingers twice. "Give it up, brother."

"I would have said fine, beautiful, and intelligent," he replied.

"Oooh, you're making me sticky, *mon frere*."

He rattled out the story. Sadao Yamamoto, a financial officer for Nippon International Investments, was found dead at Voudouxland, a grotesque amusement park that catered to the popular racist caricature of Misericordia as a land of bone-in-the-nose voudoux priests and zombies. Yamamoto's body was found, as depicted in the newspaper, by an attendant at the waterfall in the park.

"What was he doing down here?" I asked.

"He was supposedly here on business. He had some meetings scheduled."

"With whom?"

"That I don't know," he responded. "But the police believe he was killed by someone from whom he'd solicited."

"Any suspects?"

"Not as of yet."

"But the police suspect that the murderer is gay?"

"Correct."

"Was Yamamoto known to have been gay?" I queried.

"Well," said François, rubbing his face, "that's what puzzles me."

"Yeah?"

"Yamamoto had been down here several times before and the inside story—substantiated by reliable sources—is that he wasn't into men at all."

"Could that have been a smokescreen? A cover?" asked Anna. "You know, some men want to hide their 'unnatural' urges."

François shrugged, rocked his head from side to side, and turned down the corners of his mouth. "Could have been."

"Maybe he was bi?" I tossed in.

"The rumor, which has been confirmed by my sources, was that he was into women—black women."

"The darker the berry—" I ruefully began.

"The sweeter the juice," finished François. "Exactly."

"Y'all talkin' black or whut?" asked Anna, her accent suddenly tinged with ghettoese.

"We're talking about yellow liking—licking, maybe—black," I replied, and then turned to François. "Anna is the cross-gender sexuality expert. A real kink specialist."

Anna flicked her tongue over her lips, and François suddenly became erotically focused on Anna, who was sitting across from him in her hot orange tank-top dress. He shifted his legs uncomfortably beneath his desk.

"Oh, really?" he said, as nonchalantly as possible.

"*Mais oui*," I replied. Anna shot a sharp glance out of the corner of her gorgeous Asian eyes. I had never noticed before just how fabulously long her lashes were. "François?"

"Huh?" His eyes were still fixed eagerly on Mademoiselle Gong.

"So if the deceased had a thing for women, what was he doing with a black, twelve-inch schtupp stuck up his tush?"

"Experimenting?" he suggested tentatively. "Who knows? Why are you asking me?"

"Well, you're supposed to be a newspaperman in the know." François and I had been friends for years. I had first met him while vacationing in Misericordia with Luc, and later as a human rights observer. I had also helped him when he arrived in New York after the junta. But in spite of our long-time friendship, I couldn't shake the feeling that my good brother was holding out on me. And that certainly wasn't a good thing for inter-African relations.

"François, what are you doing back here?" I decided on a slight detour to the truth.

"Ah," he said, relaxing, "General Malmundo wants to open up the nation."

"To democracy?"

"Correct. And you can't do that without a free press. At

first I was reluctant, but Luc Malmundo assured me that the new government was serious about changes."

"Changes without allowing the duly elected president to regain his office and finish out his term?"

"That," said François, shifting in his chair, "is a problem that is currently being addressed."

"Nina and I met the general this afternoon," said Anna. "And the man didn't seem at all predisposed to share his power with President Bernard."

"When did this discussion take place with El Generalissimo?" he asked without the slightest veil of contempt.

"After the botched kidnapping attempt at the airport. We were the targets," I informed him. "An eyewitness account, François."

He sighed. "Yes, of course. PLAM! They are merely a nuisance."

"The situation here has reached a critical stage," I disagreed. "Armed resistance, François."

François flicked his hand in the air. "Amateurs," he scoffed. "These people know nothing about military tactics, and they are hardly a force against the army."

"Excuse me, François, but when has the army ever gone up against anyone with the will to fight back? Hmmm?"

He paused for a moment. "What are you driving at?"

"Competition," I simply answered. "Fierce, armed competition. Live ammo."

"PLAM! is merely a nuisance," he repeated.

"You're beginning to sound like a White House mouthpiece."

"Meaning what?" he said, visibly annoyed that I would challenge his journalistic integrity.

"You sound like a flak for a disreputable policy—not a newspaperman interested in the truth, the facts!"

"Look!" he informed us, "I'm living in a country that's on the brink of war, and I don't have time to entertain two American tarts!"

"Tarts?" echoed Anna. "What is that supposed to mean?"

"Code for bitches," I said out of the side of my mouth.

"Sounds like 'ho to me," she replied, looking sternly at François.

"Take it any way you want, ladies," he said without apology. "Now if you don't have any further questions."

He was hot. Pissed. Completely off-balance. I decided this might be a good time to press for information. "Yamamoto's death has something to do with EarthChem, doesn't it?" I pressed further. "Or should I say the Butt Fuck Boys? Isn't Peltrano a business partner of General Malmundo?"

The lines in François' face suddenly deepened. "Nina, there are things going on—"

"That much I know, old friend!" I tersely replied. "You have a dead Japanese businessman whose firm has invested in Earth-Chem, a big player in determining the policy of your country. I happen to know that EC owns Jeff Benton's balls. But I'm still missing some connections. If there's anybody who knows anything around here, it's you, François!"

"Go home, Nina—both of you," he said wearily. "You don't know what—"

I rose from my chair and pressed my body against his desk. "Just who are you frontin' for?"

"Somebody who cares about you deeply," he replied. "Now please leave. I have a newspaper to put out!"

With that, François booted us out of his office.

We walked around the old part of town, looking at the architecture, as well as the people and merchants on the street. Everywhere we went, we saw Papas stopping and searching people. Men were being thrown against walls and frisked without warning. Many young women were openly groped and molested by these militarish thugs.

"Open season on bitches," I ruefully noted.

We continued along a street that slowly dissolved from pavement into dirt, walked down a slightly steep hill, and found ourselves passing out of the city. Soon we had made it to the beach, the shore of sanity, the Caribbean. We took off our shoes and waded through the warm water. The white sand of the beach snaked its way for miles toward the horizon. The sun was slowly descending in the western sky. With the city behind us, blocked by a thick growth of leafy palm trees, Misericordia, the land of mercy, finally lived up to its name.

For a few minutes we walked along, laughing, splashing water, picking up shells and listening to them. The troubles and worries of the past few days disappeared. All that remained was the vision of the sea on the horizon and the sound of the waves in my ears. The reflection of the sun skipped carelessly across the surface of the water, shimmering its red-jeweled brilliance.

"God, Nina," said my friend. "It's so beautiful here."

"They don't call this place the Big Mango for nothing." My mind was reacting to the in-and-out rhythm of the waves. Should I go or stay? Find Ford or remain safe and secure with Luc? Continue investigating EarthChem or enjoy my vacation? And what was the EarthChem-Yamamoto connection, anyway? Was I just shooting in the dark?

We spent another half hour on the beach and then took a circuitous route back to the inn. By the time we reached the city, the mood had changed completely—and for the better. The air had cooled enough to make playing and partying a non-exhaustive affair. Families were parked outside of shacks and buildings, the insides of which were still too hot for comfort. *Congeros* were huddled on corners, playing rhumbas and mambos, while dancers moved rhythmically to the beat. Couples strolled along, snatching kisses as they stopped at corners, while street *urcheros* returned to hawking the things they had lifted earlier from tourists on the street. Everywhere I looked, people were enjoying themselves. An outrageous idea, under the circumstances. But here they were, having fun for all the world to see.

As we crossed the plaza, Anna noticed a woman seated in a chair selling paintings, her head tied with a colorful yellow, red, and green bandanna.

"Art inspection," she announced, linking her arm with mine and pulling me along. I wasn't going to resist. Art is good for the soul, I reasoned. Besides, girlfriend had been a good soldier since we got here and she deserved whatever pleasure she could find in this land stinking of mendacity.

The woman was unmistakably of the peazant class and displayed all the characteristics of such: studious suspicion and indifference to anyone who was a *blanc*, which included both of us. Her large eyes were partly shut, both to keep out the sun, I thought, and to prevent others from knowing what was on her mind. She was probably once a very pretty island girl, and she was still a sensuous, if somewhat chunky, woman. But her travails as a migrant to the city had clearly taken their toll. She looked tired and exhausted. Several paintings were stacked against one another in front of fruit crates that were on either side of the chair in which she sat. She struck me as an imperious island art queen, waiting patiently for her subjects to come and buy her wares.

Anna carefully examined the two separate stacks of paintings. She scrutinized them closely for texture, holding them at arm's distance. I was dragooned into playing the role of a freestanding wall: she had me hold up the paintings below my chin and then stepped away to view them at eye level. Most of the paintings were of fieldworkers cutting sugar cane. Each was painted in the classic Maerican style of a flat perspective, bright and colorful. However, she zeroed in on a portrait: a man with a child on each knee, a boy and a girl.

"Excuse me," Anna said to the woman. "Are you the artist?"

The old woman cocked her head toward her inquirer and placed a hand over her face to block out the declining rays of the sun. "*Oui*," she said in a very thick Kreole accent. "*Vous* like?"

Anna smiled, nodded, and pulled out some money, the universal language. "Yes. *Oui*. Me buy. How much?"

The woman looked at Anna, then me. "Ten Merikan dollars."

"Sold," said Anna, handing the woman her money.

"Me got *beaucoup*, ma'selle."

"Hmmm. I'll be back tomorrow. You here tomorrow?"

"Maybe," she said with a shrug, placing the money in a wallet that hung from around her neck by a black leather thong and then slipping the wallet beneath her old but immaculately clean red dress.

"Okay, then maybe I will," Anna replied. "Maybe I won't. Ciao."

Anna picked up the painting, and we crossed the plaza and turned the corner onto rue Liberté. Anna was so excited about her first island purchase, and I was so zoned out from the day's events, that we didn't hear the jeep that had rolled up on the sidewalk behind us, until it suddenly screeched to a halt.

"*Arr'te*! Stop! *Alto*!"

Three Papas jumped out of the vehicle quicker than an NYPD street-crime unit. Only a few doors down from Casa de Esperanza, we had suddenly been descended upon by tropical gangstas, with their perfunctory dark suits, trouser legs tucked into black boots, rakishly angled fedoras, and sunglasses. Smelling of beer, tobacco, and curried goat, the men arrogantly brandished their firearms in front of us.

"Passport!" one of them snapped. The man who addressed us, I assumed, was in charge, since he carried a pistol tucked in his waist instead of an assault rifle. The other two kept their Uzis trained steadily on us. One had a large cigar in his mouth and the other appeared to be smoking a marijuana blunt.

Mindful of the circumstances that have led to many a brother's untimely removal from the earth by the NYPD, I gingerly reached into the purse that hung diagonally across my shoulder, pulling out two passports and handing them to our interrogator.

"What are you doing with two passports?!" the knucklehead demanded in a Kreole accent, not even bothering to look at the passports. "Speak up!"

Anna and I exchanged nervous glances. We realized that our situation was potentially dangerous. Apparently, so did everyone else on the island. A small crowd was gathering at a respectful distance, and people were looking out from shop windows and doorways.

"Two people," I said calmly, pointing to Anna and myself. "Two passports, Monsieur Officer."

He finally opened one of the passports. I could tell right away that he didn't like the look of us. We were two *blancs*, after all, and this was his chance to humiliate us the way Maericans had always been humiliated by Americans. He read the passports and barked out our names. And each of us answered, calmly but measuredly. He snapped the little booklets shut and deposited them inside his coat pocket. "You will, of course, be searched."

"For what?" I asked testily.

"Weapons," he leered, and dropped his eyes to the two threatening missiles that I now sensed were his real objective: my breasts. He saw before him a hot, well-toned black woman, and he had only one thing on his mind. These guys were shining examples of the Papas' tough but underpaid kill-and-go squads, and extortion and rape were the perks of their trade. If Anna had been caught by herself, I could easily have imagined them holding her down and tearing through her dress with a knife, cutting off her panties with the flick of a blade. I shuddered to think of it but quickly regained my composure.

I looked straight at the man in charge. "Don't even think about it."

In response, he pulled out his revolver, a big, blue-black .357, and placed its barrel on my upper lip, right below my right nostril. The other men steadied their fingers on the triggers of their weapons. They were grinning uncontrollably. This was their routine. First the public humiliation, then they take you into custody and rape you in seclusion.

"You are a foreigner and have a subversive attitude, Ma'selle Gong!"

Okay, I thought, get out of this, girl. "She's Gong," I nodded in Anna's direction. "I'm Halligan. Nina Halligan."

"You will respect and obey the laws of this country!" he snapped, hitting me in the face with his spittle. "Hands up! Now!"

Anna, still holding onto her picture, now a quaint momento of a brief interlude of pleasure, looked nervously to me for direction. I nodded my head despairingly. There was nothing we could do—nothing that I could do. This nigga had no compunction about feeding me a bronze slug. Anna let go of her picture reluctantly, and we both raised our hands. The head moe had already tucked his weapon into the front of his pants and was ready to violate me with his claws, when his concentration was suddenly interrupted by the sound of a disapproving female voice, the sound of the universal mother.

"What is the meaning of this?!"

I glanced out of the corner of my eye. Doña Esperanza confidently approached the scene of our intended defilement and boldly wedged her body through the circle of onlookers.

"What are you doing to these women?" she barked into the leader's face. One of the Papas tried to grab her by the shoulders, but she tossed off his grip with a single, forceful shake.

"Don't touch me, you dog!" she snarled at him, and then directed her attention back to our chief tormentor. "You have no right to treat these women this way! As if they were common criminals. They are visitors to our country. Spending their money and keeping you employed!"

"This is a police matter!" said the Papa. "And of no concern to you, Doña Esperanza!"

"I will not have you terrorize my guests." she defiantly fired back. "I demand their release now!"

The head moe was about to respond when a giant shadow fell across his shoulder and onto my face. He turned immediately around to face a giant who appeared at first glance to be as wide and solid as the buildings lining the street. Without uttering a word, the giant picked the man up by his gun hand and lifted him off his feet. The giant then took the gun from the man's hand and placed it in his over-sized pocket.

"Just what are you doing, you fool?!" asked the giant.

The Papa, dangling from the air, grimaced. "Suspects were seen—"

With his other hand, the giant whacked the man several times in the face. "Monkey cunt! Do you know who you've insulted? Do you?!" He smacked the man around like a punching bag, his fist almost twice the size of the man's face. "This woman is Prosecutor Halligan! How dare you treat a real black woman like a common bandit. Like the common bitches you stick your nose into. You've embarrassed my force, you jackass!" he boomed.

Anna and I watched as the Papa took a public shellacking from the huge man. The other two Papas had lowered their weapons and stepped back from us, apparently trying to disassociate themselves from their boss. I felt Anna's hand on my forearm. Blood splattered everywhere, as the man's face was pummeled again and again.

From what I had learned since I arrived, the giant was obviously Commissioner André Hobson. At first, I couldn't figure out why he was protecting us or how he knew me. But then I remembered my reputation as a minor folk hero in the Maerican community back in New York. In the days before the coup, I had successfully prosecuted two cops who'd viciously beaten a Maerican taxi-cab driver in Brooklyn. François, I now remembered, had written about the trial when he came to visit New York. Apparently my good deeds had not been forgotten here in Misericordia—at least not by the commissioner.

Finally finished, Hobson tossed the bloodied man over his shoulder to one of his comrades, like a wet rag. "You dogs have insulted a genuine black woman. A woman who has brought honor to our people in America! Dogs! I ought to..." The man withdrew an even bigger and blacker gun than the Uzis sported by the Papas—a mack daddy cannon!

"Noo!!" I shouted at once, trying to lower his gun as I did. His arm felt like a steel crane.

"This isn't necessary, Commissioner. Please!"

Relenting, he told the two men to get back to headquarters and to take their newly stricken comrade with them. "And if I don't find you back at headquarters, remember that I know where your parents live and how many sisters you have. Get out of my sight! You monkey cunts!"

After our passports were returned to us, the bloodied body was deposited roughly into the jeep and driven away. The light-skinned giant removed his bowler and revealed a bald head. He wore a black patch over his right eye. Unlike his men, he wore a white suit coat over dark trousers, along with a bow tie. He was one suave merchant of death.

"I'm sorry for this embarrassing display of unprofessionalism, Counselor Halligan," he said as he shook my hand.

I couldn't figure out if he was referring to his men's behavior toward us or his own vicious response. "Ah, well. I thank you—for coming to our rescue. Com—"

Before I could finish, he whipped out a card, gallantly kissed my hand, and placed the card in it.

"I'd be honored if you'd call me Dre and dine with me while you're here." He returned his hat to his head, turned, and climbed into a black Mercedes. "I hope you will accept my invitation."

As his car pulled away from the curb, Doña Esperanza walked over and spat where the car had been parked. She then approached me, snatched the card from my hand, and tore it to pieces.

"Butcher!" she said.

She looked at Anna and me for a moment and then pulled us away from the scene and back to the comfort of her inn. I sized up the situation at once. Hobson was a dangerous man, who, if we let him, would eventually cause us harm or get us killed. But Doña Esperanza was a guardian, who would protect us from danger. She was a sister's sister.

CHAPTER SIXTEEN

"We are not a land of savages and brutes," explained Doña Esperanza as she escorted us to our rooms. "True, we have our problems, and things were better when Pepe was here as president. And they have been hell since he's been gone. But we have always survived."

As she led us to our room, the woman explained, apologized, and sighed about her land of mercy. I already knew the story but felt that she was telling it primarily for another set of ears, Anna's. I was picking up a lower level vibration between the two. I walked behind them as Esperanza spoke to both of us. She looked over her shoulder at me when addressing us, but I got the distinct feeling that she was trying to sell something to Anna, swaying her hips the same way I would have been doing if I wanted to get a man's attention.

Esperanza was a full-bodied woman with a café-au-lait brown complexion and mixed features: dark eyes, thick black hair, Castillian nose, high cheekbones, and full Negrita lips. Imagine a mature but still-luscious Jennifer Lopez. I liked her immediately. The woman obviously had status, even with the

Papas, and she wasn't afraid to intercede on our behalf. I was also intrigued by the knowledge that Esperanza was a flamenco dancer. It was a dance form that I greatly admired, that exuded a unique combination of elegance, sexuality, and restraint. Earlier, I had noticed a small sign in the lobby announcing one of her forthcoming performances.

"Now we have a mixed blessing," she said as we reached my door.

"What's that?" I asked, sliding my key into the hole.

"Commissioner Hobson stepped in and helped you, but that also means that he'll be around here to see if you're all right," Esperanza answered.

"And we gather that you don't approve of his presence," said Anna.

The woman lowered her eyes and then looked up at us with a very tight smile: "No." She clasped her hands tightly together.

Looking at her, I got the sense that she was hiding a story of deep pain in which the commissioner was a leading player. "Thank you, Doña Esperanza," I said.

"Please, Esperanza," she smiled, looking at both of us, though her gaze rested longer on Anna. Turning away, I noticed something pinned to the door: a stuffed voudoux doll with a photocopy of my face on its head. I pulled it quickly off the door, before the other two noticed it.

Anna thanked Esperanza again and we both entered my room. I picked up an envelope of messages that had been slid underneath the door and tossed the doll into the trashcan. I knew who sent the doll. He clearly wanted me to know that he knew I was in town, looking for his ass.

"Did you see how big that fuckin' gun was?" Anna exclaimed as soon as we closed the door.

"Which one? I had one in my face that was big enough for me." I kicked off my sandals and flopped onto the bed. Anna hadn't noticed the doll.

"Nina, these fuckers are crazy down here!" announced Anna as she went into her room through the suite door to deposit her painting. "How do these people put up with this shit?!" She began cursing in Chinese.

I lay on the bed and thought about everything that had happened: my dream, the Papas, François, Luc, EarthChem, the sex, the heat, and now the doll. I then caught a whiff of a familiarly pungent aroma. I looked up and saw Anna with a joint in her mouth. She was about to open the window. "Anna, are you crazy?"

"Hey, your new boyfriend wouldn't mind," she said, referring to Hobson, as she slid open the door to the garden. Anna walked to the center of the room and pulled on the cord to the ceiling fan. She then joined me on the bed, where she took off her shoes. I sat, raising myself to my elbows, and took a long drag.

"What do you think?" asked Anna.

"Me no wanna t'ink," I said. "What do you t'ink about Esperanza?"

Anna shrugged and turned down her mouth slightly. "Not my type."

"What?" I was surprised. I thought she had zeroed in on Esperanza.

"Doesn't do a thing for me," she said, after letting out some air. "Nice looking woman, but she's *your* type of black woman."

"Oh? My type of black woman?"

"Yeah. FBI."

"Well, she did step up to the plate—God bless her. I don't have any problems with that."

"Neither do I—but she ain't my type. Too butch."

"Butch?" I echoed incredulously. "Butch?"

"Yeah, but you know what?"

"I'm listening," I said, while reading the contents of the envelopes I'd opened.

"I think she likes *you*." She giggled like an idiot at her own joke. Good, I thought. It was better than seeing her cry or having her inquire about the doll. Still, I regarded her newfound mirthfulness a bit skeptically.

Mustapha had left a message. I went over to my bag on the night table and pulled out my digital phone. I then went into the bathroom and returned with nothing on but a light terrycloth robe. "I have a call to make, Anna."

"Okay," Anna said, placing the joint between her lips and re-igniting it. Let her get silly, I thought. In less than twenty-four hours time, we almost bought the farm twice.

Opening the screen door, I stepped into a small tropical garden and discovered that it was refreshingly cool but also humid. Walking down the path, I noticed an incredible array of tropical vegetation. Because I had been smoking, my senses were more acute, and my eyes were mesmerized by the brilliant displays of red, yellow, green, and orange. Everything seemed alive, pulsating with a lush, tropical vibrancy that I'd heretofore ignored. I felt like a mad botanist, carefully examining the leaves, petals, and stems of each plant.

I proceeded down the path and walked into a conical hut that was covered with interwoven coconut palm leaves. With two high walls on either side, the hut allowed me the privacy to disrobe. I hung up the garment and placed the phone on a small service table near the edge of the small tub. I then sank into the warm water and let out a sigh. Picking up the phone, I placed a call to New York.

Mustapha had turned over the documents that I had gotten from Fanon—the documents that she was to have given Michael the night of his murder and that had been taken from the American scientists captured by PLAM!—and they had been analyzed by an expert. Apparently, a very unique plant— the Bimbao tree—transported from Africa by slaves during the colonial period had taken root in the Misericordia clime. Its trunk and limbs were used for shelter and its roots for medicine, and the leaves as well as the roots were edible. The Bimbao was also considered sacred by the local population; it was used in voudoux ceremonies and was credited as being the source of "zombie power." This meant that the *hungan*, male priest, or *mambo*, female priestess, used it to place other people under their spell. Outside of the local population, of course, this practice had long been discounted as the stupid gibberish of "superstitious Negroes."

But the Bimbao tree also had some other interesting properties. Representatives of one American firm noticed the potential of Bimbao during the "*konchon krisis*," a swine-flu epidemic that had recently swept through the Caribbean, eradicating almost the entire porcine population of many of the islands. The nations affected by the crisis were forced to buy American pigs fed exclusively on U.S. grain, costing much more than the small-scale, subsistence farmers on the islands could possibly afford. Misericordia was the exception. Only twenty-five percent of its pigs had been affected, and those that did die were owned by the wealthy farmers who had raised their livestock on American grain. The peazants had fed their livestock garbage mixed with Bimbao roots and leaves. The firm that had noticed the heartiness of the Maerican pigs was EarthChem, the same company that was selling grains to the other Caribbean farmers—and now the Maerican farmers.

After careful analysis, EarthChem discovered that the Bimbao tree—in addition to inoculating livestock from disease (and thereby keeping the peazant classes alive)—had a genetic make-up that allowed it to be crossed with other plants to increase crop yields.

"Well," I said, expectantly. "Is that all?"

"Yes," said Mustapha after reading me the expert's report.

"Okay, let me get this straight. EarthChem's been experimenting with the plant. Finds that it can be crossed with others to provide greater crop yields. And? Duh?"

"Are you looking for a motivator? A more exact reason for Mr. Debord's death?" asked Mustapha.

"Well," I said, noticing that my toes were sticking out of the water at the opposite end of the tub, "I'm trying to figure out the connection. How would that cause Michael's death? I mean, he was investigating something connected to EarthChem. He felt that when Stone came aboard the administration's policy changed toward Misericordia. But why? What is the deal with EarthChem? What about this Yamamoto?"

"Now, that is interesting, sister," said Mustapha. "Yamamoto's firm, Nippon Investment International, has millions of dollars—almost a billion dollars, in fact—invested in EarthChem."

"And he winds up dead. That still isn't telling me very much," I sighed. "Okay. How are things with you? Have you heard from—?"

"Zee? Indirectly," he answered. "Ibrahim is coming from Paris to talk to me."

"About what?"

"Nina! Has the sun baked your head? About him and Zee! The young man is approaching me honorably. He wants to talk to the father of his bride to be," said Mustapha.

"Okay, but don't do anything rash."

"Rash? Why should I make my daughter unhappy before her marriage?"

"Oh," I said. "No reason, Colonel. Glad things are going well. If you come up with anything—"

I was about to hang up, but a thought occurred to me. "Hold it. There's a person who might be able to give you some more information about EarthChem."

I told Mustapha to contact the Rev. Neil Vandersall, the pastor of Fort Greene Presbyterian Church in (the People's Republic of) Brooklyn. The Rev. Vandersall, a former labor activist, was the chair of an interdenominational, grassroots organization that was scorned by libertarians and freetraders, the Interfaith Network Alliance (IFNA). IFNA monitored sweatshops and the new economic world order of cheap labor. He could direct me to someone who knew the 411 about EarthChem and its funny business.

"Oh, the two men who tried to kill you?" Mustapha added before the conversation ended. "Contract killers, with a specialty in industrial espionage."

Now *that* was interesting, very interesting. I placed the phone back on the tray and submerged my head beneath the warm water.

Anna and I met Luc for dinner downstairs. Casually dressed in a blue linen blazer and khaki slacks, he apologized for leaving me, telling me that he had a meeting at the ministry of education that he had to attend. I didn't say anything about our little misunderstanding with the kill-and-go squad—and not a word about Hobson. Salim escorted us to the dining area, which was packed with people. A guitarist named Flugo was playing flamenco. I remembered the sign I had read in the lobby earlier; he would be accompanying Esperanza.

We were served cocktails—each of us had a seafood appe-tizer—and we chatted about the day's events, though somewhat selectively. Anna described the woman from whom she had pur-chased the painting.

"Oh, Mama LaRue," said Luc. He then sighed.

"Local fixture?" I asked.

"She used to be a big *mambo*," said Luc, forking a large shrimp. He looked at Anna and translated, "A *mambo* is a voudoux priestess."

"You said 'used to be,' Luc," I replied. "What happened?"

"Well, voudoux has always been controversial here. If the church isn't trying to suppress it, then the state is trying to use it for its own purposes. Triomphe was famous for trying that tactic as a means of building his base. Anyway, they can be a highly independent lot, the priests, and they should be. They have to answer to the *loa*—"

"What's that?" said Anna.

"The god spirit of a particular power," Luc answered. "The *orishas*. They have to be careful about not allowing themselves to be used by corrupters."

"And Mama LaRue was incorruptible?" I said.

"And she paid a price for not toeing the Triomphe line. Her *humfo*, her site of worship, was closed down. Then when Bernard took power, he allowed Protestant ministers to run roughshod over the voudoux *hungans* and *mambos*," explained Luc. "By the time my father took over, it was too late. Mama LaRue had been out of the scene for so long she had lost her fol-lowing. When she tried to get it back, it was gone, dispersed; others had taken over as *hungans* and *mambos*.

"I don't suppose," I asked, remembering the cute little call-ing card that had been pinned to my door, "that one of the new *hungans* is Oscar Peltrano?"

Luc looked at me for a second before answering. "He's the big daddy now—and feared by all believers."

"Now she just paints and sells in the plaza?" Anna asked.

"The rumor is that she is waiting for her special *loa* to come alive," Luc replied. "A special person will come and intercede—

and give her back her position."

"Maybe I'll check her out again tomorrow," mused Anna. "I like her paintings."

"Just be careful about what you bring into your space," warned Luc.

"Why?" I asked.

"You might be getting something you didn't bargain for in the process."

"Luc, you don't believe in this superstition?" I teased. "My God, you have a doctorate."

"It's not a superstition," he said. "It's the basis of this island's religion. It's part of our heritage as a New World African people. It's part of the Yoruba religion, and everywhere the Yoruba have been in the New World, you find some permutation of that religion. We don't have the kind of identity problems that you have up in the States."

"What do you mean by that?" I felt my brow furrowing.

Luc took a sip of his cerveza and placed the glass down. "What do we call ourselves this year: Colored? Negro? Black? Afro-Americans? African-Americans? The bourgeoisie getting upset about young people using the N-word, but not really doing anything to alleviate the social condition that allows that word to become fertile. Is it multiculturalism or Afrocentrism? Is it affirmative action or black self-empowerment? We do have a certain advantage here. We *are* a black nation, and we don't make any bones about being an African-based people with European and Indian bloods. On the other hand, as the education minister, I have to fight people who refuse to recognize that the language that is spoken by ninety percent of the nation—Kreole—is a legitimate language and should be taught in our elementary schools, more so than French, Spanish, or English."

"Why is there resistance to Kreole," asked Anna, "if ninety percent of the people speak it?"

"Because anything that has an African base," Luc replied, "or anything that has an African origin, that is seen as black or predominantly black, is deemed inferior."

"You know," said Anna, who had chewed the last morsel of oxtail and crossed her knife and fork on her plate, "this sounds like the controversy regarding Ebonics."

"No, it doesn't" I countered. "Ebonics isn't a language, and they were talking about teaching it. Give me a break."

Luc said nothing for a few seconds and continued with his beer. He then focused on me. "So, you actually read the statement from the Oakland School District?"

"No. I read the press reports—"

"But you didn't read what they, the school district, had written in their resolution?"

I thought for a second and realized that I had not read the statement. As an attorney, I was supposed to do my research. And on this, I clearly hadn't. I had merely accepted what the press had reported. "No, I didn't."

"Well," said Luc, "as an educator, I've taken the time to familiarize myself with the issue. I had my assistant call California, and they faxed me the statement."

"And?" said Anna.

"All the charges by the press about Oakland teaching Ebonics are false. Granted, there are a couple of passages that do read as if such were the intent, but the statement consistently emphasized that the whole point of Ebonics was to teach students how to become proficient in standard and conventional English!"

"So what happened? If what you say is true, how did it get blown out of proportion?" I asked.

"Simple. Anything that has to do with black people becomes another example of black pathology. If you suggest black methods to black problems, you are accused, God forbid, of being a nationalist or a separatist," he argued. "I read accounts on the editorial page of the *New York Times* that would not pass a basic journalism course! They patently distorted the contents of the original document. There's one idiot who writes in a section called 'Editorial Notebook' of the *Times* whom I honestly don't think is capable of reading. And then the people who do understand this, the linguists, are not given a chance to have their views heard. But you see, that's the beauty of it. When it comes to blacks, you can have an opinion that isn't based on any knowledge, just your prejudice. Since blacks don't have a history, you don't have to understand their past; it never existed."

"If I wanted to know more about this, where should I start?" I asked. "What should I read?"

"I have a good book for you," he answered, stirring his coffee. Luc craned his neck and looked at the stage. "Looks as if things are about to get hot. They're bringing out an extra chair."

"Luc, the book," I reminded him. I had a pencil ready to take down the title.

"You won't need that," he said. "It's called *The Politics of Education*."

I volunteered the name of the author before he could tell me. "Written by Luc Malmundo."

Luc smiled. "I wished I had. No, *chica*. By Lee Halligan. Are you sisters ready? It's show time."

Now I really felt like a royal dummy. No wonder I was dreaming about my late husband whipping my ass. I hadn't even read his work. We moved from the back of the dining area and sat at the bar to get a closer look at the performance. The place was more crowded now. As the performance began, Luc explained to us that Esperanza was a leading exponent of a new dance style called Flamenco Noire.

The guitarist started off slowly during dinner, playing ballads and soothing us with his precise and delicate strumming. But as the dining ended, the tempo of the music picked up. He had begun to sing vigorously in a style that evoked the Arabic influence on Spanish culture, and rapidly strummed the guitar and stomped his feet.

Flugo was a dashing figure, with shoulder-length dreads and his brilliant white shirt and black vest crisscrossed with irregular gold stripes. He kept his classical guitar upright in the prescribed manner, the bottom resting in his lap, and shook his head fiercely when emphasizing a note. Periodically, he would stop playing entirely and beat on the wooden bottom of the guitar in a 6/8 pattern that was a signature time of West Africa, my ancestors' old neighborhood.

Listening to him play, I could easily understand what Luc meant by Flamenco Noire. Flugo remained within the distinctive flamenco style, but he also embellished certain chords and patterns with a "flash of the spirit" that was rhythmically African. He sung in Spanish, but he evoked the names of Legba, Damballah, Ogun, Osun, Obatala, Shango—and the one and only Olódùmarè, as God is known in Yoruba.

Esperanza entered the stage dancing forcefully to the rhythm. She wore a simple white peazant's blouse that broke at her shoulders and a full skirt with a floral pattern. Atop her head was a hair comb, her homage to Spain, and her feet were encased in black cha-cha heels. She kept time with a shaker and the crowd, obviously "natives," clapped, cheered, and shouted her name. Flugo stopped playing abruptly, and Esperanza took a seat beside him. I looked at Flugo and saw that he was a very handsome man. He was darker than Esperanza, but there was a strong facial resemblance between the two, and an intimate familiarity between them as they spoke before proceeding.

I tapped Luc on the shoulder and he turned his head. "*Sí?*"

"Are they related?" I asked, pointing to them on the stage.

"Brother and sister. She's older. Gypsy, Flugo's nickname, is her kid brother."

Flugo began playing and Esperanza stood up once again, her carriage erect and her head tilted upward. She lifted her skirt and began rhythmically dancing, stamping her feet. I noticed an anklet of cowrie shells. Her movements sounded like gunfire, quick bursts of staccato passion, as she swirled and turned, stepping away from her imagined suitor. She kept *clave*, time, with her hands and sang in a dark, full-throated voice. For the first forty-five minutes, the two performed traditional and *nuevo* flamencos. Eventually, they turned up the heat and slipped into Africa. Flugo began beating on the bottom of the guitar, and Esperanza began rolling her shoulders and undulating her pelvis in a provocative manner that was the antithesis of flamenco restraint.

Instead of placing her hands in the air or above her head, Esperanza placed them on her hips, rolled her shoulders, and made several sweeping arcs with her legs. She swooped down with her torso and then back up. She raised her skirt, sashayed around the stage, and then spun around, finally relaxing into a classical stance as Flugo began playing flamenco.

I had seen flamenco and had danced some forms of African dances as a student, but I had never seen the two combined. Esperanza's fluidity clearly demonstrated her comfort in being a New World amalgamation of African, European, and Indian. It was something that we sophisticated Americans — black, white, Latino, Asian, and Native — simply couldn't accept. That we, too, were a mixed people. Cultural bombs were being dropped on me right and left. Fuck multiculturalism, I thought. This has always been about kreolism!

An hour later, when the music had ended, Esperanza had removed the comb in her hair, and her rich black locks had fallen to her shoulders. The woman had kicked off her shoes and was doing an encore in her bare feet, switching quickly from castanets to shaker to tambourine. When the crowd stood and clapped for more, brother and sister bowed. Esperanza picked up one of her shoes and tossed it in our direction. The woman who caught it had only hours earlier said that Esperanza wasn't her type. By now, however, Anna was smitten and smoldering. Luc commented that he had never seen Esperanza dance with so much intensity and passion. I looked over at Anna, who had slipped off her shoe and was trying on Esperanza's.

"Perfect fit," she said, holding onto my shoulder for balance. "Guess that means I have to try on the other one."

CHAPTER SEVENTEEN

It looked as if everyone I cared about was getting ready to do *le nasté*. Esperanza would keep Anna occupied while I took Luc up to my room. Great, I thought, until a telephone call for him suddenly interrupted my plans.

"What?!" I erupted the moment he finished the call and I saw the worried look on his face.

"*Chica*, don't hit me," he said. "Something came up that I have to take care of."

"Luc, can't it wait?" I pressed closer to him, my leg rubbing against his crotch. Behind us, Esperanza and Anna were communicating perfectly without uttering a word. I was beginning to wish that Luc and I could cut out all the talk and get down to pleasure.

"*Chica*," he said, pulling my hands up to his face and kissing them. "I will join you tonight. I promise."

"Just be there, nigga," I said petulantly. "I want to wake up with you, Luc. Now go and serve your country, my love."

Luc touched my face for a moment and then was gone.

Anna, however, was still talking to Esperanza. I sat down at the bar and ordered another drink. When Salim brought my order, he also brought me the telephone. I thought he was getting cute, teasing me about having lost Luc for the evening, until I realized that I had a call, too.

"Hello," I said before sipping the gin and tonic.

"Nina Halligan?"

"The one and only—and presently lonely."

"I heard you're looking for some info on Yamamoto."

Hold everything, I thought. "Who am I speaking to?"

"A friend," said the male voice on the other end of the line. It sounded familiar but not American.

"Okay. I'm listening."

"Not over the phone. This country is a police state. I'll meet you somewhere."

I hesitated. The word "set-up" suddenly flashed through my mind. "How do I know you're a friend?"

"Because Sam Archer said you were a lady who could use some help."

"Okay," I said, deciding to take the bait. "Where?"

"At the Hôtel Nestoire. Outside the restrooms at Club Carib. Get on the phone and I'll call you. Be there at 11:15." He hung up.

I looked at my watch. It was a quarter to 10. I heard Anna and Esperanza laughing behind me.

"What's up, ladies?" I said.

"Esperanza is going to change her clothes and then we're thinking about seeing La Bomba at the Hôtel Nestoire," said Anna. "Interested?"

"Yeah, maybe," I replied matter-of-factly. Talk about coincidence.

"I won't be long," Esperanza addressed us both.

"Need any help?" asked Anna.

The two of them were getting to be a bit much.

"No," answered the more mature of the two. "I won't be long." She ran her fingers through her hair, revealing the gray swath that I'd noticed earlier. As she left us, Esperanza casually stroked Anna's arm. I watched the two of them exchange amorous glances, realizing that I was envious. In spite of all my plans with Luc, it looked as if Anna had a much better chance of getting laid than I did.

The room erupted into a round of applause as Esperanza passed through the crowd. The men kissed her hand and the women embraced her. "*Opa!*" "*Bravo!*" "*Viva Esperanza!*"

I turned to Anna, whose eyes were greedily devouring every move that Esperanza made. "Of course, she isn't *your* type.

"Funny thing," she began, "I really thought she had the hots for you, but you picked it, Nina. You got the knack, girl." She punched my arm playfully; a broad, self-satisfied smile stretched across her face. "What's with the luscious one?"

"Had an emergency educational situation," I reported. "So he sez."

"Doubt it?"

"I'll only get suspicious if he doesn't wake up with me on top of him," I confided. "Listen, someone called me at the bar and told me to meet him at the Club Carib."

"A lead?"

I nodded. "Yeah. He says he has some 411 on our dead Nipponese."

"Set-up?"

"Could be, but he said that Sam Archer told him to give me some assistance. Under the circumstances, I think I'll take my chances."

"Thanks for telling me."

"Well, we are partners, after all. But what about her?"

Anna sighed deeply. "I think I'm in love."

When Esperanza returned, she had changed into a black pants-suit, complete with a lace blouse that displayed some hefty cleavage. Her hair was still down, an obvious sign that she was off-duty. We were a fetching ensemble: me, with my soutache-embroidered black vest, bare shoulders, and black pants; Anna, in her slim, ecru-colored dress with spaghetti straps; Esperanza, in her black suit and alluring white blouse.

"Let's go, ladies." Esperanza offered us each an arm, and we strolled together into the warm night.

It was a fifteen-minute walk to the Hôtel Nestoire. The streets were completely deserted, except for the kill-and-go squads. The only other presence on the streets was the constant, throbbing rhythm of drums, the perennial heartbeat of the land of mercy.

The moon winked through a passing bank of clouds, casting large nebulous shadows. Against the background of rumbling drums, every other night sound was eerily magnified. Police sirens. The howling and screeching of stray cats. Footsteps.

"Does this always goes on," I asked Esperanza, "the drumming?"

"Yes," she smiled slightly. "It probably seems primitive to you, but it's how we survive down here. It's the only release for our people. If they took away the drums, there would be a revolution."

"Oh my God!" said Anna. "Look!"

A dead man was lying on the sidewalk, blocking our path. Blood was seeping from below his body, evidence that he was a fresh kill. His arms, legs, and head were arranged at awkward angles. As we stepped around him, Esperanza made the sign of the cross and explained that the body would probably remain unmoved for a couple of days—as a warning to would-be dissidents. But things were nowhere near as bad as the old junta, she added. Only a few bodies here and there to keep the people in line.

His body had probably been dumped on the street by one of the kill-and-go squads that had passed us earlier. It was like that in the land of mercy. Every time you experienced a moment of peacefulness or beauty, there was always something evil or odious to slap you rudely back into reality, like a knife thrust into your gut.

Minutes later we reached Club Carib and I was given my own personal rude awakening. Anna and Esperanza passed the doormen unhindered, but I was stopped by a duo of bruisers, who demanded in Kreole to see my identification papers. Also speaking in Kreole, Godmother Esperanza read them the riot act, letting them know in no uncertain terms that they would soon be answering to Commissioner Hobson for their actions. Suddenly realizing who they were talking to, the two men became visibly nervous as a small crowd gathered around us. I was immediately released without having to show my passport.

"I don't understand," said Anna. "Why did they stop you and let us go through?"

"Because I'm black," I responded. "I look as if I just stepped off the boat."

She looked at me, unable to connect with what I was saying. We were in a black country, after all.

"CHOCOLATE!!" I informed her.

"It's because of the mulattos," explained Esperanza. "They've reinstituted an old policy of discrimination against dark-skinned Maericans. Nina looks like a native."

So much for blackness. For a hot minute, I thought of how I could make money recirculating "No Niggers Allowed" signs from the old South down here. Hell, I reasoned to myself, maybe I could loop the money I made back into the island's poorest schools.

When we entered the club, La Bomba was already in full force with her all-girl band. The joint was as obnoxiously loud as any New York club; lights were flashing and dry-ice smoke was emanating from the floor. Everyone was clapping enthusiastically—the light-skinned elite, the Euro-trash tourists, the few select Negroes who had been allowed to pass through the door. The air reeked of sweat and marijuana, and the whole place was buzzing with various stages of sexual activity. A number of couples were groping intensely on the dance floor or in darkened corners. Several women had taken off their blouses and were shaking their bra-encased tits at their partners and the other people around them; others had gone a step further and were waving their bras in the air above their heads while wiggling their buttocks to the music.

Standing in front of a microphone at the center of it all, La Bomba was dressed in a red corset, g-string, black fishnet stockings, and red pumps. A young fool on the floor offered herself as a footstool and looked as if she were about to engage in some royal shoe sucking. But La Bomba kicked her away theatrically, and the crowd roared, "Kill the bitch!"

Our "slave waiter," a highly buffed black man wearing only a loincloth, led us to a table, where we sat and ordered drinks. I was really becoming tired of the S/M BS. First the escapades of Gale and the First Lady—and now this slave motif. The crowd seemed to think that they were being risqué, breaking all the rules. They didn't realize that they were simply being spoon-fed canned "wickedness." They were just playing at being decadent and had conveniently forgotten how their white ancestors used to slice off black limbs for entertainment or rape comely black wenches at the drop of a hat.

La Bomba, I concluded after about three songs, was a fifth-rate singer who had modeled her style and persona after the Platinum Slut and marketed herself as an outrageous "krazy Karibe." She strutted across the stage, flexing her tanned and toned body, and running her fingers on, across, and inside of various parts of herself. The woman barked out orders to her seven-piece all-girl band, who obediently laid out funky Latin, Caribbean, and world-beat grooves. I couldn't deny that the band was impressive; their playing flowed endlessly and seamlessly from one form of dance music—samba, hip hop, funk, salsa, meringue, son, rock, jazz—into another.

It didn't surprise me one bit that two-thirds of the musicians in the band were black. They had the talent, after all, and La Bomba had the marketing strategy. Consistent with the low-rent standards of most Western entertainment, the "sexy" people in the band were La Bomba's light-skinned back-up singers, each one of them as talentless as she. No danger of any of them showing her up, I surmised. La Bomba sang in a smoky, staccato, cigarette-ravaged voice that made me think of what Marlene Dietrich would have sounded like if she had been ordered at gunpoint to sing love songs to Hitler.

"This woman," Anna said, leaning over Esperanza and shouting into my ear, "is so bad that she's bound to be a hit back in the States!"

"She's got a good presentation," I conceded.

"But she can't sing!" barked Anna over the din.

I crossed my arms and waited for our waiter to bring my ginger beer. "That didn't stop the Platinum Slut!"

Anna held her nose. Esperanza said something to her and laughed. She moved her head over to my ear. "Esperanza's glad that I'm not impressed with La Bomba. She said we're proof that some Americans still have some aesthetic values."

Our drinks arrived. I looked at my watch: 10:45. Countdown. Fifteen minutes later, the lights went up to signal the end of the show. La Bomba was marching down the stage steps and into the audience, ignoring the crowd of fans who were trying to speak to her, touch her. Instead, she wound her way stubbornly through the throng and toward the island of the not impressed—us.

As she approached our table, I noticed that she was a short powerhouse of a woman. Admiring her red hair, full lips, faint Negro-looking nose, and freckles, I now understood why so many men licked their lips at the sight of her.

"Esperanza!" she announced dramatically. "*Hola. Como estas?*"

"*Bueno*," responded Esperanza. "*Muchas gracias*, Magdalena. *Y tú?*"

La Bomba pulled out a chair and straddled it. "Good," she answered in English. She then feasted her eyes on Anna and me, trying, I suspected, to get a quick reading as to who was available. Before she could continue, a "slave" brought over a box of Cohiba cigars. La Bomba took one and then offered the box to us. Anna and I shook our heads.

"Americans, right?" she said as she clipped off the butt of the Cohiba, and then had it lit for her by the "slave." She blew out the smoke dramatically. "You folks are too health-conscious for someone like myself. You have to enjoy life a little. Sin a little. Live a little."

La Bomba tilted her head upward and blew out a few smoke circles. "*El Cojones* gave me these. Castro himself."

She savored the taste of her cigar, and I got a fleeting epiphany: La Bomba blowing *El Cojones*. Not a pretty sight.

"So Esperanza, introduce me to your friends," she said between her puffs. "Don't be greedy."

Esperanza smiled, slightly embarrassed at Magdalena's cheap lecherousness, and introduced us.

"So what brings you ladies to our Misericordia?"

"I'm here looking at art for my gallery," said Anna.

"Hmmm," said La Bomba approvingly. "And you?" She turned to me.

"I'm here to fuck Luc Malmundo," the bad girl in me announced.

Caught by surprise, she gagged and laughed boisterously. Being the lady I am, I handed her a glass of water and felt Anna pinching me beneath the table, signaling me to behave myself. I was getting fucky, all right, a sure sign that I was about to knock someone out.

"Aiiieee! An honest woman at last!" She slapped her fish-netted thigh and stuck the cigar in the corner of her mouth. "Ah, you are Nina Halligan; *no es verdad*?"

I nodded my head.

The woman sat back and looked at me, then announced to the others, "You know, I like this woman. I like you, Doña Nina. Please, may I buy you a drink?"

I took another quick look at my watch. It was 11:05. I nodded and La Bomba bought us a round of tequila. I saw the look of a woman's woman in her eyes—not the sapphic brand that was crowding in on me from all sides—and we drank a round to *la différence*.

Drinking with La Bomba meant listening to her philosophy of life. "I believe in the battle of the sexes," she informed us. "Men and women are different. Man has brute strength and a mind. Women? We have a mind and something they want." She grabbed her crotch. "Pussy! And I say use it. It takes an acute mind to know when and how to use it!"

She laughed. Gale, I thought, would love this bitch. Same philosophy. Both of them playing games. Had Gale not been visited with her tragedy, I could envision her collaborating on some typically vapid intellectual project on S/M/gender/race/postfeminist BS with this fifth-rate Latin rock-star wannabe. But Gale's reality had been shattered. This fool, on the other hand, had no brakes at all.

Across the room, palms began slapping conga drums, announcing the third show of the night. La Bomba rose, offering me her hand. I stretched out mine, which she bent over and kissed with a wink. As she swished her ass voluptuously toward the stage, I noticed that each naked cheek sported a tattooed swastika. I stood up.

"Nina! Don't hit her," cried Anna, with a look of terror on her face. "We have to leave this place alive!"

"I'm not even thinking about her," I hissed, annoyed that she thought I was paying attention to that counterfeit dyke. I tapped my watch. "I have to make my call. I'll be right back."

I left the table and passed through the lecherous crowd. I found the passageway to the lounge, turned a corner, and came to the restrooms, a bank of telephones lined across the opposite wall. The moment I reached the telephones, one of them began to ring. Damn.

"Hello?"

"Nina Halligan?"

"Yes. Who are you?" I asked.

"Never mind. You want to know about Yamamoto, right?"

"Yes." The national phone system of Misericordia is not known for its efficiency and clarity of sound; the guy on the other end sounded as if he were bouncing off a satellite.

"He was killed by the Papas," said the man. "The commissioner ordered the hit."

"Hobson? Why? What's his motive?"

"Simple. Hobson, like most ruling members of the elite, is a thug; he's also in cahoots with General Malmundo."

"I'm listening," I said. I turned around and saw men and women in various stage of dress and sobriety passing in and out of the restrooms. I thought I heard someone retching behind one of the bathroom doors, and immediately recalled the dead man we'd seen earlier that evening.

"Hobson is afraid that the general isn't going to need him much longer. The general depends on the commissioner to repress the people, but he is depending on another person for an even bigger job."

"Peltrano?" I guessed.

"*Sí*. Peltrano is helping the military pacify the Coeur Noire region. That's a very important area, the only place where the guerrillas, PLAM!, have a toehold, and the Army doesn't dare fight the guerrillas. But the region is also the source of the Bimbao tree, and Malmundo has struck a deal with Peltrano. If he deals with the guerrillas and clears out the peazants, he'll make Peltrano a partner in the EarthChem deal."

"So why hit the Japanese?"

"He's part of the financial company that's investing in EC's Project Bimbex—that's the patent version of the extraction from the plant. He was killed by Hobson, and it's been made to look like the Butt Fuck Boys did it."

"What makes you think they didn't do it?" I asked.

"Those fools are crazy, but they wouldn't dare touch that Jap without an order from their *hungan*," he said. "Hobson knows it's only a matter of time. He's testing the water."

"For what?"

"He's gonna make a move. Seize power. It's the Maerican way. I have to go. If I find out anything else, I'll call you. Get home safely. It's dangerous out there. Ciao."

Before I could even say "thank you," he hung up. I turned and saw a man leaving one of the telephones down the hall toward the men's room. He looked a lot like Gerard Alfonso, François' assistant—the same gorgeous coal-black complexion. The man was even darker than me, and I was being carded at the door. But someone with connections might be able to get in here. Someone in the know.

I thought about going after him but surrendered instead to the more immediate demands of my bladder. I walked into the ladies' room and a few women, who were helping themselves to the complimentary toiletries, gave me a 'what is this black *puta* doing here?' look. I slipped into the stall, did my business, and went up to the wash counter to clean my hands. I was trying to fill in the gaps from what the man on the telephone had told me and what Mustapha had shared with me earlier.

The cold water felt good on my face. As I looked up, reaching for a paper towel, I saw my reflection. In the mirror, I also saw a pistol with a silencer cracking through the door. Thinking fast, I propelled myself, back first, into the door and slammed the gunman's arm.

The man screamed and fired the gun wildly, but I had his arm pinned between the door and the doorjamb. I grabbed his hand and pulled it down on my knee, breaking his grip on the gun. The gun dropped to the floor, and I kicked it beneath a stall. I then yanked my new friend into the bathroom, throwing him onto the counter and shattering the large mirror that ran the length of it. To make sure he didn't have time to collect his wits, I pulled him along the counter, knocking over the bottles of lotion, perfumes, and other feminine accoutrements arranged there. I slammed his head into a wall and let him roll onto the floor. He was a young, light-skinned, wiry guy, about twenty-five. I went over to the stall, picked up the gun, and returned to my evening's work; I rolled him over.

The door to the bathroom opened, revealing two mulattas looking to take a break from the dance floor. I pointed the gun at them and snarled, "Get out! This is a family squabble!"

The two women bulged their eyes and, without uttering a word, did a quick moonwalk back into the hall. I pulled my prisoner, who was still stunned by the fall, roughly to his feet, threw him against the door, and jacked his arm up behind his back. I lodged the gun barrel up his nostril, a technique I'd learned firsthand from the Papas. I knew who sent this son of bitch and I wasn't going to be civil.

"Who's your boss?!" I hissed, as I crammed the elongated barrel a fraction of a centimeter into his nostril.

"*No hablo—*"

That got him a deep gash against his jaw, as I snatched the barrel away from his nose and smacked him with the gun's butt. Blood splashed onto the side of the door.

"Don't play with me! All you fatherfuckers are trilingual down here!"

"Me...no...*hablo*...good...*inglés*!" he said like a frightened, overgrown puppy. He had mistakenly thought that this would be an easy job. Follow the bitch into the bathroom and pull the trigger. Simple as that. But now he had a crazed woman up in his face, beating him with his own gun. I pulled his arm up tighter against his shoulder blade.

"Who sent you, goddamn it?!" I was tired and wanted to go to bed with Luc. And this chump was wasting valuable time.

"Please...don't...kill...me," he finally croaked in passable

English. "*El Capitano*. Peltrano!"

Now I was getting somewhere. First the doll. Now him. Ford knew I'd be coming for him. "You tell your boss that I'm coming after him and no god or *loa* or voudoux is going to protect him. You tell that him that what he and every man fears, a real woman, is coming to get him. Tell him! You hear me, punk?!"

"*Sí*, señora!!" he gasped. "I...I tell him!"

Finished with my speech, I grabbed him by his hair, the gun now in the back of his skull, and shoved him out of the bathroom with my foot. I remained in the bathroom, screwed the silencer off the gun, and deposited the two in my purse. I threw some water on my face, collected my scattered wits, and left the room. The two women whom I'd chased off earlier were still standing in the hallway, talking to a cluster of other women and following me with a mixture of admiration and fear in their eyes. I was a shade of blackness they hadn't encountered before.

I passed them by and went out through the hotel lobby to get some air. I was hot and I needed to cool off. As I stepped outside, I was greeted by a chilly breeze from the nearby water. A strong wind was blowing off the waves, and I could see the leaves of the palm trees swaying. I also saw something else, something that struck me violently in the pit of my stomach. On the other side of the street, Luc was crouching into his car, another woman at his side. I froze.

I couldn't tell who the other woman was, but I could see that she was dark, like me. As the car drove off, I stood in the driveway and tried to get a better look at her. From a distance, her profile actually reminded me of Miriam. But it didn't matter who it was. All I could think of was that it wasn't me. My stupid obsession with Luc had led me to this pathetic state; I just couldn't deal with the fact that he was nothing but a lying, incorrigible cockhound. And that I was a romantic fool.

Stunned, I was walking in a daze, feeling sorry for myself, when the earth rumbled beneath my feet and I found myself momentarily rocking back and forth. I turned to see the casino two doors down from the hotel ripped apart by a tremendous explosion. People were running to and from the site. A few gamblers had straggled out of the building, blood streaming from their faces. People were screaming everywhere and sirens began to wail. Billowing smoke rose up above scattered piles of metal and concrete. The flashing red lights that soon appeared reminded me of the police activity in Brooklyn following an accident or a murder. I heard my name called and soon found myself standing beside Anna and Esperanza. They had been looking for me frantically since the explosion. Or should I say "explosions." It seemed like everything had hit me at once. Luc. Ford/Peltrano. My nightmare. The man with the gun. Earth-Chem. And now the bombing. If this is the land of mercy, I thought, heaven help us.

CHAPTER EIGHTEEN

I had an extremely restless night. I dreaded the reccur-
rence of the nightmare about Lee and my children. I had hoped
to spend the night with Luc by my side, comforted and dis-
tracted by our shared passion. But that hope was squelched the
moment I saw him entering his car with another woman at the
Hôtel Nestoire. The nigga didn't even bother to call me up and
lie to me about how he was spending the rest of his evening!

Next there was the matter of my would-be assassin—I'd
managed to save my life but not my peace of mind—and then
the explosion at the Casbah Casino, which only heightened my
anxiety. What troubled me most, though, was the thought that
the woman I saw entering Luc's car might have been Miriam.
That would mean that it was she who'd informed PLAM! about
my coming to Misericordia—that she was the one who had
placed Anna and me in so much danger. Only two people back
in the States knew that Anna and I were in Misericordia:
Mustapha and my brother Earl, who had almost certainly mentioned my trip to Miriam.

Around 8 a.m., I called my brother at his office back in

New York. Family chat. When I asked about Miriam, he said that she had gone on a retreat. It seemed that my emotionally stressed sister-in-law needed to regroup and "obtain a different perspective" following her disappointment regarding the outcome of her work with the Committee. The phone call with Earl did little to dispel my suspicions that it had been Miriam sliding into Luc's car the night before.

But if it was Miriam, what did that mean? Had she traveled all the way to Misericordia just to blow Luc? Or was she down here to fuck things up on a grander scale? If it was Luc she was after—which was, after all, a remote possibility—I could purge my anxiety and sense of betrayal by simply killing them both. I had just the method in mind for turning off Luc's lights for the last time. And I wouldn't use the traditional female weapon of choice—a compact revolver. Oh, no. I would do it the way I had once seen a love-crazed woman in a Japanese film do it—ride his cock and then asphyxiate him with my bare hands, prolonging his erection for one last, heart-stopping eruption.

More likely, though, Miriam was doing an 007, some complicated, clandestine adventure in which she would simply be one more actor in a deadly game, torquing the already tortured sovereignty of a tiny island-nation. If that was the case, then there would be no need to seek revenge, since she would probably be gobbled up with the rest of us when things really began to get nasty around here—a moment I feared was already near at hand.

In the midst of my confusion about Miriam, I was slowly beginning to piece together the complete picture of the interests and events behind Michael's death. Somewhere along the line, Mike had detected a new policy course at the White House, a tilt that had begun when Richard Stone came on board as the president's chief political consultant. I had learned from Sam Archer that Stone represented the giant pharmaceutical/biotechnology company, EarthChem, a heavy contributor to the presidential election campaign of that moral man of steel, Jeffrey T. Benton.

EC had delivered, all right, and Benton was clearly ready to reciprocate. But what did EC want? A change in policy toward the new but illegitimate government of Misericordia? But what exactly? How did it stand to benefit? What was the change in policy? A shift toward Malmundo's regime and a lessening of support for Bernard? And how did EarthChem and Bimbex fit into it all? Michael was tracking down the odd disparate elements, the bits and pieces of this change, trying to put it all together, connecting the dots. He was getting close and was axed, so to speak, by Peltrano's boys in a way that was sure to discredit him with any potential supporters.

According to "Gerard," Hobson, who feared being double-crossed by the general, had knocked off Yamamoto in order to discredit Peltrano. EarthChem could certainly not have been happy to find the representative of one of its major investors murdered.

It was easy enough to understand Hobson's misgivings. The entire country was in a state of chaos, a situation that not even a multinational powerhouse like EarthChem could easily resolve. I figured that there were numerous secret dialogues and negotiations going on right now regarding the possibility of finding a mutually satisfying outcome to the political stalemate. General Malmundo was counting on the support of two non-island players: EarthChem and the United States government.

But there was another player, PLAM! Maybe, as François argued, they were amateurs. Guerrillas often are new to the war game, but PLAM! was clearly competent enough to hold onto the Coeur Noire region, the source of the Bimbao tree. And they had one other major factor in their favor: the New Model Army of Misericordia had never engaged in legitimate combat with a motivated fighting force. If PLAM! could hold out longer, they would develop confidence as a fighting force and establish a reputation as a legitimate grassroots movement. Perhaps they could play the I.R.A. to Luc's Gerry Adams.

And Miriam?

The more I thought about it, the more convinced I was that she was indeed down here. Under the circumstances, I could easily imagine myself smoking her, as well as Luc. With Luc it would be out of an insane, erotically obsessive desire. But Miriam? I had tried to protect her from this, after all. Advised her not to get involved. I went to D.C. to talk to Bernard as requested. Even more important, I saved her ass from federal prosecution! And then she had gone and dropped my name to PLAM!, who had clearly planned to hold Anna and me hostage in order to get the government's attention. It was a cold, calculated decision. One that showed that I was the fool for thinking of her as family. That she merely saw me as one more piece to move in the Great Game.

From inside Anna's room, I heard voices and figured that things were heating up between her and Esperanza. As I approached the door, I heard a woman's voice.

"Ah! Ahhhh! Oh, yes! Oh, God! Yes! A—Ahhhhhhhh!"

I didn't move, as the moaning continued unabated. It sounded from where I stood as if Anna was getting some serious attention. I mean, *serious* attention. I walked back to my bed and sat down. I needed to get a grip on myself. Professionally, I have spied and listened in on people's conversations many times. But now I was fighting the urge, a naughty urge, to go over to the door and—

In the midst of my inner dialogue, I noticed that the door to Anna's room had an old-fashioned peephole. You've got it bad, girl, I thought. I was no different from anyone else, it seemed, no less full of desire, no less desperate.

Anna let out another muffled moan, and I was at the door and down on my knees at the peephole as quick as a streak of black light. Through the hole, I could see the back of Esperanza's head, her mass of black hair cascading down her back, as she knelt in a prayer-like position at the edge of the bed. Anna's smooth legs were hooked around Esperanza's shoulders, and from time to time, Esperanza's hands traveled up and down her thighs.

"Oh, yes, oh, yes, oh, yes, oh, yesss!" crooned Anna. "AHuuunnnhhhhh!" One of her legs went spastic and began trembling. She reached over to Esperanza's hair and grabbed two handfuls, and the dancer thrust her head more energetically into her lover's lower body. As their passion increased, I became aware of my position before the door. I stood up, turned around, and started to walk away.

I felt an odd mixture of disgust and release, but decided that I'd had more than my fill of the voyeur life recently. Turning back toward the bathroom, I heard someone mention my name. That, I thought, gave me license to listen.

"Nina?" repeated Anna. "The two of us?"

"Yes," said Esperanza. "Are you two lovers?"

My mouth opened and hung on its hinges. I couldn't believe she was about to tell her—

"No," said Anna. "We're really close friends. Sisters."

I sighed, momentarily relieved, and started for the bathroom once again.

"But we did make love once," said Anna. "And it was mighty. She's very intense in bed. Very passionate. What a body."

I almost kicked the door in. Anna was telling a stranger about a very intimate detail of my life, about a moment when I had been vulnerable, when I had needed someone to hold and comfort me.

"But Nina isn't into that," continued Anna. "It's just not her nature. I think it would trouble her having feelings for another woman. Sexual feelings, I mean. She's definitely into men, but if she knew what you had—"

"She's very beautiful," confided Esperanza. "I didn't think you two were lovers, but I needed to know. If she's really in love with Luc Malmundo, heaven help her."

That I already knew.

"Miriam?" questioned Anna, as we ate breakfast forty-five minutes later. After I heard Esperanza leave her room, I had tapped on her door and asked if she was ready for a second course. She just smiled, rose from the bed, and floated into the bathroom butt-naked.

I told her about my suspicion regarding Miriam and that I may have seen her with Luc prior to the explosion.

"Are you sure, Nina?" She plucked a mango slice from her plate and placed it in her mouth. "That's a very serious charge. We're talking about primal treason."

"Don't I know it," I replied. "But she's not at home. Supposedly on a retreat, and I'm convinced that she set us up. Dropped the dime, so to speak, and sicced PLAM! on us as a means to an end."

"But Nina, she's your sister-in-law," she argued.

"Anna, the only place where water is thicker than blood is in the sewer, and if I catch that bitch down here, that's where she is going to wind up,"

"How would you explain that to your brother?"

"Miriam collided into a dark, blunt object—me!" I replied tersely. "Don't worry. I would be ready to assume any motherly or maternal function in regard to my nieces and nephew."

Sipping my coffee, I glanced at the island newspaper. The headline article was about the bombing. Five people—all foreigners—were killed and scores more were injured. The paper attributed the attack to PLAM!, although the group had not claimed credit for the bombing. General Malmundo and his henchmen had apparently gone to great lengths to lay the blame at the guerrillas' feet, indirectly attributing the attack to President Bernard. Another article was even more interesting: The American scientists kidnapped by PLAM! months ago had been let go—and released to Dr. Luc Malmundo "as a gesture of goodwill."

"Take a look at this," I said to Anna, passing her the newspaper. I sipped my coffee and looked around the room. All the tables were occupied. Some were guests like us and others were those who had come over for a meeting or whatever. One would not get the impression that this was a nation in the throes of political turmoil. As a matter of fact, business was booming according to a *Wall Street Journal* article I had read. And a third world nation's misery index meant that it was a good place for a first world plundering. Anna lowered the paper.

"What do you think, counsel?" I asked.

"Hmmm. Carrot and stick?" she replied. "They let go of the hostages and then bombed the casino? Well, from what we know, they are capable of doing that. These are the same people who tried to kidnap us, right?"

"Yes." I was looking at the other guests in the dining room: all of them were either Americans, Euros, or Japanese. Big deals were going down. And knowing the island's history as one of the foremost kleptocracies in the region, I suspected that Luc's daddy was the gate through which these big money makers had to pass. Esperanza was making her rounds through the tables, looking fresh and vibrant as she saw to her customers' comfort. There was a new enthusiasm in her voice.

"Look at them," Anna smirked, as Esperanza made her way from one table to the next. "Look how they engage in the male gaze, watching the fluidity of her graceful movements. If they only knew," she sighed. Anna leaned over to me and was about to whisper in my ear, but Esperanza had already joined us at our table.

"*Buenos días*, señoritas," greeted Esperanza, smiling radiantly at us.

"Good morning," I replied.

"*Buenos días*, Doña Esperanza," said Anna. "How are you this morning?"

"Oh, I think you know the answer to that," she smiled. "Can I get you some more coffee, ladies?"

I told her that I was fine. Anna wanted to know if they were still going on their shopping trip together. Esperanza said that she would have to take care of a few things in the office first; she'd be ready in half an hour. She waltzed away with a wicked twitch in her hips and every male eye in the room picked up her rhythm.

"What are you two shopping for? Lesbian accoutrements?" I asked.

"Now don't get fucky, Nina. Don't blame me because Luc didn't keep his word," said Anna. "If those scientists were re-leased to him, he was probably waiting for them all night. That ought to put your overactive mind to rest—and at least clear Miriam of any suspicion in that department. Though, God knows, you may be right about—"

She cut herself off, picked up her purse, and moved to leave.

"I'm going to my room to change," she said. She leaned over and kissed me on both cheeks, continental style, the way she always did when we were preparing to separate. "If Luc doesn't know a good thing, you can always join us, sweetie. On our side of the fence, three is not a crowd."

"I'm going to smack your ass," I told her, picking up the newspaper.

"Oooh, I can hardly wait," she shivered. "Stay out of trouble. Bye."

"You're forgetting—trouble is my business."

"Oh, I have something to tell you about last night."

"Spare me the details."

"Oh, I think you're going to be interested in this detail. Ciao."

I thought about her advice. Not wanting her to worry about me, I hadn't mentioned the voudoux doll or the attack in the bathroom. She was in love, or at least in lust. I could certainly identify with both. The important thing was that she was with someone who liked her. I went through the newspaper until Salim approached me with a telephone.

"For me?"

"Yes, ma'selle." He plugged the phone into an outlet as I picked up the receiver.

"Hello?"

"What did you think of last night's fireworks?" asked the same voice from last night.

"I just know what I read," I informed him.

"Don't believe any of it," he said. "It's all a lie."

"So what do you know?"

"It wasn't PLAM!" he said.

"Okay. Who?"

"Hobson."

I looked around the room. The place was still half full, though some of the guests had gone on to their after-breakfast business. "Are you sure? The paper said—"

"Forget about the paper," he snapped. "Hobson is trying to stir up trouble by causing a split between the general and Peltrano—and by making it seem that PLAM! is launching a terrorist attack. But that's not the main reason why I called."

"Then what?" I shot back.

"Richard Stone is in Misericordia."

I thought for a second. "Things are happening because of the Yamamoto killing, huh?"

"Yes—and I wouldn't be surprised if he also became a target. The dogs are out and they don't care who they bite."

"Meaning El Generalissimo?"

"*Sí.*"

I began flicking my tongue across the edge of my upper teeth as I considered the implications of what he said. "Where's the action going down?"

"Don't have that at the moment, but I'll keep you posted."

"Please do—Gerard."

He said nothing when I used his name, and hung up. Stone's arrival meant something was up; I wondered if finding out about his business would lead me to my old friend, Nate Ford. Still thinking things over, I returned to my room, took off my clothes, and strode naked into the garden, climbing into the warm water. For a moment I didn't care about anything. Not EarthChem, not Stone, not Benton, not Claire. Not even Luc. Well, that might be pushing things.

And Miriam?

Supposing what Anna said about Luc was true, what was she doing down here? Normally, all of this—Ford, EarthChem, Miriam, Luc—would have been enough to bolt me into action. In New York, I would have leapt at the first sign of danger, but down here in the land of mercy, I decided to lie low until I had a clearer handle on things. Even at my most restrained, I wasn't prepared to just wait for things to happen. There was something else I needed to know about EC, and Mustapha had left a message with a name, supplied to him by the Interfaith Network Alliance.

A few moments later, I dried myself off, stepped into some black bike shorts, a sports bra, and sandals, and threw a flowing yellow floral-print dress over my body. I grabbed my purse and was about to head out the door when I thought about the gun I'd taken from my would-be assassin the night before. It occurred to me that Doña Nina, as I had recently been anointed by my new friend La Bomba, needed her own back-up. In the past forty-eight hours, I'd been slapped by the First Lady, almost kidnapped by guerrillas, narrowly dodged an assassination attempt, and then watched Luc slide into the backseat of his car with another woman whom I suspected was my sister-in-law. Not to mention the bombing, or the violent dreams about being beaten by Lee. The time had come, as Howlin' Wolf once sang, to be a bad girl. I placed the pistol in the small of my back and left the room.

CHAPTER NINETEEN

I was standing in front of the inn waiting for a car that Salim had ordered for me when a red Mercedes-Benz convertible roared up and screeched to a halt. La Bomba was at the wheel.

"*Bonjour*, Doña Nina."

She was wearing a very satisfied smile as she pulled up to the curb, a look that signaled that she was thinking of me and thanking the gods for her good fortune.

"*Bonjour*, Magdalena. What brings you to this part of town?"

"Actually, I was on my way to a party given by the American ambassador, and I was hoping that you'd accompany me."

"Sorry, I have an appointment," I responded.

"But darling," she countered, "this is the jam of the year on the island and the ambassador knows how to really kick it!"

I sadly shook my head. "Sorry."

"Well, can I drop you off?"

"That's very sweet of you, but don't bother."

"But I insist," she pouted. "I would most enjoy your company."

She sighed, and then lifted a magazine on the seat beside her to reveal a rather impressive handgun. Uh oh, I thought, another member of Bad Girls International. I stepped up to the car defiantly.

"Look, you don't scare me. I got one, too."

"Yes, I suspect that you do, but mine is bigger. You want to go for a draw? Act like those stupid savages we love so much? Come now, *chérie*, we are women. We don't have to act like that." She smiled pleasantly and then knowingly tapped her temple. "We have the power, *non*?"

We stared at each other for a few seconds, and I noticed that a small crowd had begun to gather on the sidewalk. Local celebrity that she was, La Bomba appeared oblivious to everything but me and the gun beside her. It struck me that this wasn't really meant to be a kidnapping; it was just her typically Maerican way of expressing herself—with a weapon. It would probably be best to go along with her and not resist—at least not yet. And besides, the Bomb had the drop on me; she could easily grab the gun and have me in her sights before I could grip the handle of the gun hidden beneath my dress. Instead, I gripped the handle of the door, indicating that I would come with her. La Bomba immediately placed the magazine on top of the gun and then moved both of them to her lap, allowing me to sit. We sat in silence for a few seconds.

"You know, you are a very beautiful woman," she said breathlessly and winked.

"Step on the gas or I'm out of here," I replied, ignoring her compliment.

"Oooh, I can see why Luc is crazy about you," she purred as she turned the ignition key and wheeled the car onto the street. "Such an *authentique* African-American woman! Grrrr."

It was only a matter of time before I would have to deck this bitch. Part of me liked her because she was bold and beautiful, a bad girl, but she suffered from the obnoxious conceit of the global ruling elite: the misperception that *they* can say or do anything they damn well please and not suffer the consequences from *us*. A case in point was the woman's driving. Standard traffic laws meant absolutely nothing to her; everyone knew her red car from a distance, and they got out of her way.

La Bomba was intrigued when she found out that I was going to the Nouveau Coeur Noire section of the city. When I mentioned that I was going to speak to someone at Global/Micro, she became positively apoplectic.

"What? Those communists?!" she fumed, taking her hands off the steering wheel as the car rounded a corner. "Those people are nothing but troublemakers. Talking about raising the minimum wage and trying to put merchants and businessmen out on the streets with their excessive demands. Half-an-hour lunch! Whoever heard of such a thing in a Caribbean culture?! They are trying to give the people the ridiculous idea that they have rights!! The right to organize! I don't understand why the general let them back in. They should have stayed in the States with Pepe Bernard. The communists! Acting as if thirty cents a hour isn't good enough for them!"

"Perhaps," I said calmly, watching the scenery change, "it is a necessary condition of a democratic society to allow people to organize, to become educated?"

"We don't need educated workers," she replied, "only oxen. After all, some people are gold, some people are silver—"

"And some people are bronze," I intoned. "I think I'm beginning to get the picture."

We had left the city center and were only a few minutes away from Global/Mirco. La Bomba slowed down the car and parked it beneath a cluster of palm trees.

"Let's talk, darling," she said, turning toward me.

I looked at my watch. "I have an appointment, and you have a party with Ambassador Blackerby."

"Fuck them." She opened a nearby compartment, pulled out a fat blunt, and began to stoke up. She offer me a hit but I declined. "For my nerves," she explained. "People have been trying to kill me."

"Hmmmm. I wonder why?"

"So, listen, darling," she said, after blowing out a lung-full of smoke, "we have to have a woman-to-woman talk."

I cocked her a questioning eyebrow. "About what?"

"You and Luc, darling. And me." She offered me another

hit, and I shook my head no. Hearing her mention the three of us in the same breath ought to have made me take a double lung-full, but I had to be stone cold sober for my meeting, not high. I decided to go on the attack. "Okay, just what is going on between you and Luc?"

"Nothing, darling. Luc and I are like brother and sister, and—"

"And fucking what?"

"That's just it. We're fucking partners—literally."

"You mean lovers?" I almost choked.

"No, not in the traditional sense," she calmly replied. "Look, this may seem complex."

"Not if you're schtupping my man," I responded. "There's nothing complex about that!"

La Bomba clapped her hands in delight. "That's what I like about you. You are such a woman! So refreshingly up-front! 'My man.' It's so womanly primitive, *non?*"

"Enough with the accolades. What's the deal between you and Luc? Is he in love with you or what?!"

She laughed and I was getting pissed, ready to slap her freckled ass. "No...we're just fuck-buddies."

"What?"

"Let me explain."

"Please do."

"We've known each other since childhood, played doctor and nurse, you know," she winked. "Luc was my first...you know. Luc is my friend and I love him—"

"And you're fucking him," I reminded her.

"No, no, no. It's not like that, Doña Nina. He's a safe fuck. I have my problems with men. You know, they want to either own you or fuck everything that moves and kill you if you do likewise. With Luc...it's relaxed. We have no ties on one another and I understand him and he understands me. It's safe. We're friends, not lovers. I sometimes want to be with a man and Luc would prefer to be with me, a woman who isn't going to make certain demands on him during this critical period. But now you're here..."

"And I'm the other *puta* in his life," I suggested.

For the first time Magdalena was not wearing her supercilious or showbiz diva persona. "I don't understand why you would think of yourself in such a way. Luc loves you, but you have come down here at a very critical time, and you may not understand the arrangement..."

"That you two are fuck-buddies? What could I possibly not understand about that?"

"That, and if there is a successful outcome to this, I may be his first lady," she informed me.

"First lady? Why not run—Hey, what are you saying? That you and Luc are going to get married?!" It hit me like a bolt: the "arrangement."

She nodded her head. "Look, I know this is difficult, but this is politics. If we bridge the two, the left and the right, by marrying, we will insure some stability. Luc loves you, Doña Nina, but there is something he loves just as much, if not more."

"And?"

"And that is Misericordia," she answered. "Luc is a patriot and will do what he has to defend and protect the other woman in his life, the mother of us all—our country!"

"And where does that leave me? Have you two decided that?"

"Look, Luc and I understand what needs to be done. The Maerican people will not accept him as their president if he marries an American. That's a harsh political reality that you should not take personally. This would be a political marriage—"

"A sham!" I spat. "A goddamn marriage of convenience—political expediency."

"It is as much a part of reality, more so, than the emphasis that you Americans place on romantic love, only to have one out of two marriages end in a divorce. Talk about family values! Besides, love is fleeting, whereas politics, concern for the community, is eternal. We're speaking of a partnership that is meant to save lives—my people's lives."

"Don't make me laugh! My lips are chapped. You begrudge the peazants—excuse me, the niggas—making less than fifty cents an hour. And now you want to call them your people? Get out of my face!"

I reached for the car door and got out, slamming it as I did. Then I walked over to a grove of palm trees several feet from the car. In the near distance was a clearing, revealing a row of buildings which I took to be Global/Micro. The sun was bearing down on me, and my anger was making me sweat big bullets. I was forgetting what I had learned as a child growing up in D.C.—sometimes it's just too hot to waste your energy getting angry about anything, especially a man.

Finally composing myself, I noticed that Magdalena, wearing an oatmeal-colored linen sheath dress and linen pumps, was standing on the other side of the tree. Peering ahead into the distance, her hand behind her back, she looked oddly like a head of state, preparing to make a policy announcement. It took me a few seconds to realize that she must have been watching Claire Foster Benton this past few months, picking up her mannerisms. The Caribbean bad girl had been attending the International First Ladies Finishing School.

"Of course," she began, clearing her throat, "we could—you and me—come to some sort of equitable arrangement."

"Oh, I see. I'm supposed to be the chick on the side. His mistress. Is that what you're offering me, huh?"

"You North Americans," she sighed, "and your twisted, hypocritical puritanism! I thought I could talk to you woman-to-woman, but like most Americans, you think that you can have it all—everything!"

La Bomba shook her head and turned back to the car. I went to the other side of the tree and blocked her movement. "Did Luc tell you to have this girl talk with me?!"

"No, darling, I decided to. The man has a lot of things on his mind, so I stepped in."

Now I was really ready to slap her. The woman had a very condescending tone, as if Luc was too busy to deal with me personally, to explain to me what was going on. But why hadn't he told me about this? If Luc did have something on his mind, I certainly hadn't heard about it. But had I been listening? Be that as it may, La Bomba had already assumed her position, knew her role: if not looking out for her man, then protecting her interests in the "arrangement."

Finished with the American, La Bomba returned to her car. She put on her sunshades and looked at me. "Well, come on," she sighed, "we both have to get to our respective appointments."

"I'll walk."

"Are you sure?"

I nodded my head. "I need some time to think."

"You've been having such a wild ride down here, why not come to the party?" she added.

"No, thanks."

"Okay. If you were anyone else, I'd feel remiss to be leaving a sister damsel in distress," she said, while applying some balm to her lips. She started the engine and then lowered her shades to flash me her green eyes. "I'll call you later."

"Don't bother."

"I thought you wanted to know," she began formally, before switching to a voice that was disturbingly familiar, "about Stone and where the action was." She winked at me, gunned the car, and blew a streak of dust in my face.

True to her nickname, La Bomba had dropped two explosions on me: first, the arrangement between her and Luc; and now, the fact that she was the phonemate who'd been feeding me information about what had been going on behind the scenes.

Turning away from La Bomba's rapidly disappearing car, I walked barefoot across a field of grass toward the compound. My destination was only a football field away, but the unrelenting brutality of the sun made me understand the importance of siestas in the region. It was hot, hot, hot, and my swollen tongue longed for a cup of water that I hoped would be awaiting me.

Global/Micro was a non-governmental organization that had been set up to help the peazants who had left the interior region of Le Coeur Noire. Years ago Nouveau Coeur Noire had been a wretched slum, with dilapidated wooden shacks, drugs, prostitutes, abandoned families, and a startlingly high crime rate. The area had been Father Bernard's original stomping ground, so to speak. He had ministered to the newly dispossessed who had lost their lands to the push for development, and who were rapidly losing their sons, their daughters, and their capacity for hope to the streets.

What had once been a maze of crumbling shacks had been replaced by a row of neat adobe houses. The simple structures looked incongruous in the tropics, but the masses had overcome their lack of conventional building materials with an ample supply of mud, straw, and palm leaves. Global/Micro had abandoned its original mission of trying to get the peazants back to their old land, and were now supporting the cultivation of garden crops and supplying computer panels for a thriving cottage industry. The village was a showcase for the New Capitalism of making micro loans to mom-and-pop entrepreneurs who employed five people or less. The newly rich techno dweebs who supported the endeavor revelled in the splashly features they regularly received in *George*, *Wired*, and a host of other crackpot libertarian policy journals. The New Capitalist model was a favorite of politicians and businesspeople everywhere, since it relieved local governments of the responsibility for providing assistance to its neediest citizens by encouraging market forces—banks, credit and loan institutions—to provide token capital to the very same people they had robbed and displaced in the first place.

Reaching the compound, I entered a large adobe building, where I found a woman typing away on an old Macintosh computer. I announced myself and informed her that I was looking for Britt-Inger Ekberg.

"Ekky?" said the woman. "She be at her house. It be siesta and her take slow. Go out and round, two 'dobies down, and find her."

I followed her instructions and came to a two-storied structure two doors down from the office. I was about to knock on the door when I heard the sound of reggae music coming from the backyard. Following the sound, I found a cozy little haven shaded by two large coconut trees. Between the trees was a hammock, supporting a woman with a suckling child at her breast. The woman had a nest of golden-brown dreadlocks spiraling into the air and down her shoulders. I was reminded of the myth of Medusa by the thickness of her corkscrew locks, the way some of them rose effortlessly into the air. I took her to be one of the island's clan of mulattoes.

She swayed back and forth with the child nursing on her breast, murmuring a Maerican lullaby in Kreole. The dark baby was feeding eagerly at its mother's breast. The baby pulled back its large head to signal that it was through, and the woman pulled down her blouse, still cradling the child's head in her palm. She then placed the child's head on her shoulder and began gently patting its back. The woman turned in my direction and discovered me, and I felt, once again, like a voyeur. For a moment, she appeared startled, but then her face broke into a broad smile.

Embarrassed, I stepped forward. "I'm sorry, but I'm looking for Britt-Inger Ek—"

"That's me," said the young woman, whom I placed in her mid-twenties. She shifted the child to her other shoulder.

It disturbed me to realize that I had been expecting someone white. "I'm Nina Halligan," I told her as I approached the hammock.

"Oh, yes. We spoke on the phone yesterday."

"Yes, that's right."

"Please have a seat," she said, indicating a roughly hewn bamboo chair. A giant wooden cable spool, the type that telecommunication companies usually abandon after use, served as a table. As I sat beneath the shaded tree at the table, the baby began crying. "I'm sorry," said Britt-Inger.

"Oh, don't apologize. I understand perfectly. A couple of months old, huh?"

"Actually, three," she smiled. She lifted the child and began softly murmuring in Kreole.

"Girl or boy?"

"A boy. Toussaint." The mother shifted her son to her other shoulder and slowly began twisting her torso left to right. "Do you have children?"

"Had," I replied, trying not to stir things up within me. "Lost them during the war."

"I'm sorry," she said. Britt-Inger blinked her eyes and then looked at me, questioning. "Ah, what war?"

"The war on drugs," I replied. "A major offensive in America."

"Oh, I see. I'll be with you in a second," she said, as she turned her attention to her child.

The baby was easily quieted. As I watched this young mother at work, it was obvious that she had, as Lee used to call it, "a smack of the black." She had enough melanin to place her in the mulatto scheme of things and her phenotype—high cheekbones, full lips, and semi-broad nose—echoed West Africa.

Britt-Inger lowered the child from her shoulder to the hammock. Smiling, she wiped the drool from its mouth and then rose. Grabbing a chair, she placed it next to the hammock and straddled it, gently rocking the hammock with one hand and turning to face me. She propped her chin lazily in the palm of her free hand.

"So what can I do for you? You said something about EarthChem?"

"Yes. I was told that you had written a report or article about EarthChem."

"Excuse me, Miss Halligan," said the woman in flawless English. "Just who are you? And what exactly do you want to know about EC?"

I thought we had covered this ground over the phone, but given the political situation here, her cautiousness was understandable. I pulled a card from my purse and told her about my investigation.

She took the card, read it, and handed it back. "Okay."

"It's my understanding that EC has lobbied—secretly, mind you—the Benton administration to recognize the Malmundo regime," I began.

"Correct." She gently rocked the hammock.

"EarthChem was—is—a major contributor to the Benton campaign."

"*Oui*. That's true."

"Now," I continued, trying to remember what Mustapha had told me and the other things I had read before I left the

States, "they have been working on something called Bimbex, based on the Bimbao tree. It is rumored to increase crop yield and food production."

"But they discovered a slight problem."

"That being?" I asked.

"Bimbex, the genetic son of the Bimbao, doesn't work anywhere except on this island."

"Why not?"

Britt-Inger hunched up her shoulders and raised her hands. "Mother Nature? No one knows why. Not even the scientists. That's what they were working on when PLAM! interrupted their research in Le Coeur Noire."

"You know about them—"

"Being released? *Oui*," she responded, neither impressed nor indifferent.

"Okay. Now this is where I become confused. If the patent doesn't work anywhere but here, why does EC attach so much importance to this regime?"

"Because the government of the United States will allow the Malmundo regime to assist EarthChem."

"In doing what?"

"In taking over the island and using it as part of its agribusiness," she said, putting on a pair of horn-rimmed eyeglasses that instantly transformed her from an island earth-mama to a new-jack intellectual.

"What?"

"Simple. Bimbex doesn't work anywhere else. It can be genetically crossed with other plants and crops to induce crop yields, but only here," she continued. "So the solution is to turn the entire island into one huge farm, growing different crops."

"But the island—no offense—is a postage stamp. It's tiny."

"Correct, but the high yield from Bimbex will make up for the small acreage."

"That's incredible."

"But there's another—"

"Problem?"

"Yes. Us."

"Us. Who is us?"

"The Maerican people," she answered. "There's no plan for the masses of people, especially those who have been removed from their traditional lands, like Le Coeur Noire. We have become redundant—and you know what the policy elites do to people the market considers redundant?"

I didn't exactly know what she was referring to. But back in the States, redundant people, usually black people, were members of the industrial reserve army—and industrialism, as the 19th and 20th centuries had known it, was dead. Now such people were slated for the fastest "growth industry" in America: the prison industrial complex.

Years ago I used to laugh at the Nation of Islam's myth about the mad black doctor Yakub, who invented the white race who later took over the world. Now I realized that Elijah Muhammad might have been offering the world a very appropriate metaphor for capitalism and technology run amok.

"What's planned for the surplus population here?"

"Urban triage," she answered.

"Triage?"

She looked at Toussaint and then at me. "Remove people from their traditional means of taking care of themselves and place them in cities where they have no real jobs or have to survive on near-slave wages doled out by subcontractors who make Pocahantas dolls for corporations like Disney. Then watch them die them from AIDS, drugs, crime, bad education, the policy indifference of the elites. It's simply the reconquest of the Caribbean, Ms. Halligan. Bernard tried to slow it down, but he doesn't understand that the World Trade Organization would consider his reforms an interference with market competition. I've read a World Bank report that explained that the rural majority has—and I quote—only two possibilities: work in the industrial or service sector, or emigration—end of quote. USAID programs are really about reducing the ability of people here to grow food in order to keep us dependent on imports."

"In other words, slow death," I said.

"Well, as Milton Friedman put it, we do have the freedom to choose. Of course, if you're black, you aren't too readily welcomed as an immigrant, especially to the U.S. or any Euro-nation. They only need a few hundred people here." She looked at me knowingly. "You know about the sheep cloning?"

"I'm way ahead of you." I was flicking my tongue again. "This is the New World Order."

"With a vengeance," confirmed Britt-Inger. "You see, the global elite wants one thing and one thing only."

"And that is?"

"*Everything*." Britt looked down at her baby, who was resting peacefully. The child was beautiful; dark curls framed his brown face and his little lips were puckered as he slept.

"Beautiful boy."

"Thank you." She looked down at him. "He favors his father. May I get you something? A glass of agua?"

"Water? Please."

Britt-Inger left me to watch her baby. I went over to the hammock. This was one of those incongruous moments that happened here on the island. One moment I was listening to an unbelievable story that led to an explanation of Michael's death, and the next moment I was watching over a beautiful island baby. *They want it all*, I thought to myself. That meant that an entire people were of absolutely no importance. Black life, collectively or individually, simply didn't matter. EarthChem wanted it all, and a handful of actors—Benton, Stone, Malmundo, Peltrano, Hobson—were willing to act as its agents. Given what I already knew, EarthChem was probably going to get what it paid for. That's the American way, after all.

A fresh island breeze swirled through the yard, swaying the leaves of the trees and the hammock. I looked into the sky and noticed a flock of birds in the far distance. As I thought about what Britt-Inger had said, a familiar sound became more audible. When I turned my head again, the distant flock of birds had suddenly become a squadron of low-flying attack helicopters. The air was whipped into a frenzy. The sound woke the child, whom I grabbed in my arms as I dashed toward the house. Britt-Inger ran out and met me halfway, and we rushed together back into the house.

"What the hell is going on?!" I asked as I handed her the child.

"Oh, nothing much," she said wistfully, stroking her son's head. "It's El Generalissimo's way of getting us ready for the New Island Order." She handed me a glass of water that tasted faintly like mango.

"I think you might find this of interest," she said, taking the glass and handing me a piece of paper.

It was a memo. While it wasn't about Misericordia, it highlighted the predatory nature of bloodless technocrats who posed as economists.

> DATE: December 12, 1991
> TO: Distribution
> FR: XXXXXXXX
>
> Subject: GEP
>
> "Dirty" Industries: Just between you and me, shouldn't XXXXXX be encouraging MORE migration of the dirty industries to the LDCs? I can think of three reasons:
>
> 1) The measurements of the costs of health-impairing pollution depend on the foregone earnings from increased morbidity and mortality. From this point of view, a given amount of health-impairing pollution should be spread in the country with the lowest costs, which will be the country with the lowest wages. I think the economic logic behind dumping a load of toxics on the lowest-wage country is impeccable, and we should face up to that.
>
> 2) The costs of pollution are likely to be nonlinear, as the initial increments of pollution probably have very low costs. I've always thought that under-populated countries in Africa are vastly UNDER-polluted; their air quality is probably inefficiently low compared

to Los Angeles or Mexico City. Only the lamentable observation that so much pollution is generated by non-tradable industries (transport, electrical generation)—combined with the fact that the unit transport costs of solid waste are so high—prevent world welfare from enhancing trade in air pollution and waste.

3) The demand for a clean environment for aesthetic and health reasons is likely to have a very high elasticity. The concern over an agent that causes a one-in-a-million change in the odds of prostate cancer is obviously going to be much higher in a country where people survive than in a country where under-five mortality is two hundred per thousand. Also, much of the concern over industrial atmosphere discharge is about visibility-impairing particulates. These discharges may have very little direct health impact. Clearly, trade in goods that embody aesthetic pollution concerns could be welfare-enhancing. While production is mobile, the consumption of pretty air is non-tradable.

The problem with the argument against all of these proposals for more pollution in LDCs (intrinsic rights to certain goods, moral reasons, social concerns, lack of adequate markets, etc.) is that they could be turned around and used more or less effectively against proposals for XXXXX liberalization.

"This is how they view us, Doña Nina," she replied with an ironic grin. If Misericordia isn't seen as an offshore cornfield, so to speak, then the Motherland is viewed as a garbage dump. People in African countries should run the risk of getting prostate cancer because they are less economically viable."
"What institution is this Nazi affiliated with?" I asked.

"The World Bank," she said. "A Brazilian secretary of environment wrote back to him and told him that his reasoning was perfectly logical but totally insane."

"Bravo," I said. Somebody was standing up to these new-age Malthusian thugs. But there was more, said Britt-Inger. Much more.

The good man also informed the World Bank official that the writer's thoughts provided a concrete example of the unbelievable alienation, reductionist thinking, social ruthlessness, and arrogant ignorance of many conventional economists. He explained that, if the World Bank kept the writer as vice president, it would lose its credibility. For the Brazilian, the best thing that could happen would be for the Bank to disappear.

However, it was he who disappeared; he was fired from his job for writing the letter. The American rose through the ranks and was now poised to become the Secretary of the U.S. Treasury in the Benton Administration, an apt place to ensure the dominance of American global economic policies.

My throat felt even drier.

CHAPTER TWENTY

By the time I dragged my tush from the bush, the siesta was ending. Normally, people would return from the two-hour break and resume their work in the shops or behind the various carts and food-stands on the street. But today was different: the streets were practically deserted, except for a few scattered corpses.

I entered the inn and inquired about Anna and Esperanza, neither of whom had returned from their outing. I figured that the shopping trip was a pretext for an out-of-the-way romantic interlude. But under the circumstances, the fact that they still hadn't returned worried me.

Upon entering my room, I noticed that the door to the garden was open; only the screen door kept out the flies and mosquitoes. Closing the room's door behind me, I heard a faint voice; someone was singing in the garden. I stepped over to the screen door, slipped my hand beneath my dress, and removed the pistol. I peered into the garden from the room but didn't see anyone. Slowly, I pulled back the screen, stepped into the garden, and walked toward the hot hut. Someone was definitely in there. I could hear the water splashing about and could smell the odor of a cigar as I approached.

"What are you doing here?" I demanded, announcing my presence to the intruder.

"*Hola!*" said La Bomba. She was smoking a cigar and reclining against the back of the tub, reading my copy of *Excellent Cadavers*, a book about the corruption of Italy by the Mafia. A glass of papaya juice and a decanter stood beside the tub. "You know, this is exactly how Misericordia is ruled," she commented, referring to the book in her hands. "General Malmundo and his gang are just a Caribbean version of the Mafia."

"You didn't answer my question," I said, lowering the pistol.

She shrugged her shoulders. "The party was canceled."

"So you dropped your ass into my room. Into my tub?"

Magdalena looked perplexed. "You sound as if you're angry with me. Did I do something wrong, Doña Nina?"

"Yes! You're in my room. Drinking my juice. Farting in my tub! And fucking my man!"

"You shouldn't let these things upset you so," she said calmly. "It's too hot down here to get so worked up."

Not amused, I raised the gun again, and she raised her hands.

"I...I was afraid," she said quickly. "Men were following me and I didn't want to get into to a fire fight, not on the streets. So I came here. I only carry the gun because people have taken shots at me, but I'm not a professional like you... And you undoubtedly saw the bodies in the street."

I nodded my head and lowered the gun, slightly. "What's happening? Where's Luc? I haven't heard from him, La Bomba."

La Bomba placed her hands back in the water. "There are secret negotiations going on, involving the government and President Bernard. That's where Luc's been. He's been trying to deal with the guerrillas. It's very difficult, and as I told you, there's the matter of Hobson, who's trying to destabilize things by killing the Japanese and blowing up things."

I didn't believe the bit about her being afraid. But then again, maybe she was finally facing up to the grim reality of being a marked woman. "Why are you really here? You could have gone to hide in numerous places."

Magdalena looked straight at me. "Be a darling and hand me the towel. I'm getting out."

Her dress was spread neatly beside the tub. I wasn't surprised to see that it covered her gun.

"Don't do anything stupid," I cautioned her, as I pulled a fresh towel off one of the wooden prongs that was studded into a beam of the hut and tossed it to her. As she rose, I noticed that she had a ring in each nipple with a chain suspended between them.

She smiled, sensing that I was watching her. "This is my chain of freedom," she explained. "It comes off when we are a freed people."

"I see," I muttered flatly.

"You know, usually women and men find me irresistible," said La Bomba, vigorously drying her abdomen.

"Well, as the Temptations loved to sing, 'I'm the exception to the rule.'"

"Are you a normal exception or an unusual exception?"

"What do you mean?"

"I mean, are you an unusual exception like Esperanza?"

"What's unusual about Esperanza?" I asked.

La Bomba stopped and stared at me. "You mean you don't know?"

"Guess not," I replied.

"She's a hermaphrodite," she said. "Got a clit that can blossom into a six-inch prong."

"You mean she's a transsexual?"

"Nonononono," corrected the woman. "She's the real thing. She has a clit, a cock and a pussy. A she-male."

But if she knew what you had. Suddenly, I remembered what I had overheard Anna say to Esperanza in the bedroom. That's what she wanted to tell me. Two for the price of one, I thought. Girlfriend had hit the jackpot.

Magdalena dried herself, wrapped the towel around her body, and walked over to pick up her dress. I watched her very carefully as she walked around the tub and came over to me.

"Well?" she asked.

"Look," I said. "You can stay here but you have to be a good girl. I'm not in the mood for antics. If you make me nervous, I will shoot you."

"*Sí*. I understand. These are crazy and dangerous times, Doña Nina." She then proceeded into the room, with me following and glancing behind for any other unwanted guests. The news about Esperanza made me think again about Anna, and the fact that I hadn't heard from her since the morning.

I offered La Bomba Anna's room to change into her clothes and then retreated into the bathroom, returning in less then five minutes, showered, dressed, and ready. La Bomba had also dressed and was sitting at the table smoking, her legs crossed and her bare feet bobbing nervously.

"Feeling better?" she asked.

"Yeah." I was still drying the last of my braided locks. I walked over to the table and noticed that she had poured me a drink of papaya.

"Why don't you sit?" La Bomba said. "We have some things to discuss."

"Look, Señorita VillaRosa, the last thing I want to talk about is your and Luc's so-called arrangement!" I snapped. I tried to turn away, but she latched onto my arm with a surprisingly firm grip.

"Sit down," she commanded. For once, the woman meant business. Her usual mischievous spark was completely gone. I tossed the towel on the end of the bed and sat.

"Luc sent me over to prepare you."

I instinctively rose, wanting to get away from what I was about to hear, but she stopped me again. "Oh God."

"You have to listen, Doña," she said calmly. "Luc has been agonizing over this decision, but if the negotiation fails and the general refuses to accede to democratic principles, he may have to remove his own father."

"How?"

She said nothing.

"You're not suggesting that he would...?"

"Things have become very drastic, Doña." She handed me

the drink. "Are you familiar with Command Decisions?"

I thought for a second. "That's the outfit operated by Carl Jaeger. Yes?"

"President Bernard has contracted him to remove the junta. That would mean a full-scale operation that would include, as the military says, 'collateral damage,' large civilian casualties."

I sat back in the chair and took in the news. General Carl T. "The Jaguar" Jaeger was "the third force." Now I was certain that it was Miriam whom I'd seen with Luc. Command Decisions was an old game, but with a new twist. In the same way that kings once commissioned privateers like Francis Drake and chartered companies like the British East Indies Company to do the dirty work of imperialism, corporations now relied on Command Decisions. Officially, it was a subsidiary of WORLDTEX, an international investment conglomerate with holdings in mining, agriculture, and biotechnology. Whenever one of its mining operations was having trouble in Africa, Command Decisions "arrested the errant development."

The Jaguar was a former U. S. military officer with counter-insurgency expertise. For work in the southern hemisphere, he had the most prized possession of all, black skin, and an army of former black veterans, including Americans, Africans, Caribbeans, and dark-skinned South Americans. They could go in anywhere they wished and be counted as brothers among the local population, restoring order while corrupt governments crumbled around them. Meanwhile, the nations they "saved" were forced to hock their patrimony to pay their bills to WORLDTEX. What made CD truly ominous was the simple fact that it, like many other international corporations, was not accountable to anyone or anything for its actions—except the shareholders of WORLDTEX.

"I don't think the United States government is going to allow—"

"According to Luc, President Benton has been checked," said Magdalena. "As you know, he has some weighty personal problems, such as Red River and campaign finance irregularities. And now there are some rumors about his wife—"

"What about his wife?" I felt a nervous twitch in my left eye.

"I don't know the exact details, but it's not the sort of thing that one would expect to hear about a First Lady," she said. "I heard that it has something to do with EarthChem."

That was enough for me. I knew what had happened—only too well. "I have to make a phone call."

I went over to my travel bag and picked up my digital phone. I strolled into the garden as I put the call through to Gale. I had given her a copy of the tape with Claire and Stone, just in case she ran into trouble with the Benton administration. Mustapha had the only other copy, and I knew that he would only release it to protect me.

"Nina, what have you found out?" Gale asked when I finally got through.

"Plenty. But you answer one thing first. Did you give the tape I gave you to anyone?"

She hesitated nervously before responding. "Nina, a situation came up...and I felt I could..."

"Gale!" I shrieked. "That was sensitive material!"

"Her behind sure as hell is sensitive now," she laughed. "The First Girlfriend is a bigger freak than me!"

"Gee, this shit isn't cute or funny." I could see Magdalena watching me from the room as I paced back and forth in the garden.

"No, it isn't, but Michael was trying to do something about that poor country. When I was approached—"

"By whom?"

"Miriam, your sister-in-law. She said she was working with you."

"Jesus Christ."

"She came asking questions about Michael, and I told her about what you were doing. She took me to see President Bernard, and I offered him my services, as one black person to another."

"Well, do you know that a *black* mercenary company may wind up dropping bombs on this *black* nation, killing a large number of *black* people?!" I asked, testily. "A *black* man may have to kill his father, another *black* man, because you put certain things in motion!!"

Gale became silent again. "Well," she began "you can't make an omelet without breaking—"

I ended the call before she could finish her sentence. I walked back into the room, threw the phone into the bag, and looked at La Bomba.

"Care to join me for a drink?"

CHAPTER TWENTY-ONE

"Where's your boss?" I asked Salim as I sat down at the bar. "And give me a double gin and tonic while you're at it."

"I don't know," he replied, quickly looking at his watch. "She's never away for long without calling. I'm concerned."

I looked at Magdalena. "I don't like this."

"You must have courage, Doña," she said. "If she has been detained by the authorities, they wouldn't dare harm her." "Why not?"

"First, she is an artist of national renown. Second, she's a major *mambo*."

"Esperanza is a *mambo*?"

"Yes. She is considered a 'big mama.' She initiated me. I'm one of her 'daughters,' a member of her family. And so is Salim. So if Anna is still with her, there's nothing to worry about. She is regarded as someone with mystical powers, a representative of the cosmic duality of life. They wouldn't dare touch her. That would be stupid ju-ju. She's the daughter of Shango, the god of fire and lightning. In voudoux and santería, Shango is represented by Saint Barbara. Given Esperanza's, shall we say, unique circumstances, it's fitting that she's the daughter of Shango."

I was still worried. Magdalena was banking on custom and political connections to save the two of them. At a time like this, all that might be thrown aside. After all, Luc was considering patricide, wasn't he?

Suddenly the cricket game that the patrons had been watching on television was interrupted by a special report from the palace. A very unsmiling Jack Malmundo appeared on the screen. The general was standing with his blood-stained arm in a sling. He wore a pained expression on his face.

Sensing that something terrible was about to happen, I took Magdalena's hand in mine.

"People of Misericordia, a foul deal has been unearthed," announced the general in a grim but dramatic tone. "On the pretext of trying to engage this government in negotiation, traitorous elements have sought to remove this government by violent means. This plot was hatched by the former president of this nation and carried out in conjunction with the Marxist terrorists, PLAM! The plot was foiled, however, due to the unique police work of our public safety commissioner. An attempt was made on my life. Most painful to me was the discovery that the attempt was made by a member of my very own cabinet. My very own flesh and blood. My son!"

The camera pulled back to reveal Luc, his face bleeding badly and his arms cuffed behind his back. The camera then turned back to the general.

"I have been alerted that our nation may soon be under attack. I assure you that the New Model Army of Misericordia will repel all such invaders, as well as dealing with this malignancy of treachery within. All those who are against the state will be dealt with swiftly and brutally. I shall show no mercy."

With his last statement, the cameras pulled back again. The general, pistol drawn, walked over to my Luc, aimed, and fired. Luc's body dropped from the camera's sight as the general emptied his pistol. Each time the gun fired, I shuddered, wishing that I could take the bullets into myself, that I could somehow deflect them from Luc.

The general continued firing, emptying his gun into his son.

There was nothing but stunned silence in the room. Right there in Misericordia, in bleeding color, the nation had sunk to a new level of barbarity. La Bomba cried uncontrollably. She rose, lifted her stool above her head, and smashed it into the television. I felt sick and suddenly began heaving into a corner of the room.

"They killed him! They killed the best man this country has produced since Nestor Morgan!" she wailed, and then placed her head on the counter and resumed crying.

No one else said a word. Stunned by what I had seen, it took me a few seconds to believe that I had actually witnessed Luc's execution on television. That the man I loved was really dead. He had been running against the clock ever since I landed, and it had finally caught up with him. Now something even worse was coming. The destruction of the nation and its re-enslavement through corporate domination. This proud black nation that had whipped the French, the Spanish, and the English would now trade in its chance at democracy and freedom for a new set of fetters.

Magdalena slowly raised her head, her eyes red and stained with tears. "He really loved us, Doña, both of us. But he was crazy about you. He began thinking about new possibilities when you arrived. Now he's gone, and these bastards will drive us into the ground if we don't stand up and act like men and women!" she said loudly. "ENOUGH IS ENOUGH! I CAN'T LIVE LIKE THIS ANYMORE! I WON'T!"

"Magdalena is right!" echoed Salim, catching the fever. "Luc Malmundo was the only politician, the only man who ever cared about us working people, and now he's gone!"

"*DECHOUKAJ!*" shouted La Bomba. She finished her drink and smashed her glass against the shattered screen.

"*Dechoukaj!*" cried Salim, pouring himself a drink and then smashing his glass in turn. He jumped over the bar with a base-ball bat, as the other men looked on.

"Well," said one man to another, "I guess today is a good day to die." They, too, drank up and smashed their glasses. "*Dechoukaj!*"

With that, I followed La Bomba and the rest of her people

out of the inn and into the street. The news of the death of Luc Malmundo traveled around the city quickly. La Bomba did more than her share to spread the news and rally the masses. At one corner after another, she jumped on the hoods of cars and shouted her orders in Kreole.

"These pigs have been squeezing and killing us for years! And now they've taken away the best man who ever lived on this island since our father, Nestor Morgan. I say from this day on we settle only for true democracy! Nothing less! *Dechoukaj!*"

The cry of *Dechoukaj* spread through the crowd that had assembled on the plaza. Gunfire was heard and a few bodies dropped at the edge of the crowd. Seeing a jeep full of Papas heading toward us, I tried to pull La Bomba out of the line of fire. But she shook free of me and stood her ground, firing quick bullets into two of the vehicle's tires. The jeep flipped over and the crowd descended on its occupants.

"Kill them!" she ordered. "No mercy. They never gave us peace, so now we'll take justice instead. Kill them all!"

The dreaded necklaces—tires filled with gasoline—suddenly appeared from out of nowhere and were immediately ignited. Bodies went up in flames and writhed in agony. No one seemed happy about what they were doing. There were no smiles on the faces of the crowd, no shouts of joy. They had seen too many friends and families summarily executed and raped with glee by authorized terrorists. They just wanted these fatherfuckers off their backs, once and for all. Malcolm X's words raced through my head: "Revolution is bloody, revolution is hostile, revolution knows no compromise, revolution overturns and destroys everything that gets in its way." The existing regime was old and in the way. Now there was only one solution. *Dechoukaj*.

The volcano of suffering from which the island had been formed had finally erupted, and the Lava-lava had begun to flow; a teeming mass of black, molten anger, pushing aside, knocking over, swallowing up anything and everything that crossed its path. At the head of the current, pressed between Magdalena and Salim, I could not share in the people's rage at their government. My sorrow over Luc's death overwhelmed any sense of purpose. The Maericans had been reborn, but their rebirth had required the death of someone I loved dearly. A rhythmic chant began to swell up from the crowd. "*Dechoukaj*! PLAM! PLAM! *Viva* Luc Malmundo!"

The angry crowd pulled down statues of previous despots. They torched the social clubs where the Papas and their associates, the Papaitos, were known to hang out. Barricades were set up everywhere, and containers filled with gasoline, called "*loco fire*," were stored for firebombs. Piano wire was strung across the narrow streets to decapitate kill-and-go goons patrolling the streets on motor scooters. A small cache of weapons was assembled as the Papas threw down their arms and fled for their lives. Along the way, we stopped to torch a police station. The officers were shot down one-by-one as they raced from the burning building.

"Find the records!" La Bomba shouted. "Place them under lock and key! We'll need a people's commission to sort out these murderers!!"

The crowd continued to grow, eventually finding its way to the sand-colored, colonial-style Hall of Justice, which had been branded "the death chamber" during the worst days of the Triomphe regime. As we reached the steps of the building, I noticed that the drumming had intensified all around us.

La Bomba raised her hand and the great crowd behind her came suddenly to a halt. She stepped forward with her pistol.

"Commissioner Hobson!" she shouted. "Come out with your hands up! You are under arrest!"

I turned around and gazed at a sea of stern but impassioned faces. I feared that the whole thing could easily turn into a bloodbath if the Papas began firing from behind their walls and the tops of buildings. I also knew that the people behind me were fully prepared to attack, to sacrifice themselves if necessary, swarming over the building like a flying phalanx of locusts descending on its prey. Taking a lesson from Zee Kincaid, I anxiously scanned the windows and the roofs for enemy barrels.

Bomba stepped closer to the entrance.

"Magdalena!" I cautioned, fearing that she was getting too

confident, too cocky. Up until that point, she had displayed remarkable leadership in controlling the flow of the crowd, but now I wasn't sure if she really knew the difference between commanding a revolution and just putting on a show.

She turned coolly and winked at me. "Don't worry, Doña. If they kill me, my people will burn these motherfuckers alive!"

She turned back toward the building. "I'm waiting, Commissioner! We're all waiting! Right, *hermanos y hermanas? Mon freres et ma soeurs?*

"*Dechoukaj*! PLAM! PLAM!" they replied, and the sound, amplified by the drums, was deafening. Bomba raised her hand and the chanting ceased, a frightening silence suddenly replacing the roar. Soon the door opened and the big man stepped out with his hands in the air. He was coatless, a pair of empty gun holsters beneath his arms. He moved slowly down the steps. At first I attributed his stiffness to his embarrassment at being humiliated before a mass of people that he and his subordinates had brutalized in the past. But then I noticed another person crouching behind his large frame, flashing the muzzle of a pistol below his ear.

"Halligan!" cried Nate Ford, a.k.a. Oscar Peltrano. "I got your partner! That other bitch, Gong! And I'm going to fuck her up the same way I had my boys do your little crumb-snatchers!"

From behind Hobson, Ford was scanning the crowd, looking for me. Since I had last seen him, awaiting sentencing several years earlier in a Brooklyn criminal court, he had grown waist-length dreadlocks and a beard. But he still had the same unmistakably arrogant bearing. He was dressed in white trousers and a knee-length Indian shirt.

I stayed still and kept my mouth shut.

"Halligan, this is the showdown, old girl!" he shouted. "I'm going to give these blood clots what they want, but you'll have to come and get me—in Le Coeur Noire! Bitch!"

Ford fired into the back of Hobson's skull and blew out his eye. A collective gasp rose from the first row of the crowd. Hobson crumbled to his knees, as Ford fired again and again, bloody chunks of skull splattering the steps of the hall. As quickly as he appeared, Ford dashed back into the building, firing at the stunned crowd as he ran. After a moment, the crowd surged forward, lifting the black iron gate that surrounded the building, tossing it roughly aside.

I reached the corner of the building and pressed my body against the wall, my left hand bracing my gun hand. Those who rushed through the door were immediately ambushed by gunmen who were hiding in the offices. I could see that it was going to be block-by-block, door-to-door, office-to-office combat. I turned and found that Salim had reappeared by my side.

"Perhaps we should try one of these explosive mangoes," he offered. I placed my hand inside the sack and brought out a hand grenade. "They're very ripe."

I pulled the pin, tossed it through the door, and we quickly returned down the stairs. A huge explosion sent shards and glass, splinters and shrapnel, in every direction, driving several wounded Papas from the building. We shot them down the moment they appeared on the steps.

Through the entrance door, I suddenly saw Ford, dragging Anna by the hair into one of the offices. One of his goons was similarly manhandling Esperanza. It was all I could do to keep myself from rushing the door—and being shot by the Papas hiding in the darkness.

"Yeah, we're down here, bitch!" screamed my dear old friend. "Come and save your playmate!" Ford fired his pistol, and we ducked behind a corner that had already been chipped repeatedly by gunfire.

In spite of the darkness of the hallway, I could make out that the left side was completely without doors, all the offices leading off to the right.

I instructed Salim to creep around the right side of the building and lob a grenade in every window on the first floor. Quicker than I had expected, I could hear the glass shattering, and then a series of brutal explosions. The gunmen who weren't killed at once didn't survive for long. Some were shot by us as they fled the building. Others were gunned down even before they reached the door by Ford and his Butt Fuck Boys, as punishment for leaving their posts.

With that hurdle cleared, La Bomba and I raced into the

building and down the hall, discarding our empty pistols and grabbing loaded ones from the dead men along the way. It took forever to reach the end of the corridor. With each burst of fire from Ford and his henchmen, we ducked in and out of the doors that lined the hall. Turning a corner, we ran to a door that was marked in Spanish, French, and Kreole, but not English. Through the narrow window, I could see that the door guarded a stairway leading down.

I turned to my interpreter. "What's down there?"

"The garage," she said, sliding a new magazine into her pistol. "Ready?"

Gunfire could be heard throughout the building. The people had gone up to the other floors, tossing grenades and cleaning out the refuse. The smoke was thickening everywhere.

I psyched myself up and told my new pal to move aside and let me lead the way. At first, La Bomba refused to budge.

"No. I don't want you taking that chance!"

"Open the goddamn door!" I ordered.

"No, Nina, I'll go in!"

I was about to bark a second time when Salim stumbled upon us, cracked open the door, and tossed in a grenade.

"Get back!" he shouted, and the three of us flattened our backs against the wall as the door was blown from its hinges.

The stairwell was even darker than the hallway. I pinched a pair of infrared shades from a body lying just inside the doorway and found two more bodies crumpled on the stairs. Salim slipped and nearly fell in the pool of blood beneath them. He used a cigarette lighter to project a path for La Bomba and himself. When we reached the ground floor, I cracked the door, but only for a moment. A frightening array of guns was pointed directly at us from over the top and hood of two cars outside the building.

"Get down!" I screamed, seconds before a fusillade tore through the door. I clapped my hand twice and shouted for Salim to toss me a grenade. I pulled the pin and rolled it through a narrow crack in the door. Outside, I heard a voice scream in English: "Get the fuck out of the way!"

Salim tossed me another grenade, and I delivered the goods

again. I waited for the impact and then rushed out of the door into the garage. Engulfed by a sudden swirl of noxious fumes and smoke, I placed the crook of my arm over my nose and mouth. Cars were smoldering everywhere. I could see that it was only a matter of minutes before they would totally combust, igniting the others. I rushed past the wreckage, ducking for cover from the gunfire behind the other cars. Hearing a car screech behind me, I knew that I was in trouble. Leaping into a cartwheel, I jerked my body out of the way just in time. But my landing was sloppy, and I whacked my head hard against a wall.

There, in the midst of the battle, I decided to take a nap.

CHAPTER TWENTY-TWO

I woke up and realized that I was lying in a bed. A good sign, I thought. At least I hadn't suddenly become fertilizer, my body dumped into a mass grave. My eyes slowly began focusing and my hearing became sharper. I was aware of people moving about, speaking encouragingly of my prognosis.

A man in white raised my eyelids and took my pulse. "Are you with us now?"

I groaned. "I'm not with the dead, am I?"

"No, you're not. You only suffered enough of a concussion to render you unconscious."

"How long have I been here?"

"Not long. Since the day of the revolution."

"Was that yesterday?"

"Yes. How do you feel?"

"A big headache, doctor," I groaned again. "A big Negrita headache."

"I have some painkillers for you. You'll be here for a couple of days." The doctor looked at me and smiled. "Well, you're the prettiest national hero we've ever had, and the first American."

"I'm not a hero, doctor," I replied weakly.

The doctor smiled, jotted down his findings, and left. A few minutes later, visitors began to stream into my room.

First there was Magdalena, now known as Colonel VillaRosa. She was wearing a new outfit befitting her new title: crisply pressed olive fatigues, an automatic pistol on her left hip, and a unlit cigar in her mouth. She had obviously been given a battlefield commission. To break out from the pack, she wore her fatigue cap backwards like a B-boy, kicking up the funk.

"Doña," she said, kissing both of my cheeks. She acted like Anna, but she still smelled like a Cohiba. "Thank Olódùmarè you are safe!" She made the sign of the cross and said something in Yoruba, "*Moddu cué.*"

"I'll live." I examined her new uniform carefully. "What's with the get-up? The hell with that! What happened? Hey! What about Anna and Esperanza?" The last thing I could remember was desperately trying to rescue Anna and Esperanza from Ford.

A nurse entered the room and told me to lie back down. It didn't take much persuasion on her part, as woozy as I was still feeling. "What happened, Bomba?"

"We won," she said energetically. "When they heard that we had risen against Malmundo, PLAM! attacked military installations around the country. Then General Jaeger swooped in with his attack helicopter squadron and destroyed Malmundo's fleet. El Generalissimo was captured and will stand trial for treason. Pepe Bernard has returned to liberate his people and—"

She snapped open a copy of *Maerican Progres* and pointed to a photo of a man wearing a flaming necklace.

"Who's that?" I asked.

"Stone, before he got to the American Embassy. He had a hot time," she guffawed. "A truly hot time. Ha! Of course, he'll be hailed as an American hero, as is the tradition in your country."

I was pleased with the results. At least Michael and Carol Bridges had been avenged, but it was only a Pyrrhic victory, with the country now in hock to WORLDTEX instead of EarthChem.

"So now WORLDTEX will be ruling Misericordia, instead of the World Bank or the IMF."

"Don't worry, Doña," said Magdalena, winking. "Some of us are working on that."

"Fine. What about Anna?"

Before she could answer, a doctor and nurse entered the room, followed by President Bernard and the two women at the top of my most-wanted-bitch list: Miriam and Gale.

La Bomba snapped to attention and saluted her commander-in-chief. "Excellency, I have the distinct honor and privilege to present to you Doña Nina Alexis Halligan."

"You left out Butler, my maiden name," I jokingly informed the newly minted colonel.

"Thank you, Colonel VillaRosa," replied President Bernard. When I last saw him, the president had the distinct aura of a pipsqueak, a vacillating Hamlet without the tragic angst. Now he was cool, calm, and decidedly in control. And the way I figured it, he had every right to his newfound confidence. The man had gambled and won, after all. Somehow, somewhere along the line, he'd finally stopped listening to Maurice North's new jack, pseudo-intellectual bullshit about reconciliation and decided to act with leadership and authority.

He took my hand and kissed it. "Doña Nina, you have my undying gratitude for the services you have provided our country."

"Thank you, Mr. President, but I did nothing," I confessed, trying to hoist myself up in the bed. Sensing my difficulty, the nurse pressed a panel button, and the bed rose obligingly to a forty-five-degree angle. I pointed to Gale. "I basically came down here to find her husband's killer."

"But," he interrupted, displaying a solitary slender finger, "it was your characterization of me as being—let's see; how did you put it?—'Pussy whipped'..."

I was mortified. He had me on that one. "Mr. President, that was a vulgar and injudicious comment on my part, and I apolo—"

"No, dear woman! It was that sort of raw wisdom that prompted me to analyze my situation," he continued, "and take bold and decisive action! You were right from the start, from the very beginning when I had read the article you wrote about our country. The entire nation owes you a debt of gratitude. If there is ever anything I can do. Anything at all."

I knew an opening when I heard one. "Yes, in fact, there is," I said. "I need to find my friends Anna Gong and Esperanza Pomona. Both of them were kidnapped before the coup by Oscar Peltrano, an ally of General Malmundo. He carried them away to Le Coeur Noire!"

There was an awkward silence, as the president looked first at me and then at the two worthless hussies who had accompanied him into the room.

"We are already looking into this delicate situation," Bernard tried to reassure me, "and we'll find a solution in due time. Rest assured."

Hearing the phrase, "this delicate situation," I knew right away that, in fact, nothing was being planned. Le Coeur Noire, after all, was a breeding ground for Bimbex; he didn't want to start any trouble in a region that was to be the island's number one source of income. I was sure that WORLDTEX had already squashed any plans for pursuing Peltrano into the region.

"Pepe," said Gale, who looked fabulous for a grieving widow in a sleek, sexy tangerine suit. She paused and then corrected herself, "Mr. President, perhaps an executive meeting could be held to look into the matter."

Gee sidled up to the man and placed her arm around him. Girlfriend was clearly a foot taller than Bernard, and he had to look up to gaze into her eyes. I knew in a flash that her grieving days were long past; she was already set to become the new first lady of Misericordia. If Bernard hadn't been a priest, it would have been easy to imagine Chantal lying in a ditch somewhere with a bullet in the back of her skull. Even so, it was clear that she was no longer part of the inner circle. And the fact that two more lives were at stake was of absolutely no consequence to any of them.

"Yes, my dear," said Bernard. "You, as always, counsel well." The president turned to me to explain the new situation. "Dr. Debord has become a special adviser; I shall have a special session called in a day or two."

"Goddamn it!" I shrieked. "Are you people deaf? They can't wait that long; Peltrano is a vicious killer! He splits people open and sews their heads up, just to prove he can. We have got to move *now*!"

Everyone in the room, except for La Bomba, looked at me as if I were crazy. How could I spoil their triumph like this? Their joyous mood? I sighed and sank back onto my bed, a crazy American who needed to be calmed down.

"I think the patient is becoming unduly agitated," said the doctor. He popped some pills from a bottle, and I decided to let him have his way.

"Nina, you have to understand," began Miriam, "the president's time is precious, with all the responsibilities of forming a new government."

I shot my sister-in-law the evilest look I could manage and pointed my finger in her face. "You don't say a fucking word to me! You fingered Anna and me to the guerrillas and they almost kidnapped us. A lot of other people died that day, Miriam!"

Shocked by my outburst, Miriam stuttered and stammered for words. "Nina, you're suffering post-traumatic stress. I'm sorry that we've disturbed you like this." Then she turned to the others and announced, "She's clearly under the influence of her medication." Miriam turned back to me, smiling beatifically, "I'll let you get your rest. Excuse me."

With that, she and the others quietly left the room. Only Colonel VillaRosa stayed behind, in spite of the doctor's misgivings.

After everyone was gone, she looked at me. "You want me to kill her, Doña?" she asked, jerking her head toward the door. She was ready, all right, her thumbs tucked into her pistol belt. "No problem."

I considered her offer for a moment, and then remembered my brother and his three children. Gale deserved it just as much as Miriam, I thought. She had suddenly become the grieving widow, calling herself "Dr. Debord," a name, mind you, she'd never even thought of using when Michael was alive.

"Don't waste your energy," I said. "What's going on,

Bomba? What about Anna and Esperanza?"

She pressed the panel, lowered the bed, and fluffed up the pillow. "Get some sleep."

She placed a thermometer gently between my lips before I could protest. "Get some rest." She sat down beside me on the edge of the bed and lowered her voice. "We're coming for you at 10 p.m., Salim and I. Through the window. Watch the parking lot and do something creative with the bed sheets. Be ready for the rumble in the jungle."

She pulled the thermometer from my mouth and read it aloud: "Normal."

Bomba winked at me as she left the room. When she passed through the door, I noticed that she had accessorized her fatigues with a pair of black leather pumps.

CHAPTER TWENTY-THREE

After my outburst, a guard was placed outside my door. I was sure they already had plans to rush me back to the States. That was fine with me. But I wasn't leaving without Anna — even if that meant returning together in separate coffins.

By 9:45, I was dressed and ready to rock and roll. From my third-floor window, I could see the parking lot was drenched in rain. The sky cracked angrily with thunder, and jagged etchings of lightning brightened the horizon. An army vehicle suddenly rounded the curve and drove into the lot. The vehicle, a black Humvee, parked and blinked its lights. I opened the window and tossed the sheets, which I had twisted and tied into a rope, onto the ground below. I fastened the sheets to the bed stand and lowered myself slowly down the side of the building, my head throbbing painfully.

Completely soaked by the rain, I stepped into the vehicle and found Salim at the wheel, dressed in fatigues. Bomba was seated beside him. She handed me a set of olive fatigues and tan leather boots.

"Welcome to the rainy season," she said. "I'm dangerous

when wet."

"What's the plan?" I asked, sliding into the back seat with my gear.

Salim drove out of the parking lot as Bomba gave me the 411: "Peltrano and his men escaped to Le Coeur Noire. They met up with a unit of PLAM! guerrillas and a fire fight ensued. PLAM! pulled back when they discovered that the *madrina* was among the hostages."

"*Madrina?*" I asked.

"Esperanza is a *madrina*," explained Salim, "a *mambo* who has a large family."

"Anyway," continued Magdalena, "PLAM! pulled back and allowed Peltrano free entry into Le Coeur Noire. There's an old church settlement there that served as a fort during the colonial period. He's using that as his base of operations in the region."

"Okay," I responded impatiently. "What's the game plan?"

"We're hooking up with a special battalion led by Fanon," said Magdalena.

"Marisol Fanon?" I asked. "Where was she when my lights went out?"

"She took the palace and marched El Generalissimo out in his underwear," replied Magdalena, taking advantage of the glare from the headlights of the automobile behind us to apply lipstick.

"Going somewhere special?" I inquired.

"To war, darling. A woman should look her best for any and all occasions." She winked at me. "You know that."

I continued to change from my wet street clothes into the fatigues as she put away her lipstick and continued with her story.

"We're meeting up with Fanon and her special unit at the steppes. They have been monitoring Peltrano at the village called Le Coeur; wedding drums have reportedly been heard—"

I stopped what I was doing, one leg halfway into my fatigues. "Wedding drums?"

"Peltrano has apparently announced his marriage to the *madrina*," confirmed Magdalena.

"What? Why would she—?!"

Bomba placed her left index finger at Salim's head, her thumb cocked back like a gun. "To save the woman she loves. She and Anna are being kept in the church, which Peltrano is using as his living quarters."

"Also," explained Salim, "Peltrano knows that Esperanza is a highly respected woman in the nation; if he marries the *madrina*, he will increase his political power, or at least decrease any political liabilities he has incurred."

"Salim's right," said Magdalena. "If Peltrano marries Esperanza, he can use her presence as a bargaining chip to hold onto Le Coeur Noire. The situation there has become quite delicate."

"How is that?"

"WORLDTEX has announced that it will invoke its proprietary rights in Le Coeur Noire and will take physical possession of the area at 0200 hours."

"You mean The Jaguar is coming in?" I tucked my shirt into my waist, realizing that the situation had already deteriorated from delicate to extreme. "So the cavalry is coming to the area—a gift to WORLDTEX from Bernard. Jesus!"

"Bernard ordered this operation, Nina," she confided over her shoulder. "PLAM! is going in to clean out Peltrano with us; the three of us are to rescue the *madrina* and Anna. They plan to hold onto Le Coeur as a sacred trust of the Maerican people."

"The WORLDTEX boys will never accept that," I argued. "There's no way that they'll relinquish their interest in the area so easily."

La Bomba turned to me in the darkness, her face barely outlined by the moon's light. Her voice was cold and to the point. "They'll only be concerned about Le Coeur if there's something to protect."

"Meaning what?"

"Meaning that PLAM! is preparing to reduce Le Coeur to ashes. They're going to burn it down." La Bomba looked at the rain pelting the windows of the truck. "Of course, that may be something of a problem in this weather."

"Magdalena, that's the island's one real hope, its main

source of income."

"And its main source of trouble," added Salim. "You know how it goes. Look, as long as we have something they want, they'll be down here monkeying with us forever. We burn it down, and poof! We're fully prepared to go about the business of being humble, poor but free."

"That's a pretty extreme prescription," I replied.

"The president has thought this through; he's willing to take his chances," said La Bomba. "He's gotten Command Decisions to provide us with logistical assistance to get rid of the junta—"

"—the third force option."

"Yes, and now he wants them out," she continued. "He played the game, and now he's acting like a leader, taking chances that might get us all killed. He's taken an old tactic from the history books. Scorch the earth."

"And then what happens after the double-cross?" The ride was getting bumpier, a sure sign that we had already moved from the paved roads of the city to the muck and mud of the back country.

"Simple. We'll grow hemp," answered Salim. "We already have people looking into it. We'll export hemp around the world."

"That'll get you pegged right away by the American Congress as a drug-trafficking enemy," I said skeptically. But I could see their point: Bimbex was trouble; it would certainly produce yet another form of colonialism in Misericordia. Growing and exporting hemp, while it wouldn't exactly give the country most-favored-nation status with its big brother to the north, would at least allow the Maericans to control their own destiny. "Who came up with this bright idea?"

The two of them exchanged glances in silence. For a moment, I heard nothing but the wheels of the Humvee churning the earth beneath us. Leaves and branches scraped the window as we went deeper into the back country. The coolness of the lowlands was seeping into the car; I felt slightly exhilarated by the fresh air.

"Luc," said Magdalena, finally answering my question. "He

was always thinking ahead, always thinking about his people. Always thinking about us."

Le Coeur was situated on a mesa that had been weathered down from a volcano by the sea's tropical storms over a thousand years. The Bimbao trees grew plentifully on the mesa's rich topsoil, helped along by the cool, humid air and tropical sunlight. The area was considered sacred; the voudoux gods had often made their appearances there. I could hear the faint rumbling of the wedding drums as we climbed the steppes. Through the darkness, I could barely make out the outline of the mesa as we approached. Soon a spectrum of lights appeared in the distance—Le Coeur. The sound of the drums grew louder and louder.

As we neared the settlement, Salim turned off the headlights and slowed down the vehicle. When we were within a mile of our destination, he pulled over and parked on the side of the road. The rain had stopped completely. La Bomba opened the door and stepped out onto the road. She placed her hand to her lips and made some type of nocturnal bird call. Within seconds, a response echoed back and dark figures emerged from the jungle's shadows. Two guerrillas.

"*Hola*, Commandante VillaRosa," said one of them, a woman, as she emerged from the shadows. It was Fanon. The two women immediately embraced and kissed one another.

"We've been waiting for you, Commandante, and—"

Fanon's sisterly goodwill quickly disappeared as she recognized me through the jungle's edge of darkness.

"What is *she* doing here?" she hissed.

"Doña Nina," said Magdalena, "is responsible for this operation, so to speak."

"She's also responsible for Raoul's death," Fanon responded. "She alerted the security forces at the airport."

I didn't know what she was talking about; Anna and I had simply tried to escape our captors. What else did she expect us to do under the circumstances? But Luc had said at the time that the whole thing had been planned by Fanon's brother; he must have gotten his ass banged at the shoot-out. But that wasn't my fault—or my problem.

"That was a stupid operation, sister," argued La Bomba. "And Raoul, unfortunately, paid for it with his life. Doña Nina is here to rescue her friend and the *madrina*—"

"Was that the bitch who was with Esperanza?!" she spat contemptuously. "I suppose you're here to try to save your friend before Peltrano and his dogs fuck her to death and then slit her throat!"

"That's enough, Fanon," said La Bomba. "We have our orders—to attempt a rescue—and you have yours—"

"And mine supersede yours, Commandante," she snarled, keeping her eyes focused on me.

Jungle girl had an AK-47 slung over her back; La Bomba was standing between us. La Bomba and Salim had equipped me with a NATO-issued 9mm Barretta, which I was now wearing in a holster around my waist. I wasn't interested in playing some gangsta bitch in the jungle, but Fanon was clearly in the mood to rumble. And if that was what she wanted, well...

"We have our orders, Commandante," said La Bomba. "This is not about personal issues. If you can't conduct yourself appropriately, I'll relieve you of your command."

That got her attention. She stepped back and looked La Bomba up and down. "Just who are you threatening, Magdalena VillaRosa? Huh? My command? I've been in the jungle!!"

"Don't raise your voice, you fool!" hushed La Bomba. "This is a military operation, and you are to conduct yourself as an officer! Now, what is this change in orders that you're referring to?"

Fanon, her eyes still fixed defiantly in my direction, opened the flap of her shirt, pulled out a folded sheet of paper, and handed it to La Bomba. La Bomba took the paper and opened it, as Salim handed her a flashlight with which to read. She studied it quickly once, and then again. She looked at her watch.

"*Merde*," she finally said.

"Bomba?" I asked tentatively. "What's wrong?"

"The Jaguar is coming in at midnight. The guerrillas have been ordered to ignite the mesa before he arrives."

I looked at my watch; it was already 11:20. "Let me go in and find them."

"No, Doña Nina," said Fanon, walking up to me. "You don't

have time for that. That would be a personal issue, and the matters of my country come before your fucking personal interest, *gringa*! So, now, I give the orders and—"

"Even if that means killing the *madrina*?" I prompted.

"Fuck the *madrina*! And voudoux! Stupid African superstition! After she dies, then we'll clear out the voudoux pestilence and start all over." With that, Fanon turned away. "The operation will commence now—without the rescue!"

"One more word and I'll blow your head off." She turned to face me and a drawn gun. She smiled and whistled. Stepping from the shadows came several more soldiers, their rifles pointed at us. Fanon continued walking.

"Bitch! Don't you move!" I croaked with rage.

Fanon walked slowly towards me. "I have you covered, woman. They'll cut you—"

"Not before I blow the glasses off your face!"

Gingerly, La Bomba approached me again. "No, Nina. Don't."

"Did you hear what she said, Bomba? They won't even give us a chance! I'll do the run—"

"No, Nina. It's too late," she said tiredly. "I didn't think it would come to this, but the revolution has already gone sour. Put away your gun. This has to stop."

"Even if it means letting Anna and Esperanza die? If they die, she'll go, too! I mean it!"

La Bomba tried to get between me and my target. But I slipped away from her, my eyes fixed on Fanon. "Don't fuck with me, Bomba!" I warned.

"No, no, no, my sister," she said. "It's over. *Le guerre est fini. Fini*, Doña. You didn't come down here to be a murderer, to be like us. This is not what Luc would have wanted. Put it way, Nina. This is their night of treachery, not ours."

I sighed and lowered the gun. I could feel Anna and Esperanza slipping into darkness.

"Get on with your devil's work," Bomba said to Fanon.

La Bomba was right. If I popped Fanon, we would all be blown away immediately. And then who could or would save Anna and Esperanza? No one. Everything and everyone was gone. Michael. Luc. Carol Bridges. Now Esperanza and Anna. And there was nothing I could do about it. I holstered my gun.

"Now," said Fanon, barking her orders into a cellular phone.

The sky suddenly lit and a ring of fire appeared atop the mesa, followed by several explosions. The guerrillas had placed a web of napalm explosives across the ridge, a mixture that was guaranteed to burn the Bimbao even in a downpour. The fire raged uncontrollably. The drums had stopped, replaced by the violent cracking and splintering of wood. We could hear the inhabitants of the village shouting.

We all stood there, mesmerized by the fire. The chemicals' odor filled our nostrils. It was a sickening smell, all right, the smell of a nation willfully burning itself to the ground. Before our eyes, what appeared to be an enormous wall of burning mud broke loose and began cascading down the side of the ridge and onto the village. A flaming mudslide. We watched in silent horror as the entire village was consumed by fire and buried by mud. The shouting and screaming of the villagers was quickly silenced by the impact of the fallen, flaming earth.

Fanon immediately called Bernard to report the outcome. She expressed her disappointment that things had not gone exactly as planned, since no one had anticipated the mudslide. Sickened, I returned to the car, where I collapsed with fatigue. Before I completely lost consciousness, I heard La Bomba tell Salim that she planned to give up smoking. Well, maybe something had been accomplished after all, I thought to myself, as my body finally gave way to the exhaustion and the drugs the doctor had given to me earlier.

When I awoke the next morning, the air was thick with the smell of burnt wood and chemicals; a thin film of smoke hovered about the ground. At dawn, Salim had driven the Humvee to the village. We surveyed the devastation. A government clean-up operation had already arrived on site. Bulldozers were at work, and shovel brigades were digging through the mud. Teams of medical workers carried away bodies coated with the wet, dark red earth. Someone handed me a shovel, and I found myself digging, reaching into the mud to extract a dead body whose arm I had found protruding from the ground.

We worked for hours, but soon discovered that it was more than we could possibly handle. Entire houses had collapsed under the weight of the molten earth, leaving their inhabitants trapped, and crushed, inside. In addition to shoveling away mud, we were also forced to pick-ax our way through wood and hardened adobe, and to cut through the metal sheeting that formed many of the makeshift shacks of the village. Extracting those who'd been smothered by the soft mud was a much less disturbing task than retrieving the bodies that had been crushed by a falling roof or wall.

"This wasn't supposed to happen this way," said La Bomba, exasperated at the carnage and destruction. "*Merde*. This wasn't supposed to happen." She stuck the shovel into a heap of mud we'd been attacking and tossed a large portion over her shoulder. It was cooler in this upper region, but the nonstop pace made us hot and sweaty. We both took off our shirts and tied bandannas around our heads.

"*Merde*. This wasn't supposed to be like this," she continued to swear underneath her breath.

I looked at the huge hill of red mud that covered the town's square. Rising out of it, at its highest peak, was a church bell tower, the only surviving evidence that a town had existed. A thought suddenly hit me. The tower was also the only means by which Anna and Esperanza could possibly have survived the fiery mudslide. The bell tower would have allowed a steady infusion of air to pass through. A team of bulldozers was hard at work, removing the mud from around the church. I shook myself. The thought was nothing more than a fantasy, I assured myself. No one could possibly have survived what we witnessed last night. No one.

"We have a saying back in the States—shit happens," I told her, hopelessly hoping that they were well.

Bomba energetically sank her shovel into the mud, but it only stuck half way in. Tired and angry, she gave the back of the shovel a swift kick, but the blade still wouldn't budge.

She was about to ram it again when I suddenly screamed: "Oh, God!" I grabbed her arm.

"What's wrong?" she said, stopping, the shovel poised in mid air. I pointed to the blood on the tip of the shovel's blade.

"Oh, Mother!" gasped Bomba. She dropped the shovel and began crying, backing away from the mud.

Salim, who had been working a few feet down from us, heard her cry and rushed over. "What's wrong?"

La Bomba kept crying, her head pressed to my shoulder. "There's a body beneath the mud, Salim. She didn't know it."

Salim looked at the shovel and understood immediately. He went over to the spot, lowered himself to his knees, and began gently removing the mud with his hands. As he got closer to the body, a small rivulet of blood began streaming from the mud. Salim turned to us. "I'll take care of this. Why don't you two take a break. We've all been working too hard."

I escorted La Bomba to a makeshift canteen area that had been erected by the government rescue workers. I fetched us both a cup of water, and we sat beneath a tree's shade. From where we were sitting, I could see that it wouldn't be long before the bulldozer would remove the last remaining large heap of mud from the church.

I turned to Bomba and placed my hand on her shoulder. "Feeling better?"

"*Sí.*" She smiled wearily and looked off into the distance. "What about you?"

"I just want to get my friend and go home."

"There's still Luc," she said.

I turned to her. "What about him?"

"The president is going to hold a memorial service for him. And I'm sure Luc would have wanted you there."

"I don't think I could handle that, Bomba. I'd rather grieve for him in a quieter, more private way. Maybe that's selfish, but that's the way I feel. Misericordia should celebrate him as a son and patriot. I just want to quietly remember him as a lover and a friend."

"I can understand that," La Bomba sighed. "Soon the state will begin to own his legacy."

"Yeah," I nodded laconically, "something like that."

We sat in silence for a while. La Bomba remembered something and dug into her trouser pocket. She removed a small case and handed it to me. "This belongs to you. Luc wanted me to give it to you, in case something happened."

I opened the case and discovered an ivory ring. A tear welled up in the corner of my eye as I handed it back to her. "I can't take this. This is obviously a family heirloom. You should keep it since you two were—"

La Bomba closed my hand around the ring. "I may have been his partner, but you were his woman."

Her touch eased some of my pain over losing Luc. But the guilt still remained.

"I have something I want to give you," said La Bomba. She then placed her hands beneath her undershirt, unfastening the chain between her two breasts. "The ring," she said.

I handed her back the ring. She placed the chain through it and then placed it around my neck.

"This way," she said, "you, me, and Luc will always be together. If not in bed, at least in spirit."

I smiled as she sat back down beside me and held my hand. I closed my eyes; as she squeezed my hand tighter, it felt as if Luc were there beside me, too. Maybe the magic was already working.

"Doña?"

"Huh?" I woke up and found Salim standing over me. I'd dozed off for at least half an hour. Bomba had gone back on line. Salim offered me a hand, and I lifted myself to my feet. I stood and dusted myself. The world around me felt different, even if everything still looked the same. I experienced a calm inside, like a soft kiss from a lover. The reasons for my visit to the island had disappeared. I fingered the ring that La Bomba had given me, thinking about Luc and what would now never be. Here, with him, I had started thinking about new tomorrows and endless nights with someone by my side. Now that was gone. I was no longer smouldering with the desire for revenge with Ford. Compared to my new loss, he had become a side issue. The main thing now was finding Anna and Esperanza, dead or alive, and getting the hell out of here and back home. I wasn't going to solve anything by making sure that Nate Ford was dead. For too long, I had used my hatred for him to assuage the guilt that I felt for being unfaithful to my husband and for causing my children's death. Now I was ready to carry on, with less baggage. My second life was about to begin, and how things went would have a lot to do with how I managed the debris from the first. The past, after all, is merely a prologue...

Although it was morning, the sky was still dark and evil-looking, with low clouds hovering overhead. There was an odd scent in the air. I was told that it was a mix of napalm and Bimbex.

"We're about to remove the last of the mud from the church, Doña," he informed me as we walked through the cleared path. Village people were still being carted off on stretchers all around us, and hundred of workers were hard at work removing the huge mounds of mud that covered the area. Heading up the path, we passed a dirt-splattered bulldozer that was scooping away mud from one of the mounds.

As we approached the church, Salim handed me my holster and pistol, and I realized that Anna and Esperanza weren't the only ones who might have survived the disaster inside the tower.

Bomba had assumed a position at the door. Realizing that the place might be boobytrapped, I held my breath and turned the knob. The door opened slowly in front of me. With my eyes adjusting to the darkness, I saw an ethereal figure walking towards me. I raised my gun.

"That won't be necessary," said the man, as he moved out of the darkness. Over his left shoulder he carried Anna.

"Anna?"

"Your friend is safe," the man assured me. He looked battle-weary; his red shirt was torn and shredded, and his exposed skin was cut and bruised.

"Anna's safe!" I shouted over my shoulder, and then returned my attention to the man. "Where's Peltrano? The *madrina*?"

"Nina, please take her," he answered. With a move of the man's shoulder, Anna tumbled into my arms. I carried her outside and into the fresh air. How did he know my name? I wondered as I stepped back into the light.

Magdalena rushed forward to help me with Anna. She looked at the man and yelped, "Oh, my Lord!!"

"What?" I turned around, ready to confront Peltrano.

"It's Shango!!" screamed La Bomba.

"Who?" I looked at the figure, who radiated the promises of the sun.

"Shango," she cried, and fell to her knees. The rest of the relief workers, soldiers, and villagers joined her, as they heard the name of one of the great *orishas* of the Yoruba. Everyone and everything stopped as they all bowed down before the man. Even Marisol. Dazed, I surmised that I was in the throes of a group hallucination. Apparently, the Bimbex and napalm were frying our brains. But if he *was* a vision, he was gorgeous.

The man looked calmly at the group on their knees before me. I just stood there, holding onto my unconscious friend. There was something oddly familiar about the man. He was unquestionably handsome, with rugged features and penetrating eyes. In addition to his white, sleeveless tunic, he wore a cowrie bracelet on his well-toned biceps. Tucked in his red sash was a double-headed axe. His hair was a massive tangle of dreadlocks, pulled back and held together by a single lock. A white streak of hair began at the crown and flowed toward the back of his head.

"You have done well, my children," he said. His voice had the quality of the warm, friendly hand of a parent, smoothing away the fear of a child. "Your father Olódùmarè is proud of you and the way that you have shown fealty to him, to your mother Esperanza, and to your nation. He salutes you and offers his thanks. *Moddu cué.*"

At that point, I decided to follow the example of the others and lower myself to my knees. It was time to give thanks to something. "Lord Shango?" I began uncertainly, not sure exactly how to address a god. "What of our mother and friend, Esperanza? Where is she?"

Shango advanced closer toward me. "What? My good woman does not cry out for the blood of Nate Ford?"

"I'd be happier to ensure the well-being of my friend's friend, My Lord."

He smiled warmly. "She is well, good woman. And will return to you shortly—with a gift."

With that, Shango raised his voice and addressed his people once again. "Rise up, you mighty people! You have great things to accomplish. And to show my gratitude, I leave you with the the gift of a new day." The apparition withdrew his double-headed axe with his right hand, aimed his left arm at the sky, and hurdled the axe heavenward. The sky split open, roaring with the sound of thunder, and the sun shown suddenly through. We all watched in wonder as the sky was transformed from gray to blue in a split second. Golden, sparkling slivers of sunlight rained down upon us.

When we turned back toward the church, the master of lightning was gone. In his place stood Esperanza. Once again, all the people bowed their heads, making signs of the cross and offering praises in Yoruba. At her feet, looking slight and pitiful beneath her, was the body of Nate Ford. She had dragged him out by the rope of his dreadlocks like a worthless sack of garbage.

I handed Anna over to a member of the medical team and faced Esperanza. The woman was radiant; she seemed completely unfazed by her ordeal.

"Are you all right, Doña?" I asked, handing her a gourd of cool water.

She took the water and gulped it throatily. "Thank you," she said. She then pulled her right hand from behind her, dragging Ford's body by its two feet of dreadlocks across the muddied earth.

I looked at Ford. Dead.

"I heard what this dog did to you and your loved ones," Esperanza closed her eyes briefly and nodded.

I continued looking at the body, but I felt nothing. The murder of Lee and the children. Luc's death. It was all over now.

"Thank you for taking care of Anna," I said, looking over my shoulder at her as she rested calmly beneath the tree, attended by the medics, "but I still need to know one thing."

"Yes, Nina," she replied, her gaze searching deeply into my eyes.

"How did he die?"

"With both of my hands around his neck, my sister," she replied calmly, "squeezing the very evilness out of his breath and pores as I rode him to death on our wedding night. He had quite a surprised look when I invoked your name."

In response, I rolled an enormous ball of saliva from the back of my throat and deposited it squarely on Ford's deathly etched sneer. It was the last mask he would ever wear.

I then took Esperanza's mango-scented hands and kissed each of them.

"Muchas gracias, Madrina."

The End

ALSO FROM AKASHIC BOOKS

Manhattan Loverboy by Arthur Nersesian
203 pages, paperback
ISBN: 1-888451-09-2
Price: $13.95
"Nersesian's newest novel is a paranoid fantasy and fantastic comedy in the service of social realism, using methods of L. Frank Baum's *Wizard of Oz* or Kafka's *The Trial* to update the picaresque urban chronicles of Augie March, with a far darker edge..." —*Downtown Magazine*

Kamikaze Lust by Lauren Sanders
287 pages, trade paperback
ISBN: 1-888451-08-4
Price: $14.95
"*Kamikaze Lust* puts a snappy spin on a traditional theme—young woman in search of herself—and stands it on its head. In a crackling, rapid-fire voice studded with deadpan one-liners and evocative descriptions, Rachel Silver takes us to such far-flung places as a pompous charity benefit, the set of an "art porn" movie, her best friend's body, Las Vegas casinos, and the psyche of her own porn-star alter ego, Silver Ray, all knit together by the unspoken question: Who am I, anyway? And as Rachel tells it, asking the question is more fun than knowing for sure could ever be." —Kate Christensen, author of *In the Drink*

Outcast by José Latour
217 pages, trade paperback
ISBN: 1-888451-07-6
Price: $13.95
(*Out of print. Available only through direct mail order.*)
"José Latour is a master of Cuban Noir, a combination of '50s unsentimentality and the harsh realities of life in a Socialist paradise. Better, he brings his tough survivor to the States to give us a picture of ourselves through Cuban eyes. Welcome to America, Sr. Latour." —Martin Cruz Smith, author of *Gorky Park*

Massage by Henry Flesh
384 pages, trade paperback
ISBN: 1-888451-06-8
Price: $15.95
"Funny, tightly plotted, and just two shades darker than burnt coffee. Henry Flesh has crafted a fine and disturbing novel."
—David Sedaris, author of *Naked*

Once There Was a Village by Yuri Kapralov
163 pages, trade paperback
ISBN: 1-888451-05-X
Price: $12

"This was the era which saw the 'invasion' of hippies and junkies and swarms of runaway boys and girls who became prey to pimps, tactical police and East Village violence... In this personal memoir of his experiences, Kapralov relives the squalor and hazards of community life along Seventh Street between Avenues B and C. The street riots of 1966, the break-up of his own stormy marriage, poignant or amusing but always memorably etched stories of the Slavs, Russians, Puerto Ricans, blacks and artists young and old who were his neighbors, his own breakdown—all of it makes a 'shtetl' experience that conjures up something of Gorki and Chagall." —*Publishers Weekly*

The Fuck-Up by Arthur Nersesian
274 pages, trade paperback
ISBN: 1-888451-03-3
Price: $13.00
(*Out of print. Available only through direct mail order.*)
"The charm and grit of Nersesian's voice is immediately eveloping, as the down-and-out but oddly up narrator of his terrific novel, *The Fuck-Up*, slinks through Alphabet City and guttural utterances of love."—*Village Voice*

These books are available at local bookstores. They can also be purchased with a credit card online through www.akashicbooks.com. To order by mail, or to order out-of-print titles, send a check or money order to:

Akashic Books
PO Box 1456
New York, NY 10009
www.akashicbooks.com
Akashic7@aol.com

(Prices include shipping.
Outside the U.S., add $3
to each book ordered.)

Norman Kelley is a freelance journalist,
author, ex-intellectual, and producer at
WBAI 99.5 FM Pacifica Radio in New
York, where he organizes arts-related
segments for "City in Exile." He has
written for the *Black Star News*, *New
Politics*, *Black Renaissance/Noir*, *The Bedford
Stuyvesant Current*, and *Word.com*, and has
also written op-ed pieces for *Newsday*. He
is the author of *Black Heat* (Cool Grove
Press, 1997), the first in the Nina Halligan
political mystery series. Mr. Kelley is a con-
tributing writer to *Gig* (Random House,
2000). He lives in Brooklyn, New York.